BLOOD VOWS

CARA CARNES

HEARTSCAPE PUBLISHING

Cover Model: Josh McCann

Photography by: Shauna Kruse @ Kruse Images & Photography

Cover Design by Freya Barker at RE&D

Content Editor: Heather Long

Copy Editor: Jax Garren

Proofing: Ink It Out Editing

For the latest information, subscribe to my newsletter, or join my Facebook Group.

❀ Created with Vellum

ACKNOWLEDGEMENTS AND AUTHOR'S NOTE

It might take a village to put out a book, but when it comes to The Arsenal I'm beyond blessed to have an army behind me. I wish there were enough pages to thank everyone individually.

Thank you to my fearless editors, who never fail to knock my words into shape. And my fabulous cover designer for always, always providing gorgeous covers that bring the world to life.

Thank you to all the experts I've reached out to throughout this series. I have learned so much from your expertise, and I thank you for your time and insight. Any errors are entirely mine.

And to The Cohorts and all the readers who have reached out about this series...You all are beyond fabulous. Your passion for these books, the characters within and the romance genre itself is why I love writing so very much. I hope that I can do justice to the world you're enjoying.

While The Arsenal series is a romance at its heart, the fiber, blood and bone of this series is a gritty, sometimes dark, and daunting rollercoaster ride of suspense, family, team and honor. Love isn't ever an easy road to navigate. While I've made every attempt to warn readers of possible triggers, please know there may very well be subject matter within this series that may be difficult to read.

Blood Vows contains references to date-rape, PTSD, adult illiteracy, mental illness, animal cruelty, and domestic violence.

1

Another dead end. Dallas Mason kicked the rotted boards along the entry wall, but stifled the curse rising in his throat. They'd searched every shack, lean-to, and campsite they ran across and had yet to find any credible lead.

"We'll find him." Viviana Chambers had turned the promise into a mantra, one she'd whispered to him shortly after she'd risked her life to get him and her now-fiancé out of The Collective's grasp.

She was a hell of a back-office operative, one of the most sought after in the business. In normal circumstances he'd take her promise as a statement of fact. There was nothing she, aka Quillery, and her partner Mary, aka Edge, couldn't do. Their recent presence at The Arsenal had thrust the covert paramilitary organization he and his brothers had started to a new level of intense—one that left him and every other operative determined to do whatever it took to keep the two women safe.

Drones whirled around him and cast bright lights across a swath of otherwise pitch-black night. They'd been hauling ass since before daybreak. He looked over at the silent group waiting out his rage. Big brothers were a serious pain in the fucking ass. The fact that he had five of them and they were all capable of knocking his ass into the new millennium if he didn't keep his shit together was the only reason he was trying.

They had no idea what'd gone down back then, back when he'd been so desperate to leave The Collective he'd willingly bedded a viperous bitch. He hadn't known what Marla had intended to do. Even as desperate as he was, he wouldn't have...

"We'll find him," Vi repeated through the com. "Come home. We'll reconvene in the white boardroom in the morning. We're narrowing the search areas. There aren't many left."

Right. Assuming Marla hadn't lied when she'd expended her last breath mentioning the Wyoming Wilderness. The woman who'd been his handler at the Collective had made him do lots of twisted shit, but none quite as foul as bedding her to earn an out from the black ops group. He should've known she'd had an ulterior motive. Maybe then he would've made a different decision. Then again, probably not. Back then out was better than the alternative—dead.

Dallas had survived more than his fair share of hellholes, but none had presented the challenges of the rugged outdoors they'd spent the past eight weeks tearing through to find his kid.

A kid he hadn't even known existed.

He rubbed his chest and forced the rage down, letting it simmer and brew. Big brother number one, aka Marshall, was one curse away from tossing his ass out of the mission altogether. Said pain in the ass crossed his arms and glanced in annoyance at his counterpart, Nolan. The fucker nodded. So did Jesse.

"Come on, man. We'll make another round in case we missed something. Light's total shit right now," Gage Sanderson commented. Sanderson was a hell of an operative, one who'd clearly been appointed his chief babysitter since the fucker hadn't left his side for more than an hour at any point.

"We're wheels up in two hours, which means we leave here in twenty. Don't make me hunt you down," Marshall said. "Vi's right. We'll find him."

Him. Everyone assumed Marla'd had a son because that's what she'd taunted him with before she died. Truth told, it was just a pronoun assigned because they'd yet to find a damn thing to indicate the crazy bitch hadn't lied about it all. No evidence of a birth. Nothing.

What if her death confession had been a final up yours as she bled out on the warehouse floor? Dallas wouldn't put anything past the woman who'd handled him and the rest of the operatives within The Collective like they were her personal play toys. Truth told, he had been. He'd been the dutiful operative, doing whatever she and the other shadowy leaders of the black ops organization ordered him to. No job was too dirty or under the radar. No kill was too far.

"How much acreage is left in this area? How much didn't we check?" Dallas growled the question into the com and waited.

"You've been hauling ass through rugged wilderness for seventeen hours, brother. We're flagging this leg of the mission. Take one last scout with Sanderson, then you're on your way back to the plane," Dylan said.

Dylan and Cord, his other two pain-in-the-ass brothers, had remained at The Arsenal compound to keep it secure. They'd learned the hard way what happened when they all left. The Collective had attacked. Fortunately, Vi's fiancé, Judson Jensen, had kicked their asses. He was a hell of a lethal operative, the best assassin around. As if summoned by sheer thought, his voice rumbled through the com like spent mortar rounds.

"You're done. The women are done. They've taken two piss breaks in eighteen hours and haven't eaten a full meal since you left. Mary has a puke bucket beside her. You're done."

"You don't get to share that level of detail with people, Judson Jensen." Vi's voice held more exhaustion than anger.

"Dallas. I'm tired." Mary's confession stifled the last of his refusal.

His brother's woman was pregnant and had been puking into a bucket for eighteen hours because he wouldn't give up.

She'd endured a hell of her own back when their paths first collided. God only knew how she'd survived. There was nothing she and Vi wouldn't do. They had a one hundred percent success rate because they never gave up. They never surrendered.

Which was why she'd been retching into a bucket while he dragged a team through a week's worth of wilderness in a day. They hadn't stopped to rest, which meant she hadn't.

But she'd just admitted she was tired. Dylan's woman didn't admit defeat, but that was too close for Dallas. He'd driven her to that finite point where surrender might very well become an option because, as much as it pained anyone to admit, there was more at stake than finding his kid.

She was pregnant.

The Arsenal had more fires burning than they should, most of them fallout from declaring war on The Collective. Sometimes to win you had to retreat, regroup, and strategize. Vi and Mary knew what the next move was. Marshall had already declared as much, but the two women had yet to close down the coms because they had his back.

They'd always had his back, Mary more than anyone.

Which was why, for now, he'd have to man up and do what neither woman would.

Admit defeat.

For now.

Because no matter what, he had *their* backs.

"We're done." He clicked off the com, yanked the headset off and charged out of the remote cabin. The sooner they got back to The Arsenal, the faster they could come back.

And they would.

Failure wasn't an option. His kid was out there somewhere.

DALLAS HEADED DIRECTLY to the operations theater when he arrived at The Arsenal. Though they were exhausted, he doubted either woman had stopped their grid search just because Dallas and the team with him had gone wheels up. Data was power, and the two women never rested their reign because HERA never rested.

The kick ass security defense system they had designed was a thing of beauty, one which defied explanation or identification. It defended operatives in the field, performed instantaneous facial recognition, surveyed hundreds of square miles of wilderness in perfect grid patterns and identified heat signatures and structures.

Simply put, it was amazing because the women who had designed it were.

Jud loomed in the entryway, a silent sentry more lethal than a pissed off gargoyle. "You're done. So are they."

"They should be in bed," Dallas commented. "Figured they wouldn't be."

"No, they aren't." Dylan muttered from behind Jud as he leaned down until his lips were to Mary's ear. "Whatever you're doing can wait, sweetheart."

"We're almost done," Mary said wearily. "If we get new search parameters established, HERA can work while we sleep and identify the next patch."

"Why the fuck can't the new girl do this?" Jud asked.

"Because she's too busy helping Cord run the missions," Vi said. "And stop growling, Jud. It's not going to make us type any faster."

"Wake Jacob up. He can do this," Jud said.

"Your nephew is exhausted. You had him crawling up and down every inch of Marville the past two days putting in cameras. Oh, and he and his dad are wheels up for a huge fundraiser in Boston. Remember?"

"Better him than me," the man responded in a husky whisper. He prowled toward Vi and sat in the chair beside her. "We've gotta make headway on the Marville situation, and I keep hitting brick walls."

Marville was a piece of shit town fifteen miles east of Resino. The Mason family had lived on their ranch land outside Resino for generations. Dallas's ancestors had helped found the town, which was one of the reasons he and his brothers had all agreed to locate The Arsenal there. No one was willing to ignore their familial responsibilities.

Dad may have passed, but it didn't mean the Mason dream of

running cattle had died with him. Mom wasn't ready to let go. None of them were.

Or so Dallas had thought. His little sister Riley had recently declared that they were out of the cattle business and taken the initiative to make it so in a big way. Their longtime ranch foreman had taken more responsibilities while Dallas's mom coordinated selling off more than eighty percent of their cattle. They'd keep just enough to keep Dad's dream alive. Juan and his crew could more than manage alone.

And Little Sister had opened up shop with Judson. A private investigator. Dallas couldn't help but smirk at the fact that the lethal assassin had undertaken training Riley. His sister didn't have any idea how deadly Jud was or what all he'd done while at The Collective.

She had no idea Dallas was more like Jud than he cared to admit.

"You with us?" Dylan asked as he slapped Dallas on the back hard enough to make him take a step forward.

"Thanks for today," he said into the room. Both women halted their typing.

They turned in unison. Blinked. Jesus. It was creepy as hell to see how in sync the two became, how disconnected from reality they were while in the zone. He often wondered what went through their heads. No wonder Jud and Dylan hadn't left their side.

The women had no clue what went on around them while they worked. All that existed was the op, the data.

The mission.

And he'd put them through the ringer the past few weeks. Attempt after attempt.

They'd searched so much wilderness Dallas couldn't imagine there was more left. They'd fanned east and north. Oregon. Idaho. Washington. Canada. Land records had been run against the database they'd seized from The Collective. Even though they'd gotten a few hits, they hadn't had any success.

The women couldn't keep running themselves into the ground. Mary was carrying Dallas's niece or nephew. He couldn't jeopardize their health by running full throttle any longer. They needed to ease off the gas.

Which meant *he* needed to ease off the gas. HERA would keep chasing leads, culling the data, and establishing new search grids. He'd chat with Marshall and divide the new grids up. There wasn't any reason for them all to go out. He trusted his brothers and everyone at The Arsenal. They were all the best trained soldiers and operatives around. They were all as emotionally invested in finding Dallas's kid as he was. It was time to work smarter, not harder.

"You okay?" Vi asked as she stood. Pain flashed across her face a moment. Jud growled and wrapped her against his side, supporting her weight before she teetered over.

"Let HERA run stuff. We'll reconvene tomorrow, figure out when and where to hit next." Dallas settled a hand on Mary's shoulder when she didn't stand. She continued tapping on the keyboard. "Mary."

The woman still had trouble disconnecting from her ops persona. He understood how a mission could overtake your life—he'd survived for nothing but the next op while in The Collective. Disconnected from family. From life.

"Mary," he repeated, his voice firmer than before. She blinked, peering up at him.

"We'll find him." She repeated the promise every time she saw him, as if there was nothing more to discuss until she'd made the statement a fact.

The woman had no idea she'd burrowed into Dallas's soul and breathed life into him by claiming Dylan's heart. People like her were the reason he'd fought and bled for his country, why he'd sacrificed even more while in The Collective. The good he'd done there had far outweighed the bad.

Or so he hoped.

"Big brother needs his beauty sleep," Dallas whispered as he leaned down and kissed her forehead. "Go tuck him in, and let my future nephew get some sleep."

"Or niece," Vi corrected.

"Or niece." Dallas smirked.

"I'm sorry we didn't find him," Mary whispered. "I thought for certain this was it."

"We'll find him." Dallas accepted the hug she offered when she rose. His gaze cut to Dylan, who stood nearby but remained far enough away to show he had no issues with the embrace or the personal conversation.

Before Mary, Dylan had been a much different man and brother. Dallas's relationship with him had improved radically over the past few months, and he had his future sister-in-law to thank for the change.

The two couples headed toward the exit, but Jud hung back after Vi left the room. The door sealed shut.

"Problem?" Dallas asked.

"A few." Jud motioned toward a file. "Marshall said you knew the players in Marville better than anyone out here. We need your input on what we've got so far."

"You've made progress."

"No, but someone thinks we have. Riley's tires were slashed outside the bar in Marville."

The Sip and Spin was a hellhole dive with a built-in laundromat. It'd been trouble since the day it opened and was also where Rachelle Garrett, Riley's best friend, had waitressed until recently. She was the reason they were looking into the Marville situation. "Rachelle say anything yet?"

"Nope. I'm thinking her being out here is more out of desire than necessity."

Dallas had thought so the first day she'd arrived, and his brothers had expressed their concerns several times since then. The woman had set her sights on hooking up with one of them—it didn't seem to matter which one any longer. Somehow that fact had flown well below Riley's radar. Little sis didn't take too kindly to women using her to get closer to them. She didn't trust easily and tended to scrape women like that off.

But Rachelle had gotten under her skin, and Dallas and his

brothers weren't willing to upset that friendship, not without a hell of a reason. They'd handled grabby women before. They'd deal with her and her brother, Cliff, at The Arsenal.

But Rachelle not saying what was spooking her in Marville was officially a problem now that tires were getting slashed. Someone was pissed and not afraid to gain their attention to make their point known.

"I'll have a word with Rachelle, see if I can get more. Riley okay?"

"She's pissed." Jud smiled. "She'll be a hell of an investigator once we knock off a couple layers of that sass."

"Still not sold on training her, but I'd rather be involved than trust someone else to do it." Which was the only reason Dallas had been working with Riley on hand-to-hand combat techniques the past few weeks whenever he was around. Jud was helping, as was everyone else.

Slashed tires could mean anything, especially in a small town like Marville, where the only entertainment was making trouble. But he wouldn't stand aside and let Riley get in over her head, not when he could help. He knew the town and those running it—or had back before the military. Before The Collective.

Hunger and his resolve to help Riley with Marville sent him to the mess hall. Even though the hour was late, the tables were filled with people, most of them from the Warrior's Path Project. His gaze swept the area as he muttered his frustration and tracked the lithe blonde heading his direction.

Rachelle Garrett was trouble in all caps. Nolan and Jesse appeared at his side as the woman flounced to a halt within touching distance. A chill spread through him as her gaze crawled appreciatively down him. A glint appeared in her eyes as she offered the same, slow perusal of Nolan, then Jesse.

Both brothers grunted their disinterest and did a half-turn that drew their attention elsewhere, into the room. Dallas did the same. Rachelle was Riley's best friend. No way in hell any of them would tread that ground, even if they were interested. Which they were definitely *not*.

"I'm sorry you didn't find him," she offered, her voice pitched high and shrill. Like nails down a chalkboard, it droned on. "Let's go grab a beer. You can unload your worries and relax. I'll take your mind off it."

The lustful glance meandering from his face to his crotch gnawed the lone strand of his patience. He didn't have time for Rachelle's bullshit. Then he recalled what Jud had said a few moments ago. They'd made no progress in Marville, and the woman standing in front of him had offered very little in the way of usable data. Riley had moved her best friend out to the ranch because "she was terrified."

Clearly there was more than one definition of terrified in play. Dallas glanced at Nolan, then at Jesse. Both brothers wore frustrated looks as they took a step backward.

"I'm thinking it's time you and I have a conversation, Rachelle." He waited a few beats, until her gaze latched onto his. Anticipation glinted in her gaze. He tracked her swallow. "Tell me about Marville."

"Why? Riley and Jud are looking into it, right? That doesn't concern you."

"Anything to do with Riley concerns me," Dallas said. "Her tires got slashed, so I've decided to help Little Sis out with this one, keep myself focused on something other than what I can't control."

Nolan grunted and slapped him on the back. "Good, was going to suggest it. Riles and Jud could use your help."

"This is ridiculous. There's nothing you can do. There's nothing to do." Rachelle's hair swished around her angelic face. She licked her lips and looked at them all. "I don't know anything."

"Then why are you scared? Why are you hiding out here?" Nolan asked. "We've been more than patient, but Riley's on someone's radar. We're wading in."

"This is all so embarrassing," Rachelle whispered. A tear tracked down her cheek.

Dallas's gut clenched at the sight. He hated when women cried, especially when it was a move to take control of the situation. He recognized the tactic. Arms crossed, he waited out the waterworks.

Lighten up. She's not Marla. This isn't a play, a mission, or an op. She's not The Collective. She's your little sister's best friend, and she's terrified out of her mind.

He'd been burned by more than Marla, though. Dallas had learned not to trust the hard way and almost lost Dylan as a result. His heart ached at the thought, but he dragged his focus back to the woman before him.

When none of them moved to console her, Rachelle sniffled and swiped at her cheeks. "You're worse than that man."

"Jud?" Jesse asked.

"Yeah, him. He keeps grilling me like I'm a criminal with something to hide." Rachelle flopped into a chair and sighed dramatically.

"Seeing as you haven't given us anything in the way of data, I can see how he'd assume you're hiding something," Dallas said. He reached over and took her hand. She latched on quick. "Give me something to go on. I swear I won't judge, and it'll stay between us. But we need to know what's going on."

"It's not my fault. I told her she was stupid. She's always been stupid, stirring up trouble when there's no reason."

"Who is she?"

"My sister, Kamren."

Rachelle had a sister? He glanced over at Nolan, whose gaze had narrowed.

"She's in trouble?" Nolan asked.

"She *is* the trouble, always has been." Rachelle swiped her eyes again. "She runs with the Marville Dogs, you know. Hell, her best friend's brother runs them from prison, or something."

"Daniella." Dallas let the name tumble from his lips as his mind recoiled from the memory of his rebellious teenage years. He'd once been tight with Daniella's older brother, Dominic.

Back then they'd been a bunch of bored punks drinking booze, smoking, and street racing. He'd heard the Marville Dogs were heavily into drugs and underground activities now, but he hadn't been over to Marville since he'd been back. There'd been no reason.

Now there was.

If little sis had gotten on the Marville Dog's radar, that meant he'd have to weigh in, warn them off, and maybe make a trip to Huntsville, where Dominic was in prison for murder, and have a word. The list of potential moves listed in his mind as he waited out Rachelle's silence.

"What's your sister into?" Nolan asked.

"No clue. She's never around. She's crazy." Her gaze widened as her voice lowered. "She scares me."

Drugs or gambling. Since the Marville Dogs were heavily into both, she'd have access to both through Daniella. Son of a bitch. He rose.

"Sit your ass down and eat," Jesse ordered as he appeared with a plate of food. "It'll wait."

Dallas glared at his brother, then glanced down at the food. His stomach pitched as his mind wandered to the fact that his son was out there. Somewhere. Had he eaten? Was he cold, hungry, and tired? Was anyone taking care of him?

"Sit your ass down and eat," Jesse repeated, this time in a tone that signaled he'd shovel it into Dallas's mouth if necessary.

Dallas's mouth fractured into a grin. He almost welcomed an ass kicking or two. Maybe then his heart wouldn't hurt so much.

2

A picture might be worth a thousand words, but since Kamren Garrett couldn't read, that didn't mean much to her. She thumbed through the newest supposed evidence she'd gathered and ignored the catcalls coming her direction from the Sip and Spin. A brisk wind whipped through the parking lot and into the open windows of her battered pickup truck.

There'd be a storm tonight, which meant she'd probably be better off crashing at the house rather than sleeping in her truck bed. It wasn't like anyone was out at the old farm anyway, seeing how Riley Mason had dragged Rachelle and Cliff over to Resino.

The Arsenal.

Kamren swallowed and let the impact of the name strike her center mass. Riley's six brothers were back from military service or whatever the heck they'd been doing. Talk around the tri-county had the lot of them flying around in capes like the new-age Superman, Thor, and Iron Man rolled into one.

No, they were more than that. They always had been as far as Rache was concerned. For Rachelle they'd been salvation. A way out of hell.

Kamren couldn't fault Rachelle for wanting more than the piece-of-shit house on the outskirts of Marville they'd been raised in. Little sis had done good for herself. She'd gotten an associate's degree and had decided to be a vet tech. How cool was that?

Truth told, Riley had been more of a sister to Rachelle than Kamren.

He's dead. None of this will bring him back. Why would you want it to? Why does it even matter? Let it go.

Rachelle's words from months ago echoed in Kamren's mind, as they frequently did late at night when exhaustion and hunger demanded her attention. When day bled into the bitter, bleak darkness where slumber fed memories, bitter reminders she'd failed Rachelle time and time again. And Cliff.

Her mom.

Her dad.

The last two were dead now, not that anyone except her cared. She sealed the thick, worn envelope shut and shoved it into her tattered backpack. Sooner or later she'd have to admit this was beyond her. Like so many things. Maybe she was too stupid to figure anything out.

Maybe Rachelle was right and there wasn't anything to figure out.

Kamren stared at the entry to the Sip and Spin. Though exhaustion demanded she spend a few hours getting much-needed rest, she knew sleep wouldn't come until she'd checked in with her best friend. She'd dodged calls for days now. Weeks.

She exited the vehicle and headed into the small building. The entirety of Marville had shown up tonight. Washing machines and dryers whirred and spun around the edges of the bar. Laundry baskets sat in a large heap in the corner nearest the door. Every table was filled. Empty beer bottles overflowed the tables as she headed toward the bar.

The bartender froze in a half turn. Angry daggers shot from her dark brown eyes. Yep, it was worse than Kamren expected.

"Where is she?" Dani demanded.

"Thanks for the welcome home, best friend. Yes, I'm fine. Thanks for asking." Kamren forced a melodic tone despite the tense undertone whipping from her friend.

Dani slammed four beer bottles down on the bar. Her long, straight black hair tumbled past her shoulders in a riotous mess, much like the woman herself. They'd been best friends since kindergarten, but that didn't mean much in these situations, the ones where the ravine between the secret lives they led became too cavernous for friendship to straddle.

"I'll ask again. It's been weeks now. Enough is enough. Where is she?"

Kamren ignored the question since the entire town knew the answer. She couldn't fix what'd happened a couple months ago when Riley rolled into town with her posse and carted Rachelle off to the Mason ranch, The Arsenal. Whatever it was, it may as well be on Mars. No one could touch that place or the men running it. All she could do now was hope Riley's move didn't backfire. Otherwise everything Kamren had worked on the past sixteen months would collapse and she'd be dead.

At least Rachelle's safe. That's all that matters.

"Get her back here, for your sake and hers," Dani clipped as she slammed a beer on the bar. "I can't weigh in on this, not when the Masons are involved."

"They aren't involved. Riley came and picked up her best friend. Do you really think any of her six brothers give a damn about Marville?" Kamren took a sip of the beer and hoped the many ears listening believed what she said, even if it was bullshit. The Masons didn't ignore trouble, which was why no one in these parts much cared for them. "I've scoped out The Arsenal. Hell of an operation, but all about private government contracts and big international shit. When have the Masons ever given a damn about Marville or anyone in it?"

"You'd better hope that's the case. Folks are nervous, the sort I can't contain—not even for you." Dani's voice lowered. "Lay low and let the dust settle."

"You know that's not an option. I'm close." Sixteen months of investigation into her father's death. "Once I find the right thread to pull, the truth will unravel."

"It's all the wrong threads you're pulling that are the problem. My brother's crew has kept quiet out of respect to me, but that respect only goes so far."

Given the fact Rachelle was hunkered down with the Masons, it was more likely they didn't want to rattle that particular hornet's nest. She glanced over at the table where Dani's cousin held court. "This isn't about the Marville Dogs, Dani."

Javier Salazar had taken control of the local gang when Dani's big brother went down for murder. Though Dom held firm leadership from his prison cell, his cousin was unofficially in charge. That bastard was ten shades crazy and a hundred layers of asshole.

"The MDs own Marville and everyone in it," Dani spat. "Back off and lay low."

"Is that a friend asking or an MD demanding?" Kamren stared her defiant friend down.

She took in the tattooed bulldog holding a bone with a lone bead of blood on her best friend's chest, just above the swell of her breasts. The bloodier the bone, the deeper the person's loyalty. Dani had earned that bead when she was fourteen, the same year her brother went away for murder.

Kamren had never found out what really happened that night, not that it mattered. It was the night she lost her best friend. The husk who remained was more Marville Dog soldier than anything.

"It's whichever one keeps your head down and out of other people's business." She wiped the bar down. "Tell your sister to get her ass in here tomorrow night or she's gone. Lonnie's pissed."

Lonnie Haskell spent the majority of his life pissed. He was a human slug whose sole accomplishment in life was being the twin brother to the local sheriff. Business at the Sip and Spin and the not-so-legal underground gambling empire he and the Marville Dogs ran cemented Lonnie's success in Marville, thereby proving even useless slugs could succeed.

"I'll take her shifts. That'll keep Riley and her brothers out of Marville, right?"

"I suppose so." Skepticism sharpened Dani's gaze as it slid to where her cousin and his crew were. "You talk to her yet?"

"No. She wants nothing to do with me."

"Bullshit. She gets whiplash scrambling to the bank when you send money."

"She needs it more than me." Kamren waited a couple seconds. "You been out to the farm?"

"A couple times, but Riley's been snooping, out there tending things like she's little Bo Peep. Figured I'd let her take it on, seeing how she's a know-it-all, do-it-better-than-all Mason." Dani slammed a beer on the bar. "Drink, then get the hell out. I don't need your trouble in here."

Still persona non-grata, even with her best friend. Great. Kamren snagged the beer and took a heavy pull. She was two swallows in when she sensed the shift in the area around her. An awkward, heavy silence descended—which was odd enough within itself. Marvillians loved their tunes and revelry, especially on Friday nights.

The scuff of thick soles across the floor too near her awakened pinpricks of unease along her spine. Tension coiled within her muscles as she set the bottle down and glanced in the mirror behind the bar. Dani was nowhere to be seen.

But it was the fierce intensity within the newcomer's blue gaze that demanded her attention. Tall, muscled, and lethal. The description translated to one name boomeranging within her mind. Mason.

She didn't know which, since she, unlike the other citizens within the tri-county, hadn't honed her knowledge of all things Mason like it was a religion. She recognized the thick, dark hair and rugged jawline easily enough. She was uneducated, not dead.

Whoever he was, his gaze remained on her longer than she liked, as though he saw through her facade and recognized the slight tremble in her hands as her pulse quickened. Why was he here? Was something wrong with Rachelle? Cliff?

Questions listed in her mind, but any move on her part at this juncture would be a weakness, one she couldn't afford to show in front of Javier and his crew. Dani may have been bitchily blunt, as she typically was when dishing truth, but she'd been spot on. The Marville Dogs were more than agitated by her activities of late.

It'd been the primary reason she'd left a few weeks before, deciding to follow leads up in Austin rather than hang around town and mourn all the dead ends she'd hoarded. They'd warned her to back off weeks ago, and she hadn't. Now that she'd returned? Well, it likely wouldn't sit well, and the man behind her had just made it ten times worse.

Having a Mason prowl into the Sip and Spin like he had every right to be in Marville Dog territory was tantamount to declaring war. A war she wanted no part of, mainly because she was already in a battle no one realized existed. Until she figured out who'd killed her dad, nothing else mattered.

Except for Rachelle and Cliff. They were all she had left now. She'd do anything to keep them safe, even if it meant declaring war on Javier and his crew. Was there a reason they were so nervous?

Likely not.

They just didn't like people meddling in their business. And she'd dived deep in their shit, so much so she stank from what all she'd uncovered. Funny how following people around gave so much insight into their secrets.

"You lost?" Lonnie's voice fractured the awkward silence. "A big-time war hero like you is best served at Bubba's. Head on back to Resino where you belong, Mason. We've got no beef with you and your brothers."

"I'm thinking you do."

The low rumble cast a heatwave of awareness within Kamren. Her gut clenched as she forced down another swallow of her beer. She'd drink an entire keg if it kept her quiet and out of whatever had brought him here.

"Get gone while you still can, man. We've got no beef with you," Javier said. "For Dom, walk away."

"Respect, Jav. That's not happening until I get what I came for."

"Have your say, then get gone," Lonnie ordered.

"Someone slashed Riley's tires today, second time."

The statement charged the air with a ripple of shock, unease, and general fear. Marville might not have an appreciation for the Mason name, but they sure as hell had an aversion to it. A downright unhealthy fear, if the truth was told, mainly because Riley's six brothers had spent many years beating down anyone and everyone who dared even glare at little sis the wrong way.

Sadly, most of those someones were the reprobates carted over to Resino due to the non-existent-past-elementary Marville public school system. Resino educated everyone in Marville past the sixth grade, so the Masons had beaten their fair quota of the local populace.

Or so Rachelle had said many a time in her I-wanna-be-married-to-a-Mason declarations. Whoever had made a move on Riley had been stupid. Really, really stupid.

Kamren laughed. The sound was low, but tumbled into the room at a loud enough volume to draw the man's attention. He angled toward her, crowding her personal space until heat wafted against her back. A firm hand locked onto the barstool near her thigh and turned it until she faced him.

Gasps echoed around her, but her lungs were in her throat. She peered up, attempting a glare, but all thoughts of anger melted beneath the intensity within his gaze.

"You find my sister's tires getting cut funny?"

"No."

"Your laugh sure as fuck says otherwise, sweetheart."

"I find the fact that someone was that stupid hysterical." She lifted her beer and saluted the room. "Besides, that means I'm not the only one spending cake on tires."

"That so?"

"Yep."

"Didn't catch a name, but I'm thinking I just found the second bullet point to my visit."

"You have bullet points?"

"I do. I'm thinking you're number two, seeing how you have the same button nose and lips as Rachelle." He leaned forward and settled a hand on each side of the bar behind her. "I'm Dallas Mason. You're Kamren."

"Is Rachelle okay?"

"She's been with us for weeks now, yet you haven't been around. I'm not sure you deserve an answer."

Ouch. The reply struck hard. She bit back the response rising in her throat. He wouldn't care. No one cared. She was on her own, like always. She and Rachelle may have grown up in the same house, but they were worlds apart. And that was good.

It meant Rache had men like Dallas Mason in her life, people who gave a damn and kept her safe.

"Thanks for looking out for her and Cliff."

"You're done."

The finality in his statement made her lean back. His lethal edge sliced through the silence as he leaned in. Hot breath trailed across her cheek.

"Whatever shit you're mired in doesn't hit her or my sister. Clean yourself up and move on. Get out of Marville, get out of Texas. Get gone whatever way is needed so Rachelle never breathes the shit you're stirring up. You're done."

"Clean myself up," she repeated.

Then the meaning of the words struck her like a shotgun blast. Drugs? He thought she was tied into drugs. Dirty.

Of course. She was from Marville. All folks from Resino thought they were better. Then again, she was a Garrett, trash by even Marville standards. Naturally, trash got tied up with drugs.

"You don't know anything," she replied in an angered whisper. She punctuated each word crisply, as evenly as possible despite the lump of emotion in her throat.

"We aren't your enemy, Kamren. Whatever you're messed up in, we'll help."

Right.

Kamren considered the offer for a few seconds but realized the foolishness. Even if they believed her, they wouldn't care. She couldn't get anyone to care because, like her, her father had been a nobody living on the outskirts of town and surviving off land he'd tended with little help from anybody.

He'd always warned her folks wouldn't want much to do with her. Kamren had always suspected he was paranoid or delusional, but he was right. She hadn't realized exactly how right until that day eighteen months ago when...

She pushed the thought away, straightened her spine, and stood. Lonnie and the majority of Marville were watching. As far as they were concerned, Dallas Mason had just declared war on her and her little mission. He had no clue what she was up to, yet he'd weighed in and declared her done, obliterated sixteen months of hard work. What little patience the Marville folk had for her snooping would be at an end soon because the almighty Masons had given them a permission slip to stop her.

"You have no idea what you've just done," she spat angrily.

"If it keeps Rachelle and those I care about clean and safe, I'm good with whatever you think I just did. You know where to find me when you're ready to wake the fuck up and move on."

He knew? The statement implied Rachelle had told him about her mission. Then again, he was a Mason. Riley and her brothers adored their father. The man's death had been a sad time in the tri-county. Even Marville folk respected Dallas's father—he'd been country through and through, a rancher to the bone.

"None of this concerns you or your family."

"It concerned us the day Riley made it her mission to keep her best friend from ghosting through life."

Kamren squeezed her eyes shut at the statement. Rachelle wasn't as settled with Riley's family as she'd initially thought. Was she taking her meds? Maybe Kamren could call Cliff, make sure.

No.

As harsh as Dallas's words were, he was right. She needed to get answers quickly, especially now that the Marville Dogs had heard the declaration. Everyone assumed the Masons were behind her because

Rachelle was at their ranch. Now? Now she was truly alone, which meant she was no longer untouchable by the Marville Dogs.

Though her fight wasn't with them, she'd learned more than she should. They'd left her be, but she suspected that wouldn't last long. Javier rose from his perch at the table and sauntered over like he owned the joint and everyone in it. In many ways, he did.

Dani had yet to reappear, which meant even she wasn't willing to weigh in on what was going down. Even best friends had limits, and Kamren was real good at shoving past them.

"We'll help you move on, but you're done. It's not healthy, Kamren," Dallas said.

What had Rachelle told them? Concern filled his eyes as he watched, waiting for a response she couldn't give. She was already neck-deep in trouble. One wrong play and she'd drown without knowing who'd killed her dad. He'd been an asshole, but he was her father. No matter what, he deserved to rest in peace.

"I'm not your concern, Mason. Never have been, never will be. I was just passing through, so I'll be gone by daylight. Tell Rachelle I'll be in touch in a couple months."

"Thinking that's not a good idea," Dallas replied. "Come out to the ranch. We've got some people you can chat with. They'll help you."

Right. Cause she was drugged out of her noggin or something. She nodded, snagged her backpack and headed for the door.

The sooner she got gone, the better. A whistle rose in the air. She froze. Javier's voice chilled her bones.

"He's right, Kamren. You're done. Get gone and stay gone. We don't need your mess in Marville."

3

Two weeks later...

SHE SHOULDN'T HAVE COME.

The realization shuddered through her in a ripple of nausea and unease as she entered the Sip and Spin. Two weeks hadn't calmed the situation Dallas Mason incited. Whispers rippled through the area as her gaze darted from one table to another. No Javier, but a few Marville Dogs sat in the appointed section.

Son of a bitch.

"You need to go," Lonnie said. "Things have calmed with you gone. Masons aren't sniffing around no more."

Because everyone had run to ground and laid low when she fled town. She'd made the perfect scapegoat to keep the Masons from nosing around Marville and uncovering whatever shady bullshit people were into.

"Just grabbing a beer and catching up with Dani."

"Gave her the night off; she's racing." Lonnie crossed his meaty arms. "You'd best head on out. I'm sure there's a room in Nomad you can crash in."

Nomad was twenty miles north of Marville and the third town in what locals called the tri-county area, with Resino and Marville being the other two. It was bigger, and no self-respecting Marvillian would crash there.

No matter. She'd catch up with Dani later. Truth told, she'd needed a break to contemplate her decision. She'd spent the past couple of weeks digging deeper into her latest suspects. Though she wasn't sure what she'd stumbled across, her gut told her she was closer than ever.

Which meant it was time to clear the air with Dallas Mason.

Though Dallas's assumptions had initially pissed her off, Kamren could understand why he'd made them. Her only friend was a Marville Dog. They weren't exactly upstanding citizens. The longer she'd thought about their altercation, the more she'd realized he'd expressed no ill intent. He had offered help. It wasn't his fault he suspected she was wrapped up in drugs or some other nefarious activity. What else could there be?

Did he even know her dad was dead, much less murdered?

It wasn't like Rachelle would've wasted a breath mentioning their father.

"I'll be back later, Lonnie. I've got questions, but they can wait."

Kamren pushed away thoughts of Dani and the Dogs. They were something else she'd left on the back burner too long. She needed to make nice with Javier and his crew soon because she didn't need trouble from them. Staying away for two weeks had probably not been the smartest play. The fact that they hadn't attempted a conversation just now unnerved her.

They were brash assholes who enjoyed public confrontations, especially if it let them preen like peacocks. No matter. She'd deal with Javier later, after she'd sorted Rachelle and the Masons.

She'd parked the battered pickup truck at the far end of the over-flowing parking area in front of the Sip and Spin. A crisp breeze flowed as she got into her vehicle and it rumbled to life. She pulled her rifle from beneath the seat out of habit, one she'd learned from her father.

Always be prepared, girl. Don't let anyone take you by surprise.

She glanced in her mirrors and flicked the headlights on. Two minutes later, she was chewing up highway and heading to The Arsenal. Her cell phone sat beside her, the number to the compound's main line already programmed in. She didn't expect to get in, not when it was already after midnight.

Waiting until tomorrow would be smart, but she'd never been smart. That was Rachelle.

The road yawned as she settled into the rolling countryside around her. She slowed as the Resino lights appeared around the bend. Headlights appeared in her rearview mirror. The Arsenal was on Mason land, which was a right at the four-way stop and five miles out, maybe seven. She couldn't remember exactly where the entry gate was.

She made the turn at the four-way and rolled her shoulders as she navigated onto the road leading to the sprawl of Mason land. She'd find a quiet space to park and catch some sleep, then she'd approach the entry gate when daylight came. Stakeouts had become commonplace for her the past several months. The who and where had changed, but sitting on her ass watching people was the same no matter the subject.

Headlights appeared in her rearview mirror, closer than before. A second set flashed on from the side and lurched toward her. She swerved left, avoiding the brunt of damage from getting T-boned—just barely.

Son of a bitch.

Someone didn't want her near The Arsenal. Did they think she meant to turn over what she had found so far to the Masons, get their help? Like any of them would ever help someone like her. They were too busy fighting wars in foreign countries and protecting America.

Marville trash wasn't worth worrying about.

Clean yourself up and move on. Get out of Marville, get out of Texas.

Get gone whatever way is needed so Rachelle never breathes the shit you're stirring up. You're done.

It'd been two weeks since her face off with Dallas Mason. He'd made assumptions she hadn't corrected. Why bother? He was right. Rachelle was better off away from her and the troubles she'd stirred.

The troubles slamming her off the highway.

It'd been a mistake going to the Sip and Spin. Coming to The Arsenal.

The truck lurched forward against a grind of bumper-on-bumper contact. Her teeth rattled, her body slammed against the seat belt. She gunned the truck and powered on. Her pulse quickened, but a calm settled over her—a steady, rumbling awareness of everything around her. She scanned the area ahead.

Lights.

The Arsenal?

Maybe.

The vehicle slammed into her truck's side. Metal crunched, but Kamren swerved into the impact and gunned the accelerator. Close. So close.

Break away. Prepare a response.

She snagged the cell and hit the call button.

Come on. Come on. Come on.

Answer. Answer. Answer.

"Arsenal." The gruff response was huskier than she expected, as if half-asleep.

She grunted as the vehicle slammed into her backside once more. Tires spun as she battled with the steering wheel. Damn it. They'd screwed up the alignment somehow.

"Who is this?" The voice—sharper, more determined—drew her attention. Adrenaline surged, fueling her thoughts.

"Kamren Garrett. Someone's after me. I'm close, but not going to make it. I'll draw their fire, but keep Rachelle safe. Don't let anyone outside Resino County get my backpack."

She doubted any of it made sense, but she had no time to repeat or play twenty questions. She angled the vehicle off the road and barreled out the passenger door as it lurched to a stop. Right hand on her rifle, left hand on her backpack, she did an awkward, curled roll into the overgrown grass in the bar ditch.

Headlights danced and bobbed as her two opponents pulled over. Voices fractured the otherwise silent night. Gasoline filled her nostrils. The fuel tank was damaged from the impact earlier. Good. Her pulse quickened as a plan formed in her mind.

She belly-crawled deeper into the grass toward the massive fence line denoting Mason land. She waited until the voices were nearer the vehicle she'd escaped.

Deep breath in. Pained breath out. She rolled into position. Up on her knees.

Aim.

Fire.

Flames shot upward from the pooled gasoline she'd ignited. Fiery rage chewed a line along the asphalt until it swallowed the truck she'd been in. Angry voices rose on the other side of the inferno. She settled deeper against the ground and waited more heartbeats than she expected.

The concussive boom rattled the ground. Flames shot out and chewed up the dry grass nearby. Shouts rose above the frenzied, fiery dance. Shadows sprinted and darted near the flame's brightness.

Aim.

Fire.

Fire.

Her ears rang. She squeezed her eyes shut a moment, willing her mind to focus beyond the shots, the flames. Voices. She needed more voices. Voices translated to targets. Targets were good. Targets kept her breathing.

The backpack.

She sat her ass on the backpack and raised her rifle as more shadows appeared beyond the flames. Headlights. A stream of head-lights and raised voices. Gunfire.

She crawled deeper into the bar ditch, sliding the backpack through the grimy mud. Cow manure filled her nostrils. She crawled along the fence line, away from the fiery inferno she'd created. A beam of light fractured the night, spewing down on her.

She rolled.

Aim.

Fire.

"Stand down, Quillery. I have eyes on her." The order was deep enough to break through the ringing in her ears, but barely.

Her breath quickened as she did another roll. Positioned atop her backpack, she aimed. The light returned, brighter and aimed at her eyes. She squinted.

Pain swept up her arm as a massive weight settled atop her. She bucked and kicked. Right hand grasped on her weapon, she fisted her left hand.

Aim.

Punch.

The figure looming above her grunted. A firm hand settled atop her right hand and pushed hard until she slammed backward on the ground. Shock detonated as she was summarily flipped onto her belly. Both hands were yanked behind her back and up until pain radiated from her shoulders.

"Stand down," the voice growled.

She squirmed and bucked to no avail. The heavy weight pinned her firmly as her hands were secured behind her back. She stared at the lights of The Arsenal.

So close.

She swallowed the regret and hoped they'd keep Rachelle safe.

Kamren grunted when she was turned over and hauled onto her knees. Knees firmly on her backpack. She glared up at her captor. Breath swooshed from her lungs as the annoying beam of light circling overhead spotlighted unruly dark hair and a muscular torso. The business end of a Sig Sauer aimed at her head demanded her attention for a few heartbeats.

Then her gaze continued its sweep. Thick thighs. Lean hips.

"Situation secured; notify local fire department." The man eased his stance slightly. He glanced over his shoulder as another figure headed their direction.

Tension coiled in her muscles.

Pick your battles, girl. Sometimes you have to lose a battle to win the war.

Anger kept her silent. Head down, she focused on the threads of sound breaking through the ringing in her ears. It was like she was sitting at the end of a tunnel.

"What the hell was this?" The second voice rose in frustration. "We've got head shots over there, clean kills."

"It looks like our girl here's good with a rifle," the first shadow commented. He shoved his weapon into a holster. "Quillery, raise the light a few feet so we can see better. You're blinding us."

Kamren peered upward as the light rose. A drone? Her stomach did an awkward somersault as she studied the figures a bit closer in the new light. Relief swarmed her insides like bees high on honey.

Masons.

She recognized the distinctive dark hair and gorgeous bodies. Was one of them Dallas? She couldn't tell with the low light and blurry vision. Her head hurt. Bad. Though they all looked alike in the darkness, she knew there'd be differences in the light of day. For now, it didn't matter.

Don't be stupid. Dallas made it clear your troubles weren't theirs. Keep quiet and get gone. You never should've come out here.

He'd offered help, too. She forced a deep breath and focused on the present.

"Sheriff's on his way," a third man said. He halted, looking down at her. "I'm Marshall Mason. This is my ranch you're trying to burn up. What happened here?"

She kept mute. He'd called the sheriff? Sheriff Haskell was the last asshole she needed out here. She shifted on the backpack. They had no way of knowing the bastard was dirty, though, and she didn't have much evidence substantiating her belief.

Dread replaced the relief as she breathed into the silence. The first shadow crouched. A firm grip forced her gaze up. She tumbled into dark blue depths.

Dallas.

He was more gorgeous than she remembered, not that she'd obsessed about their first meeting a couple weeks ago. Okay, she'd totally obsessed.

"Guess the conversation we had didn't stick," Dallas commented. "Hell of a mess you're in, Kamren. Read us in, and we'll do what we can to get you cleaned up and safe."

Right. Drugs. She'd almost forgotten that part of the ugly discussion they'd had weeks ago. She blinked and shook some of the confusion loose. Pain spread through her limbs. An ache throbbed along her side.

"Kamren, I need you to focus," Dallas ordered. He gripped her face tighter. "Sheriff Patterson is on his way. Can you tell us what happened?"

Patterson? Not Haskell? Oh, wait. Resino wasn't in Haskell's jurisdiction. Relief returned. The backpack was still secure. Okay, good. She swallowed, forcing words. "Is Rachelle okay?"

Full lips upturned into a grin. "Yeah, I'm pretty sure she's still sleeping despite the hell you unleashed on our doorstep."

Fat lot of good it did her. She was trussed up like a turkey with zero likelihood of walking away from this.

"Sorry about that," she replied with a bit more attitude than a trussed-up turkey should have. No, not turkey.

Murderer.

She kept quiet. Murder wasn't something she could explain away, even if it'd been self-defense. She couldn't involve the Masons in this mess. They were keeping Rachelle safe, which was even more important now that she'd freaking murdered someone.

But who?

Marville Dogs?

Probably. They'd been at the Sip and Spin.

Ugh. They weren't even the ones she was after. Hopefully it wasn't them. Dani's cousin was a Grade A dick, but the other guys weren't so terrible. Pain shot along her thighs, but she remained locked in place on her backpack.

If they weren't Marville Dogs, then she'd gotten closer than she'd realized, not that it mattered now. She'd be hauled off to jail and thrown into a cold, dark cell for life.

I'm sorry, Dad. I tried.

There was still hope, a long shot. If she could get hauled away and the backpack remained, Rachelle could get it later.

But her little sister wasn't down with what Kamren had been doing. She hadn't cared that Dad was dead. No. Rachelle had cared. She'd *celebrated* his death.

Emotion clogged Kamren's throat. Too many battles to wage, not enough soldiers. She couldn't wage war alone, not with so many sides to cover. She'd hoped to argue her case with the Masons, see if they'd help. Surely they would if she could convince them it was in Rachelle's best interest. They cared about her because their little sister cared.

Dallas hovered. His scrutiny bored into her, creating a nervous, frenetic awareness in her she found unsettling.

"Didn't expect her to be so quiet," one of the shadows commented.

"She's not her sister, Marshall," Dallas replied.

Marshall. The eldest Mason, if her memory served her, which was doubtful given the painful throbbing in her head. Her stomach pitched angrily.

"Are you hurt?" he asked.

The ringing continued. She blinked rapidly, willing her senses to fully return. She'd been closer to the blast radius than she realized. Her temples throbbed.

No, her head freaking hurt. Bad.

She stifled the whiny response. Keep quiet, stay focused. Nothing mattered except getting away without the backpack being noticed. Regret filled her when Marshall reached down and grabbed her father's rifle. She bit her lip to stave off the enraged response.

No one but her touched it. Ever.

"Roger, Quillery, appreciate the assist," Dallas commented. "Okay, Kamren, let's cut the silent act. Who were those men, and why were you reenacting the O.K. Corral shootout on our doorstep?"

"Cut her loose, Nolan," Marshall ordered.

The second shadow she'd damn near forgotten existed shifted from his crouch. Relief was instantaneous as he released her restraints. She recoiled when he grabbed her hair and swept it back and away from her neck and shoulder.

"Easy, I'm not gonna hurt you," he commented. "Fuck, she's clipped."

Clipped. Shot?

No wonder her head hurt. She blinked. Nolan's hand drew away from the side of her head, bloody. Her stomach heaved.

If she yacked on them, she'd shoot herself. She'd skinned deer and every other animal around since she could walk. Why would she puke now?

Because it's your blood, idiot.

"Let's get you some medical attention." Dallas put a hand under each armpit and pulled, much like one would a young, errant child. She punched and kicked until he released her.

She grabbed the backpack and hugged it to her. Dizziness assailed her as she battled to stand. Dallas and Nolan both reached for her, but she growled and announced, "I'll walk."

Eyebrows lifted. A couple men in the distance chuckled, but Kamren didn't find the situation amusing. She wasn't some helpless female. She'd been walking for thirty-one years, thank you very much.

She teetered forward.

"Jesus," Dallas muttered. A strong arm coiled around her waist. "Let me get you to the truck, and you can bust my nuts later."

"Careful, I'm thinking my girl would take you up on that." The female voice startled her a moment. She shifted focus to the tall, lithe redhead standing within a vehicle's lights.

"Your girl?" Dallas asked.

"Anyone who could take the shot she did is worth my attention." She uncrossed her arms and took a step forward. "I'm Addy. You are?"

"Kamren Garrett," Nolan responded. "She's not talking, probably because of the gash in her head."

Red and blue lights swirled in the darkness. Her heart thudded in her chest. She tugged and pulled away from Dallas's grasp about her waist.

Hide the backpack.

"Talk to me, Kamren, tell me what's wrong," Dallas whispered. "We want to help, sweetheart."

"You can't help, no one can. Besides, you warned me off, said to keep my shit far away. I shouldn't have come here." She peered up into his deep blue gaze. "But you were wrong about me, Dallas Mason. So, so wrong. If you hadn't declared war with me, they would've left me be."

"I didn't declare war, sweetheart."

"You walking into the bar, saying what you said." She glared up at him. "It was war."

The harsh lights overhead spotlighted the paleness sweeping across his face, the shock registering in his eyes. His thick lips thinned as he looked at his brothers. "Fuck, she's right. They would've seen it as a declaration."

"What you said needed to be done. If it hadn't been you, it would've been Jud and gotten messier. Or one of us," Marshall said.

"You were wrong. All of you were wrong," she said.

Her head throbbed, and nausea pitched her empty stomach. She never should've thought she was good enough or smart enough to convince someone like him to help her. If her own sister didn't care who'd killed Dad, why would the Masons?

"Then tell me why I was wrong, Kamren. Talk to me so we can help with whatever this is." He held her firmly against him as if she were lighter than a feather. Strength and confidence exuded from him. For a moment she closed her eyes and pretended they were hers to lean into and accept.

"I was so close, too close. I was too stupid to be smart about it. They won."

"Who won?"

"It doesn't matter," she whispered. Anger drowned her thoughts. Exhaustion weighted her limbs.

And it didn't. She'd be silenced soon enough. One way or another, she'd made too many mistakes along the way. She wouldn't find her dad's killer anytime soon. Maybe she'd continue her investigation after she paid the price for her poor judgment tonight, which meant she needed what little she'd gathered to be safe until she got out of jail.

Like it or not, the Masons were her only hope. A Mason's word was an unbreakable bond. Everyone in the tri-county accepted it as an established certainty. "Swear you'll keep this backpack safe. Promise me. Promise me, and I'll know."

"Know what?" he asked.

"There's still hope. A Mason's vow is unbreakable."

Dallas's jaw twitched. He stared down at the backpack as though it was a nest of angry rattlers. "Kamren, I can't make that promise. I don't do promises, not anymore."

"Then keep it safe, no vow," she responded. "It's the only hope."

She closed her eyes and allowed the blackness to engulf her.

4

Promise me.

The order from another time, another woman chased Dallas. The haunted memory rattled his grip on the past, one he didn't talk about. Or remember.

Ever.

If you hadn't declared war with me, they would've left me be.

He'd likely inherited another voice to haunt him, another bad decision to regret. He rubbed his chest and willed the words away. Was she right? Had they come after her because of what he'd said.

Fuck.

"You good?" Gage asked as he came to a halt in the narrow corridor outside the examination bay.

Kamren's muddy, shit-covered backpack dangled from Dallas's left hand. He entered the small room and cursed. Blood seeped from Kamren's head, a fact he should have noted earlier, but hadn't. He hadn't noticed a lot when it came to her the past few days.

He'd been so lost in his own troubles he'd approached the Marville situation with preconceived notions about what mess she was wrapped up in. He'd blasted her with both barrels: assumptions and biases.

Truth was, he didn't know a damn thing about the woman. At all. Though Rachelle had been a permanent presence in their lives for years now, Dallas had never interacted with Kamren. He hadn't even realized she existed. How screwed up was that?

She'd come damn close to a kill shot on him. Pride warred with anger. She'd brought trouble to their back door, and that was the last thing they needed, but he admired her fierce determination.

Unfortunately, they didn't have their doctor available. Logan had taken personal time to visit family while he recuperated from being shot in the chest not too long ago.

The former CIA doctor had helped outfit The Arsenal with state-of-the-art medical equipment so the operatives and soldiers they treated would have the best medical care possible. The massive treatment station swallowed Kamren's small form.

While Dallas supposed any one of the men gathered around Kamren could field dress a wound faster than most doctors, he couldn't get himself started on the task. She'd taken a hit to the head.

Because of him.

"Brant's on his way," Jesse offered as he got to work handling the wound.

Brant Burton was a small-town doctor and all-around great guy who'd been helping out at The Arsenal ever since Mary's dust up with her previous employer. The man was former military but made no qualms about wanting nothing more in his life than doctoring the tri-county residents. He'd agreed to help out as needed until Logan returned.

"There a reason you don't want to take her to Nomad Memorial? Hospitals do stitch people up," Nolan replied.

"She's got enough problems without dragging Nomad police into it," Dallas said.

"I called Riley," Jesse commented as he tossed another blood-soaked ball of gauze in the garbage. "She doesn't want Rachelle woken up, not until we get a better idea about what's going on."

He never should've driven to Marville and hunted Kamren down that night. He'd been in a bad place, an ugly one, and had taken it out on her. He deserved to get more than his nuts busted.

But it didn't change what'd gone down in front of their facility. "Likely Kamren's into something deep."

"She blew up a car and killed three armed combatants outside our compound. I'd say she's definitely into something deep," Nolan commented. "The entire Pentagon is going to descend on her when she wakes. Quillery and Edge are both enthralled by that shot where she exploded the car. They're looping it in the operational theater."

"It was a hell of a shot. I doubt I could've done it," Dallas commented. Kamren hadn't aimed for the gas tank. She'd nailed a clean shot and ignited the gasoline itself, which led to the explosion.

"Edge thinks it was sheer luck," Jesse said.

"Probably a combination of luck and skill," Nolan offered. "Either way, it was a sweet beauty."

Dallas had been heading toward the entrance when the explosion happened. Quillery'd had drones on site right before it happened, in plenty of time to record the *Mission Impossible* style roll out of the vehicle, the one second pause, and the damn near precision-perfect shot that had eventually ignited the vehicle.

He thought back to his high school years, but couldn't recall Kamren, which was strange. Since Marville didn't have an education system past the sixth grade, kids there were transported to either Nomad or Resino. She must've gone to Nomad, which was odd since Rachelle had clearly gone to Resino—otherwise she and Riley wouldn't have become inseparable friends.

A groan escaped Kamren as she shifted on the exam table. Jesse and Nolan both took a step back. A gasp escaped her as she recoiled. Eyes wide, she maneuvered toward the other side of the narrow bed and moved to sit up.

"Easy. I'm Jesse, you're at The Arsenal. You're safe." Jesse took a cautious step back, but settled a firm hand on Kamren's shoulder when she pushed upward. "Don't move too much or you'll likely get sick. You have a head injury."

"More like a bullet wound, not that it stopped her from nailing

Dallas," Nolan muttered. Amusement flickered across his face. "Need an ice pack, little brother?"

Dallas forced a chuckle despite the tension coiling through him. "Is there any word on the victims?"

"Marville Dogs." Nolan glanced at his phone. "Middle forehead shots, one slightly left of center. I remember Dad taking us over to Marville to hunt with Kamren's dad and grandpa when we were kids. You weren't born yet. Neither was Rachelle or Kamren here. Cliff was a baby. She's got that same natural precision."

Kamren's gaze flitted back and forth between them, but she remained still and silent as Jesse continued sopping up blood from her wound.

"Fuck, this is deeper than I thought. Kamren here was likely trained early on," Jesse surmised. "Cliff wasn't into hunting. I'm thinking she was his replacement."

Dallas grunted, noting her camo-colored cargo pants and combat boots. Mud coated the once-white sleeveless top, but his gaze settled on the thick swell of her breasts against the thin material. A woman lurked beneath a warrior facade, and he couldn't help but wonder which was real. He'd fallen for her kind before, the tough-as-nails ballbusters. They were disasters lurking beneath a beautiful, artificial frame.

He glanced down at the backpack.

Promise me.

Son of a bitch.

He owed Kamren. He'd made an assumption that'd likely triggered tonight's events. Whatever she was wrapped up in, he was partially to blame for the escalation. If he hadn't lost control and exploded in a crowded bar, the Marville Dogs wouldn't have had the nerve to make a move against her, not with Rachelle under Arsenal protection. No one in Marville understood what they did, but the Mason name carried weight.

Marshall wandered into the room with Brant in tow.

Thank fuck.

Normally they'd step out and give the doc a bit of privacy with his patient, but the woman had just unleashed hell with four bullets. Dallas wasn't going anywhere until they got some answers.

"Thanks for coming so quick," Marshall said.

Dallas offered a chin lift to Brant as he shuffled past them and over to where Jesse stood on the opposite side of the room.

"Kamren." Brant clipped the greeting as if censuring any further comment.

"I didn't ask them to call you," she said. Her already pale skin turned more so, a ghostly shade of white that drew Dallas's concern. "I'm fine."

"I'm sure you are. Heaven forbid you ask for help or do anything but what you want." Brant pulled on some gloves. "What mess are you into this time? You've been gone for weeks, leaving Rachelle to handle the house and Cliff."

Dallas doubted Rachelle or Cliff had even been out to the house since they'd crashed at his mom's house. Cliff never moved off the sofa except for when he went to hang out with his friends. Rachelle was supposedly cooking at the Warrior's Path mess hall, but she spent more time talking and flirting than she did cooking.

"Not sure how that's any of your business, Doctor Burton." She punctuated the title with a bite of anger as she pulled her wrist from between his fingertips. "Don't bother with the pulse and blood pressure check. I'm fine."

"Right. I suppose that bullet wound in your head isn't a problem either." He reached around and pressed two fingers at the back of her head.

A low growl rose from Dallas as Kamren flinched. She didn't cry out, scream, or move away, but she glared up at Brant. "Great bedside manner there, Doc. Get your hands off me. I don't need your help; it's only a graze."

"So you're a doctor now, too?" Brant pulled his hand away and ripped off the bloody glove. He reached for a suture kit on the table beside him.

"You aren't touching me. Go crawl back under whatever rock they found you under." Kamren blinked rapidly as she tilted her head to the left, then the right. She shook it and blinked harder. Lips thinned, she rolled to the side of the bed nearest the window and away from Brant. She stood.

Dallas vaulted toward her as she tumbled forward. His hands locked around her upper arms and held her in place before she could fall. He settled her onto the bed and took sentry position at the side, forcing her into place.

"Can the judgment, Burton, or get the hell out," he clipped.

"Typical Kamren. She already has you snowed," Brant commented. He sighed and regarded Kamren. "I'll set aside our differences if you will. Jesse could probably stitch you up, but he's likely not sutured anyone for years, if ever. I don't have to be your friend to treat you."

"I'd rather take my chances on bleeding out," Kamren returned.

"Let him treat you," Dallas whispered. "He won't mess with you. I won't let him."

"What makes you think I trust you to have my back?"

"You trusted me with this." He motioned to the backpack. The fear and pain in her eyes mitigated any hesitation he'd had earlier. "You wanted my word I'd keep it safe. You have it. I promise I'll keep you and whatever is in that backpack safe if you let them treat you."

"Why?"

"Because I can, and it's the right thing to do. Because no one should fight battles alone." He waited until she nodded slightly and relaxed deeper into his grip. "Are you going to sideline the attitude and be a doctor, or do I need to kick your ass, Burton?"

"Very well, I drove all the way over here. I might as well take a look. What happened?"

"We haven't gotten the details, but drones captured two vehicles attempting to ram her off the road. They succeeded a quarter mile from the gate. A shootout occurred."

"More injuries? Why didn't you mention that?" He looked over at Marshall.

"County coroner took them away," Nolan said. "I'm sure you saw the fire department outside. There was an explosion. I'm thinking she sustained a proximity injury."

Brant sighed and raised his voice. "Can you hear me, Kamren?"

She squinted but nodded. "My ears are ringing. Stitch the graze, and then you can go."

"Stop being so damn stubborn and let me finish the exam. The sooner I do, the sooner I can go. Fair enough?"

"Yeah, fair enough," she shot back.

"She's hearing you well enough, despite the ear ringing," Marshall observed.

"Not necessarily," Brant turned to face away from her. "The old man made them all learn lip reading, said every good hunter understood prey wasn't just the animal variety. He was a crazy coot, and Kamren here was his shadow. The best thing that ever happened to them was the day that bastard died."

Dallas tensed when Brant turned halfway into the conversation, intentionally letting her lip-read the last of his statement. The woman paled. A low, feral-like growl rumbled from her as she stood and almost teetered over in an attempt to lunge for Brant. Marshall intervened, keeping her upright. Nolan and Jesse cursed.

"That's it. Get out, Burton." Marshall grabbed the man's shoulder. "Whatever your beef is with her, I won't let you take it out on a patient in my facility. I didn't think you had that level of asshole in you."

"You have no idea who she is, what she's done," Brant said. He took a deep breath. "But you're right. Every doctor knows when to refuse treatment to someone. I'm afraid I can't be of help, not with her. If I'd known it was her, I wouldn't have come."

They'd known the Burton family for years; they'd grown up with the entire brood, which rivaled their own in size. Dallas stood there stunned as the man left. He'd never seen such a vehement reaction, which left him more than curious as to why. It underscored his initial curiosity. Why didn't he remember Kamren from growing up? She was about his age.

Kamren rose to a sitting position. She reached out for the backpack he held. He took a step backward and set it on the windowsill. Her gaze locked onto the pack, but he noted the watery depths. Her lower lip trembled. She blinked rapidly, but no tears fell.

He glanced at his brothers. There was more to Kamren Garrett than met the eye, but did they have the time or resources to figure it out? More importantly, did they even want to? He leaned toward no, but then guilt dragged him closer to yes.

Finding his son was the main priority, though.

But he didn't like what'd just happened. If Brant was treating her like trash overdue for getting tossed to the curb, what were others doing? He hadn't been raised to stand aside while someone needed help. Based on what they'd seen tonight, Kamren needed the kind of help not just anyone could provide.

He couldn't let anyone suffer alone, defenseless. No matter what she might be wrapped up in, she deserved a leg up.

Help.

"I'm thinking we've found Rachelle's problem," Jesse commented behind his hand.

It was a shit move, one Dallas didn't appreciate. He looked down at the woman, who'd tensed with the ensuing silence. Her gaze tracked between them, as if watching for clues as to what she was missing. He sat on the window ledge beside the backpack and waited for her gaze to settle on him.

A blue so light it was almost ice peered at him with undisguised anger and resolve. She expected to be turned away. Why had she come?

Jesse donned a new set of gloves and got to work using the suture kit. One way or the other she was going to get stitched up, even if he and his brothers had to hold her down to accomplish it.

"Why were you coming here?" he asked slowly.

"It doesn't matter, not anymore. None of it does."

Her voice had been stilted, a bit muddled at first. He recognized the response to damaged hearing. It'd happened to him and several others at the compound multiple times. He looked up at his brothers and lifted his eyebrows. Would they be dicks to her, too?

Dallas was half tempted to hunt Brant down and teach him some manners, but that'd leave Kamren alone and his protectiveness had suddenly been roused by the recent events. Whatever demons lay beneath the surface, she deserved to be treated respectfully.

"Jesse will confirm it, Kamren, but I think your eardrums are damaged. Settle back and he'll take a look, okay?"

"They'll heal," she said. "Give me my backpack and I'll leave. Coming here was a mistake. It won't happen again."

"Why did you come?" he asked.

"I wanted to make sure Rachelle was safe, that she was okay with her and Cliff being here and out of danger." She shrugged. "I shouldn't have come."

"Rachelle is safe," Jesse said as he entered her line of sight. "We'll get a room for you. You can check in on her after you get some rest."

"No." She shook her head, then grabbed it. "I need to get back to Marville."

"I'm thinking that's not a good idea. You took out three Marville Dogs. The sheriff's out in reception to get your statement."

"Okay," she said. "Do me a favor and keep the backpack safe. When I get out, I'll get it back."

"When you get out?" Jesse asked.

"From jail. Prison. The pokey." She looked around. "That's what happens to killers."

"Correct me if I'm mistaken," Nolan said as he directed her focus to him. "But they were after you. They exited their vehicles with weapons drawn. They fired first. If you hadn't responded, you wouldn't have survived. Whatever you're involved in, returning to Marville isn't an option."

"I'll talk to them. It was a misunderstanding."

"Misunderstandings don't end in car explosions and body bags," Dallas said. His brothers laughed. "Okay, clarification. Civilian misunderstandings don't end in car explosions and body bags."

"I have to return, I have things to do." Kamren moved to stand again, but Jesse settled a hand on her shoulder. "Besides, if Rachelle's out here, they need help at the Sip and Spin."

"Rachelle is more than covered. Riley hired her to cook at the Warrior's Path mess hall weeks ago," Dallas said.

"Oh." She settled back down as Jesse pulled out an instrument and started looking at her ears. Dallas drew out his phone and sent a text to Vi and Mary.

Dig into Kamren Garrett's background. I want everything on the entire family. Something's up.

On it. Nolan already requested.

He pocketed his phone and waited out the exam, remaining near her bedside despite the angry glares she sent his direction. She huffed a ragged breath when Jesse started poking and prodding her left side.

"We'll do x-rays to verify, but you have a couple cracked ribs, probably from the collision," Jesse commented. He glanced over at Dallas. "Did you hit her ribs?"

"No, I was too busy trying to save my nuts," he admitted.

His brothers chuckled. Red swept up her face, a cute tinge of pink along her upper cheeks.

"Sorry about that," she muttered.

Marshall returned, but remained out of her visual field. Arms crossed, he whispered. "I gave the security footage we captured to Sheriff Patterson. He's satisfied for now. Brant said we should keep her away from Rachelle and Riley."

"Why?" Jesse asked.

"He refused to say anything more, so we need to find out," Marshall replied. "Riley didn't indicate an immediate dislike or problem with Kamren when I called."

Which Dallas found interesting. He'd withhold judgment for now. If she'd truly come to make sure her little sister was okay, she couldn't be that bad. "Kamren, what's in the backpack?"

"It doesn't matter now. Dani's right. The answers might not be worth the hassle, not anymore. It's not like I can change anything now. Dad's dead."

He felt the clench of loss in a tightening in his chest. Not a day went by he didn't miss his old man or wish he was around offering words of wisdom Dallas had been too stupid and young to appreciate until it was too late.

"We need to run some tests and then get her some painkillers. She'll stay here where she can be observed for the night. It appears she's fine other than a lot of bruising and slight eardrum damage. I want to run tests, just to make sure." Jesse motioned toward the small bathroom. "Kamren, do you want to clean up and change? I've got some scrubs you can put on."

She glanced around the room, then over at the backpack. "Okay, but I take that with me."

Dallas looked at the mud- and shit-covered bag. He really wanted to figure out what was in it. "I promise I'll keep it safe. No one but me will touch it. I'll go find a different pack for you to transfer the contents into after you shower, okay?"

She chewed on her lip, studying the bag, then him. "You promise?"

"I promise," he repeated.

"Okay, but don't open it until I'm out."

"Fair enough." He picked it up and motioned toward the door. "There's a supply area two halls over. I'm going to get a replacement pack. I'll be right back."

She warily nodded her head. He headed out of the room as a mission list formed in his mind. Someone was hot on his heels, but he didn't bother looking to figure out which brother. It didn't matter.

Riley lurked outside the medical entrance. She glared at the two posted guards, who clearly hadn't let her in.

"What happened?"

"She'll be okay. She's got eardrum damage," Dallas said. "Brant refused to treat her."

"He didn't." She paled and her eyes widened. "Really?"

"Yes. He warned us to keep her away from you and Rachelle."

"Well, I don't exactly like the bitch," Riley admitted. "I wouldn't shoot her or anything, though I'll probably yell at her if she can't hear me."

"Why don't you like her?" Nolan asked.

"Erm, because she's a bitch?" Riley's eyes widened. "I'm not down for liking bitches, especially those who are like that to their little sisters."

"I'm thinking you'd best stop calling her a bitch," Dallas warned.

"Whatever, you'll see. She's an ice cold one, too." Riley shrugged. "I'll tell Rachelle she's alive. She's been gone for weeks. She does that, you know. Leaves for weeks at a time. Poor Rachelle has to handle the farm, Cliff, and hold down a job to pay the bills. It's disgusting."

"Why the hell can't Cliff help?" Dallas asked.

"You haven't hung around him yet," Nolan commented. "He's a lazy shit."

Yeah, Dallas had noticed that, but it still didn't answer the question. Was there a reason he didn't do anything, or was he just plain lazy? "We can do something about that. I think it's time he starts handling some chores."

"Good luck with that. I can't get him to go over to their farm and help me tend things." Riley crossed her arms. "Nole's right. He's a lazy shit."

"Leave Cliff and the farm to me," Dallas said. "I'll work the Marville case with you and Jud. That's what you all wanted anyway."

He'd read into their intentions when Jud asked for help. No operative as elite and downright deadly as Jud needed help handling anything. The man had operated as a lone wolf for his entire career. "But I'm back on the leads when they come in."

He didn't bother clarifying which leads. They all knew his thoughts would remain on finding his son. Dallas was a liability, though. As time dragged on, he'd become more desperate to find him, which meant his focus was hindered.

He was hindered.

For everyone's sake, he'd have to trust Vi and Mary and his brothers to take the lead on finding his kid. They'd flag him in when they found something actionable. And they would find something.

Until then he was on training duty with Riley. Pride rose within him. She'd been working her ass off and had done everything they asked with gusto. She trained in hand-to-hand with him and Gage and Jud. She trained on weapons with anyone who offered.

She'd already spread word around Resino and Marville that she was available to help with whatever problems people had. So far there hadn't been much in the way of serious situations. Jud had received warnings from all the Masons to keep Riley out of messy problems. The former assassin was more than capable of handling anything and everything little sis got into, which was the only reason Dallas and his brothers hadn't balked at the idea of Riley taking up detective work.

"Mary said HERA had spit out some intel. I know you're taking a backseat, but your input on the briefings would help," Marshall said. "We're boots on the ground, but you can still be read in."

Dallas regarded his brothers with a mixture of pride, love, and shame. They wouldn't understand what he'd done when he left The Collective. Jud knew. Or suspected. But the man had held true to his word and said nothing. That truth, however, was a time bomb, and Dallas wasn't sure when it was set to explode. It would, though. He just hoped like hell he could figure out a way to diffuse it first.

"What about Kamren? We can't leave her alone," Nolan said.

"I'll be here," Addy offered. "Jesse went to get knock-out juice so she'd rest. I'll handle our new guest."

Dallas regarded the kick-ass operative who'd quickly become an integral part of The Arsenal. She'd taken an immediate liking to Kamren, a reaction he not only hadn't expected, but also didn't understand. He grunted his response as he headed out.

Kamren was a mystery he might want to solve, but she'd have to wait.

5

Although Kamren wanted a shower, Jesse didn't want to risk water getting into her ears. So she settled on a sponge bath, which took quite a while because of all the blood caked onto the side of her face like a second skin. She probably resembled a *Walking Dead* extra. Oh well. She'd given up worrying what others thought of her a long time ago.

Her heart constricted. Rachelle was secure.

She entered the hospital-style room and noted the filthy backpack and a new, still-in-the-package military-style one. She sat and gingerly opened the new one. So many pockets and cool zippers. When was the last time she'd had anything new?

She swallowed.

This wasn't hers.

She'd borrow it long enough to get her other one cleaned up. Likely, if Dani was still talking to her, she'd get it cleaned up free at the Sip and Spin during a shift. The sooner she got back to Marville and handled the Marville Dogs, the better. She carefully transferred the contents into the new pack and shouldered it on. Pain shot up along her left side, but she breathed through it and kept going, just like Dad had taught her.

Weakness gets you killed, girl. Pain keeps you moving.

She was a bit surprised Dallas or one of his brothers wasn't lurking around the hospital room. She peeked out into the empty corridor and noted the double doors at the end of the hall. It was almost too simple. Then again, Rachelle was their priority. She'd shown up—uninvited—in the middle of the night and exploded a vehicle outside their facility. Oh, and she'd committed multiple homicides.

Her stomach churned.

She definitely needed to handle the Marville Dog problem immediately. It wouldn't be pretty, but she'd survive. Probably.

She went back into the hospital room and shoved her ruined clothing into her dirty backpack. With it in her left hand, she headed out into the hall and slowly navigated her way to the exit. Hopefully it wasn't one of those electronically triggered ones or something equally fancy.

Cripes, they'd had drones.

Real, honest-to-goodness drones. How freaking slick was that? Wow.

Rachelle probably loved it out here. Kamren took a deep breath near the door, relishing the fresh scents of lemon and pine.

Clean.

Her gaze cloudy with dread and regret, she pushed through the doors. The crisp breeze offered an unwelcome companionship. She was running low on time. Hunting season started in the next few weeks, which meant she would be busy handling her dad's contracts with the local ranchers. Her father had been an assistant of sorts for the rich farmers who had hunting leases on several of the sprawling ranches around Marville and Resino.

He schlepped gear, helped spot the best locales for hunts, hauled carcasses, and cleaned and dressed them. He did anything the hunters needed so all they had to do was get drunk off their asses and kill deer, doves, or whatever the hell else they had licenses for. Deer hunting was the most common around Marville. A couple of the really rich ranchers toward Eagle Pass offered pricey hunting leases for specialized game. Her dad had loved those the most, especially since he'd stopped taking work up north so much.

She swallowed the lump in her throat and froze. Damn. She was twenty miles away from Marville, and she'd blown up her truck. Someone had her rifle.

Her only weapon.

Returning without it seemed stupid, but it was likely evidence. Okay, new plan. She'd track down one of the Masons and see if she could pay for a ride back home. She had twenty bucks. Ten bucks would get her enough grub to last a week, a week and a half if she stretched meals. She'd lost her sleeping place with the truck gone, but nights didn't get very cold this far south in Texas. She'd deal.

That was what campfires were for.

Going home wasn't an option, not until she got the Marville Dogs appeased.

"Going somewhere?" The redhead shoved off the building's side that she'd been leaning against and offered a smile. "I'm Addy."

"Kamren." Stating the obvious seemed the only polite response, not that Kamren gave much of a damn about being polite.

"Figured you'd bolt," she replied. "The guys had something to handle. They're likely also discussing how to proceed with your situation."

"There's a situation?"

"Seeing how someone tried to kill you outside our compound, we're thinking so." Addy smirked and crossed her arms.

"It's a misunderstanding. I'll sort it out."

"I'm afraid Sheriff Patterson has your rifle. He said he'd return it to us as soon as possible, but it'll be a while."

"I figured as much."

"They hauled off your truck. The contents were destroyed." Addy's voice lowered. "It was pretty full."

"I'd been gone a few weeks; hadn't been back home yet," she lied. "Is there a ranch hand or someone I could give a few bucks to to get me back home?"

"You going home, or are you going to sort out the misunderstanding?"

"Does it matter?"

"Afraid you can't go anywhere, not yet. The guys will be back soon enough. There's always work to be done around here. Heal up some, then you can pick up where you left off. I'll even help."

"Why?" She eyed the redhead skeptically. "Why would you offer to help?"

"Curiosity. You're stirring up trouble, and that's my middle name."

Kamren didn't doubt it. The woman had a gun holstered on one side of her and a massive knife on the other. She eyed the latter. Military grade? She'd seen a couple when she was younger.

"Guess you're feeling a bit naked without your rifle right about now." She uncrossed her arms. "Come on, I'll show you around and see what I can do about the gear."

"I'm thinking you missed a few of the discussion points earlier, but Dallas isn't a fan. He doesn't want my trouble around here, made that quite clear a few weeks ago." Then he'd offered help a couple hours before.

Kamren swallowed. Addy crossed her arms and offered no response for a few moments. Her lips curved into a grin. "I'm thinking his stance on a lot of things has changed. Finding out about a kid you didn't know about does that to a man, I suppose. Whatever he said to you a couple weeks ago, let it go. He'd... Well, things back then were intense. They still are."

"A kid?"

Dallas Mason had a child?

Wow.

How the heck had the tri-county rumor mill missed that one? Questions listed in her mind, but she didn't verbalize any of them. Dallas wasn't her business. Nothing in Resino was her business.

No. That wasn't right. Rachelle was most certainly her business. More like responsibility. Was Cliff handling her? He shifted between helpful and detrimental in spurts, depending on his mood or whatever new video game released. Kamren grunted her frustration and looked at the main house. She couldn't imagine Rachelle being anywhere but there. She'd been worming her way into the Mason family's good graces for almost two decades now.

At least one of them had moved on from the shit they'd survived. Somehow Kamren would ensure Rachelle got her shot at the happily ever after they'd both dreamed about growing up.

"You okay?" Addy asked.

"Yeah, just thinking."

"Whatever shit you're handling, there's no one better to deal with it than Dallas and the crew out here. Give them a chance. My girls are top notch, the best in the business, and I know they'll help."

"Your girls?"

The redhead smiled. "They're brilliant, fiercely courageous and need a wrangler. After what we've been through lately, I'm feeling a bit protective of them, so yeah. My girls."

More questions listed in Kamren's mind, but she let them go. Not her business. "My troubles aren't theirs. Besides, I can't afford them."

"No one ever mentioned money. Trust me, my girls fund operations easily enough without us charging a ton to those who can't afford it. Besides, Riley's been getting word out that she and Jud are available for investigative work. She's not charging either."

Although Riley had been a great friend to Rachelle through the years, Kamren'd had very little interaction with the woman. "She's Rachelle's friend, not mine."

"Funny. I'm usually a good judge of character, but based on Brant's reaction to you and the fact that Riley called you an ice-cold bitch, I'm apparently wrong about you. Not sure that's ever happened." Addy shrugged her shoulders. "Weird."

Indeed. Kamren didn't bother defending herself. The redhead wanted a reaction, one she wouldn't get. The only person Kamren could rely on was herself. Sure, in a moment of weakness she'd considered accepting Dallas's offer of help, but that was before she found out he'd just discovered he had a child. Clearly the Masons had busy itineraries.

"Give this a chance. If you change your mind and don't want to be here, I'll take you wherever you want to go. I'm your best shot at getting off Arsenal property, though I'll admit there are a few here I'd have trouble taking down alone. Then again, I very much doubt my girls would stand aside and not help. With that crew at our backs, we could do anything we wanted."

Right. Checking out where Rachelle was staying and getting a better idea of the people she was around was a good opportunity, one Kamren couldn't pass up. Even if she should.

She didn't want more trouble knocking on the Masons' doorstep.

The sooner she got back to Marville, the better. "Fine, but I need a phone."

"Afraid phone calls for you are out of the question. They want you below radar for a while, long enough for the situation to cool down." Addy motioned toward the sidewalk. "Come on. Let's get this tour over with, then you can get some rest. You look like you need it."

KAMREN IGNORED the constant shadow she'd had the past sixteen hours. Though the *who* changed, the *why* hadn't. The Masons wanted her contained at the compound until things in Marville cooled down.

She'd managed to rest a few hours before the restlessness overrode her pain and general discomfort. She wasn't a sedentary person, and sleeping in a strange room surrounded by strangers wasn't happening.

She sat cross-legged on the ground facing the high fence along the road. They'd done a damn good job on security, a fact she'd realized this morning after walking the entirety of the compound three times. A growly dude named Gage Sanderson had kept her from straying past the barns and into the grazing lands where she really wanted to investigate.

Security was awesome along the highway, but bad guys would skulk through the back. Surely fancy-ass former military knew that. She supposed so but remained a bit unimpressed by the lack of high ground.

Why hadn't they added towers or something?

With the thought in mind, she'd commandeered a pad of paper and a couple pens and pencils from her shadow a bit ago. He hadn't been very pleased about her turning him into the local Staples, but at least they weren't moving anymore, right?

She kept the KBAR knife Addy had given her near her right thigh, just in case. She'd almost asked for a second, but figured she'd pressed her luck enough. Marshall nixed a gun, which she'd pretty much expected.

She stared up at the sun and figured she'd have enough time to hunt up a rabbit or two after she sketched out the towers. They kept appearing in her mind like things did at times. Though she hated sitting in one place for long, sometimes her restless energy ceded to the need to purge her brain of ideas.

"What are you doing?" Dallas sat beside her. "How are the ears?"

"Better. I can hear but have to focus past the ringing. It's not as bad, though. They'll heal."

She scrawled the makings of a tower and willed him to go away. Were the lines she drew straight? Heck, were they even lines? Ugh. Why had he shown up when she was trying to focus? Drawing her thoughts was hard enough without someone watching. And that someone being Dallas was...

Kamren shoved the stray thought aside. She had no business thinking about anyone with the last name Mason like that. The Masons were Rachelle's, not hers. Little sis would have a conniption fit if something happened with Kamren and a Mason. She'd claimed anyone with that particular last name to be hers a long time ago.

Even though her shadow's identity changed, Dallas had a tendency to show up a lot. Addy had showed her the cafeteria earlier and made sure she got some grub. Kamren hadn't even had to pay, which was a bit strange, but it was probably because she was with the redhead and they figured she worked there.

She would've gotten more than scrambled eggs and two pieces of bacon had she known that. Oh well, she'd go hunting later.

We don't take handouts, girl. You eat what you earn with a clean kill.

"Is that our fence line?" Dallas asked. Hot breath fell on her neck as he looked over her shoulder.

His hand settled near hers where she held the pad. Adrenaline spiked as she held her breath. No one had ever cared to see what she sketched.

"Are those blinds, like hunting blinds?"

"Kind of." She shrugged. "I know that design best, but figured I'd see what it'd look like. I was wondering why you don't have high ground for your guards. They're walking the grounds, but can't see as far as if..."

Idiot.

He's former military—knows way more about security coverage than you.

"They need higher ground to see farther," he finished. He motioned toward the tower she'd built. "We thought about something like this, but the compound looked more like a prison."

Kamren laughed. "You've got to admit it kind of is. Come on, you call it a compound. The rooms are windowless cells with freaking twin beds and a two-drawer dresser. I know because I crashed in one for a few hours."

"It's a work in progress. Most of the guys are better in those small quarters for now; reminds them of the service."

"It's a great thing you're starting, the Warrior's Path. Addy mentioned it." She continued her sketches, adding a walkway along the top. Embrace the fortress. "I'm sure it's tough to transition. Was it hard for you?"

"Everyone's situation is different. I came out of a..." His jaw twitched. His gaze grew distant, withdrawn. "My situation was complicated."

Right. There was a kid somehow created as a result of his departure. Kamren definitely didn't need details. She had enough trouble not imaging Dallas all hot, sweaty, and sexy as he...

Ugh.

Focus.

"Well, at least you're out." She switched the subject. "I'm surprised you all still run cattle. That's a lot of work."

"There's a lot of us out here. Ranch work soothes some of the soldiers, gets them focused on stuff other than the battles they survived. We're making it work for now, merging our dream with Dad's." He paused, then added, "We're cutting back on the ranching, though, over the next few months. Riley has a plan we're initiating."

"Dad wanted to lease our land out, set up a few hunting cabins. We never quite got it figured out," she whispered. "Our land wasn't nearly big enough, I suppose."

"Gage said you were trying to move past the compound grounds, into the pastures."

"Gage is a tattletale." She forced a smile as she looked at Dallas.

Damn. He was gorgeous, a golden Adonis, Thor with dark hair. His blue eyes twinkled with amusement as he waited for more of a response.

"I unwind by tracking, hunting."

"We've got a new doctor here; she'll be working with the soldiers. She's a psychiatrist for PTSD, that sort of thing. You should talk to her."

"I'm not crazy," she spat angrily.

Every one of you is gonna have a splash of crazy in you. Don't let anyone see it. They'll scrape you off like roadkill.

Dad hadn't been wrong. Kamren had an even bigger reason to go as unnoticed as possible given the fact that she was what she was. Uneducated.

Dyslexia.

The diagnosis hadn't come until she was seventeen, long after it was too late. The jumbling in her brain made reading almost impossible, which was why her parents had deemed her too stupid for schooling when she was in the third grade.

No. She was plenty educated, just not in the typical sense. Cliff had taught her what he could, and she'd picked up loads more from her parents when they weren't yelling and screaming and punching and kicking. Dani had even picked up on the fact that Kamren had troubles and done what she could to help bridge the gap so folks wouldn't notice.

She was an awesome BFF.

Assuming she forgives you for killing people in her crew. The thought soured Kamren's insides. She really needed a phone.

"No one out here's going to say that. Most everyone here's made the split-second call you did last night, Kamren. Doctor Sinclair's good at listening."

Right. She'd almost forgotten about the fact that she'd killed people. Her gaze wandered in the general vicinity of where it'd happened. Though she couldn't see the exact spot because The Arsenal compound was massive, her gut clenched anyway. Her heart thudded wildly, her mouth dried, and the buzzing in her ears got louder as the fiery inferno ignited in her mind. Flames licked her face as if the explosion had just happened.

"I didn't think, you know." Heat rose in her cheeks at the admission. "Sorry, not sure why I said that."

"Because it's on your mind. You can walk the grounds and sketch all day, and it's not going to stop streaming in the back of your head."

"You're right, it's not." She constructed a third tower, then added smaller towers in between on a whim.

"What are those?"

"Drone towers. They need homes too, you know." She smiled at the whimsical notion.

"Addy's convinced us it's time you go to Marville to make sure the air is clear with the Marville Dogs."

"Dani hasn't called. She would've called if there was trouble." The lie slipped out easily enough. She didn't need the Masons going with her, and the edge in Dallas's voice warned her that was where his mind was wandering. The sooner she snipped his helpful cord in that matter, the better. "I'll handle the Marville Dogs, and you can stay here and keep Rachelle safe. Then we can chat about what problem I may have stumbled into."

"And that problem isn't tied to the Marville Dogs?" Dallas asked, his disbelief clear in his tone and narrowed gaze.

"I doubt it. They don't appreciate snoops, though." She shrugged. "And I've snooped more than was smart."

"We're not letting you go alone."

"You can't go with me, Dallas." A Mason in Marville was tantamount to a hurricane-grade disaster. The last thing she needed was to show up with one in tow. "It's bad enough I'm out here for as long as I've been. Rumors are already hitting Marville hard, I'm sure."

"Yeah, they are, which is why I'm out here. Whatever you're mixed up in, tying yourself to us will insulate you with some folks. It'll help."

Her gut clenched. "I didn't come out here for that. I don't use people. I wanted your opinion only."

"Glad to hear it, but I think it's a solid play, Kamren. I've got history with the MD's that'll trump my last name, or should anyway."

Kamren stilled. He knew the Marville Dogs? She thought back to when that would've been and soured. It had been during her teens most likely, back when the only people she saw were her family. And Dani. They'd kept in contact even though it'd been a pain in the ass.

"You knew Dom before he went to prison."

"And Ricardo. We both tore off when Dom went down. I guess neither of us could handle it."

She'd almost lost Dani back then, too, her sole link to the outside world. Her best friend had lost so much. It'd bonded them to one another, strengthened their friendship in a twisted way.

Kamren needed to fix the fiasco she'd caused. Figure out who killed her dad, make things right with the Marville Dogs, and move on with her life. That was her new list of things to do.

For Rachelle.

For Dani.

For Dad.

Which meant sucking it up and admitting she was in over her head. She'd already been way outside her comfort zone when everything started. "I'm okay with that."

"Good, then we'll keep you out here a little longer, then we'll get to work on sorting Marville out."

Nolan and Jesse ran over. Grim lines hardened their otherwise handsome faces. They offered her cursory nods, but their attention was on Dallas. "Sheriff Patterson's calling in a favor. Bubba's grand-kids, the twins, have wandered off. They were last seen out near the back of the old Seymore place."

It'd been a while since she'd been in Resino, but the old Seymore place was the only spread between the Burton brood's land and the tail-ass end of the Mason property.

"How old are they?" Kamren asked.

"Six yesterday," Nolan offered. "Going on sixteen. They've been gone four hours, could be anywhere. Fence line's up around our lands, but not sure about the Burton's. Patterson's calling them to help, but thought he'd give us a head start."

"Get teams ready to go; let the girls know. We can use the drones." Dallas looked overhead.

The night sky was crawling up into view quick. The last thing they needed was a ton of boots on the ground screwing up the search grid before someone got a chance to track those kids. "Where were they last seen? Is it close?"

"Why?" Jesse asked.

"We should check it out first before you send a bunch of teams out in grid formation. They'll tramp all over the trail." Kamren shrugged. "Sometimes a small effort is the most efficient."

"We're down for a small strike. You in?" Dallas asked.

Adrenaline surged at the invitation. Though her entire body ached and her head still throbbed, she wasn't used to being inactive. Having something to do would help ease her anxiety. She nodded and jumped up. "We'll need supplies."

The backpack. She hadn't put it down for months, but she needed supplies more than she needed to hold onto papers like a hoarder. She looked around and spotted Addy with a group of women at the edge of the sidewalk. The redhead had been nice to her and treated her with respect, which didn't happen too often for Kamren. She ran over and unshouldered the backpack.

"Kamren!" Rachelle screamed her name and ran forward. "They

just told me you were here. Oh my God! Are you okay? They told me there was an incident. What happened?"

"I'm okay, Rache." She squeezed her tight, then pulled away to truly look at her sister for the first time in months.

Rachelle did better when Kamren didn't hover nearby, or so Cliff said. She thrived around Riley. Her eyes shown brighter than her smile. She was happy.

Safe.

"Come on, I'll show you the room I have in Mama Mason's house." Rachelle took her hand.

Damn. "Listen, I'm afraid I've gotta go. A couple kids are missing."

"But you just got here." Rachelle's voice rose. "You can't go."

"It's just for a little while to find the kids, then I'll be back and we'll catch up. Okay?"

Rachelle crossed her arms. Her lips thinned. "Fine. I guess I'll see you later. Riley and I were about to watch *The Walking Dead* anyway."

She looked at the backpack, then at her sister. Rachelle hadn't been a fan of her ongoing project, to say the least. She held it out to Addy. "Watch over this?"

The redhead's eyes flared a second. "Sure, though if I go wheels up with the teams, I'll have to relegate it to my girls here."

"Hi, I'm Vi." The blonde with red-rimmed glasses waved. "This is Mary. We run back office operations. Our drones are going out with you guys. This is Bree and Rhea." She motioned toward the other blonde and brunette. "They helped us design the drones and some other stuff. We'll watch it for you. Addy mentioned we might be able to help you with something."

She eyed the women, then her sister. "Yeah. It's time I get a second opinion and decide whether there's anything to my theories or not."

"And if there isn't?" Riley asked. "You've wasted almost two years chasing your tail."

"If there isn't, I'll drop it and move on."

"Really?" Rachelle breathed the word, as if not believing it.

Someone had tried to kill her last night. She was close and over her head. It was time she asked for help. "Really."

"Okay then. We'll wait until you're back before we dive in," Addy said.

"Thanks. It probably won't make much sense." She looked over at Addy. "Can I borrow another backpack and some supplies?"

"Come on. I'll show you where stuff is," Dallas offered.

Kamren tightened. She'd been so busy with the women she hadn't heard him come up behind her. The man was eerily stealthy, like a prowling tiger. "After you."

6

Kamren had crammed half the supply area into her backpack. She'd stocked enough supplies to undergo a three-week mission through the jungle, but Dallas admired her tenacity. She'd inspected knives and riffled through drawer after drawer with proficient speed, which was odd since all the contents were clearly labeled. Nolan and Jesse stood behind him, also watching her mad dash through the supplies. She was a cute squirrel shoving stuff into her backpack and pockets like she'd been let loose in a candy store for the first time.

She shouldered on the backpack and looked around one last time. She snagged a couple more KA-BARs. Nolan and Jesse both laughed. She'd already procured two. He'd have to get them back from her or Marshall would be all over his ass.

He looked over at Kamren when her stomach rumbled. "Sweetheart, when did you last eat?"

"Addy showed me the cafeteria at breakfast. I had some eggs and bacon."

"Nothing since then? That was more than fourteen hours ago," Jesse said. "You didn't even have much on your plate."

Red rose in her cheeks. "I didn't know it was free and didn't have much money with me. Besides, I was taught not to mooch. You eat what you kill or earn yourself."

Dallas reached into his pocket. "I can respect that, sweetheart, but as long as you're on our compound, you eat. Okay?"

She eyed the protein bar like it was a rattler, but she accepted it with a grudging nod. "Thanks."

"Eat up. We've got about a four-minute drive to where the boys were last seen." He reached into the pack he'd gotten and handed each of his brothers a granola bar. They ripped them open and started chewing along with Kamren.

"Marshall and Cord are going to work with Sanderson and Addy to assemble teams, in case they're needed." Jesse held up two small cases. "The girls sent drones, and Nolan's got headgear for us. They said it'd be a good test run for a search and rescue op."

Dallas grunted his response as they piled into a truck. He relegated himself to the back with Kamren so he could get her situated with the headgear and wrist apparatus. He doubted she'd enjoy it much since it was like wearing a tuxedo for the first time when you'd prefer a pair of shorts and flip-flops.

"Drones won't help out there. It's dark and there's a lot of land to cover. I doubt the area's been bulldozed in the past couple of decades, so brush will be thick and impossible to see through from the air," she said.

"HERA's a bit different. These drones can find heat signatures and do all sorts of cool stuff," Jesse explained.

"Oh." Her eyes flared a bit. "That's cool."

"Here." Dallas held up the headset. "Let's get this situated. Give it a few minutes before you shun it completely. It limits your visibility in your left eye until you acclimate to the read out. You can still see through it if needed. The girls will put up data in the display that they think might help you."

"'The girls' being the brainiacs back there? Vi and Mary?"

"Yeah, they're the best back-office operatives around. The Quillery Edge," he offered.

"Right." The tone proved she wasn't impressed. She was a civilian, which meant none of what he'd said meant anything.

Nolan and Jesse chuckled from the front seat. He situated the headgear on her and adjusted her ponytail so it wasn't in the way. Her hair was fine silk as it flowed through his fingers. He traced down her arm and put the wrist device on.

"What's this?" She looked down at the doodad, which was spewing all sorts of data.

"It tracks medical stats and gives you the ability to navigate the drones. If we were stuck in a heavy firefight or cut off for a long period of time, you could provide intel to them through this."

"Team leaders use it the most, usually to signal if there's a problem with one of the team members that might impact the op. They can adjust the plan accordingly," Jesse offered. "We can handle the tech and let you track."

She breathed deeply with an exhale. Relief. He almost chuckled, but then he noted the worry lines on her face. "Hey, this is okay. They probably fell asleep under a tree somewhere."

"Yeah, okay. We'll go with that. It's been a while since I've been there, but I remember the place. The crazy coot had holes drilled everywhere. There's even a cave somewhere and all sorts of traps."

"Traps?" Dallas asked.

"Hunting traps. He was a survivalist, didn't want others on his land," Nolan commented. "She's right. He was nuts."

"THERE'S ANOTHER ONE," Dallas's voice echoed through the desolate ranch land. The Mason brothers had turned finding the next set of tracks into a competition, showing the ease with which they worked together, even within tense situations.

Would her life have been different if Cliff had enjoyed tracking and the other stuff their father had done? Or Rachelle? What if one of them had been forced to take on the family legacy to keep food on the table?

Nolan crouched beside his brother, but neither messed with the area surrounding the track. Drones hovered overhead and cast light across the area. Kamren had been skeptical, but the little electronic monsters had been useful, once she'd figured out how to use whatever gunk the brainiacs were feeding to her left eye. It was a jumbled-up knot of useless data since she had zero idea what it was supposed to say. That left her unable to unscramble any of it.

But green was good and red was bad and she'd discerned numbers by recognizing a pattern she knew to be coordinates for the Resino area. And Dallas, along with Nolan and Jesse, were damn good. The three could've easily handled this without her in tow, but they'd let her do her thing.

"This one's different," Dallas commented. "Blood."

Heat fanned from his muscular form as she crouched beside him. Awareness crawled through her insides in a warmth that made her shiver. His scent, a musky oak, permeated her nostrils as she leaned her head downward a bit to focus on the tracks.

Blood droplets darkened the soil around the area and within the track. One of the kids was injured. She rose, focused on the area to the southwest from where they'd come. With a point of her finger, she had Jesse and Nolan looking east while Dallas went with her. They'd worked out the hand signals quickly once she picked up on the ones they used and started using them as well—something all three of the men found great amusement in for some reason.

She needed to find the missing boys. Exhaustion plagued her and she'd noticed Jesse's pronounced limp getting worse the farther they moved toward the Burton property. That was when she noticed what was wrong.

There was only one set of tracks.

Dread clawed her insides as her pulse punched into overtime. She unshouldered her backpack and tossed it to Dallas as she flicked on a flashlight she'd kept in her hand and sprinted back toward the last set of tracks they'd found. Nolan and Jesse followed.

"What's wrong?" Nolan asked.

"One set up there, two back here. We missed something," she said.

Blood darkened the lower edge of a bush. She stooped, running her finger across it. Recent.

"Yeah, bring the drones back this direction, Vi. Kam has something." Dallas gave her the credit over the com even though he'd been the one to locate the track and note the shift in the situation.

Kam. Dallas had started the ridiculous use of a shortened version of her name, and both his brothers had picked up on it soon enough. They were all about nicknames, though. Vi was Quillery and Mary was Edge for some reason that made no sense to Kamren. Whatever. Not her circus, definitely not her monkeys.

She studied the barely visible remnants of a rudimentary trap. The string was thin, broken. Dirt and debris covered most of it, which was probably why it'd been overlooked. Drones circled overhead, fanning lights along the area.

"Tell me what you need." Vi's voice in the headset startled Kamren a moment. They'd never spoken directly to her, not since she'd growled about the display being a waste of time and made Dallas remove it so her eyesight wasn't impeded.

"One of the boys tripped a trap. He was running faster than they'd been going. The tracks are shallower from the running pace. He's hurt." She looked toward another drone hovering above where Dallas was searching an area. "Continue past Dallas. One of them is running full-on, likely to get help. Or he's scared."

"And the other?" Jesse asked.

"That's what we need to find out, sooner rather than later." She stood. "The dark isn't going to help; it'll only get worse. There are wells and holes all in this area. Likely one of them fell in. The where will be hard to find."

"Not necessarily. Give Mary and me a moment." Vi's voice paused a beat. "Z, get in here. We need your help. We need to establish a perimeter around the current location. We're looking for holes, shifts in the geography."

"It'll be between my current location and the one before this.

We've lost a set of footprints," Kamren said as she ran toward the last location, not waiting for the fancy drones to do the work.

The distance felt like a mile but was far less than two hundred yards. In the darkness, though, it may as well have been ten miles.

"To your left. Ten feet," Vi said.

Rotted boards that had cracked in two came into view when she angled her flashlight that direction. Son of a bitch. Dallas was at her side and had the backpack undone before she had a chance to shout for it. Nolan remained quiet as he stood beside Jesse a couple feet back.

"Need you following the coordinates I'm feeding, Nolan. Drones spotted one of the boys about half a click from your position." Mary. The woman hadn't spoken much during the mission.

"On it." Nolan darted toward where they'd been.

She flashed the light into the hole, but there was no verbal response. If it was a well, it could be a long way down. The shape was wrong, though. This was more of a natural recess, something the crazy coot had probably dug from a slight sinkhole. A trap for a boar to fall in perhaps? No, it was way too deep for it to hold animals. This had been the old man's paranoia, a trap meant to catch trespassers.

"Anyone down there?" She had the ropes and equipment pulled from the backpack before she finished the question. Jesse and Dallas undid it all and worked together to get it ready. Precision perfect movements.

Without comment or discussion, the plan had been set into motion. The entry was small, too small for any of the Masons to get into. Which left her. A drone disappeared into the hole. Kamren reached up and yanked the display back over her left eye.

Kamren's heart leapt into her throat as images filled the viewing area. The boy had fallen farther than Kamren wanted to contemplate. Was he alive? Injuries were a given for that distance. Shit. There was no way she could even get that far down, which meant they'd have to wait for a rescue crew to bring equipment in.

"Okay, Kam. Vi and I aren't willing to wait for people to find a rig to haul out there and get that boy out. You ready to get down there?"

"Yeah, of course." Kamren shone the light down the hole. "I can probably find an outcropping to leapfrog from once I'm down the rope."

"We can do a bit better than that." Three drones appeared over the hole. "Dallas, you and Jesse get her harnessed. Let me know when you're ready."

"No offense, but I'd be happier if Vi was the one handling the play on this one, Edge. You're not exactly known for handling the light work." Dallas's voice was edged with concern as he glanced over at Kamren. "We're about to do something that'll sound crazy, but trust me and trust Vi and Mary. Okay?"

Kamren swallowed her uncertainty. She could do this. A broken leg or arm wouldn't matter much if she could get the boy out, right? Dallas positioned the harness around her with an ease which denoted proficiency.

"Look at me, Kamren." He settled two fingers beneath her chin and pulled up until her gaze locked with his. "You don't know us well enough to trust us, but there's no way in hell we don't have your back on this one. Okay? I give Edge shit, but she and Vi would not suggest we move on this unless they knew for a certainty we could handle this."

"Right."

Dallas's gaze narrowed. "They've dragged people out of impossible situations. Hell, Edge blew up a building with an entire team inside. They weren't even injured by the blast even though they were hunkered down in the middle of it. They have a one hundred percent success rate. They are not about to foul that up tonight. Okay?"

"Okay."

"Hook two leads up to the harness. One lead with each drone."

"She gets two? You made my brother drop off a building in San Antonio using just one," Dallas said.

What the hell? They were all loons.

"Do it." The gruff response was masculine and not pleased. "My woman's bladder is about to explode, and her feet are the size of footballs."

"They did not need to know any of that, Dylan. Get out of my control room."

Dallas smirked as the two voices on the other end halted their argument when Vi tossed out a terse order to focus. He reached down and hooked one line to each of the drones.

"Seriously?" Kamren asked.

"These little beasts are way more than obnoxious lights." The smile he offered exuded confidence and determination. "Take your time. If you change your mind, say the word and we'll get you up."

"I'm good." And she was. She wasn't leaving anyone in a hole. No way in hell.

She shouldered on her backpack and nodded that she was ready. She was about to get into position to be lowered into the hole when she was suddenly in the air. The drones were lifting her up, then lowering her into the hole. What the hell?

Shock kept her still and mute as she descended into the narrow entry. The third drone was already there projecting enough light for her to see as she was slowly lowered. She peered downward and past her feet. A small, still form was to the side about fifteen feet.

"We'll need a backboard," she stated. "We'll likely need an ambulance from Nomad."

Nomad was twenty miles away and had the nearest hospital. She hated the idea of waiting that long, though. And they'd still have to call a crew in to get a wide enough opening for the backboard. Before she could work through possible solutions, the form moved. The boy peered up and reached for her.

Movement.

Blood oozed from a wound on his head. Both his legs were pointed the wrong direction, but he was alert. And crying.

The drones lowered her gently to the ground near the boy. She sat and took his hand as she wiped the tears from his little face. "Hi, there. I'm Kamren. What's your name?"

"Sam. Where's Shane?"

"Nolan has him," Vi said in the com. "He's injured, but okay."

"He's okay. We're going to get you out and back home. Your Grandpa Bubba is mighty worried."

"He's gonna whip our butts good for this."

Likely so. Most parents would. Kamren smiled at the boy. "I'm thinking he'll likely feed you and love on you first."

"It hurts," Sam said with another cry.

"It's okay," she soothed as she ran her hand across his damp forehead. "We're getting a crew here to help you. Just remain as still as possible, and we'll get you out as soon as we can."

Kamren waited until the boy calmed a bit. "Is emergency en route?"

"Yes, but his doctor is almost there." Dread settled in a dull throb in her temples. Almost there implied close, which meant a Burton, Brant more than likely, since he'd essentially taken over his aging uncle's practice. "There are no allergies to worry about. I understand you raided the supply cabinet. Did you take any painkillers?"

"Yes."

"Good, go ahead and administer them. We have Brant's permission, not that I'd wait even if we didn't," Vi commented.

Kamren's hands trembled slightly as she removed the backpack and listened to the two women as they took turns running her through what needed to be done. Most of it was stuff she already knew, but she appreciated the calm, confident, step-by-step instructions in firm, short sentences. They kept her focused.

These were Addy's girls. The brilliant brainiacs Dallas talked about. She admired their tenacity and professionalism. If anyone could help her sort out the mess that was her supposed investigation into her father's death, it was them. She'd already decided to take a chance and try and explain things to Dallas and his brothers.

Maybe Addy was right. Maybe the women could help her make sense of stuff.

Decision made, Kamren focused on handling the situation at hand. Everything else could wait. Once the pain medicine had been administered she focused on the first task—a backboard for the boy. The ones in ambulances were too big for the small hole, and she didn't want to wait for a crew to make it bigger. She rooted through the backpack of supplies she'd taken and growled her frustration.

"It's too dark down here." One of the drone lights flashed on. "Thanks."

"Mind telling us what you're doing?" Vi asked.

"Backboard, small enough to get through the hole. I'm not waiting for Burton and whoever else is coming to figure out how to get one down here. He sees me here, he'll likely leave anyway." She muttered the last bit to herself as she pulled out the roll of duct tape. Fortunately the boy was small, so she could use some of the boards in the bottom of the makeshift pit as a board. Not exactly sanitary, but it'd do in a pinch. She kicked and punched at them until they were boy-sized bits of wood. She rolled tape around them, then yanked off her top and taped it to the board to keep the boy's skin from touching the dirty wood. It was the best she could do.

She worked the board beneath Sam, going slow enough to not jostle him too much. Whatever was in the injection had knocked him out. She hoped to hell that was the right decision. What if he had a concussion or something? No matter, Burton might hate her ass, but he was an excellent doctor. He'd sort the kid out when he arrived.

She took one of the knives and cut the boys pants where his legs were turned at awkward angles.

"Jesus," Dallas muttered into the com.

"We need to reset them while he's out," Mary said softly through the com, but Kamren was already applying traction to the worst of the injuries. The bone in his left leg had pushed out of the skin slightly, but not as bad as Cliff's back when he was twelve, but it was a nasty wound.

Kamren took two of the stakes she'd packed and positioned them around Sam's small leg. She rolled tape into position at the base of the leg, well away from the open wound. A few moments later, she had the second injury as immobilized as possible.

She glanced up at the three drones, then back at the boy on the makeshift backboard. She added a wrapping of tape around his little neck, using the last bit of her shirt to protect his skin. She was a bit surprised there wasn't yelling or talk from atop the hole drifting downward, but she was thankful for the silence.

It kept her focused on the task at hand.

"Anything else I should do?" Kamren asked the question as she wiped the sweat from her brow. "I should've grabbed one of the blankets."

"You did great," Mary said. "Let's attach the drones to the back-board, and we'll get him out," Vi said.

"Let me check it; the wood was old. It might give," Kamren worried aloud.

"It'll hold. We'll pull you up behind him so you can help support the backboard, if that makes you feel better," Mary offered.

"Okay." She took a deep breath and willed her pulse to slow. She could do this.

7

B rant had thankfully kept his mouth shut when he arrived just as Sam and Kamren were hauled out of the hole. The doctor was in full medical mode, giving the little boy the full, careful treatment he'd given to Mary months ago when he'd helped her.

The full, careful treatment he'd refused Kamren.

Dallas bit back his rage as the woman watched from a few feet away. She'd maneuvered as far away as she could, but he'd seen enough to rouse his suspicion and apparently the women had to since Kamren's actions had somehow activated the woman's protectiveness.

"Dallas," Vi whispered. "Her back."

"Think we all saw it," Jesse clipped into the com.

Yeah, they'd all seen her back because she'd shucked off her shirt and used it to help Sam. She'd been laser focused on treating his injuries, getting him safe. He'd been so wrong about her he hadn't been in the same stratosphere.

He closed the distance between them and palmed her chin. "Look at me, sweetheart."

Unfocused eyes drifted up to latch onto his. Addy ran over with a blanket in hand. The redhead halted a couple feet away and gave

Dallas the covering. He wrapped it around Kamren's exposed shoulders and ignored the rage rolling through him as he forced his gaze on her face and not the scars covering her arms, her exposed back, and stomach.

What the fuck had happened to her?

Jesse had walked away, rage evident in his gaze and stance. Dallas was beyond rage, locked within the numb zone he'd honed for years as a Collective operative.

Now wasn't the time to lose his shit. It was obvious Kamren didn't want others seeing her scars. She hunched her shoulders in and wrapped her arms around her exposed stomach while she angled her back so that no one could see it.

"Here you go, sweetheart," he whispered as he covered her fully.

"Thank you." She swallowed and looked past him, as if unable to handle whatever emotions may have leaked out within his gaze. "Is he okay? The backboard held, right?"

"Yeah, it held. Let's walk over to the ambulance. They can take a look at you before they take him in."

"I'm good."

"I know, but you'll be better once they make sure none of that shit down there got into your head wound."

She reached up and patted the gauze-covered area. "It's fine. Jesse did a good job."

Yeah, his brother had done a rudimentary field patching on her freaking head because the son of a bitch doctor they'd called had refused to help. He glared over at Brant as the doctor crawled into the back of the ambulance with Sam. He hadn't even glanced her direction to see if she was okay.

Not once had he asked if she needed emergency personnel.

Bubba and the entirety of Resino had descended on the area. By the time the ambulance had arrived, the situation had downgraded from critical to a celebration that both boys were found. Sam had a long road of recovery coming, but they'd be okay.

Thanks to Kamren.

"Come on, let's get back. You can clean up and change. We'll eat, and you can crash." When she nodded, he motioned to Addy. "Take her to the truck; I'll be there in a minute."

Jesse hadn't gone far. Dallas stopped a few feet from his big brother. The man had been through a hell he'd never fully shared, though Dallas had likely heard more than the other brothers and operatives around. Dallas stood there, patient and quiet. Waiting.

Jesse raked a hand across the back of his cropped hair and expended a deep breath. "Fuck."

Pretty much Dallas's sentiment to a tee.

"We've pussy-footed around, ignored Marville, all because we didn't take Rachelle seriously. She's been out here doing whatever the fuck that girl does to grate our last nerve, keeping Riley in the dark the whole time."

Tension coiled within Dallas. He'd taken this road quite a few times since the explosion outside The Arsenal.

"Not once." Jesse turned, rage evident on his face. "Not once has that girl said a damn thing about having a sister, one so deep in something it sends her to our doorstep, bullets flying. Trucks exploding. Freaking bleeding head wound, brother."

"And a doctor who wouldn't do shit about it," Dallas added into the thickening tension.

"Now this," Jesse spat.

This being the scars, the injuries. None recent from what he'd seen.

"Rachelle's been flitting about here in less clothes day after day, showing more skin than common sense. Not once," Jesse said, his voice louder.

Not once had they seen scars or wounds on Rachelle. Dallas could read his brother's half-speak. Jesse had a way of carving thoughts out of few words when anger struck. He didn't voice his thoughts often when he was pissed, but when he did they were often chopped into barely uttered words. You either got him, or you didn't. Big brother was the type to not give a shit one way or the other.

"She's here. We'll help her sort whatever's going on," Dallas said.

"Fuck yeah, we will."

Dallas wasn't stupid enough to believe the emotional war Jesse waged was about Kamren and her troubles, her wounds. It cut far deeper, closer to the bone. "The hole?"

Jesse tossed him a look. Though no verbal affirmation hit, the look spoke plenty. Ravaged, haunted, tormented grief he'd yet to fully air with anybody. Dallas approached, slapped a hand on his shoulder, and squeezed. Touching Jesse when he was waging hell with his demons was a bit like petting a rattler on a sunny day.

"I thought Doc Sinclair was helping you work through things," Dallas said. "You wanna talk, I'm here. Whenever, wherever, whatever."

Jesse chuckled, low and quiet. "She'd likely be thrilled I'm out here losing my shit, making all this about me. I'm in touch with my emotions, or some other crazy psycho-babble."

"Whenever, wherever, whatever," Dallas repeated as he squeezed his brother's shoulder.

"And you? When are you going to start *processing*?"

Damn. He should've expected the offer to get lobbed back like a live grenade. "I've talked to Sinclair."

"Right, about what to do when we find him, not about how he came to be."

It was a guess, but dead on. Jesse knew him. They all knew him, which was why he couldn't ever share what'd happened back then; the things he'd done weren't things the little brother they knew and loved could do. Deep inside he carried a monster, a beast born, birthed and nurtured by The Collective.

"Whenever, wherever, whatever," Jesse repeated. "I give you a piece now, you reciprocate. Quid pro quo."

Fuck. Dallas ran his hand down his face, but grunted his assent. Big brother stared, waiting for the verbal affirmation. "Quid pro quo."

"Hole I was thrown into when they were done playing with me was a lot like that; ropes around my waist hauled me up and down. Entry was small— my shoulders and sides scraped the dirt going up I rarely remembered the down." Jesse's voice barely covered the short distance between them, but neither man moved closer. Some demons needed space to breathe when they were unleashed. The raw emotion reached into Dallas's chest, and squeezed his heart and choked the air from his lungs. "Every time I felt the tug of those ropes yanking me up, a part of me wished it'd be the last time, that they'd let me eat a bullet. But carving me away, piece by piece was more fun. Fuckers even sterilized my wounds when they hauled me out, said I'd last longer that way."

Fuck.

He'd wanted an in with his brother about what had gone down. He and his brothers had all bided their time, but he hadn't expected to be the one entrusted with that in, not really. Nolan or Marshall were far more likely. Big brothers made monsters go away.

But they didn't carry the demons Dallas did, and Jesse needed to know his weren't the ugliest and nastiest in the playpen. Truth told, Dallas wasn't sure if they were or not.

Jesse looked away and added, "I died back in that hole, over and over, knowing that even if I survived, I wouldn't ever be whole again, the kind of man a good woman could accept a life with. I came back half the man I was, and I'm not sure how to fill in the holes they carved in my soul. Some days I'm not even sure if I want to bother trying."

Dallas had words lodged in his throat but swallowed them back when he saw the lost expression within his brother's gaze. Jesse had always been the one who chased the invisible monsters from underneath his bed when they were kids. He'd been the one to keep Dallas safe when storms hit and he'd gotten scared when thunder and lightning lit up the night sky.

But Dallas couldn't let a man as good as Jesse think whatever went down in that hellhole made him less than what he was before. "The measure of a man isn't what he looks like or what he can do. It's about the courage within him to pick himself up, dust the shit off, and move on. Life knocks us down, but not out."

"We're never out," Jesse finished. Their father had said the words thousands of times.

"No woman who'd put what you can or can't do with her or for her above who you are is worth having you in the first place." He slapped his brother's face and smirked. "Gotta admit we're fucked though, brother."

"Why's that?"

"Dylan raised the bar pretty fucking high hooking up with Mary. It's hard to imagine anyone out there better than her," he admitted.

Fuck. The coms were still on. The twitch in Jesse's jaw as he muttered a curse clued him in that he hadn't realized it either.

A barely audible breath on the other end was the only sound the two women running operations emitted. Dallas wasn't sure which one it was, not that it mattered. When they were running an op, they were two halves of a flawlessly cohesive unit. With a weary breath, he severed physical contact and shared the first thought that came to his mind. Quid pro quo.

But if big brother could give voice to his bad, then so could Dallas. It was time to share more about the past he'd walked away from.

"First assignment was overseas, some asshole dignitary visiting the sandbox, making nice with the bastard good men and women had died trying to find. I was fucking thrilled, thought I'd been sent to take the shot an entire country wanted." Dallas fisted his hands, bit through the worst of the emotion filling his voice, and swallowed it back.

"You weren't."

"Confirmation of my target came through. First assignment and I knew I'd made a mistake entering The Collective." He leveled a look to his big brother, and gave him a truth he'd shared with no one. "The dignitary's kid, a boy. Six, maybe seven, not much older than my kid probably is. Big brown eyes and a laugh I heard all the way from my perch. His dad had just picked him up and kissed his cheek when I took the shot."

"Fuck," Jesse said.

"My bitch handler said I deserved a bonus for effectiveness on delivering a message. Sealed my fate that day even as I knew I'd made the worst decision of my life." He rubbed the ache in his chest as he bit back the burn of shame. "I never should've taken the shot."

"We've all done shit we didn't want."

"No order justifies the things I did," Dallas said.

"I did more than my share of dark while in that hole, D. When you're trapped in hell, you do whatever's necessary to survive, to get back. Some days I prayed for death, while others I dispensed it so I could get back home, here to you. Our brothers. Mom." Jesse snagged his neck and dragged him closer until their foreheads collided. "That's what we did, brother. We survived. For family. Blood for blood."

"I see that shot every night, hear that laughter I killed." Dallas swallowed and forced out the fear he'd yet to voice, even to himself. "I'm fucking terrified of what we'll find with my boy, man. I remember what I did and can't help but think fate's decided I need to be punished, to feel the impact of my actions."

"We'll find him. Whatever the situation, we're getting your boy out and home where he belongs. Don't fuel the demons you can't vanquish."

"Back at you."

Jesse slapped him on the back as they hugged it out. "Let's get back to the truck before Addy and Nolan come over and kick our asses."

By the time he and Jesse had returned to the truck, Kamren was passed out in the back seat. Her dark hair framed her pale face and curled down onto the blanket covering her. Nolan and Addy were sitting in the front. Cool air greeted them as he and Jesse climbed into the back. He drew Kamren into his lap, but she didn't stir.

Exhausted.

He met Nolan's gaze in the rearview mirror and saw the same determination burning there that he felt in himself and saw in Jesse. Whatever Kamren's troubles were, they'd become personal tonight. None of them could handle seeing women abused or hurt.

"I'm assisting with Marville when we aren't combing a new area for your kid," Nolan said.

"Me, too," Jesse added.

Dallas had figured as much. "Let's get her home. Tomorrow's soon enough to tackle the details."

The compound was quiet by the time they arrived. Marshall, Cord, and Dylan were all near the parking area, along with Sanderson. The four men didn't demand details; likely, they'd heard enough for now.

"Marville briefing in the morning," Marshall said.

Dallas grunted his assent as he carried Kamren toward his small cottage. Jesse opened the door while Nolan went in, turned on lights and got the bedroom door open as Dallas carried Kamren. He'd need to raid Riley's closet. The thought had just swept through his mind when he turned the corner and saw the pile of clothes on his bed.

"Looks like the girls have her covered," Nolan commented as he stood in the hall, making it obvious he was there to babysit both of his little brothers.

Dallas hadn't meant to divulge so much of his past but doing so had given voice to Jesse's wounds. That alone made the risk of his brothers not understanding the things he'd had to do worth it. And, really. They'd had his back all along. Everyone at The Arsenal had been right alongside him, looking for his kid.

They'd already put two and two together and made four without him offering up details. Jesse was living proof everyone had demons. Some were darker and shittier than others, but they all had baggage they hadn't checked.

He was glad the women had taken Kamren in. Though they'd maintained their distance for the most part so far, he couldn't think of a better crew for her to get in with. Vi, Mary, Addy, Bree, and Rhea had taken Riley in. Then Zoey. None of the women were like Kamren, though. Then again, they all had their unique personalities. Zoey was a former NSA operative who'd pulled Fallon's team out of trouble not too long ago. She'd gotten burned and was now an Arsenal employee.

He wasn't sure what her skill set was, but she worked with Mary, Vi, and Jud. So, brain squad.

He set Kamren on the bed, covered her up, and sighed his frustration as he took in her sleeping form. He should wake her up so she could change into something more comfortable, but she was exhausted. She needed sleep more than she needed comfortable sleepwear.

She was beautiful, but trouble he didn't need. Not that it mattered. A man didn't walk away from someone who needed help, especially a woman. His mom and dad had raised him to help everyone, but no Mason ever left a woman needing help.

Something about her had roused his protective instincts even more than normal. He tried to recall exactly when but couldn't. Perhaps it was the quiet inner strength, or her gritty determination to handle problems on her own. He respected the hell out of that.

But he wasn't raised to let anyone fight a battle alone, especially one that could get them hurt or, even worse, killed.

Brant was a problem, one he'd handle. He didn't appreciate the man talking to Kamren like that. Whatever issues they'd had didn't justify a man ever speaking to a woman like that.

He bid Jesse and Nolan farewell, then he collapsed on the sofa and withdrew his cell phone. He had two choices on who to call. Okay, he really had four, but Vi and Mary were the top two and both had protective men capable of kicking his ass for bothering them.

But one was pregnant.

He grinned big at the thought. Mary had his little niece or nephew growing in her womb. He'd never been the sentimental sort, but knowing a little one was on the way helped ease the fear he had about raising his own kid. Soon enough there'd be a baby at The Arsenal.

His son wouldn't be the only child—he'd have a baby cousin. "What?" Jud growled the terse word into the phone in a tone that'd stop most people's hearts. Dallas took a moment to second-guess his choice of call options.

"Vi was digging into Kamren."

"Yeah, why the hell did you get her and Mary on that when we're actively trying to train Riley?"

"She and Rachelle are tight; didn't want it to get awkward."

"That sister of yours is tight with most of the tri-county. Sooner she learns business isn't personal, the better. I've put her on the dig. She's gonna brief me and you in the morning, first thing."

"Good."

"Then she and I are on the streets working this case with you."

"Riley's not ready for that level of work."

"She's observation only. The sooner they see her on the streets working cases, the easier it'll get for her to do so without me at her side. Might be a shock to you, but I've got a beautiful woman in my bed, one I'd prefer to spend time with in said bed rather than on the streets keeping your little sister breathing."

"Fine, but I'm working the Marville situation, whatever it lands out being. You can both help, but it's mine."

"Tomorrow."

Dallas shook his head and laughed when Jud hung up. Fucker had a way with words.

~

KAMREN WOKE TO BANGING. It took her more than a few eye blinks to realize she wasn't in her truck. Oh, right. She'd blown it up. Ugh. Dallas. His scent filled her nostrils, inciting a rebellious trail of thoughts that fanned heat through her entire body. A soft tap on the door bolted her upright.

The man himself prowled in. His half-hooded gaze added to the sexy half-awake look of tousled hair and barely-on boxers. Muscled flesh on prominent display quickened her pulse, proving without a doubt she was definitely not dead. Nope. She was definitely awake.

"Addy's here for you."

"Why?"

"Dunno, didn't ask." He padded into the bathroom and shut the door.

What the heck had just happened? She didn't remember even getting into bed last night. Oops. At least her bits and baubles had been covered, not that he would've cared either way. She was still in the clothes she'd worn the night before. How had she gotten inside?

Though the bathroom door was shut, she could hear the shower running, which meant she would be on her own long enough to get her head on straight.

No. Addy was here.

She didn't exactly do socializing well, so she hoped the woman got quickly to the point of why she'd come over. If Kamren counted people who cared about her on her fingers, she had exactly one friend. Two relatives. That meant three people who might give a damn about her, so she wasn't exactly well-versed in being friendly. Depending on how things shook out today, she might land out with no fingers used at all. Dani was likely pissed. Rachelle and Cliff? They drifted more toward annoyed with her existence on an average day, and they hadn't had anything remotely as good as that in a long while.

Today was decision day for a lot of stuff. One way or another she was standing at the crossroads, and for the first time in a long while, she wouldn't be deciding the direction she took. Not alone.

"You okay?" Addy asked as she entered the living room.

"Just peachy," she lied.

"Just so you know, we had World War III last night. You slept through it." Addy started making coffee in the kitchen.

The redhead set out a jug of milk and grabbed a bowl and spoon. A box of cereal appeared from the cupboard. Knots formed in Kamren's gut as she watched the scene unfolding. Her gaze swept toward the bedroom where Dallas was showering, then back to the woman making herself at home in his kitchen. She knew where he kept the spoons, had gone right to the drawer.

Like it was hers.

Addy froze as if sensing the direction of her thoughts. She chuckled and smirked as she pushed the button on the coffee maker. "Not in a million years, girlfriend. Not in a billion. No. Way. In. Hell."

"The woman doth protest too much," she muttered.

"Rhea and Bree lived here. They vacated a few weeks ago, made room for Dallas to raise his boy here when we bring him home. He didn't bother moving anything in the kitchen or anywhere else."

Addy offered the explanation and more information than Kamren's mind could process.

A boy.

Wow.

Dallas had a son. The tri-county would go wild when they discovered there was a mini-Mason running around.

"I don't shit where I live, or whatever the saying is," Addy said. "We're shooting today; got some new, potential operatives to vet. You'll shoot, too. Then we're meeting in the whiteboard room. No way around that, I'm afraid. After Marshall ended World War III last night, he declared we'd all meet to go over whatever it is we need to hash out."

"World War III?"

"The backpack," Addy supplied. When Kamren remained silent, she continued. "There was a heated discussion on who should take possession of its protective detail for the evening since you were AWOL. Mary and Vi both threw down for the right. I may have declared it was my right since you gave it to me. Cord suggested the safe, but that was thrown out as an option."

"There was an argument because of me?" Kamren didn't like knowing friends had argued because of her.

"Oh, Vi and Mary are like the yin and yang. Arguments don't happen. They're discussions with bullet points and data. Lots of data." Addy shook her head and grimaced as she poured a cup of coffee into a mug. "Vi pointed out that since Mary was preggos, her man wouldn't be down with protecting your backpack to the death, should the need arise. He'd be throwing himself in front of Mary."

"To the death?" These people were certifiably nuts. No one gave a damn about her backpack. The woman was teasing her. Surely. But Kamren had to admit it felt nice to have someone care.

"Unfortunately Dylan—he's Dallas's brother and Mary's man— walked in with Jud—who's Vi's man—right as Vi was explaining her reasoning. Dylan didn't appreciate Vi thinking he couldn't protect a backpack. He suggested they open the backpack and see if it was even worth worrying about protecting. That set Vi and Mary off. And me, if I'm being perfectly honest." She grimaced again. "Gotta say I was a bit bothered by them thinking I'd let them violate the trust you gave me, so there was a fight. Okay, a punch that was blocked and a glare that was returned."

"So a typical Thursday night?" Dallas asked as he sauntered into the room.

Wet hair and barely dried skin. His snug T-shirt was damp. The scents of soap and shampoo mingled in the air as he approached.

"Who won?" Dallas asked.

"Jud. He growled, grabbed the backpack with one hand, tossed his woman over his shoulder with the other, and left."

"Figured as much. Not sure many would go after him," Dallas replied. He smiled at Kamren. "He used to be an assassin before he came here."

Kamren blinked. Wow, okay. She remembered the name from talk yesterday. He was the one helping Riley with the Marville investigation. An assassin seemed like overkill, but she was glad someone was finally digging up the crap buried in Marville. God knew there was plenty to keep the man busy a long, long time.

"You okay?" Dallas asked. "You sleep okay?"

"Yeah, I slept great. Thank you. Sorry I stole your bed."

"I'm glad you got the rest. You'll need it. I heard there's a white-boarding session planned."

"What is that? Addy just mentioned it."

"The geeks gather round in a room filled with white boards and computer displays and arrange what they know to find patterns and holes in said knowledge. I've seen way too many of these sessions since I actually understand what I just said." Addy shook her head, as if clearing it. "The system they designed, HERA, has a computer hooked to every database around. It recognizes faces, pulls information from anywhere, and establishes patterns within seconds. Between HERA and all those geniuses, there's nothing they can't figure out. It's a thing of beauty, but I'll deny saying that if you tell them."

Wow. Kamren really wanted to see what the women and HERA

came up with. But what if there was nothing of value in what she'd gathered? What if she wasted everyone's time? Apprehension made her hope falter a moment as she looked at Dallas.

"It might not be worth everyone's time."

"Between all of us, we've seen enough to know one thing for certain." Dallas cut off the comment as if forcing her to engage with whatever he was about to say.

She huffed a frustrated breath. He smirked and raised his eyebrows. "Fine. What is for certain?"

"People don't waste bullets or manpower trying to kill someone without reason," Dallas whispered in her ear. "I know you're on the fence about letting us in on whatever mess you're in, but I think you realize you're over your head. That's why you came out here, right? To try and explain things to me since I didn't give you a shot to do so the last time I tracked you down?"

Kamren nodded.

"Okay, then. Today we'll have the conversation we should've had two weeks ago. We've also got some guns to shoot." Dallas cupped her face. "Either way, you aren't alone with whatever you're dealing with. You've got this entire compound behind you."

Wow. In that moment Kamren understood why Rachelle was so hung up on the Mason family. There was no small measure with them. When they went in, they went all in.

And they intended to go all in for Kamren.

Wow.

"We should hit the MD's first thing. I don't want to put it off any longer," Kamren said. "But I need to do this my way, which you may not agree with."

Dallas studied her a moment. If he'd run with Dom back in the day, he knew more about how the MD's operated than anyone else at The Arsenal compound. The rules hadn't changed much over the years, even if Javier's interpretation of them had.

"Addy goes with you, and we're on standby." Dallas pulled a cell-phone from his pocket. "I'll let Marshall and everyone know we're postponing the whiteboard meeting until later."

"Good idea." Addy yanked another bowl from the cabinet, tossed a spoon into it and shoved it across the bar toward Kamren. "Eat."

Kamren blinked and stared at the bowl. Her stomach growled in response as the woman filled the bowl with cereal, then doused it with milk. Although Kamren had been raised not to accept handouts and to earn the food she ate, she didn't comment. Hunger overrode upbringing, especially when she had far bigger battles ahead of her.

Like setting things straight with the Marville Dogs and reading Dallas and everyone in on what she'd been investigating the past sixteen months. She chewed and swallowed the large bite she'd taken and watched Dallas as he did the same.

God, he was sexy—so much so it almost hurt to look at him and imagine what a normal life with him in it would be like. She'd always wondered why her little sister was so taken with the Mason men. With Dallas looking like he was, hair tousled and wet, an amused grin on his face, it was easy to understand the fascination. The obsession.

"When you get there, you do what Addy says. If she says the situation's too hot and you need to vacate, you don't argue." Dallas took another bite, glancing between her and the redhead in question.

"Fair enough." Kamren blew out a relieved breath. She hadn't expected it to be quite so easy. Kamren couldn't help but wonder if she was being smart by trying to get his help with her mess. He needed to remain focused on finding his kid, not her and her troubles. Maybe he'd take a backseat and let someone else help her. Yeah. There were lots of people out here. Surely Dallas Mason wasn't the only one who could help her sort out her mess.

"You ready?" Addy asked.

"Give me five to change, then I'll be good to go."

"I'll pull a vehicle around, make sure everyone knows the plan." Addy glanced at Dallas. "'Keeping your distance' doesn't mean 'in another car on our ass'."

"Understood. We'll mic you two up, and I'll maintain my distance. They won't ever see me."

A shiver ran through Kamren. She had no doubt the man could

handle whatever Javier and his crew threw at them, but it didn't mean he should have to. This was her mess.

"I know what you're thinking," he whispered. "This became our problem, too, the moment you blew up your truck outside our fence line. Actually, it was ours to handle the moment Riley dragged Rachelle and Cliff out here. We've just been busy with other things."

Today she'd make a decision. If Dallas and the women didn't see anything in the backpack worth the hassle, she'd pack up the investigation and figure out how to move on. With that thought in mind, Kamren headed toward the bedroom.

"There's a duffel bag with clothes and stuff on the sofa," Addy said.

"Thanks." She snagged the bag. Yet another debt owed to someone. She was racking up quite the list.

8

The Marville Dogs had claimed possession of Dom's house three days after he'd been sent to prison for murder. They'd also acquired all the other property on the small road. It was a sticky situation for Dani, one Kamren had heard about countless times. Her best friend loved her big brother fiercely, so she'd avoided asking too many questions about why he'd killed someone.

Now you're more like him than Dani.

She severed the thought as she directed Addy down the narrow patch of caliche road, a one-vehicle-wide track locals called Devil's Highway, more for the freaky number of vehicles—most stolen from Nomad and Resino—and ramshackle single wides. The most trusted of the Marville Dogs earned their way into the stretch of living spaces that led to what'd once been Dani's family home.

Kamren barely remembered what the ranch house had once been like. Four street racers sat outside of the now dark blue wooden structure. Early morning sun had barely peeked over the horizon when Addy pulled up to a stop outside of the fence.

A couple of younger Marville Dog recruits stood. One let out a shrill whistle, the warning some unwanted idiot had wandered onto their hunting grounds. Kamren reached for the handle, but Addy grabbed her arm.

"You're here to send a message and clear the air."

"My best friend is tied to these assholes in a way she'll never break free. I'm here to make sure she doesn't suffer fallout for what I did. She and Rachelle stay clear of this mess."

"Then we send a firmer message. Back off or suffer the consequences. You walk in and own that yard; every asshole in it is your personal bitch." Addy's voice was edged with a slice of danger, one thicker and more confident than she'd heard—even in Dani's.

"You might want to go. I'll get home from here," Kamren said.

"I'm not leaving you here, Kamren. I'm here to watch your six. Whatever shit you're in, I'm sensing it's not your choice." Addy motioned toward the mass of bodies piling out of the house. "When we're done here, we're going back to The Arsenal and you're reading us in on whatever this is."

She nodded. "Right." And Dallas was on the outskirts of town waiting. Just in case. The knowledge kept her calmer than she should be, given the situation. She'd killed Marville Dogs.

"We all agreed long ago to weigh in on whatever was going on with Rachelle. Riley demanded it. That crew will go to the mat for her and anyone else who needs it. That includes you. Dallas has already set everything into motion. You walk in knowing you have all of us at The Arsenal at your back."

"I shouldn't have ever started this fight. I never stood a chance to win."

"Then you aren't fighting the right war. Trust us to point you in the right direction. Read us in, and my girls will figure out what's what. Vi and Mary have never failed a mission. Ever."

Kamren tasted the pride in the woman's fierce proclamation. "We'll see. It's not going to go well out there. You should stay in here. They'll...they'll hurt you."

The woman laughed. Actually laughed.

She tracked her gaze to the group of men now whistling and grabbing their crotches. A pale-faced Dani stood between Javier and his number one henchman, Ralph. Kamren vaulted from the vehicle before the redhead could stop her.

She'd faked bravado her entire life. She could confront Javier and pretend she'd snack on his balls if he messed with her again. For Rachelle. For Dani. For them she'd stare the devil himself down if necessary.

"This doesn't concern Dani," she spat angrily as she marched past Javier's idiot minions and got up in his face. "You have a lot of nerve, coming after me. What the fuck?"

"Bitch, she warned you a trip to Resino wouldn't end well."

"Yeah, she did. Newsflash, Javier, you don't own me, or her. Or the Marville Dogs." Voices rose behind her, but he held up his hand.

"I own Marville and everyone in it." His gaze slithered down her. "I'm thinking a few nights on your knees with a Marville Dog in your mouth oughta teach you your place."

"I'm thinking you best remember who you're talking to. I'm not one of your little whores. I'll gut you like a pig if you lay a hand on me or Dani." She took a menacing step forward into his space. "You fucked up, Javier. This is your one shot. Fuck with me again, and I fuck back."

He spewed off in Spanish. She let him have his say. Addy was right. She stood her ground now, or she'd never get another shot.

"You got a problem with me, you come to me. Don't send your *pendejo* tagalongs to handle it. That's a pussy move." She held the glare, but felt the men closing around her. "Marville Dogs' rules are clear. You came after me and I responded. There's no backlash. It was me and them, and I won. Fair and square."

"Ah-ah, step back from my girl or I step on you," Addy warned.

Kamren turned and noted the lithe redhead's assessing gaze as it spanned the full circle around her. Men closed the distance, but she remained steadfast in her position, gaze now locked on Javier.

"Who's your *puta* friend?" Javier asked.

"This is between me and you, Javier. No one else." Kamren's voice rose.

"The other night was your final warning. Stop sniffing around where you don't belong."

"And this is *your* final warning, Javier. Unlike your stupid crew, I don't need to be within spitting distance to pick you off. I'll drop you where you stand, and you'll never see me coming," she warned.

"Don't threaten me," Javier warned.

"That's not a threat, it's a promise. You've had a hell of a ride while Dom's been away, but don't forget who really runs the Marville Dogs. What's he gonna say when he hears about you messing with me?" She took another step forward until their breaths merged.

Disgust rolled through her, but she stood her ground. "I don't need to threaten, Javier. You aren't stupid. You know damn good and well word's already spread like wildfire and is already whispering in Dom's ear. Dani and I don't get touched by your bullshit. That was the rule, one you broke last night."

"We decide the rules, not you. Sure as fuck not Dom or his *puta* sister." Javier spat on the ground.

"That wasn't smart, Javier. You just declared war on Dom."

"Dom don't know shit. He knows what *I* say he knows." His gaze slid down Kamren with an appreciative glint that made her shudder in revulsion. "There's a new dog in charge, and I'm thinking it's past time you show him some respect."

"My respect belongs with the rightful MD leader, and that'll *never* be you. Back off, Javier."

"Or what? You'll make me?" He laughed and slid a finger down her cheek. "If you get on your knees and work that mouth the way it was meant to be worked, perhaps I'll forgive what you did to my crew."

Some of the fight vacated her bravado as fear and rage fused together and clogged her throat. "We're clear. You came after me; I responded and won. No debt owed."

"We're clear when I say we're clear, bitch."

"Javier," Dani said.

"This don't concern you, *puta*. Get in the house. I'll deal with you in a minute."

Dani's gaze narrowed. She didn't get in the house.

Addy tapped Kamren's shoulder. Two black double-cab trucks pulled to a stop. So much for staying outside town until they heard the signal for help via the mics she and Addy wore. The men around them shifted, directing their attention to Dallas as he charged through them and arrived at her side. He settled an arm around her waist and feathered a kiss at her temple.

What the hell? Jesse, Nolan and Gage Sanderson exited the vehicle, but made no move to enter the yard as Dallas curled her into his side like they'd done it a thousand times.

"You okay, babe?"

Babe? She blinked. Right, he'd said something about letting people think she'd hooked up with him, but that was before.

"Dallas." Javier shifted nervously from one foot to another as a drone appeared overhead. "Thought you warned her off, said you and your crew were done with her."

"Things changed."

"You've got shit taste in women," one of the Marville Dogs commented. "This bitch is the last skank I'd tap if I had your last name."

A drone whirled overhead and maneuvered to loom above the cluster of people. Red lasers danced from Javier's head to each man around Addy and Kamren. Taunting. Warning. Kamren wasn't sure if the drone could actually do anything, but the move was effective.

"What are you doing here?" Javier asked, his voice less confident than before.

"Not happy, Javier." Dallas's voice was lethally quiet with a slice of confident rage barely contained inside it. "You and me, it's been a while, but I thought we were good."

"We are."

"No. We are far from good. I'm not down with you or anyone shooting at women or driving them off the road. Even less thrilled you made that play outside my ranch. Big brothers aren't very thrilled either." Dallas took a menacing step forward into Javier's personal space. The man stepped back, but Dallas dragged him back with a hand fisted in his shirt. "I'm sure as fuck not good with you trying to put my woman on her knees so you can get her mouth working your worm-sized dick."

All the men glanced about as if trying to figure out how Dallas had heard that. Idiots. Kamren almost grinned as she noted the shift in the situation. All the bravado in the men gathered around Javier fled, but that didn't stop their leader from digging his grave deeper.

"Your bitch needs to mind her own business."

"Call her a bitch again and you'll be eating through a straw and shitting into a bag," Dallas warned.

Eww. Kamren swallowed and noted the tension within the MD's around them. Some reached for their weapons, but no one drew. Addy's gaze prowled each one. Jesse, Nolan, and Gage had all entered the yard and formed a half-circle around the MD's. Caging them.

"I'm gonna have a nice, long, very overdue conversation with Dom about his decision to leave you in charge of his crew. And protecting Dani. I'm thinking he's missed a few important facts." Dallas glanced over at Dani, who'd paled. "Daniella."

Her best friend swallowed. "Dallas. It's been a while."

"Too long. You good?"

"Never better." Dani looked over at Javier. "I'd like to go with you. To Huntsville. It's time I chat with Dom."

"We'll be in touch once it's arranged," Nolan said.

Kamren remained quiet, unsure what her place in this was anymore. Dallas settled a possessive hand at her waist.

"Let's go," he said.

She let him lead her toward the truck they'd come in. He opened it and settled her into the front seat. Addy slid into the back.

"What the hell just happened?" She looked over at Javier, then back at Dallas. "We had an agreement."

"I didn't like what he was saying or the way he was looking at you," he clipped. "You sent your message, then I came in and gave mine."

The truck opened and Vi and Mary crawled in. Addy cursed

when she saw the two women. "You two should've stayed at the compound."

"Hi," the blonde offered with a wave. "And you knew we wouldn't stay. And they made us stay in the truck, it wasn't like we *did* anything."

"We came to save you, but it looks like you and Addy had it under control. You didn't even need us or the drones," Mary said.

Dallas shook his head and stifled a smile with his hand as he fired up the truck. "We've gotta jet. Climb back into the other truck before Dylan has my ass."

"Damn it. The whole plan is blown," Vi declared. "We were supposed to help save her so we could earn a peek."

Mary sighed and held out the backpack like she was handing over the Holy Grail.

"A peek?" Kamren took the bag, suddenly realizing everyone's attention was on it.

"The Arsenal just weighed in on whatever your problem is," Dallas commented. "All of Marville figured that out when our trucks hit the city limits."

"This," she said holding up the bag, "doesn't concern the Marville Dogs. They got nervous because I went to check on Rachelle. They don't like you all much."

"Well, I'm thinking they're liking us even less about now," Dallas commented. "Riley was right. She said we'd turned a blind eye to our own backyard. We won't be doing that anymore, which means today was their notice. We're cleaning house."

"More like a whole town," Vi said. "Jud's thrilled. He's been sharpening knives all morning."

Oh boy.

Kamren was down for cleaning house. She'd been gathering the ammunition to burn the entire fucking town down for months now, sixteen of them to be precise.

None of what she'd done so far had resulted in answers, which was odd within itself. Surely she would've gotten at least one decent discovery by now. Right? Maybe her dad really did just have an accident.

"Kam." Dallas settled a thumb on her chin. "We need to get back to The Arsenal and figure out a real plan, one that doesn't end with you going rogue."

She winced. The ringing was still a subtle but obnoxious presence, and her head throbbed. She'd read his full lips, become somewhat enthralled by the cadence, the rhythm of movement.

Idiot. Answer him already.

"I just have to say, Mary and I have run hundreds of ops, and that move where you tumbled out of the car in a perfect roll, lifted your rifle and shot the puddle of gas? No hesitation at all? Wow! Utter brilliance." Vi waved her hands around. "Do you have any training? Like, military or anything? I started looking around into your records last night, and I didn't find anything. Weird, huh?"

Kamren processed the words for a couple beats. Tension coiled through her muscles. Heat crawled up her cheeks. She'd looked into her background and found nothing. Eventually she'd figure it out, the hideous shame she kept to herself.

Only Dani and Rachelle knew. Well, and Cliff, but he'd have to be sober long enough to remember. She swallowed back any smart-ass reply.

"Yeah, totally weird," she replied.

"Your girl's tapping on the glass." Dallas motioned toward the side window.

"I need a moment." Kamren stepped out of the truck. Dani glared into it and at Dallas. Dani was a hell of a fighter, the kind of person who came up swinging when they got knocked down.

"You okay? Maybe you should come with us," Kamren stated.

"That's not happening, Kam. I love you, but I'm not stepping on Mason property." Dani spat the name like it was a toxin. Kamren cringed knowing Dallas heard. "I'm standing my ground on this one. I appreciate the assist, whoever the hell you are, but I've got it from here."

Kamren jumped, startled that Addy had exited the vehicle and come around.

"The name's Addy." The redhead held out a card. "Here's my number. Call if there's any trouble. I'll come alone, nary a Mason with me. Gotta admit, you've got me curious since you're the first woman with a pulse who can't stand them."

"I have my reasons, and they aren't your business."

"Are they ours?" Nolan asked.

"No." Dani hugged Kamren close. "I need a moment alone with my girl. Get gone."

Addy and Nolan left; the woman climbed into the truck Kamren had exited, while Nolan went to another.

"Careful what you trust them with, girl. They did you a solid today, but that doesn't mean they'll believe you." The words were muffled, but somewhat discernible.

"I have to try, Dani. I'm close."

"I hope so." Dani pulled away. "You okay out there with Rachelle and Cliff?"

"It's a big compound. Brant was called out to check on me. He told them to keep me away from her."

"Like you're an evil leper? Bastard. I swear I'm gonna pee in his beer the next time he comes in."

"Don't you dare." It was the sort of thing Dani would totally do. "I deserve his distrust. He was there and saw the aftermath of what I did."

"He didn't know shit." Dani's raised voice made Kamren cringe. "None of them do. That piece of shit brother knows. That simpering little sister knows. I don't see either one of them speaking up."

"Dani, that's not fair. You know it's not."

"No. What's not fair is a good woman cutting herself down and chewing herself up looking into the death of a man who deserves to rot in hell."

Kamren gasped. Dani hadn't ever been that blunt, not about her father.

"I'm not saying this to hurt you; I'm saying it to wake you up. He is not worth dying over. He never was. Let it go."

"I'm close," she argued. She squeezed her friend's hand. "I can't cover shifts, not until this dies down. And Rachelle got hired out at The Arsenal, apparently."

"I'll let Ronnie know to replace her."

"Love you," Kamren whispered.

"Back atcha. Watch your back out there."

"I always do." With that, she climbed into the back of the vehicle. Addy and Dallas were up front, while Vi and Mary had returned to one of the other two trucks behind them, both of which turned around and headed out.

Her heart pattered wildly as she watched the dust trail they left behind from the U-turn. They'd driven all the way over from their ranch outside Resino in case she needed help. Damn. No one had ever had her back like that. Ever.

～

DALLAS ADDED a few more questions to his list after listening to the conversation between Kamren and Dani via the mic she wore. He should've had Cord switch it off, but they needed whatever intel they could get. The friend didn't like the father. No, she hated him. Why?

He started up the vehicle and glanced at Kamren through the rearview mirror. Her lips pursed in a thin line as she met his gaze. The other two trucks were headed back to Resino. The redhead shook her head.

Dallas nodded.

He and Addy had argued the merits of the second part of the plan vehemently the day before, but Dallas was determined they would get Kamren gone from Marville in a way she could stay away a while.

"We're going to your farm next, Kamren. Until things die down, me and a couple of the guys are going to come over and help Riley tend to things," he said.

"No. I've got it. I'm back, I'll handle it."

"Sweetheart, you can come with us when we do, but we're help-ing. It's not safe for you and Riley to go it alone. This isn't us being alpha assholes; it's us being smart."

Her body tightened.

Fuck. He'd said something wrong.

"Tell you what," he said. "Nolan, Jesse, and I will take turns going out there with Riley and you can help around our ranch. There's always lots to do, and I know you'll get it sorted a hell of a lot better than the operatives we assign to it at times. We're cutting back on the ranching part, but it'll take time."

"I know we should shut our little farm down, but Rachelle loves the animals. Mom did, too." Kamren's voice was a barely audible whisper as she turned away and shoved the visor back into position. "It's all we have left of them. It's a crumbling piece of shit, but it's *our* piece of shit."

Dallas didn't respond. Addy had warned him the house was in bad shape, but he hadn't listened. She'd driven Riley over when she'd gathered Rachelle's stuff.

Kamren's eyes were squeezed shut. Head back, she'd shut down any further conversation with him about it, no doubt thanking her ears for ringing.

Addy was right.

He was pushing too hard to get answers and a way in so he could help. Why the hell it mattered was an answer he didn't have. Truth told, he didn't give a damn.

Addy navigated the vehicle back onto the highway and turned south. The full light of day offered no shadows or masks for the squat farmhouse. Overgrown shrubs and grass engulfed what'd once been a large front yard. The fence line was in disarray around the entire house.

What looked like trash bags and duct tape covered sections of the roof. One half of the porch sat crooked thanks to a crumbled support beam. Disgust filled him as he noted the extensive repairs needed.

The list built in his mind as they parked and Addy turned the vehicle off. Dallas had grown up on a ranch his entire life. He was raised to take a certain amount of pride in your home, and provide adequate care for your stock.

He followed Addy and Kamren through the garden. At least three-quarters of it was untended and weed-riddled. A few tomato plants and onions were planted in a cleaned off patch nearest the stairs.

Kamren bypassed the house and headed toward the back. The barn's paint was chipped, but he noted the new wood along the top and near the door. Patchwork had been maintained. Some of his disgust lifted as they entered. The stalls were small, but clean and well kept.

Though he suspected he had Riley to thank for most of it, the evident care given to the area proved it'd been the focal point of the small farm for a long time. Chickens flew around in their coop when Kamren entered and tended them.

He stood and watched as she gathered eggs and fed them and checked their water. Then she sat and gathered one after another to make sure they were okay. She repeated the process with the goats, which were penned in a well-kept area to the west of the barn. A few cattle grazed lazily nearby.

He closed the distance when she headed toward bales of hay. He grabbed her by the shoulder and turned until her fiery, blue eyes landed on him like lasers. "I'm sorry, sweetheart. I don't want to push, but it's important we understand the security needs out here."

"It's not your problem." She sniffed. "I know I've failed this place. Every time I hear the floor creak under me or mop water from what was once my bedroom, I know what a screwup I've been."

"Hey." Dallas cupped her cheek. "Sweetheart, managing a place, even a smaller one like this, is hard work. It takes more than one person."

"Which is why Brant hates me. I left Rache here to handle it alone, all so I could chase a stupid notion that..." She dragged in a ragged breath.

"A notion that what?" he asked gently.

"That someone killed my father," she whispered. "No one believes me, but he was the best hunter and tracker there was. He wouldn't have gone out and gotten lost, Dallas. And he sure as hell didn't accidentally shoot himself."

"That's what's in the backpack," he guessed.

"Yes."

"The women will help sort out everything you've got; they've got a whole crew. They call themselves The Pentagon." He laughed when her eyes widened. "Yeah, I know. It sounds nuts, but they are a force to be reckoned with when they're together. Trust the process. If it's not working for you, I'll wade in and call a stop to it, okay?"

"Okay. Now, let's feed the cows. They get mean when they're hungry." Her voice resonated with determination. She needed the mundane task of feeding animals to chase away whatever demons she battled in her head.

He'd thought she was a druggie, but she was hunting her father's killer. He couldn't have been more wrong about her.

9

Kamren felt like a twelve-point buck in the sight lines of a hunter. Dallas guided her down a long hallway and into a large room. A large, very white room. The table was taller than normal and lit with a large computer display within the center. Plush leather seating, a cross between recliners and stools, sat around the table.

It was the people in the seats that terrified the living hell out of her. Large white boards and computer displays hugged every surface of the room. She gulped and sat between Dallas and Addy.

"Wow, Addy's actually sitting down for this one. That's a little—" the perky blonde gulped, "—terrifying."

"Everyone, this is Kamren Garrett, Rachelle's sister," Dallas supplied. "You already know Addy, Mary, Dylan, and Vi. The other blonde is Bree. And that is Rhea. I think you met them briefly."

The two women waved. Dallas looked around.

"Where's Riley?" he asked. "I thought she always participated in these."

"Something came up," Rhea explained.

Kamren tightened. This was a terrible, terrible idea. She swallowed the dread drowning her hope and put the backpack on the table. As a sign of good faith, she pushed it across the surface and toward Vi and Mary. They stared at it. She stared at it.

Jesus, this was awkward.

She could practically feel the bullet's trajectory as it shot straight through the finely woven strands of hope she'd created the past sixteen months. Surely one of them was strong enough to withstand whatever this was. One of them would link to her father's death.

Answers.

The door swooshed open.

"Oh, great, you both made it." Mary's face brightened.

Kamren turned. Tears trekked down Rachelle's cheeks as she closed the distance and squeezed Kamren so hard her left side screamed in agony. She bit back the pain. She'd endured far, far worse and would again for this moment.

"You're back," she cried. "I know I saw you yesterday, but it was so brief, then you were off again and I thought...I didn't think you'd be back."

Kamren barely heard the statement. "I'm not leaving again. Like I said before, I'm here to stay, I swear. I'm sorry, Rachelle. For everything."

"I'm sorry, too. I know you wanted it to be more than an accident, but I'm glad you're finally ready to see things how they are. Riley and everyone will make you see. Her brothers are really good at this stuff."

"Yes, they are," Bree commented.

Kamren glanced at Riley, whose lips remained thin. To say her sister's best friend wasn't thrilled about the reunion was an understatement. Rachelle squeezed her hand.

"Are you okay? Last night?" Rachelle asked.

"Yeah, my ears are a little messed up. I'll be fine, and the boys are safe. If Dallas and everybody here doesn't see something credible, I'm done." Her voice broke at the end. "I'll leave it be."

Rachelle looked around, disbelief evident in her wide eyes. Riley leaned forward. "What do you mean you're done? Sixteen months and you're finally ready to see reason and accept it's time to move the hell on? Just like that?"

"Riles," Dallas warned.

"No, you don't know what she's been like, what Rachelle has dealt with. She's been a maniac." Riley crossed her arms. "Rachelle finally filled me in last night. This entire thing is total lunacy."

"Maybe we should dial it back a couple notches, sis, and go over what she's gathered," Dylan suggested. "You're not here as a friend. Remember that or you're gone."

Riley glared at her brother, who was seated near Mary and Vi. Kamren shifted in her seat, suddenly wishing she was in Tibet, wherever the heck that was. Or maybe the North Pole. She could track Rudolph. Maybe become an elf and work for the big jolly dude in the red suit. Excellent plan.

"So, what are we doing here exactly? I'm afraid I missed a memo or a conversation or...something." Rhea looked around.

Kamren reached toward the backpack, then put her hands into her lap, fisting them. Today was her moving forward by giving voice to what she'd clung to too long. "My father went missing one weekend just over eighteen months ago after guiding a hunting-slash-camping expedition on a lease not too far from our property. He'd been through the area hundreds of times. He was found dead on our property. The sheriff ruled it an accident."

"She thinks he was killed," Riley finished. Arms crossed, she motioned toward the backpack. "She's been stalking all the hunters, lease owners, and anyone else she thinks might have answers. Rachelle finally explained it last night."

Stalking.

She'd hoped her sister understood why she had to get answers, closure. After everything they'd been through, she needed to know what happened. Why.

"My father managed leases and hunting trips. He guided them, provided supplies, helped determine the best locations, cleaned the kills—whatever was necessary to make it optimal for the elite hunters," Kamren said. "I wasn't the only one who thought it suspicious that he suddenly got lost so close to home and then accidentally shot himself. I'm just the only one willing to say it publicly."

When no one spoke, she continued.

"I went looking when he didn't show up on time. He was like clockwork. I couldn't find a lead, a track to follow. Then, four days later he was there, in a field I'd searched at least six times. Sheriff Haskell said it was an accidental shooting and refused to investigate."

"And the coroner?" Bree asked softly. "What did the report say?"

"Inconclusive." She motioned toward the bag. "Everything I've found is in there. I keep thinking I'm close, but I can't make heads or tails of what I'm finding."

Vi took the bag and unzipped it. Dallas had told Kamren more about the women on the way into the compound. He'd meant to reassure her, but he had no idea how much it increased her anxiety. Vi and Mary had graduated from MIT before they were eighteen. They had gotten their doctorates by the time they were twenty. Who did that? Bree and Rhea were freaking science geniuses. One had created some wicked cool energy system and the other was a biochemical weapons specialist.

Buzzards picked at her insides as Vi and Mary worked together to pull out the haphazardly organized papers. The two thumbed through the stuff she'd gathered.

"Kamren, out of curiosity, why did you organize them in this pattern?" Mary asked.

She tightened beneath the inquiry. How could she justify a hunch? An uneducated hunch wouldn't hold weight against the level of intelligence brimming within the room. She was about to be boiled alive, gutted like that twelve-point buck she'd thought about earlier.

Dallas took her chin and turned it so she looked at him. "It wasn't a judgment, sweetheart. They're going to have to ask questions."

Her eyes burned. She fisted her hands and nodded. "Sorry, this is the first time I've shared the information with anyone after..." She swallowed the rest, unwilling to risk the fledgling bond forming between her and her sister.

"I didn't believe her," Rachelle said. "She showed me when she first started, and all I saw was a bunch of pictures and nonsense. But she kept going, and I was so angry I didn't want to listen to what she was saying. That's on me. That's why she hasn't shown anyone else."

Kamren reeled from the confession. Gut-wrenching regret and guilt filled her, but she didn't respond. She deserved the blow, the angered admission and accusation-laden words.

"Dad wasn't a good man," she admitted. "I shouldn't have cared, but I did. I do."

She took a deep breath and powered through the emotional roller coaster. Eyes averted, she continued. "At first I had them organized by person, then I realized some people shared the same leases. I never determined who hired him for that trip, so I had to investigate anyone he'd worked with. I went back three years."

"So this was by lease then?" Vi asked.

Kamren nodded. "Some people share leases since they're pricey. It really depends on the land owner and what they're willing to do. Dad only worked with the large leases."

She spent the next few minutes going over how hunting leases worked. The women asked pointed questions, but Kamren found herself relaxing with each question. They didn't speak down to her or make her feel ignorant. They didn't use big fancy words she couldn't understand.

They were normal.

Nice.

"Wow, you've been busy." Rhea thumbed through the surveillance. "And thorough. Where are these pictures?"

"Austin." She swallowed. Now came the part where she admitted how determined she'd become. "Three people I've marked as the most viable leads work out of an office in downtown Austin. I spent the last few months tracking their meetings and movements."

"How? With what money? Rachelle's been eating ramen noodles the past three months, and you've been in downtown Austin? Where did the money for hotels come from?" Riley demanded.

"I took the bus from Nomad to San Antonio, then to Austin. I got a barhop gig to cover food and investigative costs like printing pictures and the like," she said. "That made sure I could send money back home."

"And the hotel?" Rachelle asked.

"I rented a storage unit on the east side of town. It was small but a good base of operations." Heat rose in her cheeks. She'd definitely entered trailer trash country now. Who would ever consider renting a storage unit to live in for three months?

Addy laughed. "That's pretty clever. I was on a four-month surveillance once and didn't think of that."

"Well, you weren't in Austin. I don't think they had storage units in Bolivia," Mary replied. "I'm adding that to our list, though. It is ingenious."

"Wait, you sent money back home?" Riley asked, gaze narrowed.

"Back off, sis. This isn't the Spanish Inquisition," Dallas said.

"It should be," the woman argued.

"She sent money, Riles," Rachelle replied. "Four or five hundred every month, like clockwork."

"Then why the heck were you eating ramen?"

"Because it's good and the money needed to be used on feed for the animals and supplies for the farm and the electric bill. Or shoes. I ate at the Sip and Spin. Dani fed me lots, too. I know you want to blame Kamren for everything, but she's been helping how she could." Rachelle shrugged as she looked down at her feet.

Kamren suspected most of the money had gone to shoes, especially since she'd just cleaned out what little money she'd had last week catching the electric bill up.

"She killed people last night, Rache. I'm sorry, but I'm not ready to believe she's changed at all, and you shouldn't either," Riley said. Kamren shifted beneath the accusation within the woman's words, but a part of her warmed. Her sister had a very protective friend in her corner.

Kamren couldn't help but wonder what that was like, then she realized she kind of did. Dallas and Addy and the other women gathered around were taking their time to look at what she'd gathered.

That was more than anyone had ever done for her, and she couldn't help but wish there was some way to repay their kindness.

Vi slapped a fist down on the table. "And this is where I take control of this meeting. We're running off into the weeds and chasing some weird-ass squirrel."

Kamren's gut soured. It'd been going decently at first. She dared a peek over at Dallas. Concern flashed in his gaze when their eyes met. He reached over and took her hand.

"Okay, we're going back to the topic at hand, but we're going to do a cone-of-silence question-and-answer real quick so the air is fully cleared here," Vi said as she glanced over at Riley. "If you don't like the results, you might want to leave. I love you, but you're destructive to this process and I can't have that."

Riley didn't comment. Arms crossed, she glared at everyone in the room.

"Show of hands in the cone of silence. Answers given here don't leave the room, but I think it's important to establish a reality for Kamren since she doesn't know us. Apparently, Riley doesn't either, so we'll hop on that right now, too." Vi held up her hand. "Raise your hand if you have directly or indirectly killed someone."

Mary and Dylan's hands went up. Kamren raised hers, not that it mattered since everyone knew the answer already.

Addy raised two hands with a shrug. "I've been busy."

Dallas did the same. Mary nudged Bree and glared at Rhea.

"What?" Rhea asked. "I haven't killed anyone."

"The drones."

"Oh." The woman's nose kinked up. Her and Bree's eyes met and widened. "Oh, wow. Okay, yeah."

Their hands darted up, leaving Riley and Rachelle as the only ones without their hands up.

"Think the point here is simple — don't judge. We've all done things out of necessity rather than desire," Mary said. "This process isn't about judgment; it's about problem resolution and getting answers."

"I'm sorry," Riley offered. "It was a bitch thing to say. I'm rattled and pinned in a corner, so I came out punching. I don't trust you being back, not after the things you've put Rachelle through. I'm sorry, but that's the way it is."

"Fair enough," Kamren responded. "I'm glad she has you in her corner."

And she was. Riley had been the best thing to ever happen to her little sister.

"Okay, so back to the topic at hand." Vi put a pair of red wire-rimmed glasses on. "HERA's in for a good feeding day. Let's get started, girls."

Vi divided up the piles of folders between her and Mary. Photographs were passed over to Rhea and Bree, who scanned them in using a cool interface of some sort on the table top. Kamren sat back, enthralled and intimidated by the process in equal measures.

Awareness tingled up her arm when Dallas squeezed her hand. She looked over and noted his soft smile and the glimmer in his gaze.

"You okay?" he asked.

She nodded, honestly not sure what the answer was. She noted Mary saying something about reinforcements, then Vi picked up a phone and started typing out what Kamren assumed was a message.

Several minutes later, the room filled to capacity as the rest of the Mason brothers entered. One of them shoved in between Vi and Mary and got to work on a laptop he'd brought in. He looked up and winked.

"I'm the cute Mason. Cord."

Kamren couldn't help but smile.

The level of testosterone in the room was a bit overwhelming. The final entrant was Jud, who looked like he snacked on nails. He walked straight to Vi and claimed her mouth.

The kiss was downright sordid in its intensity. Several of the women whistled. Nolan and Jesse laughed.

"Why are all of you in here mucking up our routine?" Vi asked.

"Curiosity," Nolan replied. "Dylan and Addy said it was a sight to behold. We're beholding."

Mary and Vi leaned near one another and started talking.

Though Kamren couldn't hear the words, she read their lips easily enough. She chuckled to herself when Cord growled, no doubt not appreciating the conversation shift as they started discussing their upcoming shopping adventure to San Antonio for honeymoon wear.

Vi wanted edible underwear and was hoping Jud would be okay with wearing a g-string so she could "experiment." Kamren covered her mouth and glanced away when Mary started sharing her latest experimentation with Dylan. Yowza, reading lips was seriously a pain in the ass sometimes. Overhearing, or in this case overseeing, people's private conversations made her feel like the lowest scum of the earth.

The hum of the machinery around them likely kept everyone else from hearing what they yammered on about. The four brilliant women worked well together, seamlessly adding Cord to the process. Marshall and Nolan walked about the room as images were thrown up onto the walls in what seemed like random patterns at first. Then Bree and Rhea started pulling out colored yarn.

"So two senators and three state supreme court justices share a lease? I'd imagine they could afford individual leases," Mary commented.

"That's not how hunting works, not for guys like them," Dylan commented. "It's amusement and camaraderie more than a sport. That's why the guys running the chopper hunts over in Nomad are doing so well."

Kamren nodded. "They're adding more exotics for this next season. I consulted for them not too long ago."

"What kind of consultation?" Bree asked.

"They hired some company to study breeding patterns and migration routes and stuff, but one of the guys didn't trust the results, said they wanted a second opinion from someone with more hands-on experience." She fiddled with the frayed bottom of her T-shirt. "I went in and recommended locations for feeders, stuff like that."

"She did more than that," Rachelle defended. "I remember that assignment. You lived out there for two weeks because you were worried about the amount of coyote tracks you saw. They paid her a big bonus for clearing out the excess predators in the area. That's how we got the barn fixed."

"You did a hell of a job tracking the twins," Jesse complimented. "We were talking about needing to take the noobs out for some survival testing."

"You're all going? Even you, Nolan?" Mary smirked. "There might be flesh-eating maggots out there."

The man growled. "Not cool, Edge. Not cool."

Dallas leaned over and drew Kamren's attention. "A few years ago, Mary saved Nolan and his team. They were in a jungle and days from an exfil. She taunted him every night with flesh-eating maggots and nasty stuff to keep him mentally alert."

Kamren chuckled. "Sadly, there aren't any of those around these parts, but fire ants can sure ruin your day."

"Do you have an ETA on this being done?" Marshall asked.

"It'll take a few more hours," Vi answered. "There's a ton of data here. HERA's pulling phone records on all these guys she's been tracking, and that's opening up records for everyone they've spoken to. Some of them have been very busy boys."

"What's up?" Dallas asked his brother.

"I'm thinking we can go be a bit more productive. We've got some new potentials to vet on the shooting range. I'm thinking Kamren might prefer playing out there."

"A gun range might not be good with her ears," Dallas argued.

Heat spread through her insides. She wasn't used to someone worrying about her. She tamped down any response as the men talked. Jesse said something about the doc. She hoped that was Logan and not Brant.

"She's clear as long as we use headgear," Jesse said with a grin. "Let's get out of this geek fest."

Kamren was down with escaping while she could. She looked over at the women who'd welcomed her so easily and listened to what she had to say. "Thank you for your help. I'm sorry if this is a huge waste of your time."

"Any chance we get to stretch HERA's legs is never a waste of time," Mary said. "We just overhauled some stuff, so it's a great exercise either way."

"Let's go," Addy said. "I'll get her outfitted with gear. You boys assemble the candidates. I say they all walk if our girl outshoots them."

Dallas smirked. "I'm down with that."

"We might want a more rigid standard," Cord commented. Vi walloped his head. "What the hell was that for?"

"For being stupid." Vi looked over at Kamren. "He hasn't seen the footage yet."

"That was a lucky shot," Kamren argued.

"Sure it was," Dallas commented. "Come on, Lucky. Let's go have some fun."

10

Addy found the most ridiculous headgear imaginable for Kamren, but Dallas found it adorable. The thick red-and-black earmuffs dwarfed her head. Her long, light brown hair was drawn back and up in a braided bun at the nape of her neck, like Princess Leia but way sexier.

The black cargo pants hugged her ass snugly and accentuated her long legs. Her plentiful breasts pushed out against the Army green T-shirt she'd stuffed into the pants. Knives stuck out of two of the cargo pockets. She'd yet to give them up?

Interesting.

The two women were laughing and talking as they stopped near the weapons Dallas had hauled out from the munitions cache downstairs. Kamren reached out and touched one of the newer rifles added to their arsenal.

"It's a new design, one that'll switch between urban and tactical settings," he offered.

"Very cool," she commented. "I'm not sure what I'm doing out here. It's kind of like the kid playing around before all the adults get busy."

"Don't sell yourself short," Dallas commented. "How old were you when your dad taught you to shoot?"

"Four or five. I followed him everywhere, like a shadow. Cliff and Rachelle never showed much of an interest, so he spent any spare time he had teaching me everything he knew." She smiled. "I'm more comfortable out there than anywhere else these days."

"Most of us feel that way sometimes. When I got back, it took me weeks to acclimate to all the people and inside lights and..." He lifted one of the rifles and offered it to her. "Go ahead, get used to it. Fire off a few practice shots if you want."

"You're serious? I can shoot it?" Anticipation shimmered in her eyes.

"You sure as hell better. We've got a pool going," he commented.

"Come on, let's get you practicing with the headgear a while. It takes some time to acclimate to," Addy commented.

Dallas watched the two women head off toward the target range someone had set up for today. Nolan moved to stand beside him.

"We've got a trip scheduled to Huntsville tomorrow," Nolan said. "We're doing this one without Dani. We'll take her later, after we've sorted things out."

Dominic DeMarco had been Dallas's idol growing up. Dom had always been a bit wilder than Nolan and his brothers. Dom had fed his wild side with fast cars and even faster women. By the time Dallas hit seventeen, he'd been running hard with Dom's crew. He and Dom's younger brother, Ricardo, had been inseparable.

Then Dom had gotten arrested for murder. Folks didn't know what to believe or who to trust. Dallas had been alienated from Ricardo, and the crew once dedicated to fast cars and street racing turned their sights onto more dangerous enterprises. Disenchanted, Dallas had entered the service like his brothers had.

"I don't think the Marville Dogs got your message," Nolan said. "Marcus spent the evening at the Sip and Spin. Things aren't calming like we hoped."

Marcus was a hell of an operative they'd recently brought on.

He'd earned his team leader stripes when he helped Jud defend The Arsenal compound while everyone had been overseas on a mission.

"Dom will handle it once he hears that tape. Javier threatening Dani the way he did sealed his fate," Dallas commented. "There's nothing he and Ricardo wouldn't do for her."

"I'm wondering why Ricardo isn't around running the MD's," Nolan commented.

"He headed out around the same time I did. I never knew where, but I figure he was as sick of Marville and small-town Texas as I was back then."

"Glad you're back," Nolan commented. "We'll get them all, brother. Everyone who touched your kid is dead."

Dallas remained focused on the two women.

The way they talked about The Collective cut too deep. Dallas was more like the bastards they hunted down than anyone realized. He shook off the thought and forged on. He couldn't look back on what he'd done and regret anything, not when it'd kept innocent civilians like his sister alive, living a happy, wholesome life.

"Dylan's worried."

Ah. Dylan had sent big brother number two after his ass. Dallas grunted. Anytime one of them was concerned about another, Nolan or Marshall was activated. The two eldest brothers were the closest thing they had to male confidants since their dad passed.

He rubbed his chest, massaging away the ache that'd settled in. "Her hunting down her dad's killer, it feels like something I've gotta help with."

"Yeah, feels like that for us all, but he wasn't a good man. Jesse got to talking last night. Cliff was in his class growing up."

Dallas filed the tidbit away. Rachelle had been in Riley's class, Cliff in Jesse's. So where the heck had Kamren been? He looked over at Nolan, who wore the same confusion on his face.

"Something about this stinks," Dallas guessed.

"Yeah, and we aren't going to like what we dig up."

KAMREN CLUTCHED the rifle Addy and Dallas had loaned her and smiled through her unease as Marshall and Dylan stood before the gathered group of commandos. A couple of women stood interspersed with the predominantly male hoard of muscled badasses. She'd yet to figure out how she fit into all this, but at least she was outside.

She breathed in the fresh air and exhaled the tension from earlier. The earmuffs were obnoxiously large but eased the ache and had prevented any unwanted reaction when she'd shot a few test rounds earlier. She wished Addy had told her how she'd done. The targets were crazy distances away, and even though the redhead had watched through binoculars, she hadn't offered any feedback at all.

"Today's objectives are simple. You're here to prove you have what it takes to handle long-range targets for an Arsenal team. This isn't the military where you have a guaranteed spotter to handhold you through the data, so we're doing today in two stages." Marshall's mouth moved slowly, as if he formed each word precisely to help her through understanding.

"The Quillery Edge is part of The Arsenal now, as you are all aware." Dylan looked around. "You're going to get to play with their latest toy during this first round. HERA will be your spotter. You'll each be given headgear, which will provide you with wind speeds, distances, and enough data to where a monkey could make the shot. That's what my fiancée said, so I expect precise hits every time."

"The second round is old-fashioned downrange shooting. No spotters, no data. Clean shots to see who can shoot the best," Marshall said. "That's where we'll cull the herd."

"Everyone get in position, three to a station. Addy, Jesse, Nolan, Gage, and Fallon are helping us out today. Listen to what they say," Dylan ordered.

Kamren waited until all the real commandos were situated. By the time everyone was in position, there was one spot left at Jesse's station. Her pulse quickened and her heart thudding in her chest. He smiled warmly as she walked over.

She had no business shooting at the station of a man like him, a hero. The compulsion to drag him into a hug was hard to beat down but she did, because he was a good man. And she felt more than a little guilty that she'd "heard" a piece of his hell, a piece he'd shared to get his little brother to give a piece of his.

Likely for Jesse, that's what family did. She totally got him because that's precisely what she did. Gave and gave and gave for blood.

"Excellent. I was hoping you'd land at my station. The boys and I have a little competition going—whose team shoots the best. Winner gets a steak dinner," he commented. "I think I might go ahead and make the reservation right now."

Her stomach rumbled its protest at the thought of food. She hadn't eaten much before arriving at The Arsenal, so the small amounts she'd managed since then hadn't fully sated her. She smiled through what she suspected had been a loud sound because his gaze swept to her belly.

"You hungry?" he asked.

Kamren shook her head. He shook his head and smiled, as if he'd suspected the answer. Fortunately, he didn't ask anything more. He reached into the pocket of his cargo pants and pulled out a nutrition bar.

"Eat. It tastes like dog shit, but it's better than an MRE." He pushed the bar into her hand. "I'll make sure Dallas shows you where the cafeteria is again when we're done here."

As if summoned by their conversation, Dallas appeared. His gaze narrowed as she inhaled half the nutrition bar in one massive bite. The two brothers did an awkward grunt, chin lift thing, then Jesse moved away to tend to his other two teammates. Dallas turned her to face him fully.

She chewed the vile bar. Jesse hadn't lied. It tasted like mud, saw dust, and grass. Blech. Dallas flashed a panty-smoldering smile, one so big and warm it damn near incinerated her. He removed the earmuffs Addy had given her, put a headset on her head, then put the muffs back on. She blinked as he essentially dressed her head like it wasn't a big deal.

But it was. He gave a damn about her hearing.

Her.

"Between this and the earmuffs, you look like an astronaut," he muttered. "The display shows you wind speeds, distances, and a bunch of other data to make shots. Just do your best and have fun, okay?"

Translation—he didn't expect her to do well. Wind speeds and distances were trajectory information. Math. Idiots like her didn't do math and trajectories. Her stomach soured at the thought.

No. Dallas didn't know about her uneducated self. Even if he did, he wouldn't care. He wanted her to have fun. That's what he'd said and meant. She watched her teammates take a few practice shots.

She matched their poses, belly down on the ground. Easy enough. She peeked through the sight via the headgear and...

Holy smokes, those were a lot of numbers streaming by. She watched them march by, unsure what the heck she was supposed to do with all the data. Really, what the ever-loving heck? She looked over, noting how everyone was tweaking doo dads on the fancy-ass rifle.

Yep, way out of your league, girl.

Should've stayed in elementary school where you belonged.

She breathed through the frustration and aimed, ignoring the displays. "Why the hell can't the display give me an arrow or something useful? Seriously, this is bullshit. If you've gotta take a shot in the heat of battle, all those numbers are useless. No one's got time to whip out a calculator in the field. You want to impress me? Give me colored arrows that make every bullet a kill shot. Talk about a waste of a brilliant tech opportunity."

Frustrated, she whipped off the headgear and refocused through the sights. Ah, much better. A presence settled beside her. She looked up and behind her where scary-as-hell Jud crouched.

An assassin? She gulped, a bit intimidated by the fact he probably knew a hundred different ways to kill someone. He glanced at the fancy headgear she'd tossed and smiled.

Crap. She'd tossed away his fiancée's fancy headgear thing.

"You have a call," he commented as he held out a com thingie similar to the one she'd forgotten was on the headgear thingamabob. "I'll verbalize for you. Viviana wants to know what you meant by colored arrows."

"Vi's busy," Kamren said. How the heck had she heard that? Yikes. Those women were like Skynet or something.

"She multi-tasks. She wants to know what you'd recommend since you think the display's bullshit." Jud's shoulders shook from laughter she didn't hear fully. "You've got to give her time to answer, Viviana."

"You call her Viviana," Kamren said. "To everyone else she's Vi."

"My woman deserves way more than a one syllable name," he replied with a grin. "Answer her question, or she's coming out here."

"I guess I expected something cooler or fancier. Like a doom-ahickey attached to the scope that'd feed into whatever fancy thing they've got. You know, like an automated arrow or something color-coded. Like green if I'm sighted right. Or whatever. Color might not work if you've got color-blind people, but ignore me. I'm not trained or anything. A doohickey that can track where the gun's pointed, measure wind speeds and distances, and zoom in the target closer and show what we're aiming at. To me, *that's* impressive."

"Did you get all that?" Jud asked, his lips thinned. "Right, will do."

He clicked off the com and offered a tight smile. "Thanks for the info. She loved your idea, Kamren."

Then why did he look like he'd sucked on a dozen lemons? She nodded as he walked away. He paused near Dallas, but they were angled away so she couldn't read what they said. She directed her attention to the target downrange. Okay, she pretended she saw the target downrange. Wowza, these folks were crazy talented to hit that far out.

Maybe the fancy headgear thing was a good idea after all. She squinted, dialing into her target, and shot. At least the dang thing wasn't moving. That'd be a serious pain in the ass. She fired another couple of shots, then surrendered to the rifle gods around her.

They were loads better.

She sat up and noted Jesse's amusement. Arms crossed, he stood beside Dallas.

"Sorry, I think I'm not ready for the deep end of the kiddie pool yet, boys."

"Really?" Jesse asked. "You hit a target twelve hundred meters out without the headgear. I'd say you swam with the sharks."

"I hit it?" Kamren turned back and squinted downrange. "No, I didn't."

Dallas squatted and offered a pair of binoculars. Heat crawled up her hand when she touched his. She peeked through the binoculars and focused. She'd hit the target, right in the center. It was more a shoulder wound than a kill shot, but not bad.

"Hell of a shooter, Kamren," Jesse complimented.

"Come on, Lucky," Dallas said. "The girls are ready to go over what they found. They're calling this exercise done without the free shooting. They tend to get a bit impatient when they're whiteboarding. Or so Dylan's assured me."

Kamren swallowed the response lodged in her throat. Vi had said it'd be hours, but they were ready way sooner.

Because there's nothing to find, idiot.

She put her hand into Dallas's woodenly and let him navigate her through the gathered group of men. Bolstered with a bit more confidence thanks to the fun shooting, she headed into the room with Dallas.

Scents assailed her. Her stomach rumbled again. A massive spread of lasagna, spaghetti, bread, and salad was along the back wall. The women all sat around the table, plates half consumed. Dallas guided her toward the food.

She'd typically turn down the offer, but she was starving. Either the bar Jesse had given her had worn off, or she was hungrier than normal. No, she hadn't eaten enough. Two bars, two strips of bacon and a couple of eggs in two days, closer to three. Oh, and the cereal earlier in the morning. Now that she'd eaten, her stomach was awake and demanding more food to compensate for the many days of very little.

She locked her hands to stave the trembling as she swallowed the saliva building in her mouth. Dallas took two plates and offered her one. The slight tremble in her fingers shook the paper tray, but he either didn't notice or didn't comment.

She followed his lead and bypassed the salad. He grabbed two pieces of meat and set them on her plate. She didn't argue. To hell with what anyone thought.

"One or two pieces of bread?" Dallas asked.

"Two, please." She swallowed and looked around as his brothers entered. "One, sorry."

He put two down. "Eat what you want, sweetheart. I should've made sure you got to the cafeteria again. I'm sorry."

Her eyes burned. She blinked rapidly as he heaved a massive pile of spaghetti and lasagna onto her plate. She hid the shameful quantity of food with her body as she edged toward the corner. As rude as it seemed, she sat and faced away from the group gathered at the table.

She ripped open the plastic cutlery and cut into the meat, not giving a damn what it was. The protein bar had staved some of her hunger, but this was nirvana. Hot food. She chewed. Swallowed. Cut. Repeat.

She sensed Dallas sit beside her but kept focused on the task at hand. Eating.

The primal urge dissipated three quarters of the way into her plate. Belly full, she swallowed the bite of lasagna in her mouth and dared a peek at Dallas. Eyes half-hooded, he regarded her without comment. He held out a bread stick.

She took it without comment.

"How long has it been?" he asked.

"I ate with Addy this morning. And Jesse gave me that bar."

"I wasn't talking about today," he replied. "Or yesterday. I know you didn't each much then. I'm thinking you hadn't had anything for a while before the explosion."

He reached over and pulled off the earmuffs. Though the ringing remained, it had subsided considerably. If she focused, she could hear his voice in the distance, as if he stood at the end of a tunnel. The warm smile he offered calmed the unease rising in her as he reached over with a napkin and wiped the side of her face.

Heat rose up her cheeks.

"Eating wasn't always easy in the field. I had a lot of assignments where I'd go days without anything except a bar here and there," Dallas commented. "We've all been there, sweetheart, but I've gotta admit it fucking pains me to see you shoveling food that fast and hiding in the corner like you're doing something wrong."

"I didn't want to get in the way." She glanced over at where her sister sat beside Riley. She fit in with everyone, laughing and smiling like she had no cares or worries.

"You don't have to justify yourself to me, Kamren. Whatever beef you've got with your sister isn't my business unless you choose to make it mine. Just know you're as safe here as she is. No hiding in corners, okay?"

"I'm not hiding," she argued.

The grin turned lazy. Her stomach did a weird flip-flop when he took the emptied plate away from her. She hadn't even realized she'd still been shoveling food in while he talked. He set her plate atop his and slowly shifted her around until she faced the room.

Okay, she'd totally been hiding. She shrank toward him as she noted how many people in the room watched her. Talk about awkward. Jesse sat on her other side. Nolan and Marshall were on his other side. Though she'd sat on the floor with her back to them, they would've seen her shoveling food quickly into her mouth.

Starved.

"Come on, sweetheart. We need to get where you can see everyone talking," Dallas said.

Kamren followed him until they were both situated at the end of the table near the door. A couple extra stools had been dragged in from somewhere. Her heart thudded wildly in her head like a drunken bongo drum as she waited.

Pictures and data filled every inch of the walls and the table display. What did it all mean? Colored lasers pointed from one display to another. Wow.

"What are we looking at?" Marshall asked.

"Honestly, we aren't sure yet. HERA has so much data to churn it'll take overnight to get final results, if not longer. We can tell you there's something very suspicious about the timeline when Kamren's father died." Mary motioned toward the table display. "Three days after the accident, which was two days before he was found, a large deposit was put into Sheriff Haskell's secret bank account."

"Secret, huh?" Nolan asked. "How much?"

"Five grand," Vi answered. "HERA's still tracing the sender, but so far the corporation is tied to the Austin crew Kamren's been following. Specifically, Henry Mills. He's a moneyman, a lobbyist of sorts for special interest groups and the like. He's the one who owns the lease you were investigating."

Henry Mills. The name didn't sound familiar. She studied his profile. Weird, she didn't remember following him. How had they connected him? Why hadn't she ever seen him around?

"I helped Dad out with the leases and never saw him."

"Is he clean?" Dylan asked.

"HERA's still digging. So far, it's suspicious enough to warrant an investigation," Vi answered. "In short, everything we're seeing so far green-lights Kamren's suspicions, but we've found zero in the way of actionable intel, other than the deposit."

"Which could've been for security work on the lease for all we know," Cord added with a grim expression. "Bears looking into, though."

"Despite some awesome reconnaissance..." Mary added, "we don't have enough actionable intel to have irrefutable answers."

"So what's next?" Nolan asked.

"We dig," Dylan answered.

"We have three threads HERA is flagging as the strongest so far. Henry Mills is the strongest. The second strongest are some foreclosures done by Aaron Patterson's bank," Vi said.

"Banks foreclose all the time," Riley said.

"Yeah, but these foreclosures were bought by our guy Henry Mills."

"Okay, and?" Addy asked.

"And it's weird. No one needs that much property," Rhea said. "One or two pieces of land, yeah. Five? No."

"Oil," Kamren said. Everyone looked at her. "Oil fracking."

"Shit, that makes sense," Cord said. He typed. A graph came up. "Here's the latest map of drill sites."

The map was settled atop the one for foreclosures. Nada.

"If suits are doing something shady, there won't be a paper trail. They aren't stupid, just greedy," Kamren commented. "If this is about oil, then the answer will be on the land itself, not in their offices and the places I've been looking. Damn it, I should've realized it was about the oil. Money and greed are always the answer around Marville."

"We need recon teams scoping out the land."

"We can drop more drones. Jacob's already installed quite a few around town. It'll be a good opportunity to test our long-range upgrades," Mary said. "Excellent feedback on the firing range, Kamren. Vi and I are going to make some adjustments this afternoon. We've already talked to Rhea and Bree."

"Drones will make people in Marville nervous," Rachelle said. "They're already nervous when a Mason truck enters the county. Y'all are worse than the law in their minds."

"Then we stay away," Marshall commented. "Jud, Gage, Fallon, and Addy can lead teams into the areas. I'm sure Kamren can offer some help getting onto the properties."

"We need to keep the heat on the Marville Dogs," Dallas said. "We're going to see Dom tomorrow, have a conversation to keep blowback contained."

"We still need more boots on the ground in Marville," Jesse said. "We won't get the data we need without more coverage. Marcus is in tight, but he needs backup."

"I'm in," Gage said. "I'll start tonight."

"Okay, now what?" Marshall asked.

"Rachelle's shifts at Sip and Spin aren't filled yet as far as I know. I could take them," Kamren said. "Just about everything going down in Marville starts there. I'll be at the farmhouse. Between there and the work shifts, I'll gather a lot of data."

"You'll be at the farmhouse," Dallas repeated. "When was that decided?"

She shrugged. "Animals need tending."

"I thought we agreed you'd be tending animals here and Jesse, Riley and I would handle your farmhouse."

"You, Jesse, and Riley at my place stirs trouble. Me at my place doesn't. This isn't up for discussion, Dallas. I'm going home," she stated firmly.

"Fine. Then I'm going with you. You're safer out here, but you at home sends a message that we aren't intimidated by the bullshit the Marville Dogs are throwing down, and I'm on board with sending that message as loudly as possible."

"What?" Breath swooshed from her lungs. She couldn't let him leave The Arsenal, not with everything going down. "You can't do this, Dallas. What about your kid? You're looking for your son. That has to be the priority."

"It is. We've got two teams searching grids now," Mary said. "We're rotating teams in and out. Fresh eyes."

"You aren't in this alone, Kamren. You leave this place, then I do, too." His jaw twitched as he made the declaration. "It's a short drive. When the teams find the target zone, there's time for me to get here so I can go wheels up."

When, not *if*. She admired the hell out of his determination and everyone's confidence. They weren't stopping until they found his son. The kid had an entire army behind him.

Kamren sat back, a bit startled. He was serious about moving into her piece of crap farmhouse. He was putting her so far up on his priorities she was impeding his mission to find his son.

"So you all believe her? Why? You said there was no proof." Rachelle shook her head. "You're wasting your time."

"We disagree," Vi returned. "It's not up for a discussion. It's a go.

We just need to know if the base of operations is here, where we're all safe and secure, or in Marville."

Base of operations.

"I know your pa likely raised you to keep your cards close, but he'd know when to accept help. With things intense, it's the only play," Nolan said. "Think on it if you want, but the decision's been made. We're not stopping until we figure out what happened to him."

Kamren's eyes burned. She cast her gaze downward as she blinked rapidly, willing the moisture away. No one had ever taken what she'd gathered seriously. Until now. She glanced about the room and noted the intense determination on everyone's faces, except Rachelle's. And Riley's. The latter seemed more confused than anything. Likely Kamren's sister had been stretching the truth.

She really needed to track Cliff down and get some answers about stuff. What'd been happening out here? Was Rachelle safe? Maybe Kamren should take her back to Marville. Dallas and his family would likely do anything for Rache, but they didn't know about her problems. No one could fix those.

Okay, no way in heck was that the right choice, but taking Dallas away from The Arsenal wasn't either. Not even for a short amount of time. "I don't know what makes the most sense. What would you do?" She asked the entire room but leveled a look at Addy.

The redhead's eyebrows rose a moment, but she crossed her arms and responded quickly. "The farmhouse. You and your boy playing house out there's likely to stir the vipers. They'll surface quicker if we're in their face constantly. We can't do that if we crawl back into our cushy compound."

"Make it uncomfortable," Jud said.

Make it uncomfortable. Kamren admitted the reasoning made sense to her, even if she hated the fact that Dallas wouldn't be here, monitoring the hunt for his son. "Okay, but the hunt for your son takes priority, no matter what. They can keep you in the loop, even if you aren't here?"

"Marville's fifteen miles down the road, sweetheart, not in Timbuktu."

Dallas made the statement gently, the tone teasing, but she blanched. It was a world apart from what he was accustomed to. Nothing in the house worked, and most of the rooms were uninhabitable. They'd be better off in a pitched tent outside.

"Fine, but if you all are helping me with my problem, I want to help with yours."

"Like you could do anything," Rachelle growled. "Come on, Riley. I've had enough of this stupid charade. I can't believe you all believe her. He's dead. Good riddance."

"Rachelle," Kamren called after her sister, but she'd already slammed out the door.

Riley looked at the glass door, then at everyone in the room. "I'll go talk to her."

Silence ticked by for a few moments, but Kamren sensed the tension crackling within the air. "Sorry, forget I said anything. I'm not a trained commando. I wouldn't be any use."

"I think you'd be a tremendous asset once we find our target zone," Jesse said. "Everywhere we've looked so far is remote, thick forest. The coordinates we were initially given were in Wyoming, but we've had to fan outward."

"Coordinates? Was the source credible?"

"Hardly," Dallas said. "We were told my kid was stashed there in the woods. The organization I was once with, The Collective, had a hidden base of operations there. But we've searched the area and fanned outward with no luck."

Kamren looked at the map as it appeared on the clear table surface before her. A large dot was in the middle of a swath of red. The red was broken into grids, but they weren't necessarily touching one another. A large tract of land was untouched by the search grids. "What's this?"

"National parks," Cord said.

"Why exclude them?" Kamren asked. Everyone looked at one another. "Dad used to go north; past few years I went, too. He hooked up with a new crew up there. They did extreme hikes for enthusiasts in the most rugged wilderness around. That area is the most remote land in the United States. It might be national parkland in theory, but that wouldn't stop people from using it. That'd help, actually. Pick a remote spot off the common trails, hunker down. If you're completely off grid, no one would ever find you. Forest rangers are spread too thin, and no one else would have access."

"It's brilliant and makes sense, but we scanned the area for encampments and heat signatures," Mary said. "We may not have hunted it physically, but planes equipped with radars searched the area."

Kamren nodded. "Survivalists wouldn't stay above ground. I'm not saying your Collective or whatever would be whacked out like some of those nut jobs, but they might've taken over someone's bunker. Maybe."

"Like *underground* bunker?" Bree asked. She darted a wide-eyed expression at Mary and Vi. "The plane we commissioned, the equipment wasn't ground penetrating, was it?"

"Nope, it sure as fuck wasn't," Cord answered.

"Son of a bitch," Zoey replied. "Does that mean the entire grid we did was bullshit?"

"No," Gage said. "We would've spotted trails, tracks, something if we'd been near a bunker, even underground."

"But she's right. We can't discount the fact that they could be in the zone north of the initial marker," Vi said. "Thank you, Kamren."

"I'm not trying to sound like one of those government conspiracy nut jobs, but there could've been underground bunkers in the park, right? We wouldn't know." She shrugged. "You said your computer was hooked up to all sorts of databases. Maybe it'd know, but Tanner and his crew would be my first go to."

"Tanner?" Marshall asked.

"Tanner Blevins. He owns Extreme Adventures, or whatever they call themselves. Hiking, hunting. The more remote or riskier, the better. They know the area better than almost anybody I know," she answered. "He'd help. Call him; tell him I told you to."

"You know him," Dallas said.

"Dad and I helped them set their business up," she said.

"So you know the area they're in, which is near this?"

"Near is subjective in land like that, but yeah. They're as nearby as anyone," she said. "Either way, if they're underground, there'd be a generator, supplies. Bunkers are typically well stocked, but supplies would get depleted if they're actually being used. Unless they're schlepping stuff in from far away, they'd buy local. Folks would remember them, especially if they aren't the typical prepper type," she said. "They won't give the info to just anyone though."

"We'll hack into whatever systems we can, ferret out anything usable and go from there," Zoey said.

Mary and Vi were typing on their keyboards. Cord's lips thinned. "I never thought about underground. Should have. Sorry, bro. That was my fuck up."

"We all overlooked it. We were told it was a remote cabin," Zoey said.

"We're getting to work on the new angles Kamren gave us. Until then there's nothing any of you all can do for that. Go away," Mary said. She put her pen in her mouth and kept typing, clearly dismissing the fact that everyone else was still in the room.

Jud rose with a chuckle, then leaned over, and kissed Vi's cheek. The woman didn't even notice. Talk about focused.

Kamren looked around the room as everyone rose. Now what?

She hadn't realized she voiced the question until Dallas put a hand on her waist and smiled down at her. "Now we wait. Thank you, sweetheart."

She hadn't really done anything but figured arguing that fact wouldn't get her far. It didn't matter. As long as Dallas's child was found, that's what mattered. Nolan and Jesse neared them.

"One problem with this plan, brother," Nolan said. "Hailey."

Dallas's jaw twitched. The only Hailey Kamren knew was Hailey Suthers, but she didn't have a connection to Dallas. Did she? She'd been with Dylan for a little while, but that'd died out a while back. Kamren hadn't ever been good at keeping up with the local gossip; that was more Rachelle's forte.

"I'll make it work," Dallas answered.

11

"I'll make it work," Dallas repeated into the silence.

Son of a bitch. Would he ever scrape Hailey and the bullshit she'd pulled off? When Dylan settled down with Mary, Dallas had hoped he and his brother had both made a clean break, but Dallas wading into the Marville situation would put him back on her radar.

Hailey Suthers had hooked up with Dylan while Dallas was away on a nasty mission. They'd been thick as thieves and he'd never known. When Dylan had left for a mission, Dallas had landed not long after. Lost in his own head, he'd somehow ended up drugged and in Hailey's bed. He'd woken up the next morning with zero memory of the night before and a pissed off family.

Fun. Times.

He sensed Kamren's gaze on him, but she kept silent.

Why the hell had he volunteered to play house with her?

Because he didn't like the thought of Nolan or Jesse volunteering. Competitiveness with his brothers had been a big issue growing up, mainly because the girls circled like he and his brothers were all roadkill. Him having the same preferences in women as his big brothers didn't help.

Though neither Nolan or Jesse had mentioned anything, he noticed their interest in the gorgeous female at his side. He didn't have the right to stake a claim, but for now he didn't want them closer. She was neck deep in trouble and until he'd waded her to safety, she was his to take care of.

Fuck. He stared at the empty plates in the overflowing trashcan. She'd attacked her food like she hadn't eaten in a week. His gut twisted, remembering those times all too well. How long had it been? She'd never answered, probably never would.

He'd have to stock up the truck with food from the cafeteria's supplies. There probably wasn't much out at her farmhouse. Did the kitchen even work? No matter, he'd set it to rights. He called up the list of things he'd noticed while out there. At least he'd have an excuse to fix a few things now.

"We'll use renovations on the farmhouse as an excuse to bring operatives in," he said.

"Renovations?" Kamren's voice was tight.

"We can't have me out there and not do some work," he commented. Hand on her back, he waited out the flash of emotions sweeping across her expressive face.

Confusion, anger, shame.

"We can't afford renovations," she commented.

"We've got more left-over supplies than we can use," Nolan said. "Using some of them up would help make way for what we actually need for the new plans out here."

Kamren glared across the table, her disbelief evident in her narrowed gaze.

"You and Cliff can help," Dallas said.

"Fine, but I'm doing stuff around here, too. I'm not a charity case," she returned.

He shaved off a few things from his mental supply list. Baby steps. Though he intended to get the farmhouse fully set to rights, he'd go slow. The condition of her house and the obvious financial woes were big triggers for her. The sooner they got their asses back to Marville, the better.

He avoided any further discussions with his brothers by barreling himself and Kamren out the side exit.

"We need to go see Dani first thing, make sure she's okay. She can handle her own against Javier, but I still want to check."

"Let's slow it down a moment and have a chat, sweetheart." He dragged her to a halt and cupped her face. "Keeping you safe while we figure out what happened to your dad is my concern. I'll take on the Marville Dogs when and if they become a problem, but I suspect they'll back down after my chat with Dom tomorrow."

"Dani wanted to go."

"She's not in on this trip; maybe next time." He noted the way she pressed her cheek deeper into his palm, as if starved for physical contact. Her eyes lit up. "You've been alone with this a long time, haven't you, sweetheart?"

"Yeah," she whispered.

"And before that? When he was alive?"

"I did what had to be done." The non-answer was answer enough. Dallas had lived years in The Collective; he could read between the lines. She'd likely hated every second of her life with her dad, but it was the only family she'd ever had or known.

"Losing a dad hurts like hell. I still wake up thinking about mine, wondering what advice he'd give on things."

"Like finding your son?" Her cheeks colored as her gaze skittered away quickly. "Sorry, forget I asked. It's not my business."

"It is. You're helping find him, so it's your business." He waited til her gaze returned to him. Something flickered there within the blue depths. "Yeah, I wish he was here to help with him. He'd know how to handle whatever we find. He'd know what to say and do. I wish to hell I'd had more time with him."

"He was an amazing man. I met him a couple time when I was young."

"Nolan and Jesse mentioned being out there hunting with him."

She laughed and looked away as her full eyelashes fluttered shut. "I got so pissed at them, you know. I wanted to go hunting with them so bad, but Dad wouldn't let me, said it was a man-only hunt. They didn't need any little girls ruining their day."

"Dad would've loved having you there. He used to take Riley out sometimes, even though she was too little to do anything but play with her dolls and make enough noise to scare everything away for miles. He never wanted her to feel left out." Dallas smiled at the memory. "It hit him hard when we all left for the service. I saw it. Being one of the last to go, I saw it and still left him here. Left everything he'd built for us."

"Dallas," she whispered, as if sensing the weight of the admission, the guilt he still clung to.

"I think we all still feel that regret, you know. It's why..."

"It's why you're running a huge-ass, whatever-it-is group on a ranch surrounded by cows?"

Dallas loved the hell out of her honest reply. Too many women chased the tags, wanting to bag a man who'd been a spec ops soldier, or whatever it was they sought. Kamren didn't know what they did, not enough to care. She'd clearly looked into them enough to have the basics, but she wasn't asking for more. What he'd done and his last name didn't matter.

But it should.

He wanted to assure her they could handle Marville, whatever they found with her dad's death. But after Marla, he couldn't make empty promises to anyone. Never again. Promises broken resulted in bad things, things that resulted in little boys being raised in hell without a dad. Or a mom.

Dallas forced away the memory of Marla bleeding out on the concrete floor of the warehouse where she'd hung him up like a piece of meat. There'd been no choice that day. Had he known about his son, would he and his brothers have made the same decisions? He couldn't afford to plow that road, not now. Possibly not ever.

THE CAMARO GROWLED as it ate up the last strip of road between her

and the Sip and Spin. Nervousness crawled through her like a restless rattler as Dallas parked toward the front, beside Dani's ride. Early
evening wasn't ever a busy time for the local bar, which left Kamren
more than a little relieved.

Then she spotted Javier's ride.

Fuck.

"This is the right play, Kamren," Dallas said as he wheeled into a
parking spot. Actually, he made a spot happen by the trashcans. "You
in everyone's face walking in there sends a message. If you aren't
ready to send it, we'll wait. Either way, your girl in there's covered.
Gage and a couple other Arsenal operatives are taking turns monitoring her. She's covered."

A relieved breath escaped her. She'd insisted they stop so she
could check on Dani. Leaving her with the Marville Dogs hadn't been
easy. Even though her best friend liked to pretend she was a hard-ass,
Kamren knew better. She'd seen the vulnerable girl lost behind the
mask. That was the person she'd come to check on, not the gangster
princess everyone else saw.

Dallas slid out of the vehicle like he owned the world. Confidence
exuded from him as he appeared at her side and draped a possessive
hand around her waist. Caliche gravel crunched beneath her combat
boots. The borrowed clothing was a bit tighter around her chest and
ass than she'd prefer, but she'd make do. The only important thing
was getting a pulse on Dani and the Marville Dogs.

She entered behind Dallas, who somehow covered her entry with
his broad body. Remembering they were supposedly a couple now,
she gave into the urge to coil her arm around his muscular chest. Her
splayed palm trekked downward until she halted at his waist. He
dragged her to his side and offered a playful grin. Heat spread
through her, an electrical awareness she couldn't explain.

"You're back," Dani commented from behind the bar. "And hooked
up. That didn't take long, but you always were a quick one, Dallas."

Kamren studied her best friend. Lips thinned, gaze assessing,
Dani looked okay, but the tension in her fisted hands and narrowed

eyes charged the room with unease. Things hadn't calmed, not nearly enough.

Dallas ignored Dani's jibe and headed straight for the Marville Dogs clustered at a table in the corner. Javier and Ralph both rose at his approach. Unease settled in Kamren's quickened pulse, but she hung back. He knew what he was doing, or so she hoped.

"Dallas," Javier said. "Didn't expect you around so soon. You'd best stay away."

"Funny, was about to say the same thing," Dallas commented.

Javier took a step forward, into Dallas's personal space. "I'm thinking you need a lesson in respect."

"Warning, lessons I give end with body bags."

The two men stared one another down. Javier broke contact first. Laughter. "Crazy *pendejo*. Never knew when to back off. For Dom, I'll leave your ass alone."

Javier's statement was met with silence.

Silence.

Lethal, unapologetic quiet.

"See you still got the look Dom taught you down," Javier said. "Go back to the ranch; suckle up to your big brothers. Marville ain't your town, *ese*."

"It's my town because it's my girl's town. Marville's on my radar now." Dallas dragged her against him.

She roped an arm around him and leaned forward until her nose pressed against his chest. Each breath dragged his scent in deeper, soapy musk and sandalwood. His fingers crawled beneath her top as though they belonged there. Fiery heat spread through her as he rubbed and stroked her side.

"Neither of us want fallout," Dallas said. "You let what went down at your clubhouse go, I make sure the recording from the compound gets wiped."

"Recording?" Javier's mouthpiece stepped forward. "What recording?"

"Insurance," Dallas said as he pulled out a phone. "Your call.

There's one copy, and I'm the one who controls if it gets to Dom. I've got zero skin in this, man."

"This is my town," Javier declared.

"You and your crew stand down and keep out of our way, we're good. My girl needs closure on what went down with her dad. The sooner we figure it out, the better it'll be for everybody. Until then, we'll be handling things at her place."

"Shitty-ass place," Javier commented. "Your girl's been up in everyone's business and not tending her own. As for her old man, Marville Dogs ain't got no part in that shit."

"Doesn't mean you don't know what went down," Dallas countered.

"Not my concern, man. Not yours either. You don't want a part in that bullshit."

Frustrated with the fact that Javier apparently knew something and wasn't sharing, Kamren turned and headed back to the bar. Dani slammed a soda in front of her. "Thought you were smarter than to hook up with a Mason, especially that one."

"Not sure what trouble you have with them, but they're good people, a fuck-load better than the Marville Dogs." Kamren sipped on the soda and looked at her friend. "You okay?"

"Javier and I cleared the air; we're good." Dani pursed her lips and looked over at the table where Dallas stood circled by Javier and his group. The fact he was surrounded didn't seem to bother the man.

Kamren's gaze roamed the building. One of the Arsenal folks was here, but she couldn't figure out who. If things went south, Dallas wouldn't be alone. Kamren wasn't the best fighter, but she could handle her own long enough to keep someone off Dallas.

"Whatever your play is, watch your back. This'll get to Hailey, and you don't need that bitch's brand of trouble on your ass."

"What's with him and Hailey? I thought she had hooked up with Dylan." She scrunched her nose. "He's way better off with Mary."

"Girl, that cow played them off one another. Her man Dylan went wheels up to parts unknown for his country and she was in Dallas's bed within two days." Dani slammed a bottle down on the table. "Don't trust him."

Shock kept her mute as she stared at Dallas from across the room. He'd slept with Hailey when she was hooked up with Dylan?

Her skin crawled. She hadn't thought of Dallas as a player, but she didn't really know him, did she? And honestly, she didn't give a damn who he took to his bed. Clearly Dylan didn't have a problem with Dallas screwing Hailey. Either that or they'd worked it out. Not her business.

So why did her gut churn at the thought of Hailey touching him? Of him holding Hailey against his side like he'd just held her.

"He's a player," Dani said. "Align with them to keep your ass covered. That's a smart play. Hooking up with him? Not smart."

"I'm not hooking up with him," she said.

"Right. That man is stripping you with his eyes every few seconds, and I've never seen you let someone touch you the way he does. He dragged you against him and you didn't even argue." Dani shook her head as she scooped ice into a couple glasses. "Keep your shit focused and get the answers you need so you can move the fuck on. The Marville Dogs are nervous, so you're clear from them. For now."

Kamren nodded. Dani was right. She needed to keep focused. Intimate relationships were a waste of time. She'd tried before, but she wasn't good girlfriend material. The only man who'd ever come close was Tanner, but he hadn't understood her need to remain in Marville. Then her dad had died, and things spiraled downhill from there.

It was a really small world. Realizing the search grid was within the same area where Tanner's operation was had startled her quite a bit. She supposed it made sense in a way. She'd always been drawn to the more rugged lands, woods, forests. Deserts. She'd briefly dated him back when she'd thought a normal life might be a possibility. For a few months it had been. She'd been up there, exploring and living life.

Then dad had called her home, said he needed help.

Then he got murdered.

"You ready?" Dallas slid a possessive hand on her hip. She tensed beneath the touch but nodded.

The sooner this was over, the better.

～

"WHAT'D SHE SAY?" Dallas asked as he pulled the Camaro onto the highway and made the turn toward Kamren's farm.

Kamren kept her gaze locked on the landscape outside. Tension crackled between them, an uneasy one he hadn't expected. She recoiled from his touch when he reached across the cab.

"I know she said something to you, Kamren. Whatever it is, there's more to the story." Dallas forced the words out despite the shame burning in him. "There's more."

"You fucked Hailey while she was still with Dylan." She crossed her arms. "I'm not sure what could be said to justify that."

He'd said the same thing to himself a thousand times. He bit back the argument lodged in his throat. "You're right. It shouldn't have happened. I pray it hadn't every night."

"He's with Mary and happy now, and you two are still close. So that's good." She bit her lip. "It's not like this thing we're doing is real anyway, Dallas. It's not my business."

"No, I guess it's not." He slammed his hand against the steering wheel.

The drive to the farmhouse was quiet, tense. He let her go up the rickety steps first, making note of which ones he'd fix in the morning once the lumber he'd ordered from Nomad arrived. She threw her weight against the door to get it open.

He'd order a door tomorrow.

Hannigan's Hardware and Lumberyard was going to get rich at this rate.

The living room was about what he'd expected. Pictures of Rachelle, Cliff, and their mom and dad were strewn about the living room. One or two of Kamren were peppered among them. A threadbare knitted throw sat atop the back of a worn-out sofa.

A lone light bulb hung from a frayed wire. Kamren flicked on a lamp beside the sofa and motioned toward the kitchen.

"Help yourself to whatever is in the fridge, but it's probably not much. I'll shop tomorrow if there's time," she said. "Bathroom's down the hall and to the left. Cliff's bedroom is a nuclear fallout zone, so I'd steer clear. Take Rachelle's bed. If we have extra sheets, they'll be in the bathroom closet."

She headed toward the room to the right. Dallas intercepted her path.

"I'm tired and not in the mood to talk. Whatever it is can wait." She studied his eyes a moment and chewed her lower lip. "Goodnight, Dallas."

"I'm heading out to Huntsville early in the morning. I'll have them pick me up here so you have the Camaro to drive if you want. Try and stay here or at The Arsenal. You'll be covered either way."

"I don't need a sitter, Dallas."

"No, but you're getting one anyway."

"I'm not your problem," she said.

Arms crossed, she was poised for a fight he was damn tempted to give her. He closed the distance between them and cornered her. He licked his lips as her gaze landed there. "For the record, sweetheart, I'd be okay with making this thing real."

She swallowed. Her tongue flicked across her lower lip as she shifted against the wall. He bracketed his hands beside her head. Hopefully the action would keep him from dragging her against him, maybe hauling her into the bed in the next room. "I'm not your kind of woman."

"I'm thinking you have no idea what kind of woman would be my kind."

"Hailey," she said.

"No fucking clue," he spat angrily.

"Mary," she whispered.

Shock stilled his gentle lean into her. "What?"

"At the rescue, I saw what you said to Jesse, before I fell asleep. I saw what you said."

"You saw what I said," he said. Shock forced him to repeat the words as his mind recalled what all they'd discussed. "Mary's a hell of a woman, so yeah. If she weren't hooked up with Dylan, she'd definitely be my type of woman. Smart, beautiful, and stronger than hell."

"Right." She shoved against him. "Maybe you should look for your own woman instead of trying to steal your brother's all the time. I'm surprised he hasn't kicked your ass."

Something in him shut down. For a moment he'd considered sharing the truth about Hailey with her, but no way that'd happen. "If you think I'm the kind of man to go after my brother's woman, you don't deserve to hear the truth. Wallow in your rumor mill bullshit."

He shoved off the wall and turned away. "I'll be gone in the morning for Huntsville. I'll see if Addy can come out with you if you want to stay out here. We'll be back at The Arsenal tomorrow night."

"What do you mean about rumor mill bullshit?"

"I'm done with this conversation, Kamren. You went in there to check on your girl and she fed you gossip. You swallowed it down and puked it all over me without even it might not be true."

"You admitted it!"

Dallas's jaw twitched. He had. He couldn't deny the fact that he'd fucked Hailey, even if he had no memory of it and certainly never wanted to. If he were a woman it'd be date rape, but he wasn't about to spill all that to her if she was so quick to listen to gossip. He hadn't even fully accepted what had happened with Hailey. This was definitely not a conversation he wanted tonight, or anytime soon.

"Whatever." Kamren went into the other room and slammed the door shut. The entire wall shook from the force.

Dallas made a note of the supplies needed to fix the door and replace the caved-in drywall he hadn't noticed earlier. Someone had punched holes in the wall nearer the door. What the hell had gone down at this house?

12

"Ouch!"

Kamren startled awake at the shouted word and grabbed her handgun. A flashlight rolled toward the bed. Two bodies loomed in the window. Pale moonlight splayed into the room and accented a blonde head of hair. The head bobbed when she picked up the flashlight and aimed it. Gun up, she waited as Bree's eyes widened.

"Uh-oh." Bree reached up and clicked a Bluetooth-looking thing in her ear. "Erm, I might need to work on my breaking and entering. I kind of broke, but she woke up before I entered. Sorry."

"Move your ass out of my way. I'm straddling the window, and it's not fun." Another blonde tumbled into the room.

Kamren clicked the safety back on her gun and threw a T-shirt on over her spaghetti-strapped nightshirt. She looked over at the door, a bit surprised Dallas hadn't already rushed in.

Her gut clenched.

Riley stood. "Girl, we have got to talk."

"You broke into my house."

"Yeah, because, I repeat, we have got to talk."

"You can't just break into my house. I almost shot you." She held up the gun.

"Oh, well, I guess we didn't predict that one," Bree said. "Though honestly, I should have. Woops."

Kamren stood up and headed to the door. She peeked outside. Dallas was sprawled on the floor, gun drawn. Rhea waved from the sofa. "Sorry, he sort of fell before I could position him. He's totally fine though."

"Start talking," Kamren clipped. She moved to Dallas's side and felt for a pulse. Strong and steady. Good. She rolled him over and settled a pillow under his head.

"See, I told you this was a good idea. If she was really mad at him, she wouldn't roll him over and make him comfortable," Bree said.

"Okay, here's the thing. My brother there has some issues, issues I can't tell you about because it's not my business to spread." Riley heaved a sigh. "But these two lame-brains convinced me we had to stage an intervention because your girl shot her mouth off tonight. They heard about it from Mary and Vi, neither of which are aware we commandeered a drone and snuck out like teenagers. So, consider yourself intervened or whatever."

Kamren rubbed the sleep from her eyes and glared at the confusing women. "Wait. Mary and Vi? How would they know what Dani said to me?"

"We have drones in the Sip and Spin," Rhea answered.

"Why do you give a damn? You don't even like me." She directed the statement at Riley.

"My brothers do. And I'm starting to see there are some disconnects between what I've been told and the truth. I mean, you're hunting down your dad's killer." The blonde's gaze watered. "That's not a crazy, irresponsible woman who doesn't give a damn about family."

Fuck. She was starting to see through Rachelle's webs. The last thing she wanted was to unspin her sister's good life. "Go home, Riley. Take these two with you. We don't have anything to talk about. It doesn't matter."

"It does," Bree argued.

"I told you this wasn't a good idea. We've told her Dallas has issues he needs to share and not to believe what she hears. That's good enough." Riley turned and headed toward the door.

"Seriously?" Rhea asked. "You didn't say anything!"

"Fine. I'm still on the fence about whether you're a good person or not, but either way, you're loads better than Hailey Suthers." Riley crossed her arms and sighed again. She tapped her booted foot and flicked her gaze to the floor. "What went down with Hailey wasn't his fault, okay? The bitch played him hard, the kind of hard a man can't remember and doesn't ever talk about with anyone."

Kamren sat and let the statement rattle around in her mind. What did that even mean?

"Oh for cripes sake this is ridiculous. Look," Bree sat on the floor. "Hailey drugged him. He woke up in her bed with no memory of getting there, okay? Our girl Mary gave her a verbal beatdown in front of the entire town. It's not like Kamren couldn't hear it from *anyone* at this point."

"Hailey drugged him?" Shock recoiled the words. They boomeranged in her brain a couple more times.

Headlights bounced through the living room as a vehicle lurched to a stop outside. Kamren motioned the three women back as she unlocked the safety on her gun and threw the door open. Gage Sanderson eyed the gun and raised his eyebrows.

"Told you she'd be packing," Addy commented. The redhead shoved her way inside. "Okay, outside. In the truck, all three of you."

"But, Addy," Bree whined.

"Outside." Her voice rose. "Now."

"You aren't the boss of me," Riley shot back.

"You're right. The bosses of you are my six bosses, and you're damn lucky none of them figured out where you three idiots went. There'll be hell to pay soon enough when Dallas wakes up. Do you really want to be here when that happens?" Addy crossed her arms. "And your boss is a bit scarier than my bosses. Wouldn't you say?"

Kamren looked at Bree, confused. Riley had a boss?

"Jud. He's her mentor to be a private investigator," Bree whispered, not so quietly.

Yikes. Kamren wouldn't cross any of the men out at The Arsenal, but Jud was definitely at the top of the list. Riley looked down at her passed-out brother and bolted for the door.

Gage chuckled and motioned toward Dallas. "You want help with him?"

"Nah, he'll wake up soon, right?"

"Yeah."

"Okay, then. I think he deserves to stay down there."

Gage glanced back at the truck where Addy had shoved the three burglar wanna-bes in. "They shouldn't have come, but they were worried you'd believe whatever you heard about Hailey."

"So what they said was true? She drugged him?"

Gage's jaw twitched. His eyes flashed fury. Though he remained steadfastly silent, she got the message loud and clear. She shut and locked the door and sat on the sofa.

Curled up under the throw her mom had made, she waited. She owed him an apology. She'd believed rumors and shut him down when he'd tried to give her the truth, even if it hadn't been her business. She'd done to him what he'd done to her back when he'd assumed she was into drugs. She squeezed her eyes shut as guilt gnawed her insides. She'd just rest her eyes a bit. When he woke, she'd apologize.

SHE'D WOKEN up alone in the house. A scrawled note was set beneath a set of keys.

At The Arsenal. Vehicle's yours to use - D

Huh. So much for the big conversation she'd hoped to have in the morning. Had he already headed to Huntsville? She showered, dressed and got to work. By the time she had the animals fed and handled, she'd come up with a tentative plan for the day. If Aaron Patterson was foreclosing on properties and Henry Mills was grabbing them up and conveniently getting rich soon after, it stood to reason there'd be drilling involved. All she needed was a list of properties.

She could probably get it from Vi or Mary, but she remembered the map Cord had pulled up easily enough. Location one was the old Gonzales farm. Nestled on the farthest area of the Marville loop, it was a decent-sized spread without much in the way of hunting leases, which meant she'd never had much reason to be out there.

Neither had Dad.

Location two had been one of her dad's past jobs, one he'd lost when old man Canales died and his son took over. Patterson had foreclosed less than a year later, mainly because Paul Canales was a moron completely incapable of managing anything, especially the family ranch. She headed that direction.

Marville ranchland was comprised mostly of mesquite and hackberry trees and black brush interspersed with copious amounts of cactus, rattlers, lizards, and coyotes. And cattle and deer. Lots and lots of deer, which was the only reason most ranches hadn't gone belly-up decades ago.

She parked the truck along the high fence line of the Canales's land and headed toward the old entry gate her dad used to use. Vines and brush grew around the unused entrance, but Kamren swung herself up and climbed over easily enough. Backpack and rifle in tow, she headed toward the old water tank Dad used to take them to. The family picnic.

Back then things had been simpler. Dad'd had plentiful work and Mom...well, she had been better. Calmer.

Kamren stifled the unwanted memory and studied the ground for recent activity, anything to show someone had been around since the bank foreclosed. The ranch house was a mile and half up the road. She headed that way since she had to start somewhere.

Shadows shifted on the ground to her left. She whirled. Aimed.

Dallas stood there with his hands up. "Going somewhere?"

"What are you doing here? You were at The Arsenal."

"Left that note a couple hours ago, sweetheart. I went for supplies, food. Breakfast. I got wrangled into helping with a few things." He walked up and grabbed her gun with lightning fast precision. He slung the rifle over his shoulder with the strap. "I went back to your place to feed you breakfast before I headed out to Huntsville and found you gone."

Wowza. That had been a seriously hot move. Her body had vibrated with a heated awareness as he approached. She stood her ground, all too aware of the way his tongue flicked out and traced his lower lip. She repeated the motion, thinking he probably tasted pretty good.

"The girls wanted to force a conversation I'm not ready for. I need you to respect that choice."

The girls. He'd figured out what'd happened last night. Guilt gnawed at her insides.

"It's not my business," she replied. "But I am sorry I didn't hear you out. I shouldn't have believed what I heard. That's no better than what you did with me at first."

"You're right, and you're wrong." He grasped her face with a hand. "We both know it'll be your business if we explore this attraction, sweetheart."

Wow. Okay, so he felt it, too. Now what? She looked around lamely. She'd never been good at holding a guy's interest for too long. Men had problems hooking up with a woman who shot and tracked better than them. She'd choose field dressing a deer over donning a dress for a fancy night out on the town.

Dallas forced her gaze up to his. "You're a hell of a woman, Kamren. I want to explore this attraction, but it's gonna have to be slow. We've got a lot on the burners right now. I'm looking for my kid. The Arsenal's still neck-deep in problems from Mary and Vi's mess. With your thing added, we've got to focus."

"Mary and Vi's mess?"

"Not my story, sweetheart. If the girls want you to know, they'll share. Though, there's a higher likelihood my sister will fill you in before anyone else gets a chance." Dallas flashed a smile and leaned forward. "We'll discuss this later, sweetheart, after I get back from Huntsville."

"You're still going." She didn't want him wading into Marville Dog crap, even if he'd once had a friendship with Dom. He was a good man that didn't deserve to be dirtied with Marville troubles.

"You're too good for me," she blurted. "I'm not a Mary, or a Vi or any of them. We can't explore this thing between us."

A growl rumbled from him as he closed the distance between them. Shock emitted a gasp from her when she slammed against his hard body. A firm hand grasped her head, and the other held her at the waist as his mouth swept against hers. The kiss was rugged, demanding, and everything she'd imagined.

Confident, firm swipes against her mouth destroyed any semblance of control she had. She softened within his embrace and surrendered to the onslaught of awareness arcing through her. God, it'd been too long since someone kissed her like this. Boldly. Hungrily.

The kiss wasn't a hesitant, exploratory probe. It was a determined invasion, a storming of her senses that left her with little doubt he'd be an awesome lover—the kind who was attentive and focused on her pleasure instead of his. She clasped his head and deepened the kiss as she followed his lead, tasting the depths of his mouth as he had hers. Fuck, the man could kiss.

It was a carnal fusion of tongues and lips. A mouth fucking that promised the real deal would be a life-altering experience, one no sane woman would pass up. Hot skin greeted her exploratory hands as they wandered beneath Dallas's shirt. She sought the heat of skin-to-skin contact.

More.

The thought ruptured her arousal even as it flared through her like a wanton fire seeking kindling. Labored breaths escaped her as he severed contact. His tongue licked his lips as if seeking one final taste of her. His dilated gaze remained locked on her.

"Tonight." He growled the word as he ran a hand through his hair and looked around. "Jesus, you're a good kisser, sweetheart. All in."

She didn't try to understand his words. It didn't matter. She wasn't the good kisser; she'd simply been following his lead.

"I know this goes against the grain for you, but I need you out at The Arsenal where I know you'll be safe. The girls have all sorts of things they want your help with. Bree alone could suck days from you if given half the chance."

"I can't help them with brainiac stuff," she argued.

"Babe, the tower was your idea. Bree wants to build one." Oh, well, that she could totally do. She nodded. "I have some supplies at my place I could take over. We could build a template, then she could redesign with fancier materials. Steel's all I have."

"Thinking we don't need anything fancier than that. We need rugged and durable. Fancy doesn't hold up under fire," he whispered. The sultry low tone made her body pulsate in awareness as her mind wandered to the subtext of his words. The molten gaze sweeping across her signaled he wasn't talking about a drone tower any longer.

"I'll pack my welding gear up, but it won't fit in the Camaro," she said as she eyed the car she'd procured from him. She was only a few miles from her place.

Dallas reached into his pocket. "We'll switch. Nolan and Jesse are at your place. We'll leave the car there, help you pack your gear, and then head out to Huntsville. You head to The Arsenal. Someone will help you unload out there. Before we do any of that, we're feeding you. Jesse's cooking bacon and eggs, and Nolan's doing French toast."

Kamren nodded. Shyness crept through her as the heat from their intimate moment dissipated. "I've never had French toast."

"Now I'm wishing I'd called dibs on fixing breakfast." His eyes drifted half closed as he cupped her face. "I'm thinking there are a lot of things you haven't experienced, and I'm gonna enjoy giving them to you."

KAMREN WAS MORE than a bit annoyed that she hadn't been allowed to unpack anything she'd brought from the truck. Gage and some guy named Fallon Graves had met her when she pulled up. They'd whistled at a group of men who looked like they were ready to go ten rounds with something big and bad. The two men had gotten into the truck and headed to Dallas's with her stuff where the men they'd whistled at were heading.

That was weird enough.

She'd blinked, watching it disappear around the side of the compound buildings for about two seconds, then the women descended on her like a pack of rabid dogs who hadn't been fed in a year. Okay, maybe not that bad, but it'd been close.

She'd started off by looking over plans Bree had drawn up for the drone house. They'd spent a good hour looking things over, then they'd spent another hour putting a rudimentary one together from the materials Kamren had brought, which a couple of the men had brought to them. The woman had asked more questions than Kamren expected. They all had.

Rhea, Vi, Mary and Addy had sat and watched from the sidelines as Kamren taught Bree how to weld. Then Rhea had wanted to learn. Seriously, they were a bit nuts, but Kamren had to admit it felt nice having people interested in what she could do. By the time she'd done her part in the construction, hunger steered them all to the mess hall.

More people than she expected were inside the large, open room. She'd been there once before with Addy, but it'd been mostly deserted. The redhead guided them to a table along the far wall, well away from the crush of mostly men and a few women. Kamren had no idea how many people were out at The Arsenal.

"We have more people here than normal because we're in the middle of vetting potential operatives," Mary said. "It's a pain in the ass."

"Yeah, but the guys need the help," Vi said.

"Come on, let's grab some food. Then you can yap her ears off," Addy said, her tone gruff even though she offered a humorous grin.

Kamren followed the redhead into the food area and followed her lead, grabbing a tray, silverware, and a napkin. Pizza, burgers, salad fixings. The aroma from across the way drew her attention, though.

Jesse was frying up taco meat. The infusion of spices made her stomach growl. How long had it been since she'd eaten tacos?

"You should let me do that. A man as important as you shouldn't have to cook his own meal," Rachelle said as she put a hand on Jesse's shoulder.

The man glanced up at Kamren's approach and offered a tight smile as he side-stepped the hand wandering across his shoulder. His obvious unease with the physical contact grated Kamren's nerves. No one should be touched without permission. The fact that Rachelle didn't care pissed her off.

"Leave him be, Rache. Clearly he's capable of frying meat without help."

"This doesn't concern you." Rachelle glared. "Jesse's had a lot on his plate, all the men out here have. I'm trying to be nice and help, not that you'd know anything about that."

Kamren set her tray down and took position at the counter beside the oven on Jesse's other side. Dallas's brother could damn well tell her sister to keep her hands to himself, so why wasn't he? His obvious unease pissed her off. The fact that he didn't say no concerned her even more. His lips thinned even more as Rachelle started whispering something.

"Leave him alone." The voice sliced through Kamren's thoughts. Her gaze flitted to Ellie Travis. She'd heard Riley mention something about her working out here now, but she hadn't exactly believed it. Interesting.

She was the sort of woman Kamren thought a Mason man needed in his life. Fierce. Brilliant. Beautiful. Loyal.

"This doesn't concern you," Rachelle replied. "Go away."

"Back off," Jesse growled as he yanked her sister's hand off his arm. "Do any of you want tacos? There's plenty."

Kamren read the subtle translation beneath the inquiry. He wanted them to hang around. It was as close to a request for help as she'd get. She nodded and grabbed a knife. "I'll cut up the tomatoes and lettuce."

"I'll get the onion," Ellie whispered, then stopped. "Wait. Does everyone want onion?"

"No," Rachelle said. "What are you even doing here? Aren't you supposed to be answering phones or something?"

"Enough," Jesse said. He removed the skillet from the burner and focused his glare on Rachelle. "I've tried polite, I've tried curt, so I'm going to go with blunt since you aren't listening to the message my brothers and I are delivering."

Oh dear. This wasn't going to end well. Kamren's gaze flitted back to the women, who'd all approached. Eyes wide, they remained silent as Riley joined their group.

"Stop touching us. Stop rubbing against us and whispering your innuendos in our ears when our sister isn't around. Stop wandering around here in your bikinis while she's at your farm doing your work. Stop bugging our operatives and flirting with the Warrior's Path participants."

"Jesse, I think you misunderstood." Rachelle took a step back and fluttered her eyes, a move Kamren had seen a thousand times.

"No, he didn't." Kamren hacked into an innocent tomato. "You were as subtle as a bull in a hen house."

"Like you'd know anything about attracting a man," Rachelle shot back. "Here's a hint. They don't want a woman whose only skill is gutting a deer."

"It's dressing," Ellie replied. "You dress a deer."

"Fuck off, cow. You don't have any idea how to please a man either. You had a good one, and he scraped you off like the trash you are. Then you lost your house and your job." She lowered her voice. "Neither of you know what I know about Jesse. It's not like I could go there with him. He's not ..."

Kamren slammed the knife into the cutting board and snagged her sister by the hair. Juvenile, but an effective move. Rachelle shot daggers with her eyes as she shifted into pissed off mode.

"Leave him be," Kamren ordered.

"Or what? You'll beat me? That's always your answer, isn't it?"

"Don't go there, Rache." Kamren released her grip. "You're out of line. Again. You have to respect people's personal boundaries. Not everything is about you."

"I wasn't doing anything," she whined.

"You were. He didn't want you touching him."

"He didn't say anything, and it doesn't matter. It's *Jesse*. Everyone knows..."

"He said plenty. He moved away. That should've clued you in." Kamren lowered her voice. "And don't ever talk about Jesse like that. Are you taking your medicine?"

"This isn't about me," she argued. It was. It was always about Rachelle. Kamren's entire life had been about her little sister and keeping her safe from herself and others.

"Honey, let's go talk."

"No. You're all nuts." Rachelle charged out of the room in a huff of tears and growls.

"Erm, what the fuck was that?" Riley demanded.

"Leave it be, sis."

"No." Riley powered forward into Jesse's personal space and looked up at her brother. Then she paled when she saw the haunted expression in the man's gaze and took a step back. "She was touching you."

"She's gone. It's over. Let's eat." A world of demands and needs resided within those words. He didn't want to chat with his little sister about what'd happened, what'd likely happened repeatedly based on what he'd said. And not just to him. Kamren's gaze swept the room.

She'd hoped Rachelle wouldn't stir up trouble out here. Clearly that hadn't been the case. "I'm sorry, Jesse."

"Don't take blame for something that's not on you," he said.

"She was *touching* you," Riley repeated, this time a little louder.

"Not the first time, sure as fuck won't be the last," Jesse said.

"Yeah, it will." The blonde took a step closer. "How long?"

The man's jaw twitched. It was a familial trait or something cause all the Mason brothers did that when they were mentally chewing on a piece of something they didn't like. Or didn't want to share.

"That long," she whispered. "All of you?"

Jesse looked away.

Riley paled and visibly recoiled. "That long."

"She's a good girl, sweetheart. She just has some boundary issues," Cord said as he entered the fray. He settled his hands on his sister's shoulders and drew her into his arms. "Our issues with Rachelle don't concern you. It's why we've never said anything."

"She's my best friend," Riley said, her voice booming with anger. "If she messes with my brothers and doesn't respect their right to say no, that damn well *does* concern me. You should have said something."

Shit. Kamren mentally reeled from the potential fallout from this moment. She wasn't sure what to do. Her entire presence within this situation wasn't good. So much of it was her fault. She hadn't been around enough to keep Rachelle in line and medicated.

"I'm sorry," she repeated. "This is my fault."

"What?" Riley whirled on her.

Kamren braced. The woman needed an outlet for the anger bleeding from her watery eyes. She needed someone to rail at who could take the brunt of her rage. "She's had problems. I'm her big sister, and I screwed up by not being around to make sure she was okay. I abandoned her, and she needed me."

Riley's intake of breath moved her entire upper body. Hands fisted at her sides, she looked away. "She's had problems?"

"Yeah."

"What sort of problems?"

"The sort that aren't my business to share," Kamren said. "You'll have to ask my sister, but I doubt she'll share. You're her best friend, Riley. Don't ever doubt that. No matter what she might try and do with your brothers or anyone around you, you are the most important person in her life."

"But her 'problems' require medication," Riley surmised. The woman's gaze locked onto Kamren. "I've been her best friend since grade school, but she's never said anything."

"It's not something she'd talk about with anyone." Kamren took a couple steps closer to the blonde. Cord backed up but remained close. "You were her sanctuary, Riley. You still are. When she's with you, she's happy, things are good."

"Clearly not without side effects for everyone around me," Riley said.

"For what it's worth, it's only gotten noticeably bad since Dylan hooked up with Mary," Cord noted.

"She messes with any of you again, you let me know," Riley ordered. "I'm thinking I'd better get to work finding a new cook for out here. I should've seen the trouble. Jud's right. I put blinders on with those I love and trust. It's a problem."

"Loving someone's never a problem," Ellie said. Red rose in her cheeks when everyone's attention settled on her. "Sorry, not my business. Carry on."

"She's right," Cord said. "Don't stop being you because of one bump in the road, Sis."

"What should I do about Rachelle?" Riley looked up at Jesse. "She's my best friend."

"Yeah, and she's likely needing you right now. Go track her down; talk it out. Don't scrape her off because of us, Riles."

"But she—"

"Don't scrape her off because of us," Jesse repeated. "She might need a visit with Doc Sinclair. We talked about it back when Mary's shit started."

"Yeah, we did," Riley said. "I thought..." She sighed loudly. "I don't know what I thought back then. I just knew something wasn't right."

And it hadn't been. She'd been lost because her routine had shifted. Kamren had upended her sister's life by shifting her own focus from providing a normal, stable environment for her sister to finding their dad's killer.

"All the things she's said about you."

Kamren returned to the chopping board and got to work on tomatoes. As if understanding the importance of moving on with what'd been a good lunch plan, Jesse and Ellie started prepping everything else.

"Answer me, Kamren."

"Didn't hear a question," she lied.

"It was bullshit," Riley said.

"No, more like partial truths."

"Right." The blonde looked around a moment, then focused on Kamren again. "I was looking for you. You're with Jud and I tomorrow hunting down answers in Marville."

Okay, wow. Unsure what to say, she nodded and then looked around at everyone. "Anyone else want tacos?"

"You invite this whole place to tacos, you're helping with more than tomatoes." Jesse looked over at Cord. "Ma's been itching to get her hands back on this mess hall. Til we get Rachelle settled, let's see if she wants to come back here."

"On it," the man replied as he turned and left.

"Thank you," Ellie whispered. Kamren stilled. "Thank you for stopping what she was saying. He's a good man. He doesn't need to be cut low by her or anyone. He has enough wounds to carry around without whatever she was gonna say seared into his brain."

"Thank you for helping," Kamren said. "And I'm sorry for what she said to you. You're a beautiful, brilliant woman. Whatever went down with you and your ex, it's your business. But from what I heard, you're good people. No way it was your fault."

The woman looked down at the onions she was cutting and didn't respond. Conversation over. Kamren suspected Ellie had a load of secrets she hadn't shared with anyone. Fortunately, she'd landed at The Arsenal, which meant they'd wade into whatever troubles she had if necessary. It's what they did, and for once, Kamren was okay with the fact they'd waded into hers.

KAMREN FOUND her quarry in the entertainment room playing a video game. She sat, waiting until the screen flashed red. Cliff threw the control onto the coffee table in front of him and glared.

Seeing her brother hurt in many ways. He looked just like Dad, from the light brown, greasy hair to the cinnamon-colored eyes. He even wore the same constantly pissed glower their father had used. He had the same stocky, tall build that would have made him an excellent football player if he'd bothered learning the sport.

Although Cliff looked just like their father, he'd inherited a lot of their mother as well. His laziness was her to the core. So was the anger. Nothing was ever his fault.

"What the hell do you want?"

"Nice to see you, too, brother. How have you been?"

"Pft, like you give a shit." Cliff was healthier than she'd expected, not strung out like he'd been a few years before when he'd been lost in drugs.

But he was far from functional. From what Kamren had seen, he still drifted through life like he always had, using what money she deposited in the family account to get whatever he couldn't mooch off friends. Or everyone out at The Arsenal. She'd hoped a few weeks around Dallas and the other operatives would have rubbed off on him, maybe instilled a fire to do something with his life.

But it hadn't.

"I see you've landed on your feet," she commented, her gaze on the new sneakers. "Nice shoes."

"It's about time someone gave me a leg up."

"You aren't owed a leg up, Cliff. You earn it, same as everyone else."

"Always the know-it-all. Don't you ever get tired of always knowing what's good for everyone?" He laughed. "That's classic fucking Kamren."

"Is Rache taking her meds?"

"Why do you care?" Cliff shook his head. "You think we can afford those useless pills? Said it a thousand times, sis. No pill is gonna take away our crazy. It's in our blood."

"Cliff, you know she needs them," Kamren whispered as she shifted uneasily on the sofa beside him. They'd never seen eye-to-eye on how to deal with their little sister. "She seems happy, but she's having troubles out here."

"That isn't my problem, sis. I'm not the one leaving for weeks on end, chasing ghosts best left dead. If you're so worried, stay the fuck where you belong and tend to her." Cliff picked up a beer, took a long swig, then slammed the bottle on the coffee table. "Better yet, do us both a favor and forget I'm here. Rachelle's not my problem. You sure as fuck aren't my problem."

"And that's *your* problem, Cliff. One day you're gonna wake up and realize you can only fly under the radar so long before you have to fucking do something. Live."

"Oh, yeah? What should I do? Chase some phantom killer of a bastard I'm glad is dead? Worry about a sister who's doing better than me and her know-it-all big sister combined?" Cliff chuckled. "I'm eating as much as I want, sleeping in a clean, soft bed, and doing whatever the fuck I want. So is Rache. The only one having a problem with all that is you. Maybe you're the one that needs to wake the fuck up and accept a few truths."

"And what truths would those be?"

"You aren't ever gonna be anything but white trash; none of us are. Dad's dead, thank fuck for small favors. Rache isn't ever gonna change. There's no pill to take the crazy out of us. That's one thing the old man had right. We've all got a splash of whacked in us. Rache embraces hers. Me? I've pickled it." He chuckled as he took another swig of beer. "It's time you shelve the high-and-mighty act and accept you're nothing but a crazy white trash whore, just like Mom."

13

It took more phone calls than Dallas expected, but they finally secured a private meeting with Dom. While Jesse remained back at The Arsenal, Nolan insisted on coming along. Personally, Dallas just wanted it done so he could get back to the compound.

Back to Kamren.

That kiss.

His entire body stirred at the memory, the way she'd awakened within his arms. He hadn't wanted a woman that bad in a long, long time. Way before Hailey. Marla.

He glowered at the door as the buzzer sounded. Restraints rattled as the prisoner was shuffled in. Nolan remained along the back wall of the small detainment room they'd commandeered for their private conversation with a man he'd once looked up to. A dull throb radiated in his gut. Back then he'd been a stupid, young punk with nothing to prove and everything to learn. He'd had the best dad around and five brothers to admire.

Yet he'd chosen Dom as a mentor, someone he'd revered. In many ways he'd been an excellent choice. He had the same raw need to rage against unjustness, push boundaries and kick the asses of anyone who dared mess with him. Yeah, Dom had once been a hell of a man. Now?

Prison had hardened him. The steely determination Dallas had once respected in the man's gaze had been replaced with controlled rage. He was bigger than Dallas remembered, well over six foot—by at least four inches. Broad shoulders had been bulked up by too many long hours of nothing else to do put pump iron. The Marville Dog tattoo had been modified, the once semi-bloody bone now filled in fully. Another one was now beneath the first, half full with the blood drops that distinguished kills for the crew he'd started.

"We doing two on one with me in chains?" Dom asked as he rattled the restraints and looked back at the guard.

"Unlock him," Nolan ordered.

"That wasn't part of the deal," the warden argued as he shifted from one foot to another. "Prisoners remain locked. This is highly irregular."

"Phone call you got was pretty clear. Whatever we want," Dallas said. "Release him, then get the hell out."

The man muttered under his breath as he nodded at the guard. A few moments later, both the men disappeared as the door slammed behind them. Dallas didn't move. Neither did Nolan.

Dom shifted restlessly as he stood his ground in the center of the room. Dallas pointed at the camera and held up a hand.

"It's down," Mary said.

"We're clear," Dallas said as he closed the distance between the man who'd once been so much of his world. He held out a hand and waited.

"What the fuck is this?" Dom asked.

"Depends."

"On?"

"On how much of the bullshit the MDs did over the past few days was you, and how much was Javier," Dallas answered as he withdrew his untouched hand and sat.

"Heard you and your brothers were back and setting up shop in

Resino." The man sat. His gaze swept the room and landed on Nolan. "You brought big brother to handle me?"

"He doesn't need my help handling anything these days, especially scum like you."

"My friend here's training Riley to become a private investigator. She started looking into some troubles in Marville recently, troubles involving Rachelle. You remember they were tight?"

"Don't give a shit what your little sister does, though I've heard she's a looker."

Dallas gritted his teeth. Nolan growled and shoved off the wall but kept his distance. They'd agreed Dallas would lead this discussion. "Sisters are off limits. Those were the rules, right? Gotta admit, Dani's filled out, too. I'm starting to wonder why she hates my family so much."

"She has her reasons."

"Those some of the reasons you're in here?" Dallas asked. "We've got shit to discuss, but I want the air cleared first. What went down that night?"

"That night's not up for discussion, now or ever. Two pieces of shit got what was coming to them. They're rotting in the ground. The law needed someone to lockup. I'm okay with taking the hit."

He didn't do it. Dallas fisted his hands and looked away as he thought back to what little he remembered. One of Dom's cousins had come out to the street they raced on. Frantic and upset, he'd snagged Dom. By the time Dallas had gotten away from the idiots he'd been racing, hell had broken loose at Dom's house. Cop cars and ambulances were there.

Two dead bodies.

Dom's brother, Ricardo, took off hours later, never to be seen again. And Dom was arrested for murder. Pled guilty.

Twenty years, fifteen with good behavior.

"Why the fuck are you darkening my world, D?"

"Tell your crew to stand down and step off Kamren Garrett," Dallas ordered. "They don't, I'll clean house in a way that'll leave you a lone dog."

"That so? You think you've got the balls for that? You grow some in the Army or wherever the fuck you ran away to?"

Dallas grinned, but didn't offer a rebuttal at first. He let the silence tick by but held Dom's gaze. There'd been a time he couldn't have looked the man in the eye—hadn't been ballsy enough to try. Now?

"You've changed," Dom said.

"So have you. The man I remembered wouldn't have been down with his crew intimidating women, slashing their tires. Warning women they won't be breathing much longer if they don't toe the line. He sure as fuck wouldn't be down with his blood saying a woman's mouth is only good for taking Marville Dog." Dallas shrugged, dragged out his cell and pushed play.

The man paled as he snagged the device. Dallas regretted the shitty maneuver because the video he'd queued up had been frozen on Dani's image. Dom's hands shook as he held the phone as if it was an alien device. Cell phones hadn't been all that small or smart back when he'd gone away. When the recording was done, he tapped on the screen.

"Again," he growled.

Dallas replayed the video several times before the man's rage was fully contained. He slammed his fists into the table, but remained locked within his chair otherwise, as if not trusting himself to move. It was simple for Dallas to put himself in Dom's place, imagine being gone for years and seeing Riley for the first time.

Hell, he'd been there not too long ago.

"Respect. We're here giving you a warning that Javier's trouble. Trouble that needs a lesson, then it needs to get cleaned." Dallas met the man's glare with one of his own. "We came back, set up shop, but didn't have an eye to our backyard."

"Now we do," Nolan added.

"I'll deal with Javier," Dom said.

"You handle him; we'll keep Dani safe. No blow back," Nolan said.

Dom's gaze flashed to Dallas. "Your word. I don't know your

brother, but I know you. Got no beef with him, but he wasn't in my crew. You were. Your word and it's done."

For Kamren he'd promise just about anything. The realization startled him a moment.

Dom leaned back in his chair. "Thinking I got played back then. You heard from Ricardo?"

"No, man. That went down; I enlisted," Dallas admitted. "You want, we'll look into him."

"Yeah. I..." He swallowed. "I need to know the truth."

"About that night," Nolan finished. "It wasn't you."

Dom didn't deny the statement, nor did he admit anything. Dallas looked at his brother. "Our crew will look into it. We'll get answers."

"Okay, boys. Reunion's over. Time to get back here," Vi said in the com.

"What's wrong?" Dallas asked.

"Why do you say there's something wrong?"

"Because you sound like you just swallowed a tank full of helium, Vi."

"Fine. While you all were en route, there was an incident. Everything's fine, but things with Rachelle sort of festered. She went after Jesse in the mess hall. Kamren and Ellie waded in, but Riley saw the whole thing. Everyone's retreated to their corners, but we could use you both back here." She paused.

Dallas stood and looked at his old friend. "We'll be in touch."

"It'll take a couple days to get things in motion, but brace yourself. Marville Dog justice is swift and furious."

Which was why Dallas had come without Dani. If they wanted Marville truly cleaned up, it meant knocking the Marville Dogs down at the ankles in a way that they'd never get back up. With one problem sorted, he'd just added another to the list.

What the hell had happened the night Dom was arrested for murder? It was a mystery he hoped Jud and Riley could solve. She needed the practice. For now, they needed to haul ass home.

He yanked out his cell when they got to the parking lot and fired off a text to the brainiacs, adding Riley and Jud at the last minute.

The man was right. It was time they started treating Riley like the investigator she wanted to be and made her do the digging.

Dig into Ricardo DeMarco. Everything. Entire family, too.

THE BED SHIFTED BEHIND KAMREN. She sprang up, but a heavy arm settled around her stomach and dragged her back down. The scream in her throat died down when her gaze settled on Dallas, whose face was illuminated from the bathroom light she'd left on.

"What the hell do you think you're doing?" Her heart thundered wildly.

"Apparently scaring the shit out of you." He ran a hand down her face. "I'm sorry, sweetheart. I figured you'd be dead asleep."

She'd tried. She'd been worried about how the visit with Dom had gone. She'd been worried about Rachelle and how she and Riley were doing. She'd been worried about Jesse. The frustration bubbled from her like a boiling vat of stew. Worries, fears, doubts, guilt and other things festered within the concoction until there was no hope she'd ever sleep again.

Dallas's heat settled along her back. She tensed within his embrace, unsure what the heck he was doing.

"Relax, Kamren. I need to hold you a minute. It's been a shit day, and the only thing I've thought of the past few hours getting back here was smelling your hair and feeling your soft curves against me. Let me hold you."

She stilled, unsure why holding her would help him. Truth be told, the physical contact was nice. Okay, it was way more than nice. The brew she'd simmered, stirred and fussed over the past few hours slowly calmed within the silence as it ticked by. His heat and the strength of his arms around her chased away any thoughts beyond the powerful body behind her.

"It went bad," she guessed moments later.

"No. Dom's handling Javier. We're keeping Dani safe."

"Good luck with that. She's not a fan of anything Mason."

"We got that, sweetheart. You know why?"

"No, but the shift in her thinking went down around the same time Dom went away," she said. "Something bad happened to her, Dallas. She never shared what, but she changed overnight. I lost my best friend back then, and I don't even know why."

"Nolan's gonna keep her safe. Jud and Riley are looking into it."

"Dallas, something happened when you were away."

"I know, sweetheart. Vi and Mary showed me the recording," he whispered in her ear. "Are you okay?"

"Me?"

"You."

"Why the heck are you asking about me? You should go find Jesse. He was the one she touched. Or Riley. She was really upset."

"Sweetheart, talk to me." He squeezed her tighter. "It's only you and me. Offload whatever you've been chewing on for hours and trust me to handle it. Whatever it is, it'll stay between us."

"You've done enough." He'd just spent hours on the road back and forth between Huntsville getting the Marville Dogs off her. That alone was enough. Add in helping find her dad's killer and the whole dealing with Rachelle and her wandering hands for God only knows how long, and she'd incurred a big enough debt with the Masons. She didn't get to offload more on them. They'd taken on enough of her crap already.

"You said something earlier today. You 'saw' what I said to Jesse at the rescue."

She tensed within his embrace. He traced a path across her shoulder and down her arm.

"You read lips. The night your truck exploded, Brant mentioned your dad teaching you all how to do it," he continued.

"I'm sorry," she whispered. "I try not to see things I shouldn't, but..." She bit off the excuse. Truth told, there weren't any excuses. She'd been too drawn to the horrors within their words, the haunted expressions within them both afterward. By then it'd seemed too vile to admit she'd spied on them.

"We left our coms on, Kam. Everyone on the line heard," Dallas said. "But if you need a quid pro quo to give me a piece of what's troubling you, I'll do it."

"Why? Why does it matter?"

"Because I'm not turning away from whatever this is between us. I haven't wanted to drive my dick into someone this bad in a long time, sweetheart. The fact that I haven't even tried to seduce you is because you're too important to me tells me this is more than a roll in the sack."

"I'm not a good woman, Dallas."

"I'm so far from a good man I can't even see the border anymore, sweetheart."

She didn't believe it for a second. Everything about Dallas and his family proved him wrong. She almost laughed, but the intensity in his voice gave her pause as the conversation she'd seen replayed in her mind. "The Collective was really bad."

"Yeah."

"Dad was really bad, but he wasn't the worst one." She burrowed deeper against him as she whispered the words she'd never shared with anyone. "Mom had problems, the kind of problems that people didn't get over. No matter what Dad did, she never got better."

"She hurt you."

"Yeah." Kamren swallowed. "Everyone thought it was Dad; sometimes it was. But Mom...she didn't handle him choosing me for his prodigy well. I was her first, the little girl she'd wanted to turn into a doll. I didn't want to be a doll. But I didn't want to be my Dad's hunter either. I just wanted to be me."

"We saw the scars, Kamren."

"I figured you had," she whispered. "She got angry easy, flew into this madness where she had insane notions of what merited punishment. Most of the time I took the brunt, but sometimes Rachelle would cry or earn a punishment. Usually I could take it for her, but when I couldn't..."

"What happened then?" His ran a hand down her hair, drew her closer.

"She'd make me punish Rachelle. If I didn't hit hard enough,

Mom would beat us both even harder, so I had to make it hurt enough to keep Rachelle from getting hit real bad."

"Fuck, sweetheart." He kissed the shell of her ear. "Is that what Brant saw in the barn?"

"Yeah. It only happened a couple of times, but it was enough. Rachelle was sensitive, she couldn't handle what we went through. What she's like is because of Mom. Dad." She reached for his hand. "Me."

"No way in hell was it your fault, Kamren."

"I hurt her."

"No. You were forced to hurt her." Dallas squeezed her face. "There's a big difference, sweetheart. Tell me you know the difference."

"I should've done more to protect her."

"You did enough. You were a kid, too." He sighed heavily and ran a hand across her stomach. "You still protect her and everyone around you. Like today, with Jesse."

"Someone needed to stop her. She's tormented you all long enough."

"That's not your fault, sweetheart. We're adults. We can handle your sister."

"But you don't because it'd hurt Riley to lose her best friend."

"We've spent so long protecting her we didn't notice she's grown up. And she's a hell of a lot stronger than we give her credit for."

"Yeah, she is." Kamren smiled. "You're a good big brother, you know. You all are."

"You're a hell of a good big sister," he whispered.

She wished it were true, but she knew better. She closed her eyes and drifted within the calm Dallas's presence created. He'd let her offload a batch of the stew simmering in her, enough for her to relax for the first time since the incident had gone down with Riley.

"My handler in The Collective was a bitch, the worst you could imagine times one hundred thousand. I knew if I stayed with them I'd never get out, I'd never get back to my family. To the good, clean, happy life I wanted." Kamren shifted in his embrace, faced him and wrapped her arms around his body. "Fuck, that feels good, sweetheart."

It did.

Pleasure danced across her skin as the heat from his exposed torso penetrated the soft shell covering hers. Her nipples tightened, but she pushed back the arousal. Tonight wasn't about sex. He'd taken on her demons. Now she'd stare his in the eyes and kick their asses.

"She blackmailed you into bed, didn't she? That's how you have a son."

"Yeah. Didn't find out until she was bleeding out on a concrete floor after she had taken me and Jud captive." He kissed her cheek and ran a hand down her back. "Fuck, you smell so good."

"Then Hailey drugged you," she whispered.

"Yeah. I'd just gotten home and was at Bubba's. I was so relieved to be home, drinking a beer and relaxing." Tension filled the muscles beneath her palms. She deepened the contact between them and kissed his jawline. "I woke up in her bed, my brother glaring down at me. Dylan went wheels up before we could have it out."

"He thought the worst."

"Everyone did, including me. Then I figured out she'd done something to my beer. No way in hell I was ready to admit that, not after..."

"Not after what The Collective bitch did." Anger seeped into Kamren's calm, but she forced it back. She didn't get to fly into a rage over his demons, not tonight. Tonight she'd keep them away from him and give him peace. "Neither of them will ever mess with you again, Dallas. I won't let them."

"One of them is dead," he said with a grin as he pulled back.

"Good." She rested her head on his chest when he settled onto his back. "I hope I get to meet your son soon."

She closed her eyes and drifted within the calm he'd given her. For the first time in forever, she had someone to share her burdens with, and he'd shared his. She'd connected with someone on a level beyond the physical. And it was spectacular.

14

Henry Mills' ranch house was vile extravagance at its worst. Kamren took in the gated entry adorned with mounted deer heads. "He probably can't even shoot a gun."

Jud chuckled. Riley shifted in the front seat. Riley had been quiet on the way to Marville, leaving Kamren to wonder how patched her friendship with Rachelle was after the disastrous confrontation in the cafeteria.

All thoughts of what'd happened the day before fled when Jud pulled their vehicle to a stop. He looked over at Riley. "What's the first rule of interviews?"

"Assess the situation before you present your questions. Watch physical reactions just as much as the verbal ones." The blonde rolled her eyes. "This isn't my first interview, you know."

"No, but this isn't someone stealing food from Bubba's, or mail from the post office. This bastard could be the one behind your tires getting slashed and her dad getting dead. We're done playing in the kiddie pool, starting today."

Wowza.

Intensity wafted off Jud as he waited Riley out. She had a streak of stubborn in her, one Kamren couldn't help but find amusing because it was so similar to Cord. She'd seen it in Marshall, too. It made her smile and wonder if Dallas had it as well.

A short man with muscles spilling out of his ill-fitting suit greeted them at the door. He made a production of touching his gun, which made Jud chuckle and cross his arms in front of his waist in the stance she'd seen many of the operatives take. She'd started calling it I-just-look-like-I'm-relaxed.

"You have an appointment with Mr. Mills?"

"Thinking he'll want to hear what we have to say," Jud said.

"And you are?" the man tried again.

"Trouble you'd best let past before I get irritated," Jud said.

"Mr. Mills is a very busy man, sir. I'm afraid unless you have an appointment, you'll have to leave, or I'll call the sheriff."

"Good, he's next on our visit list. Having them both here would save some time," Riley replied. "Go ahead and let Haskell know there's a Mason out here asking for him and Mr. Mills. Let's see how that one goes over."

"I'm afraid he doesn't know any Masons."

"That's okay; we know plenty about him." Riley crossed her arms. "The longer you wait, the bigger the chance another Mason will come wandering in. They're mighty protective and in a really bad mood lately. Someone's messing with our friends. And me. That one's got them real miffed."

The man touched his weapon again as he looked between Jud and Riley, who'd morphed into a pint-sized bad ass. She'd either been watching her brothers or simply being in the same breathing space as so many had rubbed off on her. Either way, Kamren was seriously impressed.

The man's gaze moved to Kamren. "And you are?"

"Oh, Mr. Mills killed my dad. Go ahead, make your call, and I'll wait my turn." Yep. Kamren hadn't found her bad ass, but her smart ass was definitely in place. Jud's lips twitched.

Riley's eyes widened.

"I'm sorry, ma'am. I misunderstood you."

"No, you didn't." Kamren let her voice rise. "I'll go slower this time. Your boss killed my dad. I'm here to have a few words about that. But I'll wait until the sheriff is here. We have some questions about the payoff your boss sent to him. You wouldn't know anything about that, would you?"

The man shrank backward. "I'll just go see if Mr. Mills is available."

"Great, you do that," Riley said.

The moment the door clicked shut, Jud said, "I promised I'd bring you two back in one piece. If we could maybe stow the smartass until we are in the door, that'd be helpful."

"Like you couldn't kill him a hundred different ways without breaking a sweat," Kamren muttered. "Sorry, gotta admit my mind's stewing on stuff. I've been chasing this rabbit trail a long time."

"I didn't know," Riley said. "I'm sorry. I should've known."

"Doesn't matter; we're here now." Not that it'd probably do any good. Vi and Mary had gathered very little in the way of hard evidence against Henry Mills when it came to her father's death.

Was he even responsible? Questions and doubts wore on Kamren's nerves as they waited. And waited.

The door opened. The man returned and motioned for them to enter as if they were filthy animals being let in. Kamren made a point of rubbing the dried mud caked on the bottom of her hiking boots onto the marbled floor entryway. Jud chuckled as he watched with amusement.

"This way," the man said, his lips curled. "Please refrain from touching the artwork. Mr. Mills has exquisite tastes lost on the local ilk."

"Right. Clearly a man of your cunning fashion sense knows all about art," Riley said. "Look at my friend like that again and I'll shove that too-small jacket up your ass."

"I see you've made new friends, Higgins."

Kamren chuckled. He looked like a Higgins.

"I'm afraid I didn't understand why you three are here."

"We're looking into the murder of Roland Garrett. I understand he did some work on your hunting lease," Jud said.

"I'm sorry, are you law enforcement? Sherriff Haskell hasn't mentioned new deputies," Henry replied as he undid the button to his suit jacket and sat. The move accentuated his rail-thin physique, wiry and freakishly tall. Like a weasel with a mustache that ran downward and stopped at the seam of his lips. Thick, unnaturally black hair sat atop his head like a nest. He motioned toward the sofa, but Kamren remained standing. She studied the art on the walls.

"We're private investigators contracted by The Arsenal to look into this matter on behalf of whatever alphabet agency you'd prefer. We're unfortunate enough to know all of them. Quite well." Jud sat right in front of Mills, his physical presence close enough for them to almost touch.

The man squirmed, shifting his seat backward. "Right, well, I'm afraid I don't understand how the unfortunate accident of a hand of mine is within any alphabet agency's purview. Perhaps I should contact them directly."

"Perhaps you should," Riley said. "Word of advice, Mr. Mills. You clearly don't know me, but everyone knows my brothers. You don't want to get into an address book war with them. No one does. Their contacts are plentiful, powerful, and more than willing to do whatever they ask, whenever."

"And you feel the need to boast about this because?"

Riley shrugged. "What can I say? I'm just a proud little sister. But, I'm thinking you needed that education so this conversation can move forward without you thinking you can intimidate us by mentioning some Director Schmuck in San Antonio, or wherever."

"Very well, we'll cut to the chase. I knew Mr. Garrett. He was an employee of mine, briefly. He assisted my associates and clients more than me. I prefer to remain within the comfortable indoors. But since many of my clients prefer to be outdoors, we came out here on occasion. Mr. Garrett was an exceptional asset for those visits, making sure we had whatever we needed."

"Which was?" Kamren asked. "I'll bet you don't even know where your hunting lease is."

"Don't be ridiculous. Of course, I'm sure you wouldn't understand, but my holdings are vast and keeping track of them all is a bit of a burden." He shifted within his seat. "I do recall when Mr. Garrett passed. One of my most important clients was out here. It was an..."

"Inconvenience," Jud finished.

"Yes, it was," the man admitted.

"Are these clients also part of your other business out here?" Riley asked.

"I don't believe I understand what you're asking. What other business?"

"The one where you're paying off the local sheriff to help you toss people out of their homes. The one where you're paying off the local banker to foreclose on their homes, all so you can swoop in and buy their land before the oil company leases drilling rights." Kamren smiled. "That business. If you don't remember, I'm sure we can share the pictures. Or the bank records."

The man paled. "That's hardly your business. That doesn't concern Mr. Garrett in any way."

"I'm thinking it did. See, he was my dad, and he wasn't a good man. He also wasn't one that liked rich muckety-mucks like you pushing hard working, country-raised men like him off their land, all so you can make a few more million." Kamren shrugged. "But I guess we'll see what those alphabet groups you weren't too worried about think about all that."

"I'm very sorry to hear about your father, Ms. Garrett, but I can assure you I had no involvement in his death. I was assured it was an accident," the man said.

"Henry, I heard you had some unwanted visitors."

Sheriff Ronnie Haskell made Kamren's skin crawl. No matter what she did, she couldn't ever rid herself of the disgust and unease that rattled her every time he was around. Jud rose from his seat.

"You must be Ronnie." The intentional slight of not remembering to mention his position snapped through the room like a misfired gun. Jud stared the man down.

Haskell adjusted the weapons belt around his thick waist and cleared his throat. "You must be one of those soldiers of fortune the

Masons hired. You'd best go on back. We don't tolerate your kind in my county."

"His kind?" Kamren asked. "What would that be? Hard-working, law-abiding citizens that protect and defend this country? Those kind? Or did you mean the kind that doesn't cover up an illegal gambling operations for his brother?"

"I'm not that law-abiding," Jud commented.

"I know it's hard to accept that your pa is dead, darling, but it's time you left the good folks of Marville alone with this. If you don't, I'm afraid I'm gonna have to take matters into my own hands." Haskell leered at her.

"Was it good, Sherriff?"

"Was what good, darling?"

"Did you get the five grand from this asshole before or after you pretended to look over my dad's murder scene? Did he take you out for a good steak dinner in Nomad, thanking you for your commitment to his bottom line?"

The man paled. Riley leaped into play.

"She has pictures of you two together. We dug. Deep. Deep enough to find that secret account, Sherriff Haskell. You may as well know my brothers got wind of that and said we weren't to worry about you. See, you get a pass from us." Riley smiled. "You're on their radar, and that's not somewhere anyone ever wants to be."

"I'm allowed to hire out for personal security. Nothing in my position says otherwise," the man argued.

"Like I said, I was told to stay off you." Riley looked at Henry, then back at Ronnie. "See, the way my brothers see it, and you know they're plenty smart, the Texas Rangers are gonna be looking into you. We figure they'll ferret out the truth from you, and you can flip on this asshole."

"Or not," Jud said. "Consider this your push, gentlemen. We'll be in touch for answers. First one to give us the details we want gets a pass. The other one swings."

∽

Vi LOOKED around the room at the gathered group of women. "No! I didn't believe Jud when he came back. He was laughing so hard I damn near died from curiosity. I mean, he just doesn't lose it like that."

Kamren had been commandeered by a very demanding Bree shortly after they'd returned from Marville. As far as Kamren was concerned, the day was a waste of time. But Jud had said they'd pushed. Now they had to wait.

She glanced around the small cottage as she sipped her beer. Addy, Vi, Mary, Bree, Rhea, Zoey, Riley and Rachelle. The latter was a bit cold with Kamren, but everyone had been civil so far, which kept the awkward in the room at a manageable level.

"You just announced you were there because he killed your dad? Just like that?" Rhea asked.

"Yep." Riley grinned. "I almost died. I don't know how I didn't. The man's face alone made me wish we'd had a drone to record it."

"Clearly the bastard's hiding something. We fielded calls from his attorney, some schmuck in the local FBI field office in San Antonio, then another attorney." Mary leaned back and rubbed her belly. "He's definitely nervous, which unfortunately proves what Vi and I suspected."

"He's not the one, is he?" Kamren asked.

"No, but he's definitely dirty. Then again, he might be guilty for all we know. That's what an investigation's for," Vi said.

"Are we done yapping about the boring stuff? I want to get to the fun part of the night."

"Fun? What fun?" Rachelle asked. "Are we going shopping?"

"It's midnight. Where the hell would we go?" Addy asked as she entered the room and dumped a bag in Kamren's lap.

"Addy! We discussed this. I was going to go back in the bedroom and wrap it," Bree said.

"Geez," Zoey whined. "I spent ten minutes printing out wrapping paper."

"So get the damn thing and wrap it," Addy said. "My girl there isn't like you all. You drag this shit out too long, and she'll get awkward and nervous."

Kamren had passed awkward and nervous a while back. She offered Addy a small smile of thanks and looked down at the box. Rachelle's gaze narrowed on the bag the box was in. Kamren recognized the logo as a place in Nomad that sold phones and computers and stuff but wasn't sure.

"What's this?" Kamren asked.

"Open it!" Bree exclaimed.

"Warning, don't freak out. We all talked it over. You're doing investigations with this crew; we need to be able to be in contact with you. This is a tool, just like any other in your backpack. A weapon when needed." Addy's voice was low, but in a tone Kamren knew meant business. A lecture so she wouldn't freak out.

She opted for silence rather than a verbal response. She opened the bag, then the box. Shock kept her silent as she pulled out the cell phone. It was thin, but small enough to fit in a pocket.

"We know you lost yours in the explosion, so we replaced it. It's on The Arsenal plan. They get this really awesome deal," Rhea said. "It's a smartphone."

"Pft, that's ironic," Rachelle muttered.

Tension corded around Kamren as she glared at her sister. Truth be told, she'd always wanted one but hadn't been able to afford anything more than a cheap one from Walmart that flipped up. She'd never gotten many calls anyway because back then she hadn't had many people to call her.

Now she did.

She thought.

She had friends.

"That wasn't nice," Riley said as she punched Rachelle's arm.

"What? It's true, okay? She probably won't even be able to operate it. I love her, but she's not like you all." Rachelle looked around. Arms crossed, she halted on Kamren. "Tell them."

She should. But for once she wanted to fit in, wanted to be like them. "I can't read. My education stopped in the third grade, so I suppose she's right, but I pick up on stuff fast and learn what I can."

"You're smarter than most operatives we have worked with in the field before coming here," Mary said. "There's book smarts and street smarts. You've got the latter in spades. Everyone out here says so."

"Thank you," Kamren said as she glanced down at the phone. How the heck did she get it set up? She'd never had one before.

"Now we can set it up and enter our numbers in. We'll take pictures to program in so you see our faces when we call. And your address book will show pictures, too," Zoey said.

"We can teach you to read," Rhea said.

"Yes! I can make a word a day app," Bree said.

"There's like hundreds of those," Rachelle said.

"Yeah, but this one's just for Kamren. When she's used the word twice, she'll get another. Words I know she'll want to know."

Emotion formed in her throat. "Thanks. This means a lot to me."

"The guys want to make sure you get all their numbers into it," Riley said. "I told them we were doing this, and they want to make sure she's got everyone's numbers."

"On it," Addy said as she whipped the phone from Kamren.

Rachelle's gaze narrowed on the phone. "Why is she getting everyone's number?"

"Because she may need them," Mary said. "And Rhea's right. We can teach you to read, if you want us to. It's entirely up to you because you are what matters, not what you can or cannot do."

Kamren believed her. She looked around the room and saw the same quiet resolve within everyone's expressions. They'd respect whatever decision she made because they respected the fact it was her choice. She was so far beneath their league, but she didn't want to be. She might be street smart, but she wanted to be far more than that.

"I'd like to learn, maybe get my GED."

Bree's eyes widened, and she erupted into a big grin. "Yes! Okay, girls. I'll get an action plan together and assign us each a grid of knowledge."

A grid of knowledge? Kamren gulped. What had she just gotten herself into?

"Why do you get to be the decider of the grid?" Rhea asked.

"Because I have time on my hands, and I know a thing or two about teaching adults how to read," Bree answered quickly. "I taught my grandma, you know."

"You did?" Kamren asked.

"Yep. She was raised country, in the Appalachian Mountains." The blonde locked gazes with Kamren. "So I've got this. *We've* got this."

She nodded. Maybe she wasn't that different from them after all.

15

"What are we doing?" Kamren asked as she followed the women up the stairwell leading to the top of the roof. The women crouched, so she did too.

It was the next morning, and way too early as far as Kamren was concerned. They'd stayed up into the late hours talking, laughing and getting to know one another. She loved how down to earth all the women were, even though they were all so freaking brilliant in their own way.

They helped her fit in.

If conversation steered to weird science mumbo jumbo, Addy shifted it back to common ground. So did Riley. They talked about hunting and stuff, too. Bree wanted to know more about hunting blinds and tracking techniques.

When her question went unanswered, she repeated herself. "What are we doing?"

"War games," Vi said. "Operatives get bored easily around here, guess we've raised the bar pretty high on the adrenaline scale."

"No shit," Zoey muttered. "Stay low. We don't want anyone accidentally looking up here."

War games didn't sound like something anyone would want. Kamren stared down at the large group of people exercising in formation down below. Funny, they didn't look ready for war games. No guns. Hardly any clothes. She gulped as the thought slammed into her. She glanced down and winced as she took in the pale pink Star Wars jammies.

Addy was easy to spot in the group because of her red hair, but the woman hadn't noticed them. As far as she could tell, no one had. She crouched down, using the ledge of the roof as cover as she looked over at Vi and Zoey.

"Well, what are you waiting for? Shoot them." Vi did a shooing motion with her hands as she reached up and fiddled with her com. "She's chickening out."

"I'm not chickening out," Kamren groused. "Just tell me what I'm doing again."

"You're shooting them. What part of that is hard to understand?" Zoey turned a screen to Kamren. It had a number one in green on one side and a one hundred on the other. "I'm calling it 'One Versus One Hundred', but I think there's a bit more than one hundred. And they're worth different point levels. I figured that's only fair. Like taking out Marshall is worth way more than one of the potentials. And Jud? Well he's worth one hundred points. Dallas and Gage are seventy-five. Oh, and Fallon and Addy. Actually, we'll make it simple. Any team leaders are seventy-five points. Everyone else is twenty-five."

Kamren eyed the gun skeptically. No way in hell was this a good idea. "And the point of this?"

"They're getting slack with their security," Mary said in the com. "Not a single one of them has a weapon on them. Not one. It's shameful."

"It's six a.m.," Kamren argued. She glanced down at her jammy bottoms and bare feet. She couldn't shoot people while wearing jammies.

"If you aren't up for it, I'll do it my damn self, but that's not gonna be very effective."

"And me up here on a rooftop where I can't get down is?" Kamren shook her head.

"Okay, smartass. We go when you think you're in a good position you can defend. Let us know, and we'll start," Vi said. "Zoey and I will stay up here and keep score. Don't get dead. There's a pool."

"A pool?"

"Yep. One thousand bucks big," Zoey said.

They were certifiable. The thought made her wince. Certifiable wasn't the best thing to think about given what'd gone down with Rachelle. Fortunately, Riley and Rachelle had ironed out their differences. The woman had even convinced her sister to talk with Doctor Sinclair, a psychologist they had on hand at the compound. The two had gone into town with Momma Mason to do some modifications to the upcoming wedding plans.

Last night had been a bit awkward with her sister, but Kamren was glad they'd gotten to spend some time together. She and Riley were still tight, and that was what was important. Once she got the medicine she needed, she'd be back to herself in no time.

"Shouldn't you and Mary be in town with Mrs. Mason doing wedding stuff?" she asked.

"No," Mary growled into the com. "Dylan and I should've eloped."

"Don't you dare do that. You dragged me into a big wedding, missy. I'm not doing it alone."

"She dragged you in?" Kamren looked at Vi.

"Dylan proposed to Mary. She said yes. Momma Mason started planning a huge shindig. Jud and I hooked up, fell in love. He proposed. I said yes." She sighed. "Then he got with Dylan and Mary and decided we could get hitched on the same day. They all agreed. I got shanghaied." The love and adoration in Vi's gaze told Kamren all she needed to know—the woman was thrilled about being "shanghaied."

"The wedding is Momma Mason's jurisdiction. We all want it that way," Mary said. "So, are you in position? Time's ticking."

Kamren sighed and eyed the bag full of paint pellets for the gun they'd given her. Bree had modified one of the fancy rifles to shoot paint pellets instead of bullets. She'd assured everyone the distance would be comparable to a real bullet, but Kamren had her doubts. If she was going against over one hundred well-trained operatives with nothing more than colored paint, she needed a better plan than standing on a rooftop and firing down at them.

"Give me half an hour." She didn't wait for a response. She scurried down the roof via the fire escape on the far backside of the building. She unshouldered the backpack of extra supplies she'd packed when this disastrous idea of "fun" had formed a little while ago.

Over breakfast.

Kamren couldn't help but smile. She'd woken in Dallas's arms. They'd spent a long few minutes kissing, then they'd progressed to grabbing breakfast. He'd gotten waylaid with drills, but the women had dragged her into their group and the plan had formed.

She opted to stay in her jammies to not waste valuable time. The traps were rudimentary and far from precise, but she didn't need perfection—she needed functional and quick. The more the better, given the number of targets. The protective blind she'd been working on would be a perfect position to work her way back toward. It sat in the back against the electrical fence and had a defendable one-hundred-eighty-degree view. With the traps and other surprises she'd set out along the way, she should last a while.

Assuming the dang gun worked.

Her pulse pounded in her ears as she climbed into the blind. She sat on the small stool and sighted the unsuspecting targets. She listed the higher point values in her head. Everyone was present, the highest targets up front leading the rest. It was almost too simple, but she knew they were well-trained operatives. They'd act swiftly and brutally.

"In position."

"You're green for Operation One to One Hundred."

And so chaos ensued. She got in six head shots before anyone realized what was going on. Then she stared Jesse straight in the eye as she shot him in the forehead. Bree had ensured her the shots wouldn't hurt. Much. So head shots were clean, swift kills.

Panic commenced.

Marshall, Addy, and Dallas were the only high value targets remaining. Jud had been the first shot, mainly because the man freaking terrified her. She didn't waste ammo, but shot whenever her next target's gaze swept away from her location. She counted the targets as Zoey and Vi kept her apprised of how many remained.

"Someone's coming up at your nine," Mary said. "Ouch, that's gonna leave a mark. What kind of traps do you have laid out? He just went down hard."

Kamren angled her rifle downward, shot him, then refocused on the crowd heading her direction. Fish. Meet barrel.

"What the fuck are you doing?" Dylan's voice growled in the com.

"You can't talk. You're dead," Mary said, her voice a monotone, like she was reading off a grocery list.

Kamren chuckled into the com as she took down Marshall and two others. Oops. Time to reload. Damn it. Not that she should complain since she couldn't recall ever using a weapon that held so much ammo. Bree's creation was pure genius.

"Thirty-four left standing," Zoey whispered.

"What are you doing?" Dylan repeated.

"Teaching everyone a lesson," Vi supplied. "Now be a good dead person and keep quiet, or she'll shoot you again."

"Son of a bitch."

The man's voice was met with silence as Kamren continued about her work. Someone had set out some paint rifles along the perimeter near the building. Though a couple of people had managed to get one, the metal blind she'd insulated herself in ensured they wouldn't breach her area easily.

Because those who stood a chance were already dead.

One man remained standing. He'd hunkered down behind a barrier and waited out her firing. She tracked his progression as he slowly made his way toward her location.

"Crap, I fucked up," Zoey whispered.

"What?" Mary asked.

"I sort of forgot Marcus was a high level. I had him flagged in her view as a ten and he's definitely at least a fifty."

"His training, he's a seventy-five. If not more," Vi said. "He's a team leader, newly promoted."

"Great." Her victims weren't good dead people. They cheered him on and offered him advice as he moved on her position. Damn mouthy corpses.

Really, it was nuts. No way in hell would she have done so well without the element of surprise on her side. And the women.

"He's too good at hand-to-hand, but he's slow in rapid-fire situations," Mary supplied, like it made any danged sense.

"English, please."

"Give him more than one thing to target at once, then strike."

Right. That she could do. Maybe. With her gaze sweeping between her target's last position and her bag, she used some of the cord she'd pocketed to jury-rig the weapon to go off. She headed for the door. She shimmied down the stairs and fell to her belly in an awkward crawl. She so wasn't a soldier. How the heck did they do this shit every day? Oye.

"Why did you leave the blind?" Zoey asked. "Get back up there."

"Quiet," Vi ordered.

"He's still firing at the blind. Holy shit! Wait. Who's firing the gun?"

"Zoey, shut up," Mary ordered.

Kamren let the women duke it out via the com as she pulled the handgun she'd loaded with paint pellets. Colored gas grenades were in her other hand. She tracked her target's new location, ten feet to the left of his previous location. Smart man had realized the gun wasn't manned any longer, which meant she didn't have long to act. It was now or never.

Adrenaline spiked within her as she lobbed the first grenade so it landed with a hard thud behind his current position. He whirled toward it. She lobbed the second near the first. She jumped to a crouch and lobbed a third, this time to the right. He was almost within range. She lobbed the final one right at him.

He turned, rifle in hand. Red filled the air between them. A pellet shot past her head, where she'd been moments before, but she was already firing. She didn't stop until his entire chest and forehead were splattered with pellets. She dropped to her knees as a loud whoop sounded from atop the building.

Though Bree had remained quiet during the "game," she was quite vocal now.

"And we have a victor!" the woman shouted.

Marcus wiped paint off his face and smirked. Dallas laughed loud and long, his amusement filling the tension-charged air around her. He closed the distance and hauled her against him. His mouth swept down on hers. The kiss was long, hungry and filled with the same desire she'd experienced the last time they'd kissed.

"Damn, that was spectacular, sweetheart." He dragged her head against the crook of his arm and turned them both to face the gathered hoard of people she'd just pseudo killed. "And what did we learn today?"

"Not to leave my woman alone with yours?" Dylan asked as he crossed his arms and scowled. "And pink is the new commando color around here."

"Try again," Mary said as she appeared with Vi and Zoey. Bree was still shouting from the rooftop. "Never assume HERA has you covered. None of you had a weapon."

"And if we did, she'd be dead," someone said.

"Hardly." Vi pointed at the blind. "She had the element of surprise, but that doesn't excuse the chaos I saw from some of you. She took out all the leaders first, knowing they would get to her otherwise. All the rest of you? You've got a long day ahead of you. Hit the showers, then be back out here in an hour. That'll give me time to chew your leaders out while you aren't here to hear me."

When they didn't move, Mary added. "Now, unless you want another lesson from me and HERA."

Everyone shuffled out quickly. Kamren turned and noticed Fallon, Nolan, and Jesse looking over the traps she'd set as a man she'd never met hobbled away. Oops.

"These are clever," Fallon admired. "Simple, but very effective."

"If you pack the holes with nails or something else painful, they're more effective. Dad learned how to set them from survivalists up north." She pulled out a knife and got to work removing them. "Sorry about all this, by the way. I told them it was a bad idea."

Kamren stood as she finished the apology and shifted her gaze beneath the intense scrutiny of those gathered around her.

"You were brilliant, sweetheart," Dallas said. "Though not sure I'm down with our teams seeing your jammies."

"They're Bree's. I think."

The appreciative smile and his half-hooded gaze as it meandered down her, slow and assessing, killed any further response.

"He's right." Jud smiled. "You worked the field perfectly and established a defensible position. Given enough weapons, you could've likely stayed up there a long time if you had hand-to-hand training. It was a hell of a job."

"And to think she has no formal training," Addy said with a grin. "That's my girl."

"No, that's my girl." Bree sauntered up with a huge wad of cash in her hand. She held it up to Mary and Vi. "Told you! I freaking told you she'd clear them all. But no. You were naysayers."

"I said ninety percent," Vi said. "That's hardly a naysayer."

"Pft. Please. She was ninety percent through with them before they even knew what the heck was happening."

"I'm thinking you'd probably be better off taking that money inside," Kamren suggested.

Bree looked around. Her gaze widened. "Right. See ya later. We'll do this again. Double the odds."

"I'm thinking this is a one-time thing," Kamren said.

"Are you really pissed?" Mary asked Dylan.

"No," he said with a grin as he hauled her close and kissed her. "We deserved it."

"Yeah, you did," Vi said. She shoved Jud. "She took you out with one shot."

The man looked at Vi and smiled. Then laughed.

Everyone followed suit. Conversation flowed easily as they compared "wounds" and moved closer to inspect the blind she'd constructed. In typical man fashion, they decided to test the blind with real bullets. Kamren shook her head and walked away with the women. She flashed Dallas a smile and waved as she left. The intensity in his gaze as he returned the grin promised more kisses later. She couldn't wait.

An obnoxious buzzer sounded from Mary's pocket. She looked at Vi, then snagged a device from her back pocket. She looked back at Dallas. "HERA has a hit, in the deep of the black we'd excluded."

Oh my God. They'd possibly found Dallas's son.

Vi whistled, long and loud, until all the operatives gathered around the blind turned to look at her. "Wheels up in thirty. We've got a hit. Pack a bag, Kamren. You're going with them. We've been in touch with your friend, Tanner. He was on standby for the hit. Now that we have it, he and his partner are meeting us there. We'll form a plan en route, but you're part of it."

"I am?"

"Yeah, no way in hell they're going without you. If you're tracking is half as good as your ability to lay traps, we'll need you in the field. Tanner said you're a natural, one of the best he's ever worked with."

Whether the admiration her ex-boyfriend offered was real or not, Kamren appreciated it. She just hoped she could live up to expectations. More than anything, though, she hoped they'd find Dallas's son.

"YOU'RE GOOD." The voice startled her almost more than the compliment.

Kamren turned and watched Jud prowl toward her. He reached down and unstrapped one of the sheaths on his thigh. "Addy suspects you're as good with knives as you are guns. She noticed you were drawn to them."

She swallowed, unsure what to say or do. Leaving the small room wasn't an option since he blocked the lone exit with his massive frame. She'd gone to the supply area to fill her bag in case she needed supplies. She wasn't sure what to anticipate, and even though Tanner was often prepared for anything, he wasn't a thinker like her. He relied on luck more than she cared for, and The Arsenal had some seriously slick gear.

"I'm hoping you don't have a reason to need this, but if you do, I want you to have it." He held out the weapon. "When we get back, I'd like to train you on hand-to-hand, assuming Dallas agrees. I've been working with Riley."

"Thanks, but there's not much need for hand-to-hand when I'm tracking deer."

"These days, you never know," he said. "Besides, the way things are going, I suspect you'll be around here a lot more. Sooner or later my Viviana will hit you up to join a team. Sharp shooters are hard to come by."

"Oh, I'm not trained, not former military or anything."

"I'm not former military. Think about it. Either that or you can help Riley and me. You have a gift. It'd be a shame to waste it." He settled the knife into her hand.

She withdrew it from the sheath and lost the ability to breathe. It was...magnificent in its simplicity. The perfect survival knife. The fixed blade was a plain, single-sided, thick drop point belly. It was lighter than she expected, but durable enough to last a long, long time, even with rugged use. She swallowed back the emotion in her throat. The man was a total stranger and he was offering her a knife so gorgeous it defied belief. The etched hilt drew her attention. Though it was a simplistic style, nothing about it was without precision quality.

"I can't take this."

"I insist. I've heard the plan and know you're going on a different team than me. Addy's gut's never wrong and she says you'll be as good with knives as you are with guns. If that's the case, I want you well armed with the best." He held out a second sheath. Two hilts emerged from double pockets. "These are the twins. I've got more than a few sets, but these are the best. Custom made to my specs, but they should do."

Do? The man was a loon. She withdrew one knife and immediately noted the differences between them and the first weapon. The blade narrowed on both the sharpened side and the spine, then flared out again, only to curve inward on itself at the end. This weighted the weapon's profile toward the tip. Throwing blades. She swallowed.

"I hope there's no reason to use these," she whispered into the room.

"The fact you say that proves she's right. You know knives."

"Dad met a few people who showed me some stuff along the way," she commented. "Survivalists who did stints here and there, mostly up north."

"You run into anyone who means you or anyone in your group harm, don't hesitate. There's nothing you'll do my woman can't cover if needed. We get that boy home, but we do it sending a lesson. No one messes with The Arsenal."

The weight of his words powered through her. Everyone else was likely already on board with a declaration like that. How many times had she said she needed to send a message to whoever was messing with her? The Arsenal had done exactly that for her. She sheathed the weapon, setting it beside its twin.

"Thank you. I'll return them when we bring him home," she said.

"They're yours. Think about what I said."

She nodded, unsure if she could form more words in her throat. She had a lot to think about.

16

"Stop glaring at my man, or I'll dart your stupid ass," Vi warned over the com. "It's knives, Dallas. Get over it."

"She hasn't stopped messing with them. It's..." Dallas didn't know what the hell it was. "Unsettling."

"It's sweet," Mary said.

"It was uncalled for," he argued as the man currently on the top of his shit list smirked from across the aisle. He was one laugh away from an ass kicking at ten thousand feet.

Dallas looked over at Kamren, who'd sat next to Addy a few moments ago to show off her new knives. If he'd known she wanted new knives, he would've gotten her some. And really, who the fuck gave anyone throwing knives? That was like giving a sniper a...

Fuck.

He was losing it.

"Deep breath, brother," Dylan said from The Arsenal, where he'd remained to protect the facility while all the other team leads had gone wheels up. "This isn't about knives, Jud, or even Kamren, even though I do find your jealous streak amusing."

"Stay out of this."

"Afraid that's a no can do. Get your head on or I'll have to narc you out to Marshall."

"This lead feels different than the others." He gave voice to his biggest fear and rubbed at his chest as the plane began its descent. He peered out the window but saw nothing aside from rugged wilderness. "My kid's out there somewhere. I feel it in my gut. This is it, and I'm fucking terrified."

"We've got this. More importantly, you've got this. I've got a vested interested in bringing your son home. He's my kid's cousin. He's coming home with a huge responsibility to teach my kid shit he shouldn't know."

Dallas couldn't help but chuckle. Dylan and Jesse had used to teach him shit that got him in trouble with their dad every single time. Then the fuckers would feign innocence when he tried to rat them out, which he rarely did. Brothers never snitched on brothers.

"Bring him home, brother," Dylan said.

The com clicked off into wait mode as the plane made its landing on a makeshift runway carved out of the thick forest. Kamren was at his side before he'd gotten the seatbelt unbuckled. She grasped his hand and squeezed until their gazes locked.

"We've got this, Dallas. I won't let you down."

"I never thought you would, sweetheart." He settled his forehead against hers. "Sorry I've been a jealous dick."

"I kind of went a bit gaga, probably too much so." A cute blush rose in her face as she leaned in and whispered, "It's the first gift I've gotten from anyone."

Shock kept him mute because, honestly, that made it worse. He cupped her face and squeezed the ugly emotions rising in him until he'd choked them out. Jud had given Dallas's woman a memory, something that tied her to The Arsenal in a way she'd never forget. She needed more memories like that to burn away the bad ones. He kissed her lips and groaned his frustration.

"If I don't get you in a bed soon, I might combust."

"Please don't. We'd start a forest fire, and those aren't good."

Laughter rolled through him at the seriousness in her voice, but it was her smile that killed the last of his worries. No way in hell the team with him wouldn't find his kid. Failure wasn't an option. Everything they'd studied from HERA's initial findings indicated this area was it. Ground Zero.

Mary and Vi had established contact with Tanner and his crew. The ugly jealousy monster reared its head as Dallas made his way out of the plane. Although Kamren remained at his side, hand in his, a tall, muscular man with close-cropped dark hair closed the distance quickly. Fucker dragged her into a tight hug. A rumble rose from Dallas's throat. When the hug tightened to the point that her tits squished against the man's chest, Dallas contemplated a hundred ways to end the bastard.

"Play nice," Vi said in the com. "Don't kill the guide."

They didn't need a fucking guide. They'd reconned the other areas just fine without Tanner.

Jesus. He needed to get his fucking head on straight. The man was an expert tracker and had done work for a lot of the same agencies The Arsenal worked for. He took in veterans and gave them sanctuary within the wilderness in a non-profit meant to help PTSD survivors. On paper he was a hell of a man, and so were the men he'd employed, one of whom watched the reunion between Tanner and Kamren with amusement.

"Buddy, I'd take a couple steps back before you get your ass handed to you," the man said with a chuckle. "Though I'm thinking he'd whack a piece of you off at the front first. A lot more painful."

Tanner broke contact and glared back at his friend. "Get your ass over here and greet Kam. What's gotten into you?"

"I'm more worried about what's gotten into her. I'm good right here. Thanks." The man waved. "Hey, Kam. Welcome back."

"You're still as crazy as ever, Brace." Kamren tossed her backpack down and ran over to the other guy, who got bonus points for keeping the hug short and loose. His icy blue gaze never left Dallas. Kamren separated quickly and returned to Dallas's side.

"Tanner, Brace, this is Dallas, and his brothers Marshall, Jesse, and Nolan. We've got his other brothers Cord and Dylan on coms, along with Mary and Vi. Over here we have Fallon, Addy, Gage, and Jud." She smiled at everyone. "Tanner and Brace are a couple of the best trackers I've met."

"Except you; never could touch your natural talent," Tanner stated as he crossed his arms and glanced at Dallas. "We've worked some of the same circles as you all. I've heard good things about your operation. Glad to help you out on this. We just went through one of the most thorough briefings I've ever gotten. Your operations team is good."

"Vi and Mary are the best," Dallas said. "So you know the plan."

"Yeah, we went through the details, switched them up a bit. They'd organized two teams of five, but we'll cover more ground split-ting into three," Tanner said. He glanced at Kamren. "Sorry, Kamren. Vi and Mary wanted me to take the lead, but I threw you under the bus and said you'd be better. I'm man enough to admit your better than I'll ever be. They're keeping Dallas on your team. Nolan's on mine and Jesse's with Brace. That'll give us two trackers per team. Addy and Fallon are with Brace. Marshall and Jud are with me and Nolan. Gage is with you and Dallas. Three's a bit short size-wise for the swaths we're running, but with you handling the tracking, Dallas and Gage can handle security and clearance."

Translation—the man trusted Kamren to miss nothing and not require a second set of eyes in a forested area he and Brace likely knew better than her. As if sensing the direction of his thoughts, the man looked at him.

"We got out of the service and decided to start this operation up. My family was connected with a tracker down in Texas. We made some calls. This chick showed up with her dad. I took one look at the two of them and shook my head. No way in hell they knew more than what we'd already learned." Tanner chuckled. "Her dip-shit dad made us do an escape and evade exercise against her. All we had to do was find her."

"How long did it take?" Addy asked with a grin.

"They didn't find me," Kamren answered. She glanced up at Dallas. "Guess it's a small world, huh?"

"Yeah, guess so." Then again, some worlds were small because people remained connected. Spec ops teams were like that. He could see trackers, survivalists and the like being the same way. She likely knew every tracker in the country worth knowing.

"Nightfall's soon. We can crash here, get started in the morning. We brought what gear we had, supplies and the like. I know you all did the same. We'll run an inventory and split stuff up as needed," Brace said. He winked at Kam. "Assuming Kam shares."

"I'll run inventory," Kam offered quickly.

"I'll help," Fallon offered. "I'll make sure our toys get in each set of packs."

Dallas nodded. That'd leave the rest of them to go over the plans a few more times with Tanner and Brace. Clearly Mary, Vi, Cord and Dylan had been busy while they'd been en route.

"Gotta admit I've got a concern with this breakup." Tanner looked around at them all.

"What's that?" Marshall asked.

"The trio team's short a medic," Brace said. "Jessie and Tanner are the only certified ones we've got. I'm a little nervous, too."

"Mary? Vi?"

"We're clear," Mary said.

"We're clear," Vi confirmed.

"We're clear," Dallas repeated for Tanner and Brace.

One by one, everyone from The Arsenal affirmed their belief Mary and Vi could get them through any tight spots. Most of them could handle rudimentary field patches. God knew Dallas had done more than his fair share over the years. They likely all had.

"All right, then let's go over the plan," Nolan said.

"Here," Fallon handed her a small zippered kit that resembled a sunglasses case. "Put one of these in each team's gear pack. We'll make sure we have it all back when we re-board."

Kamren looked at the ordnance expert and gulped the inquiry

perched on her tongue. Did she want to know what he was sneaking into the packs like a ninja? Nope. Nowhere close to wanting to know.

"It's from Rhea, just in case it's needed," Vi said.

"Okay." She dragged out the word because that seriously didn't answer anything, it only added a question to the list.

What serious shit could a biochemical weapons expert concoct to go in a field gear pack? Kamren shoved one in each of the packs she was inventorying. Fallon added C4 and an assortment of other explosive stuff she didn't want to contemplate, much less carry. Things that went boom weren't her thing.

"You're on Brace's crew. Who handles ordnance for the other teams?"

"Jud for Tanner's. Dallas for yours. Or Gage. You're double covered. All three teams are since Jesse and Nolan are qualified, too."

"Okay."

"I'm more worried about traps. You can make them, so you can undo them. I'm not sure about Tanner's crew. Jud could probably do it; any of them could with instruction."

"I taught Tanner," she said. "Dad and I did."

"Your man's strung tight," Fallon said. "Advice?"

Kamren wasn't sure she wanted his advice but nodded anyway. Arguing the point of Dallas being her man was moot. In man land, she was.

"Keep close to Dallas tonight; stay away from Tanner and stow the knives."

She mulled the "advice" over, more than a little aware of the fact the knives were apparently an issue. She hadn't ever assumed they would be. Jud was with Vi. It was a nice gesture, one Vi herself had loved. She let the knife issue go, though. And Tanner? Dallas had no reason to worry in that regard. She and Tanner had ended things somewhat amicably, but the divide was there. He'd wanted her to pick him over family, which proved he'd never truly known her. He'd actually expected her not to return home when her father said he needed help making ends meet.

What kind of daughter would she have been if she'd refused to help her starving family? Tanner hadn't understood, though.

You can't keep living for them, Kamren. Stay. Make us the priority, not them.

But she hadn't been able to do as Tanner asked. There was never any picking someone over blood.

The Arsenal packs were beyond perfection. They knew exactly what to pack as far as she was concerned. They had just about every scenario covered in duplicate while also maintaining a tight, as light as possible pack. It was still damn close to seventy-five pounds for each one, but that was to be expected. No telling how long they'd be out. She had no intention of leaving if she saw even one sign of a kid out there.

She added assorted thicknesses of string and rope to the packs along with snare wires. There was a metric ton of MREs, but in a pinch they'd need to trap food. Flints. There were matches, but they weren't exactly easy to replace after use. Shoelaces. Ponchos. Extra paracord. She grunted as she rifled through her pack. Where the heck were all the zip ties? She added some to each bag.

Grrr.

She powered toward the clustered group and glared at Tanner. "Your packs don't have hatchets."

"Damn it. Sorry, we've got a noob. He must've forgotten to pack them."

"You should've checked. He also forgot shovels and vaseline. We had shovels and vaseline."

"We had vaseline?" Addy asked. "I'm admitting I have no idea, so I'm just gonna ask. What's that for?"

"Ointment," Brace said.

"Fire starter," Kamren added as she turned and headed back to the bags.

Dallas snagged her by the arm and dragged her into a hug. "We're okay with the hatchets, sweetheart."

"I didn't bring any welding kits. I should've thought of that in case we have to cut into a bunker or something."

"I'm thinking Fallon packed enough explosives to blow half the state, so we're covered," Dallas said.

"What if we forgot something and your son needs it? What then?"

"Then Vi, Mary, Cord, and Dylan talk us through a workaround." His voice lowered. "You aren't alone."

"You were a wreck earlier, and now you're calm."

"Because I saw you in there rifling through the packs like a rabid squirrel to make sure we were covered. And because when I got over the nervousness about my kid likely being nearby, I realized this isn't anything we haven't done a hundred times."

"Which makes my worrying about a hatchet pretty stupid," she muttered into his neck.

"No, it makes you smart," Dallas said. "But we'll be fine."

Kamren inhaled his scent and stilled. Scent. Shit. Surely since they'd been on hundreds of missions they knew scent was critical. Some of them smelled so damn good she could track them from a half mile away from that alone. Normally that was a good thing, but not in the woods. Not when the slightest out-of-place scent gave away your location. Out here any smell other than a natural one was foul. Translation? They stunk like city. No way in heck was she telling Dallas, or any of them they stunk. No way in heck.

She imagined someone telling Jud he stunk and snickered into Dallas's neck.

"What's so funny?"

"Nothing," she lied.

"I'm thinking you just lied," he said. "Maybe I should interrogate you."

Kamren squealed and shoved away when he started tickling her sides, but he held her firmly in place. She bucked and kicked but couldn't get away. "Dallas, no!"

Instead of stopping, he carried it one step further—by hoisting her up and carting her toward a thatch of trees a ways away. Oh no. He was not going to take her away where everyone knew he was going to...

She froze as anticipation fired through her system. What *was* he going to do? "Dallas?"

He set her down a few feet into the wooded area. For the most part they were still in the lower plains leading to the rugged wilderness they'd be searching, which meant there were far fewer trees at this point. Pleasure ignited within her as he claimed her mouth. The kiss was slow and all-consuming as the impact drifted within her, a sensuous curling of awareness after a long numbing sleep.

He taunted, toyed, and tantalized with his tongue as it swept, flicked and laved her mouth, neck, and downward. Confident hands wandered beneath her shirt and stroked upward in a slow, patient glide that left her growling and grabbing at him. The timing was horrible—they were about to head into rugged wilderness for no telling how long—but Kamren couldn't deny the connection between them.

He sat on a downed log and dragged her forward until she straddled his lap. She cupped his face and claimed his mouth as she ground against him, letting him know she didn't want to stop. She needed way more than a few languid kisses to fuel the inferno within her. A groan escaped him as he yanked off her shirt and held up his hands with a grin as she did the same to him.

"Erm, guys?" Kamren froze at the voice in her ear. "Yeah, erm. Mics. Off. Please?"

"Sorry, Zoey." Dallas yanked the small bud from his ear and pushed something on it. He repeated the process with hers. "Sorry, Kamren, I should've remembered they were in."

She didn't let herself think about who had heard what they'd been doing. Thank God she hadn't said much, if anything. "I need you, Dallas."

"My first time inside you isn't going to be in the woods," Dallas whispered against her skin as he trailed kisses down her neck. He dragged her into him as he removed her bra. "But we can sure as hell make you come."

Her toes curled in her boots as heat suffused her nipples. Awareness arced through her in a surge of heated tingles arrowing downward to where she ground herself against the prominent bulge in his pants. Sex hadn't ever been a driving focus in her life, which was probably why she'd never had a long-term relationship. Her few months with Tanner were the extent of her experience in the keeping-a-man endeavor, and that'd failed miserably.

She didn't want to screw things up with Dallas. She swallowed the thought as he severed contact with her nipple and dragged her face downward until their lips merged. It wasn't a merging as much as it was her melting into him. He rolled both her nipples between his fingers and looked up at her when the kiss broke.

"Gorgeous," he whispered. "I can't wait to spread you out on my bed and feast on you for hours."

Her pussy clenched as his words activated her imagination, but it was the way he stroked down her belly as he maintained eye contact that made her pulse pound. He undid the button on her cargo pants. She swallowed, leaned down and kissed him. But he kept his eyes open, watching her from so close it felt as though they'd crawled inside one another and set up camp.

"Dallas," she whispered against his mouth as he undid her zipper and dipped his hand inside.

A moan escaped her as he cupped her sex and glided deft fingers against her slick entrance. She cut off his appreciative groan with a kiss as he thrust two fingers inside her. He nipped her lower lip and shifted focus to her clit. She cried out against his mouth and sank her nails into his back and shoulders as she rode his hand.

Dallas was lethal to the senses.

"Come for me, Kamren." The gruff voice pushed her closer to the edge as her entire body trembled with the need for release. "Look at me. I want to see your face when you come on my hand. Pretend it's my cock."

Kamren complied but ran her hand between them and reached for his pants.

"Don't. This is about you," he said.

"That's not fair," she quipped, her voice breathless as he rolled his thumb across her clit again. Any semblance of thought died beneath the onslaught of sensations as she exploded. There was no other way to explain the strength with which her orgasm struck. As she rode the dregs of pleasure, she looked down into Dallas's eyes and knew he'd taken root deep inside her.

She hadn't even noticed his presence until just now, but he'd settled in at some point. In a way she knew she'd never recover if he decided to pull up stakes and vacate her life. Her heart thudded wildly in her chest when he brought his fingers up to his mouth and licked her arousal from them. The act, her watching, their eyes locked...her entire body trembled beneath the weight of awareness encasing them.

"You're beautiful when you come, Kamren."

She stroked his face and leaned down until their foreheads pressed together. "I can't wait to be under you, in your bed, feel you buried deep inside me. But before that I'm gonna take you deep my mouth, taste your arousal as I look up into your eyes. I want to watch you come for me, Dallas."

"Fuck, sweetheart. I'm harder than a spike as it is."

"Then let me."

"No, not here. You deserve more than a wilderness romp, and there's no way in hell I'd stop if I got your mouth around my dick."

There was no way she'd stop either. She sighed her contentment as he closed her pants. Together they redressed and cleaned up with some of the disposable wipes she had in her cargo pants.

"You would've made an excellent Boy Scout, you're prepared for anything." Admiration reflected in his voice, a confidence in her abilities he'd demonstrated by letting her divvy up supplies earlier and not having anyone double-check her work. And he'd wanted her out here helping find his child.

He trusted her to help.

"I'm leaving nothing to chance. We're not leaving until we find your son."

"YOU SHOULD BE ASLEEP." The voice on the com startled Kamren a moment. She blinked and looked around. None of the Arsenal crew stirred. Had they not heard Vi's voice?

"It's just us. You, me, Vi, and Mary," Zoey said. "They think you're stewing on something."

"How would you know that?"

"The drones," Mary answered. "You kept pacing earlier, after everyone ate and settled down. Our teams are the best around because we don't ever keep things to ourselves. Whatever you're stewing on, spit it out."

"Is it about Tanner?" Zoey asked. "He's really hot."

"No. It's not about Tanner." She slid from Dallas's embrace and took a moment to check on him. She was surprised he hadn't stirred.

Jud and Sanderson were taking the first shift of security, along with the drones. She'd heard them work out the schedule amongst themselves earlier. No one had tried to work Tanner or Brace into them. Though she understood, it didn't bode well for them trusting the two men.

"They don't trust Tanner and Brace," she said.

"No. We don't know them, but we trust your judgment. If you say they're good enough to lead our men through this, then that's good enough for us," Vi said. "But that doesn't mean Dallas's brothers and the other men are going to be welcoming Tanner and Brace into the group. They're unknowns, one of which clearly had a close relationship with you. They won't accept those two until Dallas does because they've got his back."

"There's no reason to have his back," she argued.

"Given the things Dallas and Dylan went through, there's reason, but I doubt that's what's keeping you up," Mary said.

"It's stupid, and I..." She took a deep breath. "I can't keep obsessing over it. It won't matter anyway." Probably.

"What?" Mary repeated, her tone still patient. Calm.

"Everyone smells. Soap. Cologne. Man." She swallowed. "Scent carries a long way out here. One whiff of them and our location may as well be a bullseye with flashing neon arrows. I could track them from a mile out, if not more, on that alone." And really, what was she doing spewing all that? The women had led tons of operations. They likely knew more of this stuff than she did.

"Okay, that wasn't what I expected," Vi said, amusement evident. "So, to clarify. You can't sleep because my man and the others smell?"

"I didn't say that," she said quickly.

"Yeah, you kinda did." Zoey snickered. "Oh, please, please, please let me be the one to tell Sanderson he smells. Holy. Shit. I love this job."

God. This wasn't going to go well.

"Kamren, take a deep breath. Your pulse is through the roof," Mary said.

Kamren glanced down at the damned wrist thing Dallas had put on her earlier in the evening. She'd forgotten the women could monitor her vitals now. How embarrassing. "Sorry, I shouldn't have said anything. You all had it covered, didn't you?"

"Honestly, no." Vi paused a moment. "We've searched a lot of grids for Dallas's son the past few months, and it's easy to forget the setting isn't our typical op. With all the scents in a forest and wilderness environment, I have to admit I didn't think they'd stand out, but now that you say it, it seems extremely obvious."

"And hysterical," Zoey said as she continued her laughing fit. "Oh, God. We can't say anything until the drones are in place. Hold on, I'll get them in position, then you can wake everyone."

Wake everyone? Wait. "No. Let them sleep. We've got a long trek ahead of us."

"Yeah, in less than a few hours. They need to handle this while they're up on their security detail, which means we have to tell Sanderson and Jud at the bare minimum," Mary said. "Unless you want to."

"I'm not telling them that shit," Kamren shook her head and swallowed. "I really wish you'd forget about it."

"No way in hell," Vi said. "Thank you. Thank you for having my man's back out there. Now get some rest. We'll handle the stink issue."

"I put some wipes and bars of hunter soap in the packs. You know, just in case," Kamren supplied.

"Thank you," Mary added. "Rest. We've got your six. You aren't alone."

And she wasn't. She peered out into the inky night, then settled back into position beside Dallas. Tomorrow they'd set out, and she wouldn't stop until they found his son. He was out there. Somewhere.

17

"You've got a hell of a woman," Jud commented. "Mine took a certain amount of pleasure informing me and Sanderson we all smell, and Kamren was too worried about us smelling up the woods to sleep."

The man slammed a small bar of soap and a pack of wipes against his chest. "Creek's a quarter click east, colder than hell. Thinking you could use it."

Fucker. Dallas gritted his teeth and ignored the blood surging southward when he thought about Kamren's sweet body against his when he'd woken moments ago. Darkness sealed the area off like a tomb. He glanced back at where she still slept. She'd stretched closer to Jesse's sleeping bag, likely seeking the natural heat of another body in her sleep.

"She should've woken me, told me."

"Thinking she didn't want to tell her new man he stinks like city." Jud smirked. "Gotta admit, it hadn't occurred to me. Figured a little civilian soap wouldn't hurt."

"Can't be too careful," Dallas muttered as the revolting stench radiating from the small bar entered his nostrils. Pride rose in his chest, but it was shoved aside by another far deeper emotion, one he didn't want to think about. She'd been deep in her head worrying about every little detail to find his kid. He glanced down at the foul stuff in his hands. "She bring this?"

"Yep. Smells like deer piss or something else I'd rather not think about." Jud glanced at the campsite. "You cool with Tanner?"

"Yeah." He hadn't been at first, but she'd yet to approach the man who'd once had her. Fucker was an idiot for letting her go.

"Should've cleared the knives with you first, man." The man's voice was low but edged with sincerity.

"Made too much out of it." Dallas looked the operative in the eyes and gave him something in return. "Said it was the first gift she'd ever gotten. That hit hard. You're a hell of a man to give her that."

"Fuck."

"When this is over, I'd appreciate you showing her how to use them. With the shit that surfaces around us, can't hurt for her to know whatever she can."

"I'm thinking she could teach us a few things," Jud said with a grin as he crossed his arms. "Consider it done."

Dallas looked down at the second bar and set of wipes with a raised eyebrow. Jud's grin returned, along with a wicked gleam he'd started to recognize, one that'd appeared thanks to Vi. The woman had unearthed the man beneath the lethal machine created by The Collective.

"Figured you could inform Tanner of his issue."

Dallas chuckled. Fuck, but he loved his team.

He found the bastard skulking not too far from where Kamren slept. A pot of coffee was brewing on the campfire. He motioned the man toward the wilderness, and like the trusting dumb fuck he was, he followed without comment. In another lifetime, Dallas would've relished handling the situation a little differently. Bullet to the brain. Knife to the throat. The possibilities listed in his mind, and he was sorely tempted to use one as he halted not too far away.

A drone followed.

Fucking Vi and Mary. They hadn't said anything through the

com, but they were silent witnesses. The conscience he'd gladly set aside for Kamren without hesitation.

"Problem?" Tanner asked, a smug smirk on his face.

"A few." Dallas clipped the words as he shoved the soap and wipes at him. "Clean the smells off before we head out."

"Kamren always thinks of the little things," Tanner said, his voice fucking reverent.

"That's problem two." Dallas waited until the man's gaze locked with his. "Want to make sure you hear this loud and clear. Back the fuck off."

"Come again?"

"Kamren isn't yours. I won't have her hurt because she's helping me find my kid."

The man crossed his arms, looking back at where they'd left everyone else. "For the record, I fucked up. I made her choose between me and her family, demanding she stay with me rather than go home when her dad said he needed help. I tried to keep her away from the shit at home."

Dallas had to admit he would've likely tried to do the same thing —keep her away, especially if he hadn't ever been in Marville and seen firsthand how folks there grew up. Family came first, no matter what. It was the same upbringing he'd been raised with.

Except his family hadn't used fists and left scars. The guy hadn't made the right decision, but he'd tried to keep her safe, which stifled a lot of Dallas's distrust and dislike for the man. He'd tried to keep her safe.

"It sounds like you did what you could. I'm not sure what I would've done if it'd been me back then. I have to admit things are different now with him gone."

"Maybe so, but a lot of what went wrong was on me. I was young and dumb. I wasn't prepared to fight to a relationship, to give her the time she needed to experience a normal life. I wasn't the man she needed to be the woman she could be. I made her choose because I didn't understand what else I could have done."

"Strong woman like that doesn't want a man fighting her battles. She doesn't need a hero."

"I saw enough, toward the end. She was good at hiding the evidence. He was a mean son of a bitch," Tanner said. "Getting between her and family was the wrong play."

Truth told, Dallas wasn't sure how he would've played it if her father was still alive.

"Woman like that, strong and brilliant, deserves a man who stands at her side. Saw that with my brother. Fucking hardest thing he's ever done was stand back and let her fight her own battle. Had no fucking clue the balls it took for him to do that when it went down. Now I know."

An intake of breath on the other end of the com was the only indication Dallas had that he and Tanner were not alone. Didn't matter. "Balls of steel to let the woman you love look her nightmare in the eye and kick its ass. Learned that from the women on the coms. I thank whatever twisted fate brought them to us, because I learned from watching their men how to pull my head out of my ass and be the man Kamren needs, not the one I think she should have. I'm sorry you didn't get to have that insight when you were with Kamren."

"Even if it meant she stayed with me?"

"If she stayed with you, she likely would've had a good life. A happy one. That's what matters."

Tanner was quiet longer than Dallas expected, likely replaying all the ways he'd screwed up. "You're in deeper than I ever was. The woman I knew never would've crashed, damn near comatose. You and your crew are bringing out the woman I fought to find. You hurt her, and I'll bury you in these woods."

Fair enough.

Dallas watched the man leave, then he went to the creek and scrubbed the city stink off for his woman. He'd just arrived at the creek when a low voice on the com dragged him to a halt.

"A man like you at her back, there's not a nightmare in existence Kamren won't kick in the balls," Vi said.

"Love you, Dallas." Mary's voice was cracked at the end.

His gut twisted as he heard the emotion through the com from the woman who was ice cold precision during a mission, no matter what went down. Pregnancy had loosened the reins on her emotions. Dallas couldn't wait to welcome his niece or nephew into the world. The kid had a hell of a mom and dad.

"Love you, too," he replied. "Fucking thrilled he has you. Fucking thrilled we all have you both. Now get that drone away from me so I can scrub the city stink off."

THEY HAULED ass as a group for a full day and camped east of where the trail they'd used ended. Kamren had been impressed with how fast the large group moved. The Arsenal folks were in excellent condition and clearly used to rougher terrain.

Which was good since the area was a rugged span of millions of wilderness acreage interspersed with plains, forest, and mountains at the south end of Yellowstone where the Teton Wilderness yawned on until eventually ceding its swath of existence to the Washakie Wilderness and the Shoshone Forest. Their search grid was massive, to say the least.

Mary and Vi had established zones based on the recent dump of scans they'd obtained from somewhere. Based on their conversations, Kamren didn't want to know where the women had procured the resources to scan whatever landscape they chose. All that mattered was they had target zones.

They'd opted to use a drop point that was farther away than actually necessary. They could've shaved a day off had they dropped nearer the target zones, but the element of surprise was important. Planes made noise, and Kamren had been okay with not jumping from a perfectly functional plane for a LALO (which she found out was a "low altitude, low opening jump"). No thank you. She'd haul ass for an extra day.

Since each group had gone their separate way mid-morning, she,

Gage, and Dallas had fallen into a routine of their own. Gage remained at her left, Dallas to her right. Though they let her remain in lead position between them, neither of the men's attention ever diverted from patrolling their perimeter as the sagebrush along the open plain gave way to lodgepole and white bark pine, spruce, and fir trees.

Mule deer and elk darted in the distance, as if sensing the growing tension within their small group as they headed deeper into the remote region. No one had mentioned the possibility of losing coms, but she suspected Mary and Vi had that covered since they'd been more than a few steps ahead of them the entire way so far.

Stopping hadn't been on the itinerary. Hard paces gave way to slower trudges on occasion, but conversation wasn't ever necessary since they let her set the pace. Sound carried farther out here, where man was often at the mercy of the terrain, the sheer wildness of the world humanity hadn't fully tamed.

A distance of half a day's hard haul would separate the groups from each other by day's end. Kamren studied the changing land-scape as she headed deeper in the forested area. So far, they'd seen no sign of humanity aside from hikers and campers, which had been yesterday. They were well into the bowels of the wild now.

They'd gone another two hours before she caught the first glimpse of something abnormal. Bones. Carcasses in assorted states of decomposition. She squatted, withdrew the survival knife Jud had given her, and inspected the newest kill. Maggots and critters crawled within the foul stench. She breathed through her mouth, which left a vile taste on her tongue when she swallowed.

"Human kill, a couple days ago," she said into the com. She let the adrenaline spike within her bloodstream before she shared her suspicions. "They played with it first."

"How?" Dallas asked.

Kamren pointed at what had once been a baby deer. No self-respecting hunter would take down a fawn, much less one this young. Disgust rolled through her. "Baby deer, all four legs are broken.

Skinned along its haunches. Judging by the large pool of blood, it was still alive."

"They stabbed to kill after they were done playing," Gage commented as he crouched beside her and Dallas and motioned to the binoculars he held. "There are a few more to the west."

"A killing ground, likely squatters." Kamren stood. "Unpredictable."

"Erm, what's the different between a squatter and a hunter or a survivalist or whatever?" Zoey asked.

"Survivalists live off the land, taking only what they need. Preppers stock for the end of days, or whatever disaster they fear the most. They hoard resources, the more the better. Hunters kill for the thrill, but typically adhere to rules and clean their kills, then use the meat, or give it away."

"And squatters?" Zoey asked.

"They ravage the land, take what they want, and don't give a damn about the ecosystem around them." Her stomach soured when they continued forward, and she inspected the swath of death carved out in the landscape. "This is a pack."

"How can you tell?" Gage asked.

"Kills are different—some hesitant, others confident and brutal. This is fun and sport for them." She looked around. "They're trapping the animals elsewhere, then bringing them here." She motioned to the remnants of fires around them. "Been here a while. They'll be back."

"They aren't who we're looking for," Vi surmised.

"No, but they may have seen others. They're often paranoid assholes who'd either prey on more innocent folks that they run across or they'd steer clear of a bigger opponent." Her stomach turned. "Doing nothing about these bastards isn't an option."

"No, it's not," Dallas said. "Gotta ask, sweetheart. How do you know so much about guys like this?"

"Been raised wilder than civilized most of my life. Dad worked for guys like this some seasons when things were lean; any money was good money." She didn't offer more. Likely he and everyone else listening on the com could fill in the holes.

"That before, after, or during your stint here with Tanner?" Dallas asked.

"Before mostly, though some during," she answered honestly.

"Jesus, there's damn near twenty kills within my visual range. How big of a group are we dealing with?" Gage asked.

"Surprised they didn't leave someone there," Vi said on the com.

"They're cocky. With nothing left to protect, they'd all rather enjoy the hunt, come back, play and kill. Then do it again tomorrow." She peeked up at the sky. "They'll be back soon. Night will fall in a few hours."

"So we wait," Gage said.

"And prep our own little surprise." She shouldered off her backpack and looked at Dallas as he grinned at her.

"Tell us what to do, sweetheart."

BY THE TIME NIGHT FELL, they'd set enough traps to down a small army. Dallas grinned as Kamren tied off the last snare and stood. She'd been amazing. He could almost hear the thoughts radiating from her as she inventoried her environment for weapons for her traps. Bits of bone had been scavenged from the older kills. Rocks, sticks and other jagged debris had been accumulated. Her instructions had been quick, concise and focused.

He and Gage had spent the past couple hours digging holes, filling them with more revolting shit than he'd rather remember, and watching her construct something within the tops of the trees above them. Mary and Vi had shown her how to use the drones to position the massive snare she'd constructed from paracord and rope.

"Everything's ready. Now we wait," she whispered as she settled on her belly behind the blind of foliage and small branches he and Gage had constructed. She admired their handiwork a moment, nodded and added, "Good job."

"We learned a thing or two about blinds thanks to you," Gage said with a grin.

Silence descended as they waited. Sound was the ultimate determinant in landscapes such as this. Unchecked, it echoed a warning great distances. Their quarry didn't bother to remain quiet as they made their way to their playground. Dallas's pulse quickened as he noted eight heat signatures within the headgear, a larger group than he'd expected.

"Let's refrain from lethal," Mary requested.

"I make no promises," Kamren said.

Dallas chuckled. "I'm liking her blood-thirsty streak."

"Oh boy, this isn't going to go well for those assholes," Zoey said.

She wasn't wrong. The first idiot stumbled on a trip wire and into the target zone and tumbled forward. His head struck the large rock Kamren had them roll into position.

"Jim? Jim?" Voices rose as the men ran to their downed comrade. Another stumbled and landed in the same unconscious position.

"What the fuck?" One of the men looked around. "Someone's here."

"Well, isn't he the brilliant one," Vi quipped. "Want the drones to handle this?"

"No," Kamren answered quickly. "These guys get off on playing. I think it's time we make them the prey."

Before Dallas could stop her, she rose from her position behind the perch and sauntered out. There was no other description for the sultry way she moved her hips and thrust her chest out. She demanded their attention, and she got it quickly.

"Well, looks like we have a visitor, boys." The man looked around. "I'm Billy. You lost? We might help, if you're nice to us."

Dallas growled, but Gage grabbed his arm and shook his head. Right. They'd wait and let her do whatever the fuck she thought she was doing.

"You boys like to play," she commented as she angled back a couple steps. Her right foot bypassed a snare without pause.

The men took menacing steps forward. Another landed in a trap dug into the ground, much like the pit Bubba's grandson had fallen into, but shallower.

"Get your ass over here. What'd you do to our camp?" Billy asked.

"You want me?" Kamren asked. "Come get me."

The taunt sent the five remaining men forward in a loud burst of movement and battle cries.

"Jesus, they're pathetic," Mary commented. "Drones are in position, Kam. Let us know if you need them. Cord's ready."

Dallas and Gage rose from their hiding spots and engaged two of the biggest combatants, which left three chasing after Kamren as she wound herself through the maze of snares with rabbit-quick reflexes. With a grin, she jumped onto a large rock and sat, knives in hand.

One more fell, slamming forward into the rock she sat atop. She glanced down at him as he crumbled to the ground, then reached over and yanked a rope. The large net she'd constructed ripped from its hiding hole beneath the foliage and entombed the two remaining men in the final trap. Their cries of rage and shock echoed within the area as they were hoisted upward.

"Now," she said into the coms.

Drones flitted about and wound cord around their ankles. The netting fell to the ground as they fell a few feet down, then snapped to a stop as the hoist from a rope hung between two of the largest trees held them in place. Dallas moved quickly and, with Gage's help, gathered all the weapons they found on the men. He left zip-tying them to Gage and dropped all the weapons near where Kamren now sat on the ground.

She looked up at the two hanging men and began unknotting the paracord net she'd made.

"Bitch! Let us down or you'll be sorry."

Dallas snagged the KA-BAR from its sheath on his thigh, hauled the man up by his mangy hair and pressed the tip against his jugular. "Call my woman a bitch again and I'll give her a lesson in how to skin a human. She's been wanting to learn."

"Aww," Kamren said. She set the unwound cording down. "You're so sweet to me, babe. You know what I really want, though?"

Her eyes were wide, her voice pitched shrill-high and loud with excitement. Dallas chuckled as Gage approached, an amused grin on his face.

"I'll give you the world if you only ask, sweetheart," he said dramatically. "You want a trophy from your hunt? We'll carve something off. I bet they've got something small enough to turn into a necklace. You want one, sweetheart?"

She kinked her nose up and shook her head, sighing loudly. "They smell bad."

"We'll burn 'em then," Gage said as he kicked some sticks beneath the two men. "I'll get some tinder."

"What the fuck?!" one of the men shouted.

Kamren drew out her knife and scraped it through the ground at her feet in a wide circle. "I'm gonna be honest with you, Billy. See, we're out here hunting, same as you. Thing is, our prey's a bit smarter than your kills. Way smarter than *you*."

The two men wiggled like worms on a fishing line. Dallas dropped Billy's companion.

"I figure you all have been out here rounding up your toys and having your sport with poor, defenseless babies because you aren't men enough to take on real prey." She shrugged. "That's kinda sad. But you're just a sad sack of shit, aren't you, Billy?"

"I ain't got no beef with you," he said.

"See, you do. Cause I don't take too kindly to idiots like you wrecking an ecosystem for fun." She stabbed the knife into the ground mere inches from his face. "So here's what's gonna happen. My man and a buddy of his are real good at skinning anything. I'm thinking there're two of them, two of you. And I really wanna learn."

They wiggled harder. One pissed his pants.

"Jesus. They always piss their pants," Gage muttered. "Remember? The last one did that, too."

Dallas chuckled. "That's only the start of our fun, though."

"True," Kamren said. She crouched down. "Here's what you're gonna do for us, Billy. You're gonna tell us all about what you've seen out here. Every little detail. When, where, who, how many. *Everything.*"

"We ain't seen nothing!" The other man's voice hiked up. "Let me go!"

"You're a smart man, Billy. This is a good trade. Your life for info on assholes you don't give a shit about. Give us what we need, and we'll cut you down." She shook her head. "Keep quiet, and I'll be forced to get mean."

"You're crazy!"

"Probably," she admitted. "But I know how to draw every grizzly in these parts here. You two would make fun toys."

"Okay, okay. We've seen lots of folks. There's a trail a couple days from here."

"Don't fuck with me, Billy. The crew we're hunting has hunkered in; they're mean and nasty. The sort of asshole you steer clear of 'cause you ain't got the balls to play in their yard."

"Past where the Thorofare spills into the Yellowstone River."

"Use Bridger Lake as a landmark," Mary said.

"Starting point is the campground at Bridger Lake. Where from there?" Dallas asked.

"East. East of Bridger," the other man said. "You don't want to mess with them."

"Why not?" Gage asked.

"They're crazy."

The answer said a lot since both the men strung up were nuts. Dallas grunted as he cut them both down and nodded for Gage to secure them.

"We'll notify someone to come and collect the trash," Vi said. "Sending coordinates for everyone to converge near your current location."

"And if his intel is bullshit?" Kamren asked.

"Then we go back to the initial plan, but the area is within your search grid," Mary said.

Kamren glanced at Dallas. He understood the look on her face without her saying anything more because his mind was already there. "No convergence. We'll proceed to the coordinates and scout the area, then we can converge if needed."

"Agreed," Nolan said via the com.

"Agreed," Jesse said.

"Okay. Marking a route for you, most direct path," Vi said.

Dallas clicked the com to standby and got to work helping Gage and Kamren clear the traps and repack supplies.

"You can't leave us," Billy screamed.

"Someone will haul you out when they have time. Until then you can hang there, wondering if the grizzlies will get you first." Kamren shrugged on her backpack. "Guess it's not as much fun in your playground when you're the prey."

Dallas chuckled as she turned and headed out like they hadn't just left eight men-zip tied in the wilderness. Gage shook his head. "Your woman's a handful."

Yeah, she was, and he couldn't wait to get her home.

With his son.

"We're close," he said into the com.

"We're close," Mary confirmed.

"It's a larger group than expected," Vi said. "The other two teams are en route, but it'll take a while and they're breaking down their encampment."

Kamren heard the information and ignored the clutch in her gut. She'd suspected as much based on the movement within the encampment and makeshift lean-tos at the edge of where the plains gave way to an outcropping of new tree growth. They'd counted eleven structures, but there was no sign of a bunker. They hadn't been hunkered down, simply on the move. Structures were in assorted stages of being broken down.

They were leaving the area, which meant she, Dallas, and Gage couldn't wait for backup. They had to somehow slow them down.

"We have a plan," Mary said. "Or the start of one."

"Read us in," Dallas said. "Any signs of my kid in that mess?"

"Not yet, but that's part of the plan."

"Go on."

"The small case of vials Fallon had packed in the gear is a new drug Rhea created. It should knock them out and suck away the memories right before they fall asleep. That'd give us time to search for your son and for the teams to arrive." Mary paused. "A hard entry could jeopardize him if he's in there. They're too spread out for drones to act efficiently."

"So how do we get the compound dispensed?" Gage asked.

"I go in," Kamren replied, somehow knowing that was the best answer.

"Yeah, that's the part we've been discussing," Vi said. "Or arguing, rather."

"No way," Dallas said, his tone rough and his voice lethal in its evenness. Kamren reached out and squeezed his shoulder. "Use the drones, knock their asses out that way. Hell, kill them all for all I care."

"Drones can't get the bad guys all in one swoop because of the layout of the encampment. You two are good, Dallas and Gage, but there are over twenty-five armed combatants spread out down there, maybe more. We considered sending you two in as an option and nixed it as viable. The pockets within the lean-tos are sporadic at best. There's no clear line of sight for them all, which means no matter the entry, there's too much time."

Time for someone to get to Dallas's son and kill him.

"Dallas, let's at least talk it through. I know I'm not trained, but I learn quick. All I need is a plan."

"We need to stall them. The compound would do that if we dosed everyone. Then you and Gage could go in, Dallas." Mary's voice was firm and even, and bolstered Kamren with confidence. She could do this.

Kamren studied the images the drones had obtained. The lean-tos were sporadically placed, entries and egresses spread throughout a complicated maze. Too much of the interior was unknown, which meant too many foreseeable problems. Two men versus twenty-five? She knew the two men were good, but that wasn't good odds.

"How long til the other teams arrive?" Kamren asked.

"Half a day at their current speeds, which is way faster than is safe," Vi answered.

"And we know the assholes inside are who we're after?" Gage asked.

"Facial recognition has identified five with the encampment as Collective so far. So, yes. We haven't gotten clear shots of the others. We've counted twenty-five, but there could be more within the structure," Vi said.

"And how is sending an untrained woman into an encampment full of men a better play than sending Dallas and me in?" Gage asked.

"Because she's not an obvious threat," Mary answered.

"Fuck." Dallas ran his hands through his hair. "I'll go."

"No," Mary said. "They'd shoot you and Gage immediately. You're a threat no matter how much you feign otherwise."

"They'll hurt her," Dallas growled. "We wait it out. A group that big, they'll move slower than us. The teams will catch up; we'll give chase."

"You're okay with waiting," Vi said.

"I've waited months to get my kid; I'm not gonna turn impatient and be stupid now. And I'm sure as hell not sending Kamren in like a sacrificial lamb to buy time." Dallas's face turned red. "We wait."

18

Kamren's heart thudded wildly in her chest as she feigned discomfort because of the massive backpack she half carried, half dragged behind her. Though her gaze remained a couple feet before her, she knew where every target was based on the last scan of the encampment.

Addy trudged beside her. Her hair was muddy and matted, her eye blackened from the punch she'd taken somewhere en route after the tentative plan formed. The woman was certifiable, and Kamren wasn't sure who she'd convinced to punch her in the first place. The effect was perfection, though. The damaged area already showed signs of healing, thus lending a bit of credibility to their story.

Talk about effective results. A few tears of their clothing and they were the poster women of dick boyfriends who'd abandoned them in the middle of nowhere. Kamren had even taken the story further and emptied one of the packs, used what they could in the way of extras like blankets and stupid shit city women would try and pack. All weapons were left with the men, except for the knives Kamren had and a small pistol Addy had tucked away at the small of her back.

Although Dallas and Gage had been dead set against the plan, Vi,

Mary, and everyone else backed it. She trusted Dallas, Gage, and the rest of the men, who were all in position around the encampment.

Going in hot—whatever that was—would risk Dallas's son if he was in there. All she and Addy had to do was give the small cameras mounted to their shirts as buttons a visual inspection of as much of the interior as possible.

They got bonus points if they found a way to dispatch the compound they each had tucked away in a pocket of their shorts. Shorts. Addy had two pairs for some reason. The woman was brilliant to have brought them, though. They fit the cover story perfectly.

She waited until she was within shouting distance of the encampment and stumbled to her knees with a plaintive cry. "Help!"

Addy followed suit.

Like vultures on a dead carcass, the men converged on them. Hands hauled them both up. Kamren slammed against a man with a beer-belly and a small splotch of red hair atop his otherwise bald head. "You okay, honey?"

"No," Addy whined. "My—" Tears shimmered from her eyes and swept down her bruised face.

Jesus, the woman was *good*.

"Easy now. Come on and have a seat. Tell Gomer all about it."

Gomer? Seriously?

Addy feigned sniffles as she blotted at her eyes. "My boyfriend, he ditched me, said I wasn't worth hauling around any longer. And her man..."

Kamren hid her face and shook her shoulders as she forced tears to her eyes. "They wanted us to swap, then do each other, and I said no. Then Addy's man punched her and they kicked us out of camp."

There'd been a heated discussion about the merits of a sex-based story. It brought out the men's baser instincts, made them think with the wrong brain. But it also sexualized her and Addy, which presented a risk within itself. But Addy had assured them all she could handle any fallout if that happened. Surprisingly, none of them argued beyond that.

"You poor girls." Gomer rubbed Kamren's shoulders. "You're safe now."

She looked around at the men gathered around them. No kid. "I can't believe we actually found someone. We wandered forever."

"You don't look like the hiking kinda girls. Your men never should've brought you out this far. It's not safe," one of the men said.

"Yeah, well. We were stupid, thought it'd be fun." Kamren sniffled as she looked around and spotted the large vat of beans simmering on the stove. "I-I'm so hungry."

She recalled the shame of being hungry the first time at The Arsenal until heat filled her cheeks. Her stomach rumbled on command, by sheer luck or determination. "I'm sorry; forget I said anything."

"Nonsense," Gomer said. "Come on, we'll get you two settled."

Kamren's stomach churned for an entirely different reason as the group escorted her and Addy into the encampment. They wound through narrow corridors constructed with wood, thick burlap-like material. The twisty route spilled into a large common area with a small area open up top, like a rudimentary teepee.

A small cooking area was along the far "wall" of the common room. She kept her gaze cast downward and took comfort in the fact Addy appeared calm and at ease despite the fact all the men were clustering around them.

The plan was working.

Moths to a flame. We're the moths.

Addy's words from earlier echoed in her brain and served as a reminder to play the part of a terrified woman. That was pretty simple since she *was* a terrified woman.

"Get the girls a couple bowls. We were about to eat anyway," Gomer ordered.

Kamren smiled and ignored the lecherous hand rubbing her knee. Gomer's gaze swept down her exposed legs. "How long were you with your man, honey? He do that to you?"

She glanced down at the scars going up and down her legs. "I can be stubborn."

"You don't worry none. Gomer's gonna take good care of you both." Gomer referring to himself in the third person was way creepy. Revulsion shuddered through Kamren, but she remained silent as she accepted a steaming bowl of beans. A meat of some sort was mixed in with it.

Addy had the tear thing down, so Kamren would handle the rest. She plowed through the bowl, shoveling spoonfuls of the beans and deer meat into her mouth, barely taking time to chew before she swallowed. She maintained eye contact with Gomer and his goons the whole time, measuring the effectiveness of her mock starvation.

She burped real big, which made the men laugh. Some turned their lecherous attention from Addy to her. She eyed Gomer hopefully as she shifted closer to the vat of beans. "May I have a little more, please?"

The plaintive request sliced through the room.

"Just a little more, honey. I don't want you to get sick." Gomer motioned toward the dish. "Help yourself. We don't starve our women."

"Thank you," she whispered.

Making her way slowly to the food, she palmed the mysterious compound she'd kept tucked away by wiping her face with her torn shirt. She feigned shyness and huddled her body over the vat of beans as she filled a ladle, then dumped the compound vial into the beans and stirred. She turned, set her bowl down. "Can I get you some? I hate eating alone, and I feel bad taking your food."

"That'd be mighty fine, honey."

Addy was still eating her bowl and watched as man after man lined up to get a bowl and a smile from Kamren. She sat after the last dish was taken. Thirty-two men, way more than twenty-five.

"Anyone else?" she asked.

"No, honey. Not anymore." Gomer's grim statement thundered through the area.

"Rhea, you wanna fill us in on what that shit does?" Dallas asked.

"Um, wow. Okay. So she dosed them all. Didn't expect that to actually work." The woman appeared flustered but recovered quickly.

"They'll get drowsy, but it's a bit like truth serum. I'll skip the science 'cause Vi and Mary are glaring at me. They'll talk. So ask questions."

That she could do.

"Not anymore?" Kamren swallowed a spoon of beans as she reached out and squeezed Gomer's knee. "I'm sorry. You seem sad."

"Not sad, honey. Just pissed. A woman I cared about very much died. I'm sort of lost without her."

"Bingo," Mary said.

"That sucks," Addy said. "My brother got killed not too long ago. Fucking guts you."

"Yeah."

"Sweet setup here," Addy commented. "Looks like we almost missed you. You heading home?"

"No, that's not an option," one of them said. "Can't get found, or we get dead."

Kamren ate a piece of meat. "This meat is good. What is it?"

"Deer?"

"Wow. You..." She forced a pause for effect. "You can hunt? That's so cool. I always wanted my dad to teach me, but he wouldn't, said I was a girl and shouldn't know that stuff. I don't think he knew how, though. He was a car salesman."

"Sounds like you need a real man to show you how things should be." Gomer adjusted himself. Yawned. "My woman had a couple kids, you know. Boys. I was showing them how to shoot. Track. Youngest wasn't all that bright, but the other one, he was good. Had a lot of potential."

The other one? She forced her mind away from the tidbit as her mind settled on the rest of what he'd said.

"Had?" Kamren didn't have to feign tears. They streamed out as her brain focused on the past tense of his conversation. "They...they died with her?"

"No, but we had to leave them behind. They'd slow us down, and it wasn't safe. Folks who hurt my woman, we don't want to mess with them. The kids were a tie to us we couldn't afford," someone said.

"What the fuck?" Gomer glared over his shoulder. "Your mouth is running fast and loose."

"Where were you? You left them somewhere? Alone?" Addy's accusatory voice thundered through the room.

"They'll be fine. Cabin's remote. No one will ever find 'em." Gomer yawned again.

"How far away is it? I could use a place to lay low. Her boyfriend's nuts. He'll hunt us down."

"You leave that bastard to me if he shows up. You ain't got no business hiding out in that cabin. Closest town is a shithole with two hundred folks at most. Rude-ass fuckers called it Friendly Junction." Gomer yawned again. "Shit, I'm beat."

Kamren knew they had what they needed when hell broke loose moments later. The take downs were swift and simple thanks to the drugs pumping through their systems. She latched onto Dallas. "We have a location. We have a location."

She drew back, expecting to see smiles from the men around her. The grim expressions made her insides clench. "What?"

"The woman he was talking about was Marla, my ex. My son's mom. She died eleven weeks ago."

Shit. Kamren swallowed the fear rising in her throat. She wouldn't give it a voice. "He said they could hunt, track. The other kid was good. Maybe that was your kid he was talking about. Either way, they can hunt."

"You think assholes like that left a gun for a kid?"

"No, but I've been that kid, Dallas. I've been lost in the woods alone with no weapon except a dull knife, no supplies except a ball of string, a filthy blanket, and a backpack. So I know you can live for eleven weeks if you have the skills and smarts to do it, because I did. *Repeatedly.*" She looked up at him as she squeezed his arm. "Shake that shitty look off your face and clean up this mess so we can move out."

TJ CROUCHED beside the dark hole. "Lilly?"

"It's dark; you shouldn't be out here. Go back inside with your brother before they spot you out here." Her voice was weaker than before. She stopped halfway in between to cough, the sound was long and deep. "Go back inside."

TJ looked around. The bad men who'd stayed at the cabin after Gomer and his men left were away again. He hoped they'd stay away for good, like Gomer and his men. But Mo and his goons were real mean and didn't wanna leave, said it was safer to hunker down, whatever that meant.

But Mo and his goons always left to hunt and get supplies. They always stayed away a couple sunrises, so TJ knew there was time to check on Lilly. Back when Gomer and his guys were there, too, someone had always stayed behind, which made it hard to sneak out and get to the hole where they kept Lilly.

At least Gomer was gone. It'd been way easier to get out of the cabin with no one there. He and DJ would leave, go to town and ask for help, but that hadn't gone too well last time he tried. He'd gotten hauled back, and Mo and his goons beat him and DJ real bad.

"There's time." He lowered his voice, just in case. Last time he'd gotten caught, he'd been whipped. His bottom still hurt. "I caught a rabbit, exactly where you said. Nearest tree to the slow water. I did just what you said. DJ helped me skin it. We even got the guts out right this time."

"That's good, baby. Really good. I knew you could do it." She coughed harder. "You know how to cook it, right? You have the flint you found? You gotta cook it and eat real quick before Mo and them get back. Outside, so the smell isn't in the cabin."

"Yeah. DJ found sticks and stuff. We cooked it good." He held his hand out. The bag dangled. "We saved you some."

"You keep it; eat it for breakfast."

"We got two eggs from the hens you taught me to catch. They're hidden in the cave we found," TJ said proudly. He'd learned a lot from Lilly. "Eat or we won't."

Lilly didn't like him and DJ not eating. When the mean men had gone away and left them last sunrise, TJ wanted to go into town and tell someone about Lilly in the hole, but then he'd remembered the guy from town.

Lilly had tried to get him and DJ to leave without her, said there was another town four days toward the sun when it was up in the sky. She said no one could know she was there, it was too dangerous. So he and DJ should go without her. Forget about her. His tummy and insides hurt real bad thinking about leaving her behind.

She said it was 'cause he was brave. He didn't understand her fancy words, but he knew it wasn't right to leave someone in a hole. Hungry.

Scared.

At first, he'd been real scared when the mean men went away the last time 'cause when Gomer and the others left they'd never come back. The mean woman hadn't been around in a long time, and then Gomer got scared, said she was dead. TJ knew what dead was. He'd seen lots and lots of things get dead because of the mean men. Lilly said it was his job to keep him and DJ fed, watered, and safe.

And he had.

Because of Lilly.

Mo and his goons didn't much care what he and DJ did as long as they didn't try and get away. They were real good at finding things and said he and DJ would get hurt real bad if they tried to run while they were out hunting. TJ and DJ could hunt at the creek for fish. If he was quick he could sneak into town, even though Lilly didn't trust folks there.

She said one day they'd all get away so they could be taken to a good home with lots of family and plenty of food. He didn't know what a family was.

But Lilly was good to them. She'd kept the mean men from hurting him and DJ. She'd fought them again and again and again. The mean men said food wasn't free, you had to earn a hunt. TJ didn't know what all that meant, but she always left the hole they kept her in when his and DJ's bellies hurt, and she'd go away. Sometimes she'd come back hurt, but she always had food.

The mean men had loud things that killed easy. Guns. They'd taught TJ how to use them, but Lilly never got one. And they'd taken all the guns away. But she had made TJ hide a knife. She was real good with it, too. She killed a grizzly with one the last time she went out, said it was either her or the bear.

TJ was glad she won.

Even if bear meat wasn't all that good.

TJ remembered when it had just been him, the mean men and the woman. His mom. Whatever that was, she wasn't good. She was the reason Lilly was in the hole. She'd said the woman needed a lesson.

She was always telling Gomer and the other mean men he and DJ needed lessons.

DJ had been the only good thing the mom-woman did. She'd dumped him in TJ's lap one day, said he was his brother. Whatever that was, TJ knew he had to figure out how to keep him alive. Safe. He'd been too little to chew. He didn't have teeth, and he pooped all the time. TJ hadn't done too good taking care of DJ at first, but Gomer had thrown bottles at him every now and then. DJ liked whatever was in them.

Then Lilly had showed up and he'd learned what to do. How to make the smelly poop go away. How to keep him from screaming. At first DJ had been easy to handle. He ate. He shit. He drank his bottle. He slept. Then he pooped again and then ate.

That was a long time ago.

Now DJ was big and way easier to handle. He learned quick, too.

Lilly finally accepted the fact that TJ wasn't leaving until she ate the food. She called it stubborn. He was lots of that. It kept her fed and DJ clean and their bellies full.

Most of the time.

He'd looked everywhere for a key, the small thing they needed to get the thing off Lilly's neck and legs and arms so she could leave the hole. But Gomer must've taken it with him when he went away a long time ago, right after the mean woman didn't come back.

TJ couldn't find it. He'd found a place in town that had lots and lots of keys. It was a long walk that hurt his bare feet, but he'd made it a few times and gotten keys when the old man wasn't looking. He never left without paying, though.

Lilly said that was stealing and bad. Real bad.

He figured he didn't want to be bad like the mom and the mean men. They were real bad.

Lilly said good people paid for what they needed. He didn't have money, whatever that was.

So he left meat.

Or eggs.

They had three chickens now, which meant they always had one egg each to eat now.

DJ was a good fisher, too, way better than TJ.

"We're fishing at the creek tomorrow."

"You be careful out there and get back before the sun comes up too high. Mo and them will be back. And the bears are awake; you don't have any business taking their fish. They'll get mean if they see you, especially the mamas. They have babies to take care of."

"I know. I'll be safe. DJ's real quick." TJ lowered water down to Lilly. She never took much, said they needed it more than her. But at least she'd take some. Mainly 'cause of that stubborn he had, whatever that was. It always got him what he wanted with Lilly.

He waited until she tugged on the rope. He raised the cup, dropped the keys he'd taken from the old man in town into the empty cup, then lowered it again. All those keys. One of them had to work. He waited a couple seconds. "Well?"

"Afraid not, baby. It'd be really small."

"I'll go again tomorrow, after we fish."

"I want you to take DJ this time and find a policeman. Tell him you're lost and need help." Lilly's voice raised. "It's time to get you away from this place. You heard what Mo said before they left."

He looked back at the cabin to make sure DJ hadn't followed him out. "Yeah."

"He's gonna leave soon, too. Then you and DJ…" She cut off the words, but he knew. They'd be dead and so would she. "It's time to get to town or head to the one I told you about. Find a policeman there."

"Not leaving unless you are."

"Such a stubborn little man."

TJ smiled. He liked when she called him a little man. One day he'd be like one of the superheroes on the shows he sometimes got to watch when Gomer, Mo, and the mean men drank too much of the smelly stuff.

"Fine. Tomorrow, you go into town and tell the first person you see with a badge about this place and me. Bring them out here." Lilly's voice lowered. "Policemen have guns on their belts, and a whole bunch of other stuff. Look for the badge."

"Dunno what that is."

"It's a shiny piece of metal they'll be wearing."

"Oh, okay." That he could find. "Town's small. Don't think they have that there."

"Then find someone you think is nice, someone you feel in your gut is a good person. You've got one hell of a gut, TJ. It won't steer you wrong."

It'd steered him wrong last time, but she was right. They had to be gone before Mo and his goons got back from their hunt, which meant he had to try again. Surely not everyone in the town was bad. Right?

THEY MADE a four-day trek in two out of sheer determination. Mary and Vi had vehicles waiting for them, along with a fresh supply of clothes and replenishments for gear. They'd found a small roadside gas station and taken turns cleaning up with the hose outside the bathrooms. By the time they were done and on the road, it'd been an hour since they'd hit civilization.

Friendly Junction wasn't on any maps. No land records indicated anything resembling a homestead. Per computer records, the town simply didn't exist, which was why they hadn't notated it earlier. HERA was the best tech around, but tech was only as good as the databases it was connected to, and since the speck of a town was so small, they'd missed it entirely during their grid search.

The coordinates they'd been given were off. Way off, leading them all to suspect there'd been a relocation somewhere along the way.

But they had a location now.

The town was a small gas station across from what looked to be a general grocery and hardware store rolled into one. Dallas wheeled the vehicle holding himself, Tanner, Jesse, Jud, Kamren and Nolan to a stop in front of the latter, while Marshall parked the other SUV by the gas station. A couple of other small buildings peeked out from the trees nearby. A small diner was on the side of the gas station.

"Didn't realize this was here," Tanner said.

"Thought you knew these parts," Dallas commented.

"Me knowing all of the Wyoming wilderness is a bit like me assuming you know all of Texas," the man replied.

Nolan chuckled as they entered the small store. An old man leaned forward, both hands on the wooden counter holding an antiquated register.

"Evening," he said.

"Evening," Dallas replied as he pulled out the identification the FBI had offered them back when the hunt for his son initially started. Consultants. If it greased people's mouths, he'd flash just about anything. "We're working with the FBI to track a couple of missing children. We received some tips indicating there's a cabin in this area, likely inhabited until recently by a large group of men. Not too friendly. Kept to themselves."

"I know the crew you're talking about. Always ripping through town, taking whatever they want, even got their kid doing it. Haven't seen them around, but that brat's been around. Stealing the dangedest things, too."

"Like what?" Kamren asked as she wrapped an arm around Dallas.

"Keys." The man motioned toward the back wall. "Keep them for the hunters when they need extra sets made. Lots of remote cabins in these parts, I'm afraid. Not sure which they're in, but they're trouble. Every last one of them."

"Keys?" Mary asked.

"Keys," Jesse confirmed. "You ever ask him why he's taking them?"

"If I catch the little cuss, I'm gonna wallop his butt. No excuse for stealing." The man's jaw moved a few beats even though he didn't speak. "Gotta admit, he's been looking a little worn thin, if you know what I mean. Dirty. Skinny. Always been skinny, never that dirty. Leaves smelly meat and eggs on the counter."

"Barter." Kamren's voice was low. And pissed. Hands fisted, she took a step toward the old man. "Boy brought food in exchange for those keys. Likely the only thing he had of value, which means he's skinny because he was giving away his only food for what he needed more."

"Huh, never thought of that." The old man's jaws worked as he looked at the woman. "Guess I shouldn't have thrown it away."

Dallas left the building before he beat the man. What the fuck was wrong with people these days that they'd see a boy in that kind of condition and not do anything? Before the rage got the better of his common sense, Kamren was at his side, arms around him.

"We're close," she said. "He was in here just yesterday. That's a good sign."

She was right. It was. Marshall whistled from the other side of the narrow road. Dallas and the others crossed the street.

"Got a hit. Gas station owner saw a young boy, dark hair, ragged, walking north along the road. He was gonna go see if the kid needed help, but he was gone by the time he pulled free from customers." Translation—he'd taken his time.

"North. Anything else?"

"No, but it's a start." Brace looked around. "Your women got a map of this area; we can start knocking on doors til we find the right one."

"We'll grab some real grub first," Fallon said. "We throw some cash into the local economy, maybe lips will loosen."

"Makes sense," Addy said. "Gotta admit, food smells way better than the MREs."

19

Kamren broke off from the group as everyone headed toward the small eatery. Keys. She couldn't beat back the sense of dread that settled within her. Why would a little boy steal keys? He was bartering, which meant he'd learned the value of items from someone. The bastards they'd met earlier wouldn't have bothered. So who had taught him to pay for items? And why would he need keys?

Because he needed to unlock something real important.

She swallowed back the fear clawing her throat. Dirty. Scrawny. Hungry.

She remembered those times growing up, never knowing where the next meal was coming from. Or when. Or what.

"You okay?" Dallas asked. He cupped her face. The intensity in his gaze seeped into her.

"No." She splayed her palm across his chest. "He gave away his food for keys. I..."

"It hits close to home. You remember being hungry."

"Yeah. I remember bartering for things I needed to survive. That's a skill, Dallas. Someone taught that boy the value of items. Gomer and those bastards we caught wouldn't have done that."

A smile broke on his face as his amusement boomed in the area.

Heat rose in her cheeks. He'd laughed a lot about what'd gone down at the campsite. They all had.

"Stop laughing."

"No way, sweetheart. You took Gomer and all those men down. Fuck, I could live to be a thousand years old and never see a sight like you plowing through those beans like it was the first meal you'd had in a year. And the way you dished out that shit to knock them out, all so you could get what we needed to find my kid? Fucking beautiful." He cupped her face. "Just like you."

Movement to her side drew her attention. A young boy with dark hair stood there looking at the knife strapped to her side. His shirt was in tattered strips along his little torso. Mud, twigs, and debris filled his hair. His dark chocolate eyes latched onto her. "You a policeman?"

She swallowed. "No, honey. Afraid not. I can get one for you, though. I'm Kamren."

The boy looked up at Dallas. His eyes widened when he saw the dog tags Dallas wore. "That a badge?"

Dallas crouched, putting himself on the same level as the young boy. "In a way, yeah. Got these fighting bad men and keeping people safe. That's what I do. That's what we all do."

The boy's gaze swept the area. He took a hesitant step backward as he eyed Kamren skeptically a moment. A world of nightmares resided within those depths. She crouched down.

"You know Gomer. I heard you." His little dirty hands fisted at his sides. Anger seeped into his tense stance. "Gomer's mean, a bad man. Mo is, too."

"Yeah, he is," Dallas said. "But he's not ever gonna hurt anyone again. My woman here made sure of that."

"We all did," Kamren clarified, but the impact had already taken seed within the boy.

"You fought Gomer?" He looked at them. "What about Mo? You fight him, too?"

"She didn't have to. She outsmarted him and all the others,

knocked 'em all out," Dallas said, pride evident in his voice. "I'm Dallas, she's Kamren. What's your name?"

"TJ." His gaze remained on her thigh, the knife Jud had given her. She took a chance, pulled it from its sheath as the crush of her team rounded the building and froze.

"Stay back," Mary ordered in the com. "Let her do this. Nice and slow."

"A friend gave this to me. I..." She wasn't sure what to say, but she knew trust was essential. Whoever this kid was, he was too old to be Dallas's boy. He was probably eight or nine, not five. "I had a rough upbringing, was raised in the country, the wild."

"You good with that?" His voice was soft, hesitant.

"Yeah, pretty good. My friend back there's probably better, though. He said he'd show me a few things, but I'm not gonna let him unless I can show him a few things in return. I'm a real good tracker and hunter."

"Figured. You smell like you are 'cause you don't smell."

"Yeah. You wanna hear a secret?"

"I guess," the boy whispered skeptically as he took a step toward her.

"I'm with a group of people right now," she crawled one step closer to the boy and lowered her voice slightly. "We came out here looking for someone real important. They trusted me to lead them through the woods and find him."

"Yeah, sounds like they need you to show them some stuff. It's a good trade." The boy's eyes turned sad. He looked down. "Lilly said it's important to have something big to trade when you need something."

"That's how I was raised. It's bartering," she said softly. "Sounds like Lilly is a good friend. You know her long?"

"No. Bad men brought her." His voice lowered. "She needs my help."

"She's lucky to have you," Dallas said.

"I ain't got nothing left to trade, though. Lilly said I needed to come to town, bring DJ, and find a policeman." His gaze settled on Dallas. "That you?"

"No, but I'm better than a policeman," Dallas replied.

"Why's that?" TJ asked.

"Policemen have rules, things they won't do to keep people safe." He pointed to Kamren and then the others. "Me, my woman, and our team? There's nothing we won't do to keep someone safe from the bad men. That's what we do."

"You got a key?"

"A key, huh?" Kamren tried to play it cool when all she wanted to do was scoop the boy up, hug him tight, and make all his hurt go away. Movement from behind them drew her attention. "Who's that with you?"

TJ's eyes widened. "You are good. You heard him?"

"I did," she said. "Wanna know how? I'll show you."

The boy shifted from one foot to another, looked around, then nodded.

"Everything makes a shadow when the sun is out. If you know where it's at in the sky, you know where something is when a shadow moves. It's real important when you're tracking or hunting. You watch the ground, you'll see the shadows. If you watch them, know what they mean, you'll see someone or something coming up behind you."

"Oh, yeah. Wow, I didn't know that."

"Birds also flew off when he rustled the branches. Animals flee an area when an unknown threat is there," Kamren offered as the boy's gaze looked upward. "When you're somewhere you don't know well, watch the animals. Listen to what they're doing. Animals don't ever lie; they'll tell you what's what if you pay attention."

"Huh. You track 'em?"

"Yeah, when I need to, though it's better to leave some animals be. Respecting them is important. You respect them, they'll respect you."

"You hunt?"

"Yeah, when I get hungry. I was raised with the rule you don't eat what you don't kill."

"You must be good." The unspoken statement that she'd eaten

plenty made the women on the other end of the com laugh. She couldn't help but smirk.

"Yeah, I'm good." She looked back at the shrubbery Dallas's gaze hadn't settled off of. If she didn't get answers now, he'd likely give chase, and that was the last thing two terrified boys needed. "Is that DJ? Is he your brother?"

"How do you know his name?"

"My man here. We've been looking for him. He found out that bad people took him away." Kamren's voice lowered. "I'm thinking you're his brother."

"I guess. The mean woman said he was; not sure what that is, though."

"My man's got five brothers. Three of them are back there," she motioned. The boy tightened when he saw so many people nearby. She settled a hand around his tiny body and continued. "Bet you can guess which ones are brothers. They all look alike."

"DJ don't look like me, but he does them. A lot." TJ sniffled. "Guess she lied. If brothers look alike, he's not my brother."

"Not necessarily. See, I've got a sister. That's like the girl version of brothers. She's got hair that's really blond, and mine isn't. We look nothing alike because she looks like our mom. And I look like my dad."

"I don't look like her either."

"Well, that probably means you look like your dad, and that means DJ and you have different dads."

"What are those?"

"Moms and dads keep us safe, love us no matter what, take care of us, and do everything we need to become just like them one day. Some are really good, and some aren't."

"She wasn't good."

"Sounds like it," Kamren admitted. "My mom and dad weren't good either. They tried, but they weren't good."

"They tried?"

"Yeah, they taught me what they could. I hunted, helped keep us fed." Her voice cracked beneath the enormity of emotion assailing her. "My dad taught me to shoot, use a knife. Hunt and track. So, I guess they were a lot more good than I realized."

"Suppose so," TJ said. His gaze swept back to the group. "Which of them knows knives?"

"Well, I'm thinking most of them. They're all real good with guns, but I can hold my own with them." Kamren wrapped her arm around TJ and pointed. "That's Jud. He's the one who gave me this knife."

"I got a knife. I been finding food for me and DJ since the mean men went away. Lilly told me how. Lilly keeps us safe and fed."

"Is Lilly here with you too?" Kamren looked back at the woods and somehow pushing back the urge to race into the thick over-growth and snatch DJ up. "You think DJ wants to come out and meet us?"

"Was he the something important you were looking for?"

Kamren smiled. "He is. And you are too. We just didn't know until just now."

"Lilly said a policeman would take us somewhere with a good family. Lots of food. We'd be safe from the bad men." He looked at Dallas. "You make bad men go away?"

"We do."

"You from where he's at?" TJ asked her.

"Yeah, pretty near."

"And you hunt there? Get food?" The boy rocked back on his bare feet.

"Yeah. There're rules, but you can hunt for food." She lowered her voice. She'd been the scared, determined big sibling before. "Dallas and his family don't do things like you and me. Adults provide the food and keep people safe."

"What's an adult?"

"Old people," Kamren said with a grin.

"So, like you?"

"Yeah," she said as the women on the com laughed again.

"I can help. We don't eat much," he said.

"You and DJ eating a lot would help me and my brothers out. Our mom loves to cook; she always makes too much food," Dallas said.

"Suppose we could help with that," TJ offered.

Dallas smiled. "Oh yeah? Well, that sounds like a pretty good deal. How about I take you and your brother away from here. We can work the details out later." He held his hand out. "In my family our word is our bond. When we say we'll do something, we do it. We shake on it, and it's a vow we always honor it, no matter what."

"You'll keep us safe from the bad men?"

"Yeah, I will. We all will." Determination and confidence. Dallas exuded both qualities in his stance and his voice.

"And we'll help eat your mom's cooking. She any good?" TJ asked.

"Yeah, she's the best around."

"Then it's a deal." TJ put his hand against Dallas's.

"It's a deal."

TJ smiled, turned, and motioned. The brush moved. Breath swooshed from her lungs as a mini-Dallas entered the clearing. His hair was matted and filthy, but the distinctive Mason-dark. His bright blue eyes swept the area, then latched onto TJ. He rushed forward in a fast sweep of unsteady limbs.

Kamren reached out and kept him from falling when he got close. "Hi, I'm Kamren."

DJ looked around, his gaze riveted to the large group of people. She noted the tension in his little body and unshouldered the pack. "You know, I have something for you. For you both, actually. My friend over there has one of them."

She hoped to hell someone with a pack took the hint. "When we set out to come find you, I wanted to have something to give to you. My dad taught me never to show up without something, a gift."

Jesse had found what she'd tucked away in each team's pack. She pulled hers out and held it out to DJ as Jesse approached TJ with the other small teddy bear. The boys stared at the bears, then slowly reaching out to touch them.

"I'll save mine for Lilly. It'll make her laugh," TJ said. "She killed a bear with a knife like yours. It hurt her real bad though."

"Find out where she is," Vi ordered. "He's worried. Ask about the key again."

"TJ, honey, we can help Lilly, okay? Why do you need a key?"

"The bad men kept her in the hole. I can't get her out." The boy's eyes watered. "We tried and tried, but I can't find the key to the things around her neck and her feet and arms. I give her food and water, and she tells me how to catch stuff and how to fix it. But I need a key."

The boy's voice rose. Nolan approached and knelt. "We'll get the key. Show us where she is."

TJ looked at the two men, then reached out and touched their dog tags. "You fighters, too?"

"Yeah," Jesse said. "We all are."

"You'll take her, too? Make her better?" DJ asked.

"Yeah, we will," Dallas said. Jesse and Nolan stepped back and stood behind their brother as he crouched in front of the two boys. Tears glinted in his blue eyes. "Hi, boys. I'm Dallas. I'm here to take you home."

"Like a dad?" TJ asked. "You aren't my dad."

"I am now," Dallas said.

The boys vaulted forward and hugged him close.

"Lilly said someone would take us to a good place. I won't go without her," TJ said. "We have a deal; it includes her."

"Deal. Take us to her," Nolan said.

The boys sprang toward the tree line. Kamren, Dallas, Jesse, and Nolan kept pace while Mary and Vi barked orders at the others. Kamren's heart thudded wildly in her chest.

They'd found Dallas's son. He was okay.

But questions remained. Who was Lilly?

Dallas picked his son up and drew him against his side as TJ continued sprinting toward the destination. How much farther was it? How often had he made this trek? Darkness began sucking the daylight from the sky.

≈

"There's a small cabin half a click west-northwest of your location."

"Copy." Vi's statement gave Dallas something to focus on aside from the fact two kids were running through the woods without shoes. He gripped his son tighter as he chased Kamren, who'd snagged TJ and was in an all-out sprint for the location. He wasn't sure how much the kid was helping and how much she was figuring out for herself. Either way, he didn't want those two arriving first. "Get her to slow down."

He caught up with her at the edge of a clearing near the target location. She'd set TJ down and was whispering for him to get down when Dallas arrived with DJ. The two boys crouched low to the ground and clung to one another as he and Kamren surveyed what lay before them. A drone whizzed by and headed around the side of the small, run-down structure. Another slipped into the open door.

"You left the door open?" Kamren asked.

TJ shook his head. "Mo and his goons must be back. Guess you didn't fight them after all."

Fuck.

Dallas slipped on his headgear and noted everyone else doing the same. He looked around and made a split-second decision as he caught Tanner's attention. "Get the kids out of here."

The man looked over at Brace, who nodded. They snatched the kids and tore off back toward the small town. A drone followed. Thank fuck. The two men had handled their own in the wilderness, but he wasn't sure either Tanner or Brace could fight. Until they figured out who was at the cabin, he didn't want the kids anywhere near the area.

Jud and Gage crouched beside a grouping of trees to his right, while Jesse and Addy were to the left. He didn't see Marshall or Nolan, but they were likely with Fallon and circling around. The headgear flashed on and images assailed them as the drones provided visuals. Seven heavily armed targets, which wouldn't be a problem if there weren't more heat signatures arriving from the north.

"Engaging second group," Jud said as he separated from Gage and headed that direction.

"I'll cover his six," Addy said as she broke off.

"Fallon, we have a possible location for Lilly around the back. Marking the location on your display."

"Roger."

"Stay here," Dallas ordered Kamren. Fuck, he should've had her go with Tanner and the kids. Then again, he doubted she would have.

Though her eyes narrowed, she didn't offer an argument. Thank fuck. He motioned to the rest of his team to move in as he edged forward. Angered shouts thundered within the clearing.

"Gonna beat your butts 'til you bleed. Get back here." The massive brute slammed the door shut behind him as he stormed down the rickety entry to the cabin. Dallas sighted the fucker with his rifle. One shot and the takedown would commence, but death wasn't in the mission protocol.

They needed answers.

Were there more of them? The Collective was much larger an operation than he'd initially realized. No matter how many they took down, more sprang up. It was like playing a twisted game of whack-a-mole without the mallet. No matter. He had fists, bullets, knives, and years of unspent rage.

"Go," he made the call as soon as everyone's lights within the headgear turned green to show they were in position.

Ten minutes later, Dallas wished the take down hadn't been so simple. He wanted to hurt the bastards who'd kept his kid rat holed away like a prisoner. But they'd taken the bastards by surprise, which made the entire mission go from green to done within ten minutes. By the time he had his two targets secured, the rest of the team had made their way to him with their bloodied and secured prisoners.

He sneered down at the bastard who'd threatened to beat his son bloody. Sons. No way in hell Dallas would separate those two boys. He was a Mason. End of discussion.

He pulled his KA-BAR and settled it against the man's jugular. "Time for a game, boys. First one to talk lives. The rest?" He shrugged. "Suppose you know how this goes if you've been on Marla's payroll long enough."

"Fuck you."

Dallas severed the man's jugular then moved to the next asshole. "You really don't want to piss me off. You know who I am and you know why I'm here."

"The crazy-ass bitch said you'd come after him, said we'd best make sure you never found him if we wanted to keep breathing. I guess she should've listened to her own advice," the man said. "We don't know where the fuck they went. They were here when we left. Swear to God they were. Gomer wanted 'em dead, but we weren't killing no kids."

"How many of you are there?"

"Seven, but we called in another team. They were right behind us."

"'Were' being the operative word," Jud said as he entered the clearing. "Second team is handled."

Addy ambled up behind him. Both raised their eyebrows at the dead man at Dallas's feet.

"He pissed me off," Dallas commented. "Our man here was about to share everything he knows about the kids. Start with TJ. Who's his dad?"

"Fuck if I know. Bitch put us out here on babysitting detail. Then she brought the other bitch. At least then it got fun."

Lilly. Dallas silently cursed. He'd forgotten about the woman in his haste to get answers about the kids. "Fallon, status?"

"In process." He paused. "Fire in the hole."

A boom echoed through the clearing.

"Fuck, need a medic. Hold on, Lilly. You're safe." The man's voice softened over the com. "Addy, Kamren, I need one of you back here."

"On my way," Addy said, her voice tight as she jogged toward his position.

It took Addy less time than they'd expected to get Lilly out of the hole. The possibility of freedom had a way of stifling fear, Dallas supposed.

His gaze swept the area and settled on Kamren. She offered a smile and motioned toward where Tanner and Brace had taken the kids. The tightness in his chest from the past several months eased. He'd found his son.

"Come on. Let's get my nephew home," Jesse said.

"Nephews," Dallas corrected, making sure the com line was open so everyone heard the declaration and adopted it as their own. "TJ is as much a Mason as DJ. No exceptions."

"Damn straight," Marshall said. "Make sure Mom knows."

"On it," Cord replied. "Mary and Vi are on calls, cutting through the red tape to include TJ in the arrangements they'd made. It's gonna be a bit tougher since there's no biological link between you and him, but they can move mountains with a pebble. They'll get your sons home where they belong."

Sons.

"We need to find out who TJ's father is. I don't want a surprise showing up at The Arsenal."

"I'm on it, though a DNA swab will go a long way," Zoey commented. "I've got scans from the drones, though. HERA's running facial recognition. So far, nothing has popped."

"Likely won't," Kamren said. "He's been out here, living wild."

Dallas put an arm around the woman and hugged her close. He suspected the kids out here, living the way they had, cut close to the vein for her in a lot of ways. Then again, she hadn't been a prisoner of The Collective.

Fuck. Lilly.

He glanced back as Fallon and Jesse guided the woman around the corner of the house. She appeared to be about Kamren's age, but the dirt, grime and injuries made it difficult to estimate. Her skin hung on her thin frame. Matted dark hair framed her hollowed face. Thick, bloody gouges in her throat and wrists drew his attention.

"Fucking restraints were so tight Jesse had to rip skin to get them off," Nolan commented as he arrived beside Dallas. "She didn't even scream. Just stared up at him and Fallon like they were avenging angels."

"In a way they were," Marshall muttered. "Not sure who she is, but we've gotta take responsibility for her."

"Talk to Tanner," Kamren said. "The Arsenal's secure, but not good for her. You've got over one hundred trained male operatives at your facility. That's not a good location for anyone in her condition. You've got a psychologist. Ask her. Better yet, Tanner's got several on his staff. See what they say before we haul her back and make it worse."

The protectiveness within her voice, the fierce determination made Dallas's chest swell. "That's the plan, sweetheart."

"Oh, okay then."

"Though, we hadn't considered Tanner and his crew. You say they're worth looking into to use beyond this one op, we'll make that happen."

"They're worth looking into," she whispered as she looked up at him. "Until you know who she is, she's safer out at their facility where she can have the privacy she needs to heal. They've got teams of doctors who specialize in PTSD, Dallas. She's not their typical case, but their remote location will help her."

He didn't point out they had a similar setup at The Arsenal, because what she'd said earlier was true. They had a lot of people at their compound. Most of them were men. Until they knew Lilly's story, keeping her safe and isolated was the best option, which nixed any idea of taking her back with them.

But she was still their responsibility to protect. Whoever she was, she'd been an enemy of The Collective, which made her a significant person of interest as far as Dallas was concerned. Specifically, she'd pissed off Marla. Why else would she have been dragged out into remote wilderness, secured like an animal and brutalized?

"Even if they're equipped to handle her treatment, they likely aren't ready for security. Cord, notify my team they're on standby. I'm staying up here to assist Tanner with security, but I want them here assisting," Marshall said.

Dallas wouldn't have pegged Marshall's team for the task, but he wasn't going to argue. The sooner they got back to civilization, the quicker he'd get the kids settled.

Home.

20

Dallas had never been so glad to see Resino or the lights of The Arsenal. Each breath he dragged in drew him farther and farther away from the past few days. The red tape associated with bringing DJ home was surprisingly light. Dallas was his biological father. End of discussion. TJ was a totally different mountain of red tape. Vi and Mary had called in what favors they could, but the fact no one knew anything about TJ made the FBI and every other alphabet agency was more than a little "concerned."

They'd eventually navigated their way toward home and gotten out of Wyoming, only to come to a grinding halt in San Antonio. Two days of paperwork, meetings, court appearances and enough red tape to choke out humanity, Dallas had two exhausted boys officially within his custody.

Maria Mendez, the boys' CASA advocate, had been a godsend. She'd made both boys feel equally important, which was enough to declare her a saint in Dallas's book. Little TJ was beyond lost. Terrified. Alone.

No.

He had Dallas and everyone at The Arsenal.

The two boys had gone from having only each other and Lilly to a huge family on a sprawling compound.

The FBI and several other government agencies demanded TJ be placed under their care. Fortunately Vi and Mary had secured legal counsel months ago and any attempts to take Tj were trumped by the overarching desire to keep the two children together.

The entire process was different than customary routine because of security concerns surrounding The Collective and TJ's unknown identity. Nothing about TJ was typical, which made how he was processed through the system entirely unique.

"Those two boys were rescued from reprehensible conditions by a family of war heroes, men who not only fought and bled for your country but continue to do so in ways I will not pretend to understand. I have seen the work they are doing for our veterans, and the other work they do. I find the mere mention of removing TJ from their care offensive and severely damaging to his already delicate emotional health. He's a child, your honor, not a threat to national security." The attorney's words as she'd stood before the judge still resonated with Dallas. He didn't even know the woman's name, but she'd defended his right to keep TJ.

For now, the kids were home. They'd undergone batteries of tests to confirm (or in TJ's case establish) identities. All data gathered was shared with Mary and Vi. Until HERA or the agencies had more information, Dallas was focused on what mattered—bringing normal to his sons. He looked over at TJ.

Though exhaustion plagued him, the boy had yet to sleep. If anyone was near his little brother, he was sentry. Watching. Protecting. Dallas's chest swelled. "Proud of you, TJ."

The boy's head snapped up. His drowsy eyes focused on him via the rearview mirror, then shifted over to Jesse, who sat on the boy's other side in the back seat. Kamren was in the front seat beside Dallas, quiet but astute—as she'd been since they landed in Texas.

"I had lots of big brothers growing up, so I know a thing or two about what a great one is. I lucked out, had a lot of good ones. Gotta say, you're the best big brother DJ could've ever gotten. The way you took care of him, kept him safe—I'm proud of you, we all are." Dallas waited for the little boy's weary brain to take in all he'd said. The doctors had all mentioned that neither boy was used to lots of conversation. They were significantly behind where they should be in many ways yet accelerated in others.

"You aren't alone anymore," Jesse added. "You have a huge family now, by blood and by brotherhood. Whatever you and DJ need, we're all here. You aren't alone anymore."

"I know." The boy's cautious voice filled the cab. His gaze slid up to the front, focused on Kamren, and remained locked on her, as if willing her to hear his unspoken question.

Kamren. Dallas reached over and squeezed her hand. She'd been amazing, after she'd gotten over her initial concerns about meeting with Mrs. Mendez. TJ had spoken about Kamren with enough curiosity, interest, and reverence the advocate had wanted to meet someone who had made such a profound impact on the young boy so quickly.

There were many similarities between his boys and Kamren, the way they were raised, living off the land. Fending for themselves. Jesus. He hadn't realized some of the shit she'd gone through until he heard the conversation she had with Mrs. Mendez. Her father had forced her to hunt to eat, even when she was as young as DJ. Rachelle and Cliff didn't go through it, mainly because he'd already had Kamren beneath his thumb.

It was the questions she'd refused to answer about her mother that concerned Dallas. Although she'd shared a lot about her father and the things they'd endured at his hand, very little had come out about their mom so far. Why? It was one of the million things he intended to find out about the woman who'd become important to him and the two boys in the back seat.

"You know your dad and uncles were all soldiers, right? Most everyone here was at one point." Kamren's voice filled the cab. She looked back at TJ and smiled. "They do things as a team. Everyone has a strength, but they also have weaknesses. Like me? I can shoot and hunt with the best of them, but I'm not good with numbers and book-learning stuff. But Mary and Vi? Rhea and Bree? Those four are really, really smart. But they can't shoot worth a damn."

TJ snickered, like he couldn't imagine someone not knowing how to shoot.

"So alone, we aren't as good as we are when we help one another. A team."

"DJ and I are a team," the boy said.

"Yeah, you are," Jesse said. "But all the rest of us are part that team now, too."

"That means we trust one another," Dallas said. He hoped the kid understood what they were saying. "We have each other's backs. When one of us has problems or needs to tap out, to rest and recover from being in protective mode too long, we flag someone in to take our place. Past few days have been scary, but it's okay to rest now. We're tagged in. You can rest. Nothing's gonna happen to you or DJ, not here."

The little boy's lips thinned. Gaze narrowed, he sat up higher in his seat when Dallas parked the truck in front of the ranch house. He turned it off, slid out of the front of the cab, and opened the back door. He looked back at Jesse. "You get TJ, and I'll take DJ."

"Right." Jesse held out his hands to TJ. "You ready for a pony ride, little man?"

Little man. Lilly had told them it was a nickname the boy liked. She was still wrangled with red tape. Her recovery would be slow, and one which was not suited for the facilities they had at The Arsenal. She needed something more private, secure. At Kamren's suggestion, Tanner had offered the woman a spot in one of his remote cabins. He had therapists who worked with the people out there. The woman had agreed quickly, as if realizing it was the best option.

For now, she was simply a victim they'd rescued. Nothing aside from that mattered, especially since her identity was as much a mystery as TJ's. But Dallas wasn't taking chances that it wasn't an elaborate ruse. Marshall and his team would be wheels down tomorrow to Tanner's facility, providing security and helping out with an ongoing issue they had.

Dallas waited until TJ was situated on Jesse's back before he took DJ out. Kamren smiled at them as she remained nearby, but distant enough to give the boys the space they needed. He kept each movement slow and visible to the protective older brother. He glanced at the porch as his mom walked out. She was dabbing at her eyes and smiling big.

Some of the pain and fear within him vanished. His son was home.

No. His sons.

He didn't know the first thing about healing them or raising them. But he had the best damn family and friends around. Together they could do anything.

"Get the door, Mom," Dallas whispered as he carried an exhausted DJ toward his childhood home.

A sleepy but ever-watchful TJ tightened his lock on Jesse a few steps away. The older boy's gaze slid to Dallas's mom and widened slightly as the woman reached out and clasped his head in her hands. Before Dallas could stop her, she leaned in and kissed his little forehead.

"You poor, sweet dear. Welcome home, baby," she whispered through watery tears.

TJ's gaze darted to Dallas, then swung to Jesse. "I didn't do it."

"Do what?" Jesse asked.

"Make her cry," he said softly.

"Oh, baby." Mom yanked the boy from Jesse and wrapped him into a big hug as she headed into the house. "We've been looking for you ever since we found out about you."

"That's DJ." TJ pointed at his little brother. "I'm not nobody."

"You're God's gift to me, you and your little brother both. My babies are all home, and now our family's growing." Her voice softened. "I made up the room Dallas used to share with Cord. You haven't met him yet, but you will. There's lot of people here who love you both. You won't ever be alone or scared again, baby. Never, ever again."

Jesus.

Dallas glanced at Jesse. Kamren's eyes shimmered with unshed tears. She nodded, as if assuring him things were okay and headed where they needed to go. His sons were home. He and his brothers had discussed their mom's involvement with the boys at length from the moment they undertook the mission of finding him. Doctor Sinclair was adamant she would be a tremendous asset. While Dallas had no doubt that was true, their mother didn't have a filter on her mother-hen syndrome to the point it bled into everything within a one-hundred-mile radius of her nest. She'd mothered everyone within the Warrior's Path Project and all the Arsenal operatives, despite numerous attempts by them all to get her to ease off on the mothering. Not everyone could handle the level of attention she doled out.

"I called Ray Burton. He's got two boys about your age, and he assured me I couldn't go wrong with superheroes for the bedding. I wasn't sure which ones you'd want, so I got them all. You don't want Spiderman, say the word and I'll switch them out." Dallas's mother set TJ down, then glanced back at him. "Set him on the bed, dear. The poor thing was so tuckered out he hasn't even moved."

Dallas settled DJ onto the bed and smirked as his mother flitted to a dresser. She opened the top drawer. Pajamas spilled out, enough to outfit all of Resino.

"Ma," Jesse said, his eyebrows lifted.

"Hush. These are my grandbabies. I've waited too long to spoil them as rotten as I can, so I figure I've got loads of making up to do." She handed over a pair of pale blue pajamas with red Spiderman images on them, her eyes watery. She handed another pair to TJ. "The bathroom's down the hall and to the right. You change, and we'll get your brother changed."

TJ tightened. He gripped the clothing in his arms, but his gaze latched onto Dallas, then slid down to DJ. A century of wariness exploded within his little eyes. "I'll help, then I'll change."

"Okay," Dallas said quickly, knowing the big brother wasn't about to leave them alone with his little brother. "Appreciated."

Dallas didn't know a damn thing about changing little boys so asleep they resembled comatose patients, but between him and TJ they had his tiny clothes shucked off quickly. TJ's widened gaze slid to Dallas when they got to his wet pants.

"He was scared," TJ defended.

"It's okay, bud," Dallas said. "I was pretty scared, too."

"We've never been in a plane before, or in the city, or any of it. And all those people were nosing around, asking things. He doesn't like strangers. Or noise." TJ took a step away when Dallas's mom appeared with a package of wipes.

By the time they had DJ pajama'd and tucked into the bed, Dallas could tell TJ was about to pass out, but the little boy stood beside the bed, a sentry looking out over his little brother. Emotion welled in his chest at the protectiveness.

How many times had one of his brothers done the same thing when he'd woken them because of a nightmare? He glanced back at Jesse.

"You know, when I was DJ's age, I used to have nightmares just about every night," Dallas said.

"What?" His mom's eyes widened. "I don't remember that."

"That's because he'd come in and wake me or Nolan, sometimes Marshall," Jesse said. "We took turns coming in and checking under the bed and in the closet for the monsters. Then we'd crawl into the bed with him. Safety in numbers."

TJ looked at Dallas, then Jesse. His little lips twisted as he knelt and peeked under the bed. Jesse helped, whispering as he pointed out potential hiding spots behind the dresser and around the bed. Behind the curtains.

The sweep was thorough and extensive. By the time TJ walked to the closet and opened it, the fear in his eyes had been bolstered into big-brother confidence. He spent a good three minutes looking through everything. He glanced about the room and nodded his approval.

"I'll sleep with him," TJ said. "I'll keep him quiet if he wakes up yelling. He won't know where we are."

Why would a little boy wake up yelling? Dallas bit back the question. "You need anything, I'll be across the hall. We'll leave the lamp on low for you," he said.

"Good. Then he'll know we aren't in the pit," TJ commented as he crawled in.

"The pit?" Jesse asked. "The one Lilly was in?"

The boy's body tightened once again. His gaze darted from Jesse, to Dallas, then to their mother. "Doesn't matter. Forget I said anything. Don't mention it to DJ or the lady. She'll ask him. Doesn't matter."

Dallas settled on his haunches and waited for the boy's gaze to slide to him. "Everything about you and DJ matters to me, to Jesse, to Mom, and everyone else here. I know you don't know us yet, but we'll listen. We won't ever judge or get angry. There's nothing you can't tell us, any of us."

The boy's head bobbed as he drew the sheet and blanket over himself and his brother. Conversation over. Dallas smiled down at the two boys. TJ's gaze tracked him and Jesse to the door. Dallas's mom leaned down and kissed the boy's forehead and whispered something in his ear.

They left the door half open and headed downstairs to the living room. Riley and Cord stood at the bottom of the stairs.

"They're asleep?" Riley asked, disappointment heavy in her voice.

"Just about," Dallas said. He braced as she vaulted into him. He took the impact with one step back and a grunt. She squeezed him tight enough to force breath from his lungs. "They're okay, Riles. They're home."

"Damn straight they are," she muttered into his body. "You good?" Her voice was soft, gentle like it'd been back when he'd first returned from The Collective.

"I'm getting there," he admitted.

"Good. Good." She looked at their mom. "I know you want a big family breakfast, but it's up to Dallas. He'll know if the kids are ready for the crazy that is a family breakfast."

Riley shuffled off, leaving Dallas, their mom, and Jesse. And Kamren, who hovered nearby. Warmth resonated in his chest when his mom put her hand there and peered up at him with a teary expression, then beamed a smile. She did the same with Jesse, her other hand on his chest. "Proud. He would've been so proud of you boys."

Jesus.

Jesse beat him to the hug Mom needed. Dallas waited his turn, then drew her into a tight, long one that'd let her give them whatever tidal wave of loss had stricken her. They were fewer and farther between, but recent events had activated them frequently. Dylan getting married. Mary being pregnant.

Now Dallas bringing his sons home. He looked over at Kamren and her teary-eyed expression. Had she ever had moments like this with her family? Doubtful. "Wish he was here giving advice on how to be a good dad. He was the best."

"We'll figure it out." Jesse reached over, grabbed Dallas's neck, and squeezed hard. "Together. Practice for Dylan's kid. You know it'll be a brilliant hellion, those two's genes running through him."

"Or her," their mom supplied with a sniffle. "I'm hoping for a granddaughter, seeing how I already have two grandsons now."

There it was, affirmation she'd already brought TJ into the fold.

"Go. Get Kamren fed. Jesse and I'll sit with the boys. That thing Cord put in makes me nervous."

That thing? Dallas looked at Jesse, who shrugged.

"He said Doc Sinclair suggested it, said we'd know if one of the boys got up, or was restless. A drone in the house seems a bit much." His mom's gaze was on the stairs. "Suppose I'll go up to my room. Love you."

"Love you, too," Dallas said as he kissed her cheek. Jesse did the same.

A drone in the house. Made sense. Dallas wished to hell he'd thought of it. He dragged Kamren closer, cupped her face, and kissed her. Blood surged southward when she melted into him without hesitation.

"Go. I've got this," Jesse said.

Dallas chuckled and took Kamren's hand. "Come on, sweetheart."

21

The shower was sublime, the latest word Bree had taught her. She couldn't believe Dallas had actually left the ranch house. She'd expected to fend for herself tonight, but if she was being perfectly honest, she was glad they were going to spend some time alone. As selfish as it might seem, she needed time with the man who'd snared her in a way that she knew she'd never be the same.

The past few days hadn't been celebratory. They'd been beyond stressful in so many ways. With all the government agencies crawling through every crevice of Dallas's life, his family, and questioning the boys, the sheer stress of not knowing what was going to happen, she'd been a wreck just observing it all happen. Most was centered around The Collective from what Kamren understood. Very little had to do with either of the boys.

The boys. They were a mess. They'd gone from quiet and downright terrified some moments to insolent and demanding in others. They both missed Lilly terribly. They both wanted to go back to the cabin, where they weren't watched by so many people.

Translation—they were confused and terrified.

Then she'd gotten dragged into it somehow.

At first, she'd been worried. Dallas and his brothers didn't need her anymore. Heck, they hadn't ever truly needed her help, but she was glad she'd been there to help find the boys. She'd expected to be ignored or even forgotten once the authorities swarmed like a pissed off wasp's nest.

But Dallas and his brothers, all the team, had remained at her side. She hadn't been alone the entire time they'd been back from the woods. No matter what went down, they'd kept her within their central core, apprised of everything.

As if she mattered.

Warmth spread within her.

Dallas was a good man. The Masons were good people. She could see why Rache was so drawn to them.

Rachelle. Kamren squeezed her eyes shut and willed thoughts of her sister and the troubles she'd left back in Marville away. For tonight, she wanted to pretend there weren't problems awaiting her on the horizon. Tonight, she'd spend what time she could with Dallas and celebrate the fact they'd found his son.

She shut off the water, toweled dry, and donned the T-shirt and drawstring shorts. Both swallowed her, but she didn't care. She peered into the mirror long enough to finger-comb the worst of the snags out, and then headed down the hallway into the living area. Dallas was returning from the kitchen, a plate in his hand. He wore a matching pair of drawstring shorts, but they definitely weren't swallowing him.

He hadn't bothered with a shirt, which left the broad sweep of his shoulders, muscled chest and arms, and the steely ridges along his stomach on prominent display. It was a visual feast spotlighted by what little material he did wear, since it clung to his body in all the right places and ended in a soft hug of his thick thighs. The distinctive bulge in the cotton made her entire body warm as his gaze raked over her with the same hungered appreciation.

He set the food down on the coffee table and headed toward her.

Anticipation drummed within her, a steady, rapid beat that pattered wildly beneath her skin as he drew her into his arms. The kiss was demanding and uncontrolled, much like her emotions for

Dallas. She wrapped her arms around him and deepened the fusion of tongues, the taunting of lips. His damp hair brought forward images of him wet in the shower. She couldn't help but imagine being in there with him. A shiver rolled through her body.

"What are you thinking?" he asked, his voice husky with arousal.

"You showered, too."

"Yeah, two bathrooms." He grinned. "I'm thinking I should've joined you."

Kamren curled her toes and smiled shyly. The man was a temptation she had every intention of exploring. Enjoying. "We should go back to the house. What if the boys wake up?"

"The day they had, they'll be out for hours. Jesse and Mom are there if they wake up," Dallas answered as he lifted her up until her legs wrapped around his middle. "I'm gonna fuck you, sweetheart. I need you too much for it to be sweet and slow."

Awareness tingled within her. She was okay with not getting it sweet and slow. She claimed his mouth as he carried her to the back bedroom. Something ignited within her, as if a part of her sensed the importance of this moment—her chance to have Dallas Mason. Every inch of him was hers.

He severed their kiss long enough to set her on the bed. He pulled back just enough to sweep the shirt over her head and toss it across the room. A flash of insecurity scraped her insides as his gaze swept across her naked torso, but then she saw the warmth there.

"I'm not all that..." She halted when he placed a finger atop her lips, the contact so soft that if she hadn't been watching, she might have missed it altogether.

"You're beautiful," he whispered.

She didn't bother arguing. Her mind was too focused on the scars Dallas wore, ones she hadn't ever gotten the chance to notice. She leaned forward and brushed her lips across a long white scar along his side. Knife.

A puckered white patch a few inches lower. Bullet.

Then she was done because Dallas tossed her deeper onto the bed and covered her. The move was swift and the result everything she needed. Dallas's weight settled on her lower body as he claimed her mouth again. She ground against him, promising him with her body what she had no words to describe.

Even if she could speak.

Breathless, she looked up into his intense gaze.

This was really happening. Him. Her.

It'd been so long since she'd been with anyone. She swallowed the insecurity, somehow knowing Dallas would make it good, even if she somehow screwed up.

The next graze of lips was slow and sweet, exactly what he'd said he wouldn't give tonight. She followed his lead; each stroke of her body was met with a touch of his. Pleasure sparked within her wherever he licked, tasted. An arrow of awareness shot southward on the same line as his hot mouth. He nipped, licked, and sucked. She held her breath as he stripped off the shorts and ran deft fingers along her slit.

"Fuck, you're wet for me." He growled the statement in an appreciative tone that shot awareness where his fingers were. Two thrust inside her as she cried out. She reached for him, but he pushed her back on the bed. "I've been thinking about this for a long time, sweetheart."

Thinking about what?

A groan escaped her as his tongue and mouth replaced his hand. Pleasure replaced her initial shock as she threaded her fingers into his hair and held on. Every kiss, flick, and suck coursed sensation through her entire body. The world narrowed until all that existed was him. Her.

She floated in a sea of bliss so raw and wild, her eyes burned with unshed tears. She blinked them away as she tumbled into a crashing wave of ecstasy. But Dallas's ministrations had only begun. The attention continued in a slow foray of tongue, mouth, and hands as he taunted, tasted and toyed with every inch of her body.

"Dallas," she pleaded, unsure what she needed more of. She reached for his thick, hard cock. He severed the contact long enough to strip his shorts off.

She attacked. It was the only word for the speed she used to get what she wanted. Her hand on his cock. Her mouth around the thick shaft. His precum greeted her tongue as he emitted a groan so deep it was a growl. She reached between her legs, slickened her hand with her arousal, then returned it to his length.

"Fuck, that's hot." He grasped her head firmly as she sucked him off. His entire body reacted to the slightest touch of her hands. Her mouth. Every inch of him was hers to explore and enjoy.

And she did.

"Every night, every day," she whispered as she popped his aroused flesh from her mouth.

"What's that?" His voice was ragged, breathy as she looked up into his dilated pupils.

"Gonna suck you off every day. I want you fucking me so hard I pass out every night," she demanded. "That's what I've been thinking about, Dallas."

"No way in hell I'd say no to that, sweetheart, on one condition," he whispered as he yanked her hair. "I get to eat you out whenever I want."

Her entire body trembled with need. "Fuck me, Dallas. I can't wait any longer."

He stooped down and pulled a condom from the pocket of his shorts. She snagged it, ripped the foil packet open with her teeth, then rolled it onto him. Protectiveness flared within her. No, it was way deeper than that. Possessiveness. He was hers. She would never let anyone hurt him again. Or take advantage of him. She was thankful Marla was dead. And Hailey? Well, Kamren could handle that cow.

"I like the way you look at me, my dick," he admitted.

"Oh yeah?"

"Like you own me and it."

"Maybe I do. You got a problem with that?"

"No, which terrifies the fuck out of me." He lifted her leg and swatted her thigh. "Shimmy back, Kam. Gonna fuck you so hard you forget everyone's name but mine."

The slow and sweet Dallas was gone, replaced with a ravenous, all-consuming brand of passion that left her entire body shaking with the need to be fucked by him. She clawed, squeezed, and gripped whatever parts of him she could, but he was totally in control.

He powered into her in one thrust so hard and deep her entire body reacted. With her knees drawn up and spread wide, he looked down with a gaze so consumed with raw hunger she orgasmed. Her entire body shook from the release. A slow, smug satisfaction rolled across his expression.

"Glad I turn you on so much, but we're just getting started." He rolled a nipple between his thumb and forefinger, and pinched as he settled into an intense pace.

Kamren squeezed his cock, thrusting herself upward. But Dallas growled, pinned her down at the hips with both hands and increased the frenzied pace.

"You sure you wanna claim me, my cock?" He powered into her, staying seated deep in her, so deep she almost came again simply thinking about it. "You want me fucking you like this every day?"

"Yes, Dallas."

"Then you gotta know that means you're mine. In every way. Mine to pleasure. Mine to protect. Mine to make love to. Mine to fuck breathless." He twisted her until she was on her knees. Then he slid into her, slow and deep. "Mine."

"Yes. Yes." Head down, ass in the air. "Fuck me, Dallas."

"So fucking hot for me. Don't ever guard yourself in my bed, Kamren. This is what we are together. Alone. Anything we want. Whenever. No boundaries. No defenses."

God. Yes.

He pounded into her. Flesh slammed against flesh. The bed shook beneath them. Her cries filled the room as he whispered, "Come for me, sweetheart."

She collapsed into his grip as she orgasmed again. He growled and followed her soon. His front to her back, he followed her into the floaty bliss of truly amazing sex, the kind that shook the foundation of everything she'd ever known or wanted.

She was in deep with Dallas Mason and couldn't imagine being happier than in this moment, the one after he'd left the bed just long enough to dispense with the condom. The one where he dragged her against him and them to where they were fully connected. He sighed into her throat.

"Never had this," she whispered. "No one ever came close to giving me this."

"Fuck, sweetheart. So sweet after I fuck you." He wrapped a protective arm around her.

"Glad you've got your boy. Now you can move on, scrape off what that bitch did to you." She swallowed.

"Marla liked collecting playthings, toys. Making men like me, capable of ending anyone a thousand different ways, kowtow to her whims," he said. "She'd angled to get me in her bed a while, but I'd dodged it, knowing she was a piranha that'd chew me up and not ever spit me out. She sent me on a mission with someone who set me up to take a fall, one big enough to rattle the foundations of a powerful ally. It'd leave everyone I cared about at risk 'cause the people who'd come after me wouldn't have stopped 'til everyone I loved was dead."

She squeezed his hand. She couldn't imagine a life like that. All alone.

"It didn't go the way she'd planned because I didn't fall. I struck back in a way that left me standing and The Collective twisting in the wind. I can't give you details. Even if I could, I wouldn't. That level of nightmare haunts you every night, and I want you sleeping sweet against me."

God. She squeezed her eyes shut. "Want you sleeping sweet against me, too, Dallas."

"I will. 'Cause the bitch is dead. She sent Jud to kill me. He was an assassin for them, way deeper than I ever was. The best around. He saw something in me; I never asked what. Never found out why, but he took my side in a way where the only maneuver Marla had was to let me walk away from The Collective. She gave me an out, one she'd never given to anyone."

"But it came with a price," she guessed.

"Yeah. A big one." He sighed. "I'm man enough to admit I was terrified and exhausted, so deep over my head and missing my family I couldn't imagine staying another single day. I looked that bitch in the eye and gave her the best damn weekend of her miserable life. Never knew the fallout until she was dying."

"KAM." She moaned, snuggled against the warmth, then realized Dallas wasn't behind her. She blinked and heard his voice again. "Need you to wake up, sweetheart. We gotta get moving."

"Huh?"

"Get dressed, baby." Dallas moved. He dragged on cargo pants. A shirt. Sat on the edge of the bed and had shoes and socks on before she had wiped her eyes. That's when she felt it.

Tension.

"What's wrong, Dallas?"

"Something happened, an attack on the Marville Dog compound. Need to get you to your girl."

Dani. Kamren bolted out of bed. She snagged the clothes Dallas held out for her. Fear crawled through her throat. He wasn't offering up any more information which either meant he didn't know anything else, or it wasn't good.

No. No. No.

Years. For years she'd begged and pleaded with Dani to leave that life behind, let the Dogs have their patch of the world. She needed to move on, even if it meant leaving Marville and Kamren behind in her dust.

"Look at me, sweetheart," Dallas ordered.

Watery-eyed, she peered up as he cupped her face. "Your girl is okay. That's all I know. Our man inside the Marville Dogs wanted me to wait for more, but I'm not ever gonna be the guy standing between you and what you have the right to know. You don't need me fighting your fights."

Wow. He totally understood her. "She's okay."

"Yeah, sweetheart, she's okay. Marcus was there. You remember him? The guy who was the last one standing in your one-woman war." Marcus was a good shooter. He'd lasted longer than anyone. "He kept her safe."

"Who...?"

"We're assuming Dom, but we've gotta get to Marville, sweetheart." He set her shoes on the ground. "Get dressed."

They left as soon as Kamren got dressed. Dallas drove like a madman. Each minute that ticked by on the illuminated clock increased her worry. Shouldn't Marcus have called back or something? Why hadn't Dani called?

Police lights and headlights flooded the area. Shadows moved within the lights as people walked around on the lawn of Dani's childhood home. Dallas parked closer than Kamren expected. She exited just as he arrived at her side. Arms around each other, they walked toward the line of police tape strung around the gate.

"Mason, turn your ass around and leave. This isn't your business," Haskell ordered. His gaze raked over Kamren. "It sure as shit isn't yours, unless you've got a lead on who did this. Was it you?"

"Step aside, Haskell," Dallas ordered. "Not fucking with you or your shit tonight."

"I'm Sherriff in this county. I'm the law. Get lost."

"You might be the law tonight, but we both know it won't last much longer," Dallas said. "We're here to check on Daniella. We'll stay out of your way."

"She's around the corner sitting on the truck bed. I need her to give me a statement. So far she's had some guy dragging her off every time I try and get one." Haskell glared in the direction he'd pointed. "Ten minutes, then I'm coming over. Either she gives me a statement, or I'm hauling her in as an accessory."

"On what grounds?" Kamren asked.

"Pissing me off." The bastard walked back into the house.

Kamren let her gaze sweep over the area. Blood and carbine. Her sensitized smelling picked the scents up easily. She clung to Dallas as he guided them around to where the sheriff had indicated.

Dani was wrapped in a blanket and sitting on the tailgate of a brown Ford truck. Marcus did a half a head turn and lifted his chin as they approached. Kamren raced to her best friend.

"Kam. I wanted to call, but he wouldn't let me go get my phone."

"Told you I called her, woman. There's no way in hell you're going back into that house." Marcus looked at Dallas as he crossed his arms. "Thinking Dom reacted to your visit."

Dani tightened. "You saw Dom? When?"

Dallas's jaw twitched. Kamren squeezed her best friend. "Look at me, honey. Don't go there. Don't lay blame where you know it's not gonna settle. You know. You know this is on Javier. He set this into motion the day he stood in the yard with Dom's crew and said my mouth was only good for Marville Dog. Your cousin saying that about me while he's supposed to be protecting you? No way Dom would let that ride. Disrespect."

Dani sniffled. Her shoulders trembled as she buried her face in Kamren's neck. Unsure what to say beyond what'd already been said, she remained quiet and let her friend cry it out. She could count on one hand how many times her best friend had cried.

The first and last had been the night they arrested Dom.

Once.

Before tonight.

"Are you okay? Do you need a hospital?"

"No." She shook her head. "It all happened so fast. One minute I was getting a beer from the fridge, then I heard noises. And this brute tackled me. Then gunfire. Glass everywhere."

Kamren looked at Marcus as she pulled Dani back into a hug. "Thank you." She mouthed the words and got a chin lift in response.

"I'm thinking someone didn't realize she was in the house," Dallas said.

"He'd better not ever find out," Dani growled. She stood, wiped her face off, and glared up at Dallas. "He doesn't ever find out."

"He?" Haskell asked. "Dare I hope you know who did this?"

"Afraid not. I was minding my own business, having a beer when gunfire exploded around me. I fell to the ground to protect myself and didn't see a damn thing, Sheriff."

"Afraid I'll have to bring you in for questioning then, ma'am."

"That's not happening," Dallas said. "You want to chat with her, Haskell, you phone out to The Arsenal. We'll arrange it. Until then, no one gets near her. Understood?"

"You don't run this county, boy."

"No, but you sure as shit don't either. She's done. You want a conversation with her, call The Arsenal." Dallas waited until the man backed away.

"I'll be in contact in the morning, Ms. DeMarco."

"She's coming with us," Dallas said.

Dani tightened. "No, I'm not."

"Don't be loco," Marcus said. "You aren't staying here."

"I'll go to Sylvia's."

"That the same Sylvia whose brother was just whacked inside?" Marcus asked. "That Sylvia?"

"He's right, Dani. I know you've got your issues with the Masons, but you've gotta have a safe place to crash."

"Not going out there. Don't ask me to go there, Kam. I can't, not tonight." She swallowed. "You know Sylvia wasn't tight with her *familia*. She wasn't. She'll let me crash."

Marcus cursed in Spanish. Long, loudly, and rather creatively. "Fine. You go to Sylvia's, I go to Sylvia's."

"No, you don't."

"*Mamita*, you're chewing through my last nerve. I'd pick your battles. This isn't one you're winning." Marcus stared Dani down.

"Okay, I suppose you can come, too."

God. Kamren squeezed her friend closer. "I'll come too, make sure you're settled in."

"Sweetheart, I need you back at The Arsenal where you're safe," Dallas whispered in Kamren's ear.

"I can't leave her. She's my best friend, Dallas." She looked up at him. "We'll be with Marcus. Just a few hours, then you can come and get me."

"Fine, but you call if you need anything." He kissed her lips, then looked over at Marcus.

"She's covered," the man said. "Both of them are.

With that, Dallas left.

The phone.

Kamren rose and raced after him before he could leave. She saw headlights from another reflect on the truck, which was odd because it was typically one lane road. Then again, it was probably an ambulance or cop car. She shifted to the side.

Brakes grinded. Pain exploded along her side as she was yanked hard. She landed headfirst into the back of a large cargo van. Tires spun.

She looked up into the eyes of Henry Mills. He grinned down, then put a smelly rag over the top of her nose and mouth.

22

"Fuck!"

Dallas slammed his fist into the wall of the compound's waiting room. Whoever had taken Kamren was smart enough to have a plan in place. They'd had a total of four white cargo vans fan out at the Y leading out of Marville. By the time Dallas had realized what the hell he'd witnessed, the van was far enough away for the diversion to work. He'd given chase to one while Marcus and Dani took another.

She'd been in one of the other two.

Rage consumed him.

"We'll find her," Mary said.

"I shouldn't have let her stay there. I knew it wasn't the right call," Dallas said.

"You did it for her. For me," Dani said. "That's why you're the right man for her."

He looked over the woman who'd set aside her aversion to all things Mason because her best friend was now missing. Kidnapped from right under Dallas's nose.

"Shouldn't have let her run off like that," Marcus said.

"That's not on you," Vi said. "Or Dallas. Or anybody. Someone was clearly watching the situation, recognized the opportunity, and took it. Now let's get busy finding her. Henry Mills is our most likely suspect. He's got several properties in this area. We just have to find the right one."

"You think he'd take her to somewhere tied to him?" Marshall asked. "Not very smart."

"No, but arrogant as fuck, which he is," Jud said. "List the properties out. We'll split up, hit them all. We can roll out in twenty, be there in ten."

Dallas was down with that idea.

"I swear once we get her back, I'm strapping you all down and Lo-Jacking your asses," Bree said. "Seriously. No one else is ever getting taken. Not on my watch."

The blonde stormed out, tears in her eyes. Everyone watched her slam the door leading to where her lab was.

"I'll go," Rhea offered.

"No, let me." Addy headed that direction. "Though Lo-Jacking us is a good idea."

It was. Dallas looked at Mary and Vi, who were already looking at one another in that contemplative way. Yeah, they'd be chipping everyone soon enough. Never again would one of theirs get taken.

～

"THIS WASN'T VERY SMART, HENRY," Kamren said. She glared at the man sitting across the small shack. In his expensive three-piece suit and fancy tie, he looked out of place in the old Canales supply shed. "Let me go, and I'll pretend I got lost."

"You've cost me a great deal of money." Rage filled the man's words.

"What's wrong? Did your investors pull out when all the authorities started asking questions?"

"You bitch, you have no idea what you and your stupid old man stepped into."

"No, but I wanna know. Why did you kill him?"

"Stupid, stupid bitch. I didn't. I didn't give a damn what he did or didn't see because I knew as long as the money was flowing his mouth would stay shut. Who do you think was telling me which plots of land would be the smartest to get? And which Marville resident was hurting the most?"

No. Her dad may have been a bastard in many ways, but he wouldn't have betrayed his neighbors like that. Then again, had he really been close to any of them? She squeezed her eyes shut and forced the skepticism away.

Ha. First use of the new word of the day.

Thoughts of Bree brought on the realization that The Arsenal was going to be mighty pissed. Dallas. Oh God, he'd been right there. Chasing after her.

Anger rolled in. Her man had been through enough. The kids had been through way, way too much. No more. She assessed her surroundings as she shifted awkwardly, raising herself to her knees.

The knife she'd tucked away at the small of her back was still there in its sheath. So were the twins. It'd become a secret ritual, one only Dallas noticed. She always, always kept them on her. A reminder.

She was strong.

She was fierce.

The thoughts bolstered her confidence. All she needed was patience. Let him spew his hate and rage. She'd take whatever he dished, then she'd strike when she got a chance. Get the hell out. Away.

Dallas would find her.

He just needed time.

Henry Mills had bought up lots of properties in the area, but there were lots of Arsenal teams and they were a short fifteen miles away and armed to take on third-world militaries. The stupid, arrogant ass spewing his bullshit wasn't a match for them. She almost pitied the asshole.

"Heard you're quite the tracker," Mills commented. "Some of my clients enjoy some rather daring activities. I think you'd make an excellent game, wouldn't you agree?"

Rage fired within her veins as the bastard nodded. Two large hooligans hauled her up, dragged her out of the small shack, and untied her hands.

What the hell?

"You want to go back to your man?" Henry grinned. "Go. You have two minutes. Then my clients give chase. You don't want to get caught by them, Ms. Garrett. They aren't very nice."

God. God. God.

"Time's wasting. Tick tock, Ms. Garrett. Tick tock." He looked around at one of the other goons. "Start the timer. Two minutes. Then phone them, let them know their prey is on the run."

Kamren fled. Mesquite bushes scraped her skin, leaving a trail of fabric, skin, and blood in her wake. Didn't matter. Not yet. Distance was what she needed now.

It'd been years since she'd been at the Canales farm, but she'd once known this stretch of land well and had helped her father with its maintenance for a long time. They wanted to turn this into a playground? Damn bastards.

They'd never find her.

She retracted the knives from their sheaths along the curvature of her back. Idiots hadn't even made sure she didn't have weapons. She was sorely tempted to circle back and kill the bastards. Embrace her inner Jud. Or her inner Dallas. Yeah, that sounded pretty good.

But she wasn't Jud or Dallas.

So she ran like hell, making sure she left as little a trail as possible. The extra seconds she took covering her progression could save her life. She didn't know what his clients had in mind. Was it a giant mind fuck? Was anyone even giving chase?

That's when she heard them. Catcalling. Screaming her name.

Terror rolled through her, then she remembered Mary's lethal calm. Vi's confidence.

Addy's deadly stealth.

Those three wouldn't ever run in terror. No, they'd plan. Fight.

Kill.

"WE'VE GOT ANOTHER ONE," Jud shouted from a few feet away.

Dallas sprinted that direction. His gut twisted as he eyed the prone body. The man squirmed. Blood coated his pants from the savage knife wounds along the backs of his knees.

"Help me. The bitch is crazy," the man said.

They'd caught Henry Mills on his way out of town, but the game had already been set in motion. *Game.* Disgust filled him as he remembered what the man's bodyguard had shared. Seven hunters were looking for her.

"That's three down," Addy said, her pride evident. "I'm thinking she could teach us a few things. She's got a natural instinct."

"Thinking I'd rather not have my woman running for her life in a fucking pasture," Dallas spat angrily as he sought another clue.

Jesse had been the one to notice the first one, back with the first man she'd taken down. A small heart with an arrow carved into the ground. Dallas spotted another and vaulted toward where the arrow pointed.

"This was fresh. We're close," Nolan said. "Jesse and Marshall took one of them down, that leaves three in play."

"Make that two. Marcus and I just got another," Cord said. "Pretty fucking impressed they're all still breathing. Your girl's good with traps. And knives."

"Starting to really appreciate those knives you gave her," Dallas admitted to Jud.

"Me, too."

Together they continued in the direction of the arrow. Drones whirred past them.

"She's circling back around toward..." Vi's voice halted. "I think she's going to her farm."

"She'd know the land," Zoey said.

"Justice, where it all started," Dylan said into the com. "She's going to stand her ground where the bastard killed her father. That's what I'd do. Bleed him out where she found her father."

"Country justice," Jesse offered.

Fuck. Dallas sprinted toward where her farmland started. They weren't far if they cut through brush country. The headset displayed their target location: where her father died. Dallas's beautiful, brilliant woman was biding her time, hoping they'd show up in time.

"Erm, just a friendly reminder our girl is damn good at the whole escape and evade thing. So, traps," Zoey said.

"Understood," Gage said. "Fallon and I are coming up on the target zone from the west. Dispensing more drones."

"Roger," Mary said. Moments later, the woman's voice returned to the com. "Final two targets have been spotted, in pursuit of our package."

Son of a bitch.

"Drones have target in range. Firing," Vi said. "One target down."

The video feed spewed into his headgear as Dallas pressed on. Close. His lungs heaved air into them, expended it. Labored breaths entered and exited. Weapon drawn, he shoved through overgrown shrubbery, not mindful of the thorny thickets. Nothing mattered except getting to Kamren.

He pushed through the final patch of brush and entered the edge of the clearing where her father had died. The bastard was fighting with her. Drones buzzed and whirred, preparing to fire at him, but Dallas didn't wait.

He knelt.

Aimed.

Fired.

He didn't wait to confirm the kill. He never missed, especially not when it mattered.

Kamren rose from the ground where the bastard had punched her until she fell. Blood seeped from her mouth and nose. She looked at the dead man, then tracked the bullet's trajectory. Her gaze narrowed, then she ran.

She powered into him in a crush of trembling limbs. "I knew you'd find me."

"The swath of bodies was hard to miss," Jud commented dryly as he and the others converged on their location. "Great job, Kam."

"The man was a loon. He...they..." She forced a few deep breaths. "They were hunting me. Like an animal. They were nuts."

"Looks like there's another facet to the Henry Mills investigation," Mary commented. "Get our girl home. We'll take it from here, Dallas. Nolan, Sanderson, you're point. Texas Rangers are inbound, along with the FBI. A couple of our girl's captures are wanted in Louisiana."

THREE DAYS LATER...

Things calmed after Henry Mills and his crazy clients were arrested. According to the FBI, the crew had been hunting people a while, mostly in the Louisiana bayou country where they were from. As far as the investigators could tell, Kamren had been their first hunt with Mills, which meant that hadn't been the reason her father was murdered.

Though the *why* was still an unknown circling around Kamren, she'd reconciled herself to the fact that she'd done enough to get answers. She'd taken down Mills. Soon enough authorities would be picking over the rest of the Marville assholes, like Haskell.

She'd spent the couple days following her ordeal with Dallas and the kids.

Living.

Loving.

Being loved.

By the morning of the third day, she was restless. The women had convinced the men to let them have a girls' adventure. This hadn't gone over well, but the guys had grudgingly agreed since there were drones in place and since Jud would go with them.

Yikes.

Kamren rode her high of fantastic morning sex with Dallas all the way into Resino and straight into Bubba's. To hell what anyone thought. The women around her laughed and chattered amongst themselves on the way over. There'd been a lot of talk about Mary's and Vi's upcoming nuptials. With Dallas's sons home where they belonged, they both had ring bearers. That was Momma Mason's latest declaration.

They were two drinks into their merry excursion when conversation shifted to Kamren. And Dallas.

"You and Dallas were hot and heavy last night," Zoey commented. "Cord and I saw you two sneaking into the mess hall for a late-night snack. Must've worked up one hell of an appetite."

Riley choked on her beer. Kamren wasn't sure whether it was a good idea to divulge details about her late-night romp with Dallas, especially since he was Riley's big brother. That. Ventured into TMI and downright weird territory. Since the woman's eyes were bugged out and Rachelle looked like she was about to puke at the thought, Kamren opted to keep her reply short. "We had a good time."

"Pfft," Bree replied. "A good time is a nice steak dinner, maybe a walk in a park or something dull. What a good time isn't is me and Cord having to take sound down on cameras in the cafeteria when you two decide you'd..."

"Woah!" Riley held up her hand. "Thrilled my brother has a good woman that brought him back to who he used to be, but I do not need details about how she's doing that."

"You want them together?" Rachelle asked, sputtering as she set the beer down.

"Well, first, I learned a long time ago that I will not ever get a say in who my brothers bed. Second, yeah. I was skeptical, but after hearing all the shit she did to get my nephews home, she's earned my respect and my vote."

"TJ isn't even your nephew," Rachelle retorted angrily.

"You shouldn't mention what you see on feeds, Z," Vi said. "We respect people's privacy. Otherwise, Mary and I could ask you what's up with you and Sanderson, seeing how he's had you pressed against..."

"Okay, point made," Zoey replied quickly. "And there's nothing going on with me and Gage. He thinks I'm up to something, and he's determined to keep you two protected from little me and my bad self."

"Are you?" Mary asked.

"Nothing bad. You know where I used to work. I have secrets I can't divulge, things I've done I can't ever talk about."

"We get that," the two women answered simultaneously.

Everyone laughed.

It was well into the third drink when the atmosphere within Bubba's shifted. Everyone around them silenced, as if prepping for an apocalyptic event. Hailey Suthers and her cronies walked in. Addy chuckled. Bree and Rhea shared wide-eyed stares at one another while Mary and Vi growled. Riley and Rachelle looked at Kamren, but her focus was on the parasitic bitch who'd date-raped her man.

She'd drugged him in this very fucking joint, gotten him into her bed, and *raped* him.

Since the high of her pleasure with Dallas was still humming within her veins, the rage hit fast. She didn't want the bitch in the same air space as her man. Or Dylan. Neither of them deserved having to handle her existence within their world. The thought surged her forward as her focus tunneled on Hailey.

She was across the small room and had the woman pinned against the corner wall before anyone could stop her, not that she'd thought anyone would. The two women Hailey had entered with were already a good four feet away and looking over at Addy, who'd followed the flow of Kamren's wake. The redhead was shaking her head and her finger in a don't-even-think-about-interfering kind of way.

"She's crazy!" Hailey shouted. "Someone call the sheriff."

"You know me," Kamren said, her voice low as the knife she'd drawn scraped against the woman's cheek.

"Yeah, you're the crazy Garrett, the one who can't read, right?"

"Suppose that's true. What I can do, though, is carve you up, gut you like a deer. I'd probably get it mostly done before you bled out."

She looked down as if assessing the possibility, then grunted. "Yeah, think I'd figure it out."

"Let me go."

"Why? You scared? You don't want to be here? You don't want my blade scraping your pretty face? You don't want my filthy, uneducated hands on you?"

"Oh boy," someone muttered.

"About damn time," someone else replied.

Kamren didn't know the patrons commenting, but their statements didn't surprise her. The Mason were respected, especially in Resino. She was a bit surprised someone hadn't already set Hailey straight about what she'd done to Dallas. Then again, Mary had at some point when she and Dylan got together.

Hailey's eyes widened as realization settled into her pea-sized brain. Kamren was pissed and no one in Bubba's was gonna stop her from doing whatever she wanted to do.

"Yeah, I'm thinking I'm not the slow one in this conversation, so I'm gonna break it down for you real easy so you can keep up."

The woman trembled as Kamren pressed the tip of the blade into her cheek.

"Rule one, you do not ever come in here again. You see a Mason truck in this lot, you keep going. For that matter, you see a Mason truck at the post office, at the grocery in Nomad, *anywhere* in the tri-county, you keep riding past. You don't and I hear word you breathed the same air as my man, I'll scrape the skin clear off you. I even know someone who'll teach me how." She motioned to Jud, who'd moved to stand nearby.

Arms crossed, he smirked as he quirked his eyebrows, leaned back against the wall, and watched.

"Make no mistake, Hailey, you breathe the same air as my man or any of his brothers, I will find out. There's not an inch of the tri-county you can hide in because I know it all. If I can find a little boy in millions of forested acreage, I can damn sure track your worthless, man-raping filth down." She paused for effect. "Nod so I know you understand."

Hailey glared. Kamren pushed the blade just a bit harder, enough to prick the skin. Hailey nodded.

"Good. Now, rule two's gonna be a bit harder for you to follow along with, but we'll go slow. You do not ever speak about my man or his brothers or anyone out at The Arsenal. I've heard the shit you've been saying about Dylan. And I know the shit you've said about the woman he's marrying. You spew that filth all over the tri-county. If I even get a whiff of that shit coming from your mouth again, getting skinned will be the least of your worries. I can shoot a grape from a thousand yards. You're way bigger than a grape."

She gulped.

"Now, should you or anyone else feel the need to share this conversation with someone or should anyone ask about your past experience with my man and his brother, you had better set the record straight so that everyone knows you're a man-raping scumbag bitch who does not ever deserve good men like them." She released her grip. "Now get the fuck out of my space before I get pissed."

She sheathed her knife and glared as Hailey and her two friends scurried out of Bubba's. She returned to her seat, took a swig of her beer, and looked at the women around her. Startled expressions greeted her assessing gaze. "What?"

"Girl, you just earned free beers for life," Bubba declared. "Already earned free food finding my grandbabies."

"Can't keep handing out free shit, Bubba," she counseled sagely, like she knew how to run a business. "Besides, it was my pleasure to set that cow straight."

Bubba's big hand settled on her head as he set a fresh beer in front of her and took the warm half-empty. "Thrilled he has a good woman taking his six."

She cleared her throat and took a sip of beer, unsure what to say.

"That was..." Zoey started, then halted.

"Awesome!" Bree finished.

"Wow," Riley said. "If you didn't have my vote before, you sure as hell have it now."

"They're right," Mary added, her tone confident and authoritative.

"I still remember the way he and Dylan froze up when that bitch was near them. Taking care with the women around them is so engrained they don't know how to turn it off and keep themselves safe when they're the prey."

Although the woman's gaze remained locked on Kamren, she sensed the shift in everyone else's to Rachelle. None of them had forgotten her episode with Jesse.

"I hope they all find a woman who'll have their backs like you just had his," Mary said. "I told him he'd find a good woman one day, but I don't think he believed me. I'm thinking he does now." The woman's eyes twinkled as she picked up her tea, raised it in a toast, and sipped from the straw. Her gaze swept upward and a smile spread across her face.

A warm hand settled on Kamren's back. She looked up and froze as her gaze locked with Dallas.

And Dylan.

Fuck.

Dallas leaned down and grinned as he claimed her mouth in a kiss so hot her beer bottle should've melted. He nipped her earlobe. "Babe."

"Don't be pissed," she ordered.

"Not pissed, but you'd best finish that beer. Seeing my woman in action has me harder than hell."

Wow. Suddenly she was being pulled from her chair. Dylan paused their progression to give her a hug.

"Bubba's right. I'm thrilled he's got you in his corner."

And she was totally in his corner, no matter what. She looked around and realized they'd all been there for Dallas. One more than anyone, yet she doubted he'd ever been thanked or even acknowledged. She powered forward before she could think the urge through fully.

Jud grunted from the impact as she wrapped her arms around him and squeezed tight. "Thank you for having his six. Thank you for saving him so he could come back here to his family."

"Jesus," the man whispered as he returned the hug.

23

F *our days later...*
Both of the boys were acclimating to life at the Mason house fairly well. Momma Mason had cooked enough food for a hundred grown adults, but Kamren sensed Dallas and his siblings weren't about to say anything to the woman who'd taken her new role as a grandma very, very seriously.

Doctor Sinclair had spent the past week and a half working with TJ and DJ. Tests. Games. Everything centered around establishing their physical, mental and emotional health and determining how far behind they were educationally. Kamren's stomach soured at the last bit. She knew a thing or two about being behind and never catching up.

It was nearly lunch. She'd spent the day wandering the back acreage with Dallas and both boys, who'd taken to tracking the coyote, deer, armadillo, and rabbit tracks like proverbial ducks to water. They'd asked pointed questions about how she could tell what kind of animal, the sex of the animal, the age.

Though she suspected Dallas could've easily handled all the answers himself, he'd included her. The fact he'd thought to do so made her heart warm. No matter how much she tried, she couldn't deny that she was head over heels in love with Dallas Mason. He personified everything good she'd always wanted—craved more than the air she dragged into her lungs.

And the way he looked at her...

She flashed him a smile when she caught his gaze on her again. He did that a lot, watching her. Somehow, he managed to divide his attention between her and the boys, never letting her or them feel as though they weren't his sole focus.

"You two hungry?" Dallas asked.

"Yes!" DJ shouted.

"TJ? You ready to eat?" Dallas asked.

"Yeah, I guess. You gonna eat, Kam?"

She nodded. Dallas had mentioned something about her going with the kids somewhere. For barbecue. Her stomach rumbled at the prospect.

"Piggy back! Piggy back!" DJ shouted as he reached his arms up to Kamren.

Her side ached at the prospect. Before she could respond, Dallas had his son up and tossed into the air. Merry giggles and laughter echoed as the boy landed, then was carefully set on Dallas's wide shoulders. Kamren couldn't help but smile at the wide smile the boy beamed. He waved wildly. "Jesse! No!"

She chuckled at the abbreviated term for Nolan as the two men arrived at their side. "His name is Nolan, DJ. *No* is an important word, not a name. Okay?"

"Okay." The boy grinned. "We're going to go eat."

"Bubba's?" Jesse asked.

"Yep," Dallas. "You two in?"

"Sure," Nolan said. He set a hand on TJ's shoulder. "You want a ride to the truck?"

"Nah, I'm too big."

"Nonsense." The man hoisted TJ into the air and settled him atop his shoulders.

TJ looked down at Kamren, then over at Dallas, as if seeking approval to relax and be a kid. Her chest squeezed tight. Every move, every action had likely been so filled with danger he'd never been anything but wary. She smiled up at him. As if the slight gesture loosened the stranglehold he'd maintained, he dissolved into a peel of laughter as Dallas and Nolan started a mock tickle fight between the two boys.

The boys crawled into the back of the truck with Nolan and Jesse, who both insisted Kamren sit up front with Dallas.

By the time everyone was buckled in and the vehicle rumbled onto the highway, Kamren's mind had calmed.

She squeezed her eyes shut. It'd been nice having someone there, strong at her side. Even if she'd had no business expecting it of him. The last few days had been the best ever, and she was terrified it'd all suddenly end. That Dallas would realize he was wasting too much precious time with her when DJ and TJ were the only ones who mattered. As long as they were safe and healthy, well, that's all that mattered, she supposed.

What time she'd had with him was a gift, really. She had no business thinking it'd ever be more than that. She wasn't the kind of woman who could keep a good man like him happy. She certainly wasn't good mom material for those two boys. What could she do, really? She couldn't help with homework. She couldn't even cook all that well.

She hunted.

That was about it, and there wasn't much call for that sort of thing at The Arsenal.

"You okay?" he asked. An invisible fist squeezed her heart. He always sensed when her mind wandered into the dark thoughts.

She forced a smile and a nod even though the answer was a resounding no. No, she wasn't okay, because for the first time in her entire life she was happy.

And it fucking terrified her.

Nervousness settled in her gut as Dallas wheeled the truck into a parking lot already filled with tons of vehicles. The building was small, way too tiny to hold everyone in all those trucks. Even if there was just one person per vehicle, well...she wasn't good at math but that was way more people in one small space than DJ and TJ had likely ever handled. Except for maybe at The Arsenal a few times.

But that'd been different because they'd been secure. Her gaze roamed the area as she assessed exit strategies and spotted makeshift weapons. A pipe by the trash bin. A cement cinder block three steps from where Dallas parked. The kids weren't ready for this level of exposure. Were they?

She peered into the back and saw the curious smiles on their expressive faces. TJ had forgone the little man syndrome and remained a curious boy. The hope gleaming within their gazes squashed her worries. No matter what went down inside, she'd handle it. They'd be safe.

"Sweetheart, it warms my heart and soul to see you worried about my kids, but not a single person in this town will do them harm. Or you." Dallas's voice was a startling whisper of hot air against her cheek. He'd leaned into her, and she hadn't noticed. "This is Resino, not Marville."

Right. The fifteen-mile distinction was a huge one. She'd never really explored Resino much, but Bubba's barbecue was sublime. Heh. Bonus use of the word, which meant she could get an extra one from Bree and have two words in play.

He unlatched the belt strapping her in.

"It'll be okay. No way in hell anyone in there will touch the boys. They do, you have my permission to kick their ass."

She nodded. Good enough for her.

"Assuming me and my brothers don't do it first," he said with a grin. "Come on, let's eat."

Any semblance of little boy radiating from TJ died when they exited the vehicle. DJ latched onto his big brother and activated protection mode. Kamren stifled her own need to protect the boys as Nolan and Jesse took point behind them. Dallas settled a hand on TJ's shoulder as he stood on the other side of DJ, effectively book-ending the boy. The protective attention to detail before they'd even stepped into the building deepened her love for Dallas.

He was already a damn good dad. It radiated within him naturally; he exuded it in every alert sweep of his gaze, every gentle rub on the boys' backs. Dallas put his other arm around her waist and drew her close, as if shrouding her in the lethal confidence he exuded like a second skin. But she'd never had someone shroud her in anything, and she had a real hard time forgetting that she shouldn't get too used to it. She angled to the side a step, enough to separate her from the pack.

Dallas reached the door first and opened it. Music drifted from a large glass jukebox in the corner. Conversation hummed within the air like an explosion. Details of the words on people's lips drifted into her brain as her gaze flitted about the room. Then a still, deathly silence descended in the building. Every eye in the place landed on them.

Tension coiled within her as she noted the threats within the room. A pack of four tall, muscular men in the corner nearest the eastern sector of the bar. A cluster of three nearest their position to her right. Lips started moving as whispers filled the room. Conversations sifted into her brain as she deciphered the unheard words.

Mason's boy.

Jesus. He looks just like him. Wait. There's two?

No way the second one's a Mason. No fucking way.

I heard he's taking both on.

Crazy-ass bitch to saddle him with this.

Hell of a man taking on a kid he didn't know or want.

Was it true? Did he not want the boys there? Sure, he hadn't known, but why would he hunt them down if they were such a burden? Did the strangers gawking at them know Dallas and his brothers well enough to judge the situation?

Did it matter?

"You okay?" Dallas asked.

"Fine." She shoved the word out through clenched teeth as her gaze continued scanning conversations around her. Sit where the smallest threat was.

Easier said than done. There weren't any open seats. Then she spotted the empty table in the far back of the room, nearest a narrow hallway leading to...a secondary exit. Perfect. It was where she'd sat the day before with the women. She made a beeline for the table, squeezing past the two tables of gawking people rudely discussing TJ's darker skin tone and possible heritage.

Did Dallas knocked up two different women?

Anger seeped into her as the unwanted inquiries listed in her brain. She couldn't help but note their existence. She'd trained her entire life to assess a room, analyze potential threats and react as necessary—all without giving away that she saw every conversation, spied on every utterance in three languages fluently. She hadn't picked up reading, but she'd studied her ass off mastering the ability to please her father, who'd spent hours reading dictionaries to her, making her memorize the lip movements of each word. Hours upon hours for years.

Kamren waited for everyone to sit. She wanted her back to the hall on the outside of the large bench. When none of the men moved, she sat where she wanted and glared up at Dallas, daring him to question her decision. His lips twitched, as if he understood the war she was willing to wage. Jesse and Nolan both chuckled as they motioned TJ and DJ into the middle of them on the opposite side.

Though the bench was plenty big for Dallas to not sit close, he settled right beside her. Right. Against. Her. Heat danced beneath her skin where his jean-clad thigh brushed against hers. Memories of their lovemaking the past several days flashed through her mind and burned away some of the anxiety pulsating within her like a second presence. She'd always hated crowded places.

Dallas made her pulse quicken for an entirely different reason she didn't pretend to understand. Was she scared? No, not of him. So why was her entire awareness settled on the way his thigh felt against hers?

Because you're in love, idiot.

An older, bearded man with a large belly headed straight toward them. Bubba. He shoved through the swollen crush of people, and his mouth spread into a barely-visible grin as he stood at the table. "Always makes my heart swell seeing you Masons at your table. Add in the woman who saved my grandbabies, and it's a fine day at Bubba's."

Their table?

She looked up and noted his gaze was still on hers. "You gonna skin any bitches in my bar today?"

"No, today's my day off." Her attention swept to the two young boys with them. Cursing around them didn't seem like the smartest move, but she powered on. "How are the twins? They good?"

"Thanks to you they will be."

"Why?" DJ asked.

"My grandbabies, about your brother's age, they got themselves lost. One of them fell into a hole, got hurt pretty bad. Kamren and your pa and uncles found them."

"They're good at finding people in holes. They found Lilly," DJ offered.

Red rose in Bubba's face as the horrors within the innocent reply swept through the room in a not-so-hushed wave of whispers.

"TJ and DJ," Dallas motioned to each one. "This is Bubba, the best damn barbecue master around and a great guy. If you are ever in trouble or separate from us and in town, you head over here and find him. Okay?"

"Does he have a badge?" TJ asked.

"No."

"So he's like you? No rules."

"When it comes to family, no rules," Bubba replied. He looked around the table. "You boys, your pa and all his kin, you're family as far as I'm concerned. You ever need me, I'm here."

The boys nodded quickly.

"Spitting image," Bubba said. He reached up and wiped his eyes. "Fucking thrilled for you. Your ma's lighting up the phone lines, keeping everyone apprised. She's invited me and the boys out, says everything out there's wheelchair accessible, so Sam can get around easy."

"Love to have you and your family out, anytime," Jesse answered.

"I've held most folks off, but there'll be a contingent hauling stuff out there tomorrow. Can't hold 'em off any longer since you've come in. Told 'em they'd have to wait until you surfaced." Bubba's loud laughter boomed in the area as he added, "Good thing you've got a big spread out there 'cause I think you're about to get half of Resino's stuff."

Shit. Nolan mouthed the word as he pulled out his cell phone, likely alerting someone to what they'd just learned. The Masons took security seriously, so Kamren suspected a contingent of well-meaning folks wasn't exactly a welcomed gesture.

"Plates'll be out in a minute. What'll you have to drink?"

"Sweet teas all around," Jesse said.

"Gotcha."

"What's tea?" DJ asked.

"Hush. You eat and drink what you're given. Those are the rules," TJ clipped in a hushed order.

"Is it better than juice?" DJ asked. "And what's barbecue? What animal is that, Kam? I hope it doesn't taste like squirrel. I don't like squirrel."

Bubba hadn't left. He remained frozen in place as DJ's little voice rose in frustration as he offered his insights into squirrel. She peered up at the burly man and noted the red rising within his cheeks. She didn't know him, but it wasn't a huge leap to realize he didn't like knowing a little boy had ever eaten squirrel.

The man left without comment. A moment later a loud crash sounded from within the back. Nolan rose from the table and headed that direction. Everyone watched Dallas and the boys. DJ remained blissfully unaware of the scrutiny, but TJ's little body was tight, his gaze frozen to the hallway. The exit. He'd be ready if shit hit. He'd get himself and DJ out.

She recognized the protective sweep of his gaze, the tension within the men at the table as they did as well.

"It's okay," Dallas said. He reached over and took the boy's hand. "Remember what I said? About us taking shifts?"

"Yeah."

"This is ours. Relax and enjoy yourself."

TJ's gaze slid to hers. Though she still didn't fully understand why, he always sought her approval or opinion. She took a deep breath and nodded as she forced back her own anxiety and worry. Dallas was right. This wasn't Marville. It was Resino, where anyone with the last name Mason was practically royalty.

$\sim$

DALLAS WAITED until Nolan had gotten both boys halfway down the hall that lead toward the restrooms before he leaned into Kamren and whispered, "You okay?"

"Yeah. Fine." The words were clipped and forced as her gaze pulverized the room once more.

Jesse glowered behind him. "I'm thinking your woman's not liking the conversations around us much."

Fuck. Of course. He'd been so wrapped up in the boys and enjoying the softer side of Kamren, he'd forgotten she read lips. She'd likely become privy to every thought about every facet of his life the past few years, if not longer. Resino residents had long memories and plenty of opinions to share with whoever would listen.

"I don't give a shit what they think about anything, Kamren. You shouldn't either."

She nodded and wiped her mouth. A tremble radiated in her hand. "I was fine with them yapping about the boys or speculating about me."

Dallas flashed Jesse a look and glared at the tables around them. They were likely chatting about Hailey at this point, possibly Jesse. Plenty of speculation about both subjects had been bandied about.

"Doesn't matter," Jesse said. "My family's given enough to this community, our country. It's about damn time people stop prying."

His voice boomed within the area, but Kamren's body tightened. Determined to drag her away from whatever mental war she waged with everyone around them, he cupped her face and claimed her mouth. The kiss started off as a gentle swipe of tongue across the seam of her lips, but her immediate surrender emitted a moan from him as she deepened the contact.

Whistles and cheers erupted around them, but he didn't give a bloody damn. Kamren and his family—most especially his two sons— were all that mattered. He severed the fusion of tongues and mouths even though all he wanted was to cart her home and keep going. "That protective streak is one of the ten thousand things I love about you."

"W-what?"

"Think you heard me," he whispered. "We'll chat tonight. I think it's past time I make sure you know where we stand. To be clear, it's the kind of conversation highlighting how you are a big part of my life, Kamren."

"Dallas, I don't think..." Her voice lowered as her gaze swept the room. "Why are we having this conversation in a barbecue place with everyone watching?"

"Because the sooner they see this is serious, the quicker they'll shut up and leave us be." He thundered the statement into the room. To hell with being polite. He'd catch hell from his mom, but he'd take the heat if it put his woman and his kids at ease. "Thinking I should've given you the same assurance I did TJ."

"About what?"

"Relax, sweetheart. I've got this. Enjoy your meal. When you're done, we're going over to get more of your things and check on the farmhouse. The boys wanted to see the goats."

"They do?"

"Yeah. In case you missed it, they see a lot of themselves in you, sweetheart. Doctor Sinclair's even noticed how drawn TJ is to you, says you're one of the reasons they've acclimated so quickly at the house. He watches you and follows your lead. You got in deep with him back in the woods." He kissed her mouth. "Another one of the ten thousand things I love about you. You went all in without reservation, giving him a piece of you he isn't ever letting go."

"We cool?" TJ asked as he, DJ, and Nolan returned to the table from the restroom.

"Yeah," Jesse said. "I think it's time we talk Bubba into giving us some peach cobbler."

"Don't tell Mom this." Nolan leaned into the boys as he sat with them at the table. "But Bubba's cobbler's better than hers."

Dallas smirked, knowing full well their mom was already aware of the secret. The entire town was because she bragged about the man's cobbler to anyone who'd listen. Riley suspected she was sweet on Bubba. Dallas had half a mind to believe it was true. He looked over at Kamren and couldn't help but grin.

He hadn't understood the depths of Dylan's emotions for Mary, not at first. Love was something they'd been raised seeing between their parents, but it'd been a long time since he'd felt it for someone outside his family.

Fuck.

Had he ever loved someone? Really and truly loved them to the point that he'd die for them?

His family? Fuck yes.

Anyone else?

He glanced at Kamren and knew the answer. For her and his kids, he'd do anything. He took a sip of his tea to wash down the emotion clogging his throat. Son of a bitch he was in a sappy mood today. It'd been a long time since he felt this level of happiness.

The Collective and the things he'd done for them weren't weighing him down any longer. His brothers knew, and they'd helped him find his kid. Everything Marla had put him through, the bullshit Hailey put him through when he'd gotten home was over and he was happy. His kids were safe.

The smile on TJ's face and the grin—so much like Dallas's—on DJ's face made it all worth it. The woman tearing up beside him as she watched the boys sealed the fact he'd go through it all again if it brought him back to this point.

This was love.

Son of a bitch. He looked over at his two big brothers, who both wore amused expressions. Fuckers knew he was a goner where

Kamren was concerned. They'd called it back in the woods, way before he'd realized it himself.

She was a hell of a woman, and tonight he'd make sure she knew where they stood.

She was his.

～

BY THE TIME they'd stuffed themselves on barbecue, all the fixings, and dessert, the boys had acclimated to the noises of the "city." Calling Resino a city was amusing in many ways, but true for the boys. Kamren remembered how hard it was to return to society when she'd been young. Adapting to the extra noises of so many people within one space. The smells.

"You all ready to go visit my goats?" she asked as they headed toward the truck.

"Yeah!" both boys shouted as Jesse and Nolan helped them into the back seat.

Dallas pressed her against the open passenger's seat door. Heat spread through her like a brushfire. "When we get there, Jesse and Nolan will handle the feeding and showing off the goats."

"Why's that?"

"Because I'm in the mood to have an extra dessert," he whispered against her neck.

Laughter tumbled from her. The man was beyond incorrigible, tactile to a fault. She loved that he enjoyed sex. More importantly, he enjoyed it with *her*. Anticipation beaded along her skin as she wrapped her arms around his shoulders and grinned up at him. His kiss was playful and full of tawdry promises. She couldn't wait.

The boys shared their thoughts on farms as the truck growled down the highway toward Marville. Nolan and Jesse answered the questions, which were plentiful and way more insightful than she expected boys their age to be, not that she knew much about boys their age. She looked over at Dallas. "I should call Dani, let her know

I'll be in town. I haven't gotten a chance to touch base with her since..."

Since hell had broken loose.

Kamren still couldn't believe Javier and his crew were gone.

"Then we'll call, sweetheart." He reached over and pushed a button on the console, then another when a list appeared.

"Yeah." Dani's voice over the truck's loud speakers startled her a moment.

"Dani." Kamren bit back the rush of words on her tongue, the inquiries. "You're on speaker. Dallas's sons are with us, and we're on our way to the farmhouse. I wanted to see you while I was there and make sure you're okay."

She forced a breath after the spew of words vacated her. Silence descended on the other end of the line. "Dani?"

Dallas tightened his grip on the wheel beside her.

"I'm good, but not good. Thinking you need to turn around and leave those boys with their aunt. She was just here checking on me. Give her a buzz, have her take them to the compound, then we can chat," Dani said, her voice low and in a tone Kamren recognized. Guarded. "Thinking you should get some of those fancy-ass teams your man leads to come with you."

Oh no. No. No. No.

"Dani."

"I'm okay. Love you to the bottom of my heart and back. Wherever you are, stop and do what I say. You do, then give me a call when things are in place. Wanna make sure my girl's covered."

No. No. No. No.

Kamren's eyes burned as she blinked back the denial thundering through her mind. Something was terribly wrong. Dani wanted to make sure she was covered, thought she needed fancy-ass teams. The woman hated everything Mason and wouldn't normally consider them a solution to anything, which meant the trouble was big.

"Dani."

"I'm okay. Know you've got the boys there, so I'll be short on the details. Riley has Burton Construction all over fixing the fallout from what went down at my house," Dani said. "I wasn't down with that, but she has a way of talking people around. I'm thinking it's time I set aside my hate of all things Mason. They've had your back in a way I couldn't."

"Dani."

"You had theirs, found the boys," Dani whispered. "Which makes what I've gotta share now cut deep because I can't patch this; it's too big for me to handle. Get those crews en route. Riley left; I just got a call. No one's verified, but Sylvia sees buzzards flying and diving over your place."

Sylvia sees flying and diving over your place. Kamren squeezed her eyes shut again and willed the denial away, even as her mind formed an explanation. Vultures. While they didn't circle dead animals like people believed, they did ride the warm pockets of air and watch situations. Carrion. They preferred their meals fresh. "How many?"

"More than we've seen in a long time," Dani whispered. "Get your man's crew assembled. I'll meet you out there. Call when you're on the way."

The line went dead. Nausea rose in Kamren's stomach as the vehicle pulled to the side of the road. She wanted to climb out and purge the contents from her stomach, but that wasn't an option. Two small boys had hung on every word in the backseat. They'd been through enough hell. She wasn't about to shove them neck deep into whatever was going down in Marville.

Dallas tapped a few buttons and the line rang again. Riley's voice filled the cab. "Hey, I was about to call you. You all still heading over to Marville?"

"Thinking we need a change in plans. Jud with you?" Dallas asked.

"Yeah, why?" Riley's voice shifted, turning alert. "What's wrong?"

"We're three miles out of Marville. Come pick up the kids. Have a team meet us out at the farmhouse," Dallas said.

"Okay. I'm guessing there's more to the story."

"There's more to the story," Dallas confirmed. "Jud's with us when you arrive. We aren't waiting for the team. We're at the curve, just past the Brannigan farm."

"Something's wrong," TJ said. His voice rose when the line clicked off. "You said we were part of the team."

"Yeah, you are," Jesse said. "But we need you and DJ at the compound."

"Why?" DJ asked.

"Cord needs help flying the whirlies," Kamren lied. The boys loved the drones and had been demanding to fly them.

Dallas's jaw twitched, but he didn't refute her claim.

"We can fly them?" DJ asked.

"Sure," Nolan replied. "Riley will take you there."

Most of their troubles had settled, but Kamren suspected they'd yet to face today's real monster. Something was wrong at the farmhouse.

24

It took less time than she'd expected for The Arsenal to arrive where Dallas had wheeled to a stop less than a mile from her familial homestead. Though he'd said they weren't gonna wait, what they'd seen so far had charged the truck's cab with unease and tension so palpable, it was a sixth companion within the cab. She'd moved to the back to sit between Jesse and Nolan, despite everyone's argument otherwise. Jud had grudgingly taken her place up front.

Though her visibility was somewhat limited from the center of the back seat, she'd seen enough and recognized the telltale signs to know what that many vultures in an area meant.

Four black, double-cab trucks arrived and paused their progression long enough for Dallas to move into lead position. The fact that it'd taken so little time to assemble four trucks of bad asses assured Kamren they'd deal with whatever was at her home.

No.

The place hadn't ever been a home, not in the real sense that made something more than a shelter from the rain and the cold. It hadn't had the warmth Dallas's home had. The love.

She had a new home.

A new family.

The truck bobbed and lurched as Dallas navigated the potholes of the driveway leading to her house.

"Was here yesterday evening with a couple guys. Nothing out of the ordinary," Jud commented. "Cliff said he'd handle the morning feeding. Anyone heard from him?"

Fear crawled through her. Cliff.

They all exited the vehicle as Gage, Addy, Fallon, and teams of operatives she'd never formally met exited the trucks behind them. The three team leads motioned, and everyone fanned out, weapons in hand. Dylan, Cord, Mary, Vi, and Zoey exited the last vehicle. Drones rose into the air around them.

"Gear," Dylan said as he passed out cases she knew held the headgear HERA used. Nolan, Jesse, Dallas, and Jud geared up, but Kamren stared numbly overhead.

"I promised I wouldn't stand between you and your fight, but today, out there, I need you to step back for me so I can step up and handle the next few hours. Hold onto me and let me take the lead for a little while, okay?" Dallas's whispered plea was soft against her neck.

Unsure what to say, she remained silent.

He continued on.

"I'd prefer you stay here, but that's your call, sweetheart. All I'm asking is that you let me take the lead on this for a while."

She nodded.

He took her hand. "Let's go. If it gets to be too much, you let me know. There's no shame in tagging out."

You don't ever let someone else fight your battles, girl.

Kamren ignored the voice in her head. For the first time in a long while, she took a chance and let someone else take the lead.

THE HEADGEAR DISPLAYED what Dallas expected. Death. As far as the drones could sweep. Someone had laid waste to everything Kamren held dear. Rage rose within him. She hadn't been here because she'd been with him and the boys. What if she'd been here? Alone? Unprotected?

"This is a significant escalation," Vi said. "Henry Mills is in custody, and nothing we know about him indicates he'd be capable of this. He's a white-collar thug wanna-be. It doesn't make sense."

Psychopathic carnage rarely did. Despite protests, Vi had insisted on coming along. Dylan had managed to keep Mary at the compound, but she was watching via drones already circling overhead.

"Maybe you should hang back with me, Kamren," Zoey suggested.

"No. I need to see." Her words were icy steel caged in a quiet rage he felt in her stance and noted in the firm set of her jaw and determined gaze. "Let's go."

Dallas headed around the side of the house. The teams had fanned out, but Addy, Gage, and Fallon remained with Dallas, Nolan and Jesse as Kamren navigated them toward the first evidence of trouble. Kamren halted and knelt. "A vehicle was driven back here, an ATV perhaps. Thick, fat tires."

A drone appeared and snapped photos. They continued on. The coppery stench of death assailed Dallas's senses. A lone hen squawked and fluttered about in the bloodied carnage in front of the house. Feathers covered the exterior and floated in the breeze nearby.

Pale and trembling slightly, Kamren stepped forward, coiling a hand through the chicken coop's wire frame. Her gaze scanned the sprawled bodies of her chickens, then tracked outward to the white, red and brown feathers scattered about.

"Knives—some to the neck, others to the heart. They didn't know how to kill a chicken. They bled, but died slow," she whispered. She looked over at Mary and Vi. "Feathers. Get them all. Fingerprints."

She wandered away, deeper into the carnage. Dallas glanced at his brothers. Their glowers matched his. She had no business going into that barn, but they respected her too much to hold her back. Women like her didn't want to be protected and treated like a dainty princess.

"I wouldn't have thought about the feathers," Nolan admitted.

"I'll hang back and image them. We'll have to leave them for the crime scene unit, if they even bother showing up when we call," Dylan commented. "Sheriff Haskell is a lazy shit."

Kamren walked toward the barn and paused at the door where a warning had been written in what appeared to be blood.

Stop or die.

She reached out, put a finger to the sticky red and licked it.

"Okay, that was gross," Vi admitted.

Dallas chuckled.

Kamren looked back at him. Face expressionless, eyes flat, voice monotone. "Paint."

She stooped down, picked up a small branch, and pulled the door open. He grabbed her arm. She looked down at where his hand touched her.

"I need to check the area first, sweetheart."

"Right." She nodded and took a step back.

He entered hell. Goats were hung by ropes along the insides of the barn. Blood dripped. Drones whizzed by.

"Dallas, the far right corner. Hurry." The urgency in Mary's voice through the com pushed him forward. That's when he saw it. A horse pulled itself upright. Blood leaked from its side.

"Brant, yeah, it's Jesse. We've got a situation out at the Garrett farm. I need your uncle out here immediately, but keep it under the radar for now." His brother's voice halted. "The vet, not the doc. Whatever your issue is with Kamren, set it aside."

Dallas calmed the agitated beast before him. Obviously in pain, the horse whinnied and stamped a foot in warning. Kamren shoved past him. He watched as she calmed the beast and stroked it. Tears ran down her face as she whispered to the animal.

"He'll be here in ten with his uncle," Jesse said. "I saw a trailer out back. I'll make sure it's ready to use."

More warnings were etched within the interior. He ignored the stench of death and stood beside Kamren as she stroked the agitated horse, who'd somehow survived the carnage.

He glanced out the back exit and spotted two dairy cows gutted. Nausea pitched his stomach, but he'd seen worse. By the time Brant and his uncle arrived, Vi had surveyed, scanned, and recorded every crevice of the ranch and a quarter mile around.

The teams walked the perimeter of the small farm, but no evidence was found aside from ATV tracks.

Brant's uncle Bart was a vet and a sourpuss of a man who'd rather spit on you than shake your hand. Dallas and his brothers moved out of the way as he shuffled into the stall and took Kamren's place with the animal.

"What the hell happened out here?" Brant's voice thundered in anger. "What the hell has she gotten into now?"

"None of us are in the mood," Dallas warned.

"Step back and check the attitude or I'll have Addy teach you some manners," Vi ordered.

"It'd be a pleasure," the woman returned quickly.

"Rachelle shouldn't be exposed to this violence. Whatever mess Kamren's in, she doesn't have any right dragging her into it," Brant growled.

"The most violent thing that girl's dealt with was when my girl over there made her stop fondling Masons," Addy said. "Advice. Take a few steps back and assess the situation with your brain instead of your dick, Doc."

The man stormed from the barn. Kamren wandered out in time to see him stamp away.

"I see I'm still his favorite person," she replied.

Dallas was sick of the man's attitude. It was clear he didn't fully understand the family history or the shit Kamren had endured. Whatever he'd heard or seen from Rachelle was a drop in the bucket. Though it wasn't his place to share, Dallas couldn't stomach much more attitude from the surly prick. He sure as hell wouldn't let Kamren take it much longer, not on top of everything else.

Dallas followed her to the winch that'd obviously been used to hoist the animals up and into position. She studied the line and looked over at Vi again.

"This system's old, jerks fast on the start. There's blood on the line," she commented.

"Someone injured themselves?" Vi asked.

"Possibly," Kamren muttered. She clutched Dallas's belt loop again and motioned toward outside. "Why? Why would someone do this?"

"I don't know, sweetheart, but we won't rest until we figure it out." He kissed her forehead and drew her to his side. "Come on, let's get you back to The Arsenal. I think you've given everyone enough to go on for today."

Kamren rested her head against him and looked over at Vi. "Thank you. Thank you all."

"You two go on out. I'll call Sheriff Haskell and report it. I think we have enough lead time on evidence gathering," Nolan said.

"I'll make some calls, figure out what to do about cleanup," Dylan said. "Jesus, this is fucked up."

Dallas watched as Vi steered Kamren toward the truck. Good. She needed to be away from here, sooner rather than later. "Thanks, man."

His brother's gaze settled on Brant as the man shoved his cell phone into his pocket and glowered at the women near the truck. "Not liking his treatment of the women much."

"Yeah, think it's time he and I have a chat."

"Sanderson and Jud will stay back with you. Addy's team is maintaining a protective detail," Dylan commented. "We'll get Kamren to the compound."

"Appreciated." Dallas closed the distance between himself and Brant. "A moment."

"Not sure I have anything to say."

"Good, because this is a one-sided conversation. You lay into my woman again, I'll lay you out."

"She's an abuser."

"Thinking you need to rewind what you remember, replay with the brain God gave you. Whatever you saw, I've seen the scars. The burns, knife wounds. Whip marks. Only one of them is a walking road map for abuse, and it's sure as fuck not Rachelle." Dallas fisted his hands. "Kept my mouth shut too long, letting you take gouges out of her she can't afford to lose. No more."

"She beat her sister," Brant spat angrily.

"Probably. Horrible shit goes down in screwed up homes like the one they lived in." Dallas clenched his jaw, glared at the man. "Shouldn't have to tell a doctor that shit. You know."

"I'll steer clear as long as you assure me Rache is secure out at your place."

"Gotta admit I'm not sure how the fuck she is. Last time I saw her, she was grinding up against me, making it clear she wanted way more of me than I was willing to give. Seeing how she's done the same with most of my brothers, I'm thinking you get where her mind's headed." Dallas crossed his arms.

"Rache isn't like that."

"Maybe not the Rachelle you know, but the one we see? She's got more issues than anyone realizes, except maybe Kamren. She's seen plenty of her sister's trouble."

"Guess we'll have to agree to disagree about that," Brant said.

"Long as you keep your distance, that'll do."

"How is she?"

Dallas stared at Zoey as he sat at the remaining seat in the white-board room. For a brilliant woman, she had a way of asking things better left unspoken. Gage glowered at him from his lean against the wall. The man was mighty protective of Vi and Mary's new hire. On a different day, Dallas would find it amusing.

There wasn't much amusing today, though.

Exhausted, he expended a breath and looked at the brainiacs at the head of the table. He hadn't seen much of Rhea or Bree lately. While the former had been working on some secret government contract, the latter had simply been AWOL, working on a "secret project" within her lab. They'd both joined the fray once word about what went down at Kamren's home spread at The Arsenal.

They bookended Mary and Vi. Cord and Zoey closed off the genius side of the table. The six had been at work for several hours with the datasets spewed out by HERA while he and everyone else worked to put the Garrett farm to some semblances of right, if there was such a thing. Personally, he was sorely tempted to raze the damn place.

Rachelle hadn't surfaced. She'd been deep within her head since they'd all had a come to Jesus with her, but Riley assured them all she was okay.

He looked around. "Anyone find Cliff?"

"Yeah, he took it harder than I'd expected," Nolan said. "Said we should look into Wayne. Cliff did some work for him a while back, then cut himself loose. He thinks it could have something to do with him. I asked him about Mills in case he knew something we hadn't gotten from him. He didn't. All he said was it might've been Wayne."

"That's doubtful. He's a lazy shit," Dallas said. He'd met the man a couple times. He was Hailey's cousin, and the drug-dealing bastard who'd supplied the drugs that she'd used to...

Not now.

"What'd HERA find?" Dylan asked.

"Some of the kills were hesitant, while others were almost savage in their..." Rhea swallowed. Eyes wide, she continued. "Right. So, at least two perpetrators, possibly three, though we think the hesitant one grew more confident."

"It took time," Jud said. "Lots of noise. No one heard anything?"

"My team and I canvassed neighbors, but folks aren't saying anything. If they heard, we won't be privy to details." Addy knocked her fist on the table. "Though, I'd go back and knock heads together to get our girl answers."

"Thinking there's a line forming for that right," Jesse muttered. "Her shit simmered on the back burner too long while we were away."

"Possibly, but the timeline isn't making sense to us. I mean, she went eighteen months digging into her dad's death. Aside from pissing off the Marville Dogs, she had very little in the way of elevated danger to her directly," Vi said, "until we pushed Mills, then he pushed back, and we shut him down."

"Fallout from Dom's hit against Javier?" Gage asked.

"Doubtful. Marcus barely got Dani out of there. Dom didn't leave anyone standing that'd react against him or his sister," Jud said. "Street justice—swift, fast, untraceable."

Dallas wouldn't have expected anything less from the man he'd once called a friend. Truth be told, he was glad at least their mess was off the list of shit they had to handle. "We're missing something."

"Yeah, which is why we gave what we knew to Doctor Sinclair. Figured a psychological approach might be in order at this point," Mary said. "Especially since the why is escaping me."

"So it's not about the hunt for her father's killer?" Bree asked.

"That's the thing. Why kill him in the first place? That *why* has never been answered," Vi said. "Kamren found lots of dirt on local folks, shady things, but HERA's yet to find a hard line between any of it and Kamren's dad."

"Except for Mills. He reacted swiftly to the push," Addy said. "I thought he and his cronies were connected."

"Kamren dug deep, uncovered lots of vipers, but they aren't necessarily the nest we're looking for," Mary said.

"Meaning?" Dylan asked.

"Meaning they may have been involved in something her dad stumbled across, but that didn't get him dead," Zoey said. "We're missing the path leading to the why."

"It was personal," Vi said. She glanced about the room, but her gaze settled on Dallas. "Kamren's hiding something important."

"She's not the only one," Gage commented, his gaze on Zoey, whose face reddened.

"It's likely something she's either embarrassed about, or it's so dark and ugly she doesn't want to breathe life to it," Nolan said. "She was raised to keep things to herself, relying on no one."

"The mom," Dallas shared. "She's mentioned stuff, that she wasn't a good woman. Abusive."

The women looked at one another. Zoey bit her lip. "Yeah, about that. They all lived pretty off the grid, except for Rachelle and Cliff. But the mom didn't have any form of paper trail round about the time Kamren went off grid."

"And by 'off grid' you mean 'stopped going to school'?" Jesse clarified.

"Right. So we all know the Marville school system goes to the sixth grade, then they're bussed to Resino, or Nomad. Kamren stopped going in the third grade. She's shared that much."

"Because of the dyslexia." Dallas's jaw twitched. I was hard to imagine a kid not getting the help she needed to learn. Pissed him off to think her parents hadn't bothered trying. She'd been too much of a burden. Too much trouble.

TJ and DJ were both significantly behind. Heck, TJ wasn't far away from the age Kamren had been when her parents gave up on her. He couldn't fathom not giving them everything he could in the way of help.

"Doctor Sinclair thinks the mom had severe issues, issues that'd explain some of Rachelle's erratic behavior. She can't give us many details, but she did say we needed to find out more about the family history." Mary's voice lowered. "She's concerned."

"I'll talk to Kamren tonight and get some more details."

HEAT SETTLED against Kamren's back as Dallas covered them both with a thin blanket. Darkness encroached from the window she'd stared out the past couple of hours as life continued around her. A young man she hadn't met yet named Jacob had taken TJ and DJ under his wing as the rest of The Arsenal handled the carnage at the farmhouse. That was about the extent of what Kamren knew.

Weak as it might seem, she'd left the details to Dallas and everyone around her. The firm grip around her waist redirected her thoughts to the man behind her, at her back in every way she'd needed today. "Thank you."

The soft utterance tumbled from her.

He sighed deeply and kissed her shoulder. "Shit day, Kam."

Yeah. Shit day indeed.

"You want details of what we have so far?"

"Yeah."

"First, we checked on Dani and made sure she was secure. Things are calming with the Marville Dogs. The crew left is loyal to Dom, so that'll likely keep your girl's world a lot calmer than it's been in a long time. She's worried about you, so much so she's coming out here tomorrow."

"Good. Then she can see you're good people. She means something to me. You mean something to me," she whispered. "Did...did Juniper make it?"

"Yeah, Bart phoned, letting us know he'd bring him over in the morning. Riley and Cord have already made room for him in the barn." He ran a hand down her hair, then kissed her shoulder again, as if knowing she needed the physical contact, a connection to reality so the horrors of today didn't rip out the last of her sanity. "How long have you had Juniper?"

"He's Rachelle's," she commented. "A gift from mom right before she..."

"I'm gonna have to ask some hard questions right now, sweetheart. No easy way to broach this subject, but we need more information about your family, your mom. Rachelle. I know you said your mom hurt you more than your dad, but I need more."

"Why?" She already knew the answer. "You think it's related."

"There are some concerns."

"Mom and dad had issues."

"Think I figured that much out, sweetheart. Their issues are all over you, literally."

"He was a mean brute, but not physical. His punishments were challenges, survival and tactical. Lessons meant to make me stronger, not break me down."

Dallas tightened as he processed between the lines of what she hadn't said. He couldn't understand the level of evil her mom had become toward the end. "Your mom hurt you."

"Dad tried getting her help lots of times. Pills. They just made her worse," Kamren whispered. "She hated me, said I ruined everything. I stole him away from her."

Memories engulfed her; things she'd never given voice to spilled forward in a rush of words. "She was beautiful, the same hair and eyes like Rachelle. The prettiest voice. Sometimes she'd sing, back when I hadn't stolen him away and I was just her little girl. She'd dress me up in pretty dresses with matching shoes."

"Then she changed."

"No," Kamren argued quickly. "Dad changed. I changed. Cliff changed. He didn't want to be the little hunter; he didn't want to be much of anything. He hated the outdoors, hunting. Tracking. Anything to do with Dad."

"So Dad took you out."

"Yeah, said I had a natural talent, just like my grandpa." Kamren swallowed, focusing on the swirls Dallas created on her arm and down her back. "That's when she changed, turned mean."

"And Rachelle?"

"She loved Mom so much. She was the little princess, doted on. Loved."

"What happened to your mom?" Dallas asked as he drew her closer. Kamren turned and wrapped her arms around his strength as a flood of memories assailed her.

Face buried in his neck, she gave him the skeletons she'd buried. Literally. "It was the summer after second grade when Dad hauled me east, into the Appalachians. We were gone a long time, months. When we got back, things hadn't gone well with Mom. She'd gone into her head, where things made sense only to her. Dad went to the bank to catch the mortgage up. Mom dragged me out to the barn, the post where..."

Dallas tightened, as if bracing for what was to come. She let the rest of the sentence die. He read plenty of the shit between the lines without her filling them in.

"I must've passed out. She went way longer than normal, but we'd been gone way longer, too. I had months of beatings to take."

"A shotgun blast woke me up. Dad had come home, found her still laying into me. Rache was in the house crying. Cliff was standing there, staring down at all the blood. Mine. Mom's." Kamren swallowed. "Rache came out. She was so young. Her little mind must not have been able to handle what she saw. Mom dead, Dad holding the gun, and me bleeding from my beating. She wasn't the same after that. I know I mentioned the pills before, her needing help."

"Jesus."

"Mom was born off grid in the Appalachians. Dad buried her in the northwest corner of the property by where he'd bury our dogs. Said that's what she deserved for treating him and his kids like animals."

"Jesus."

"Before that I'd had some freedoms, friends. After that he didn't let me go anywhere. I was in charge of the house. Hunting. Trapping. I didn't have time to be a kid. Have friends." She ran her hands down Dallas's back. "Dani never gave up, though, came out every night to check on me. She didn't know what happened with Mom, but she knew it wasn't good."

"I crawled into my head after Dad died, needing answers even though they didn't matter, not really. Our family died that night," she whispered. "Riley said Rache was ghosting through life. She wasn't the only one."

"Do you think..." He pulled her tighter into his arms and whispered the rest against her cheek. "You think she hurt your Dad?"

No. She shook her head; the vehement rebuttal died in her throat, though. Somewhere deep, deep down the thought took root and grew as leaves of truth she'd refused to see branched outward, until all she was left with was the truth. "God, I hope not."

"I hope not too, but whatever we find out, we'll deal. You aren't alone with this anymore, Kam," he whispered. He feathered kisses along her forehead. "Gotta go get the girls working this. We need to track Rachelle down. She's been AWOL, but in contact with Riley. Cliff mentioned Wayne. Was she close to him?"

"Dunno, maybe. He hung out with Cliff at the house sometimes," Kamren admitted. "You think Wayne did this?"

"It's possible, but the women think there were at least two people out there."

Dread burst within her, an explosion of what-ifs she couldn't voice. "I'll find her."

"Take Addy with you," he ordered as he rose from the bed. "We'll track down Wayne and bring him in to get some answers."

"Dallas, it can't be her. I..." She shook her head. "No way. She told Riley she'd get help the other day when they had the big confrontation because of her touching Jesse. It can't be her."

"I'm hoping to hell not, sweetheart. But hearing what you just shared about your ma and what happened with her..." Sadness filled his gaze. "We've gotta brace for the possibility."

The likelihood. He didn't say it, but Kamren knew that's what he meant. Woodenly, she rose from the bed. Dressed.

She didn't know what to think or believe. Could her sister have killed their dad?

The why was obvious. She'd hated him for taking their mom away, but that didn't make her a killer. Did it? "Henry Mills and them. They're behind all this. Vi and Mary said as much. He kidnapped me."

"He was up to squirrelly shit that's earned them a focal point in a statewide investigation and a spot in a cell for taking you, but nothing ties any of those assholes to your dad's murder. What happened at the farmhouse was personal."

Personal. Kamren looked at the man who'd finagled his way into her heart, the same heart that was dying beneath the toxic trail they were chasing. "Juniper was hers. He survived."

The grim expression on his face denoted he'd already realized as much. Whether Rachelle had done the horrible things Dallas was afraid she'd done or not, Kamren needed to find her.

25

K amren stared down at the buzzing cell phone in her hand, then slid her finger across the screen to answer. "Hello?"

"Kam." The woman's voice was broken with gasping tears. "It's not her fault; she's sick."

"Riley. Where are you?" Kamren looked around the compound, but most everyone had moved out, tracing Rachelle's and Riley's cell phone signals to Marville. The Sip and Spin. "Everyone thinks you two at the Sip and Spin."

"She dumped the phones. This is a disposable." The woman cried out. "Let me go, Rache. Let me get you help."

"Rache! Let her go." Kamren screamed the order into the phone.

"You want her, big sis? Come and get her. Follow the trail if you can."

No. No. No. Kamren punched her way through screens on the cell phone the girls had given her until she came across Dallas's picture. She hit the phone icon as her heartbeat thudded in her ears. Tears burned her eyes, but she didn't get to make this about her, not when Rache had Riley. And the situation sounded far, far away from calm.

"Kam? You okay?"

"Rache has Riley, said I had to follow the trail. They aren't at the Sip and Spin."

"No, but Wayne was out back behind the trashcans." Dallas's tone tightened the unease in her gut. "Dead."

No. No. No. "Dallas."

"We're on our way back. I'll get everyone in ops on it."

"On what? She didn't give us anything to go by," Kamren said. Agitation rose within her. "She has Riley."

"I know that, sweetheart. We'll find them."

This was her fault. She'd ignored her sister too long, focusing on the fallout rather than the chief cause of her illness. It'd been simpler to ignore that Rachelle was troubled and needed more than some cursory drugs and a new environment. What'd happened long ago may not have been Kamren's fault, but it was definitely her problem, which meant she needed to calm the hell down and work through what to do.

Find Rachelle.

Follow the trail.

Riley had moved out to the newly built college beside Dallas's. Kamren sprinted toward the small structure, which was within walking distance of the Mason home.

Kamren's gut clenched.

Blood droplets.

Heavy boot steps thundered around her. She glanced up, noting Cord and Jud coming to a halt near her. Addy came from the other direction.

"Yeah, we're here with her," Cord said. "Dunno; she's found some-thing, though."

"Blood," she whispered tightly. Though she didn't want to believe her sister would cut her own best friend, she didn't get to judge the situation. All she could do was track the trail and hope to hell she wasn't too late.

A flashlight settled in her hand, along with a knife. She hoped to hell she didn't need the weapon but offered a chin lift in gratitude to Jud as she flicked on the light and got to work chasing the trail.

"Z, need you backpedaling footage in the perimeter nearest this location. Look for Riles and Rachelle," Cord said into his com as he held out one to her. She put it on quickly, thankful they always seemed to have the important things covered when shit hit the fan.

A team.

Family.

"On it. Mary and Vi are dispatching drones. We're running a heat signature grid," the woman said. "Teams are spread out. We'll find them."

Maybe, but would it be soon enough?

Kamren's gaze swept the area as the last blood drop ended in the middle of nowhere. No. She looked back to the main house, then the buildings nearest the new location. "The barn."

"Come again," Jud said.

"The barn. Peanut. Rache made us get Juniper when Riley got Peanut." She glanced at Cord. "Are drones in there?"

"No," he said. "Riley thought they'd spook Peanut."

"And she goes in there to talk to the horse a lot," Mary offered in the com. "She may have taken Rache in there to share that with her."

Fuck.

Kamren's focus narrowed as everyone converged on the location. Jud and Cord took point, weapons drawn as they opened the entry to the barn.

Then froze. Flashlights swept across Rachelle holding Riley at knife point. The two women were so close it was hard to tell where one ended and the other began because of the darkness within the barn.

"Take one more step in and she's dead. This is between me and Kam," Rachelle spat. "Get in here, sister. Close the door behind you."

"You aren't going in there," Jud declared.

"To hell I'm not." She looked at the crush of armed operatives around her. Dread settled into a tremble deep in her bones. "I have to. This isn't going to end well if I don't try."

"We'll get drones in there."

"And until you do, I'll keep her talking." Kamren looked around, trusting everyone around her because Dallas did. "That's the smartest play. Right?"

Cord glared at Jud, who glared at everyone around him.

"Honey, she's right," Vi whispered. "She won't be alone. We have a solution in play, but we need time."

"One hint of bad and I'm going in," Jud warned.

Kamren nodded and wiped her palms on her jeans. Her heart thudded wildly in her chest as she slid in, unarmed except the sheathed knife she'd stuck onto her waistband.

"Rache? What's wrong, baby?"

"You know damn good and well what's wrong, sister." Anger mottled her voice, deepening it to a feral growl. "Why couldn't you just let him fucking die?"

"Let Riley go and we'll talk it through, just you and me, okay?"

"No. She's gotta know. She's gotta understand." Rache yanked on Riley's undone hair, hair so similar to Rachelle's the two blondes blended into one another within the darkness. Riley's hands were bound in front of her. The knife glinted within the narrow scant shaft of light from the flashlight. It remained against Riley's throat as if it'd become a part of her.

"Honey, you can't do this. Riley loves you; she's your best friend. You don't want to hurt her."

"Oh yeah? You know she told me you were good for him. Said you brought back the brother she'd lost; the Dallas she loved was back." Blood ran down Rachelle's hand as she thundered the rest of the accusation. "*Because of you!*"

Tears seeped out of Kamren's eyes. She took a step closer, silently wishing for an answer out of this disaster. How had she missed how ill Rachelle truly was? "I'm sorry, Rache. I should've been here for you. I was wrong."

"Yeah, you were. Years! I've waited for years to have one of them as mine, finally get the good I deserve. Then you had to go and ruin it all, coming out here, involving them in your stupid, stupid hunt for answers. No one gave a shit that he was dead. He deserved it. He deserved it." Rachelle glared. "So did you. You always ruined *every-thing*. He took her away because of *you*."

"Why? Why now?"

"He heard me with Wayne, knew I had a plan, a real good one that'd get me what I deserved. But he said I was stupid, nothing better than him or you." She glared at Kamren when she took another step closer. "Get the fuck back, or I swear I'll kill her."

"Tell me what you want, Rache."

"Everything!"

"Okay," she said, unsure what the fuck 'everything' meant. What-ever it was, she'd figure a way to get it. "Let Riley go."

"No. Not until they know. She's gotta know. He's gotta hear the truth."

"What truth?"

"About you. Mom. Dad. Everything!"

"He knows, baby," she whispered. "They all know, except Riley. They've seen the scars. They know."

"You liar!" Blood coated her hand, but Kamren couldn't tell whose it was. Rachelle's grip on the knife was firm, but not correct. If there was such a thing as a correct grip while holding a weapon against your best friend's throat.

"Dad shouldn't have kept us away so long. I begged him to take me back to you. To Mom."

"It was always you. Mom loved him so much, but he didn't give a damn. You took him from her. From me. You were always such a greedy, demanding little cunt."

Kamren recoiled beneath the hatred, words that echoed her mother's from long ago.

"Rache," Riley pleaded, her voice weak and pained. "It hurts."

"Good, you gotta learn your place. You picked her over me, said she was good for him. He's mine. They're *all* mine! Bad enough that fat-assed bitch came in and sank her claws into Dylan. Now there're fucking brats running around here getting their attention." Rachelle's eyes narrowed. "You brought them here, found them. You fucking fucking cunt."

"Please fucking tell me there's a firing solution," Jud said through the com.

"No. Do not!" Kamren shouted the words into the com but held her attention on her sister. "You need help, Rache. This isn't your fault, honey, but you've gotta drop the knife and let Riley go. If you're pissed at me, fine. Take it out on me, but she's been the only good, clean truth in your life. Do not fuck that up with this."

"It's too late," she whispered. "You fucked it up the day you started digging into Dad's death. Knew then this would have to happen. Knew then there wasn't any other end."

"Honey."

"Then you brought the brats here. No one pays attention to me anymore. They don't care, all 'cause of you."

"No solution."

"No solution."

"No solution."

The voices in the com all repeated what Kamren already knew. Except for the lone beam of the flashlight she had trained on the women, there was no light. No open doors. No windows. No way into the hell her sister had unleashed on the Masons. On The Arsenal.

"They love you, Rache."

"Liar!"

"They do, you know. You're their baby sister's best friend. They'd crawl through the fires of hell if you'd only ask. But you've gotta know this isn't right. Somewhere deep, deep down, you know this isn't the answer." She sobbed, openly crying, and prayed the tenuous grip she'd lost on her emotions helped the situation, made her sister see this wasn't good. "It's not too late to move past what happened to us."

"Kamren, she's cycling fast. She's burrowed into a corner where we can't get eyes behind her. We shoot through the wood, it won't be good for her or Riley. The drone we have in position has a lock, but it's on Riley. There's an eighty percent chance it'll knock Riley out. And a fifteen percent chance it'll hit nothing but air and make the situation worse." Mary's voice was calm, even and filled with enough determination to fuel an army. "We're going with the eighty percent here, so I'm gonna give you an order you aren't gonna want to hear."

No. No. No.

"We tranq Riley, you take your sister down. Whatever it takes, Kamren. You. Take. Her. Down."

No. No. No.

Kamren shifted on her feet. Hands at her side, she waited and prayed there was another solution. Emotion clogged her throat and lungs, but she pushed it back. She didn't get to break down, not now. Not when her sister had a knife to Riley's throat.

"You took on Hailey without hesitation. You found his son in millions of acres of woods," Mary's voice was calm, the focal point of Kamren's brain, even though Rachelle continued screaming words she no longer heard.

"There comes a time when emotion can't play a part in your actions, a time when hesitation is certain death. You've been there before, Kam. I need you there again, or Riley isn't gonna make it."

"Okay." It was the only word she could press out as she shifted again and focused on her sister.

"I love you, Rache, but I can't stand between you and the world, not anymore. Let her go, Rache. We can fix this."

"Aim for her hand if you've got a clean hit," Jud said in the com. "Muscles will seize quick if the hit is hard enough."

God. God. God.

The grip was wrong, kept her palm fully hidden, which meant the target would have to be her wrist. Clean through.

She closed her eyes a second, long enough to curse her father for giving her this lesson, the skill that'd been one of the many reasons he'd driven a wedge between her and Rachelle ages ago. He'd made her his shadow, the most important part of his life even though the rest of his family desperately craved his love and attention—something they never got.

Kamren hadn't either, but Rache wouldn't ever understand or believe that. "I love you, Rache. Let her go. We can fix this."

"You're wrong. They gotta learn. Dad always said the best lessons are those that hurt to the bone, burn your marrow and settle in permanent-like. They're gonna learn."

"Now!"

Kamren wasn't sure what to expect. A crazy-looking device shot from beneath the ground near the corner. Peanut whinnied. The machine whirred, then fired a dart. It all happened within one breath.

Riley dropped, her weight too much when unconscious. Kamren pulled her knife and threw. The savagely sharp blade plunged precisely where she'd aimed, her sister's wrist. The weapon she'd held clattered to the ground as Rachelle growled and screamed, then slammed into Kamren.

Blood.

So much blood.

Light shafted into the barn as both doors exploded open and Arsenal operatives stormed in. Two incapacitated her sister, while Cord and Jud hauled Kamren backward. Jesse and Nolan surged in and collapsed beside their sister, whose blood ran freely from a neck wound.

She looked down at the blood coating her hands. Riley's. Or Rachelle's.

"Fuck." Dallas swept her into his arms. "I've got you, sweetheart."

DALLAS PACED the narrow corridor of Nomad Memorial Hospital. He glanced back at the waiting room where the entirety of The Arsenal and Mason brood waited for word about Riley. Kamren was huddled in the corner with Vi, Mary, Zoey, Rhea, and Bree. The women had converged like the force they were and swept her into their loving fold. Gage and Addy had remained back at the compound to deal with the loose ends and keep everything secure, including the boys, who'd thankfully slept through the entire ordeal.

Jesus. There'd been so much blood.

"Come back into the waiting room, man. Your pacing is making my woman nauseous," Dylan said as he clapped Dallas on the back. "She'll be fine. Our sis is strong and stubborn, just like us."

"We should have seen that crazy," Dallas whispered. "Should have known she was trouble."

"She's gonna get the help she needs."

Dallas glanced over at Kamren. "Maybe, but at what cost? Fuck, man. She didn't even hesitate, threw that knife dead center. Took out her sister's wrist to keep ours breathing."

"It was the only call. If she'd hesitated, we'd be here for an entirely different reason, a much worse one."

Fuck. Dallas clenched his teeth. It was over. He rubbed his chest and looked at his brother. "Can't help but wonder what the fuck is next. The Hive. The Collective. Marville Dogs. Then this."

"Think we're due for a break. A couple of weddings. Maybe three." Dylan's smirk turned into an outright grin. "She's a good woman. Warning, though. There's been talk. Jacob had an idea."

"Shit. Now what?"

"They're going to help her learn to read and get her GED."

"She might not be down with that," Dallas said. "Her decision, not theirs."

"Agreed. They'll approach it slowly, but either way, we think she'd be good on the teams. Nolan and Jesse want her field-training survival and tracking techniques to the noobs."

Dallas had expected as much. She was kickass in the field, a vital asset. Pride settled deep in his chest, then warmed. Fuck, he loved her. The double doors he'd staked out opened. Brant sauntered through, gaze weary and mouth thinned. Clad in operational scrubs and green booties, he waited until the entire waiting room clustered around him. Dallas and Dylan put hands on their mom's shoulders as she shoved her way to the man.

Dallas put his other arm around Kamren, kissed her neck, then nipped her earlobe. "Love you, sweetheart. Don't ever forget that."

She melted against him. "Love you, too."

"Well? Spit it out," Bree ordered.

"Riley made it through surgery. It was touch and go, lots of blood loss, as you know. Jesse's field patching saved her life," his gaze settled on Kamren, "as did the rapid response to secure her."

Translation: Kamren had saved her life by not hesitating.

"Recovery?" Rhea asked.

Dallas's mom held her hands to her mouth. Eyes wide and tear-filled, she looked up at Brant as he looked down.

"She won't be singing in the choir anytime soon, and there'll be a scar."

"Thinking little sis can accept that," Jesse said.

"Thinking so," Nolan agreed. "I'll phone Marshall, let him and the folks back at The Arsenal know."

"She's asked to see you," Brant said, his gaze on Kamren; then slid up to Dallas. "And you."

Kamren glanced at Dallas's mom. Pale, she whispered. "I won't be long, Mrs. Mason, then you can go back and sit with her."

Dallas held onto his woman as she rocked back into him. She expended a relieved breath as everyone returned to the waiting area. No one would be leaving anytime soon. A Mason was laid low. Nomad Memorial was lucky the entirety of Resino hadn't converged in the small facility. That'd likely happen in a few hours, once word had spread. They'd need to double security at The Arsenal to handle well-meaning folk dropping off even more casseroles and healing wishes.

"And Rache?" A tremble ran through Kamren, her voice so soft he'd barely heard.

Brant froze his half-turn. Shock rippled through his expression. Along with regret. "She'll recover, though it's still touch and go on whether she'll keep the hand. She was stabilized about an hour ago. She's being transferred to a psychiatric unit in San Antonio where a specialist will determine next steps for her injury. Doctor Sinclair's already been in touch with the chief psychiatrist there. He's one of the best in the state."

"Good." Kamren nodded, burrowed deeper against Dallas, and squeezed his arm, as if asking him to continue voicing the inquiry stuck in her throat.

And he did. He knew his woman needed to know the full extent of her sister's situation, good or bad. Right or wrong, she'd done what was needed and had ended so much. "Should we try and see her?"

We. He emphasized the word, letting Kamren know she wouldn't be alone in this or any of the rest to follow.

"She's sedated," Brant said gently. His gaze moved to the cluster of women behind Dallas. They hadn't left Kamren's side. She was one of them now, had been since she'd exploded the car outside their compound. "Work it out through Doctor Sinclair. Once she's settled and medicated, then yeah. It'd be good for her to see you."

"Thank you," she whispered. "I'll just go see Riley quick like. Then Momma Mason can go back."

Kamren trundled past Brant. Dallas followed.

"Kamren." The doctor's voice boomed within the narrow hallway.

Dallas tensed when Kamren turned. Everyone in the area did, as if poised to strike the man down if he said anything about the decision she'd made, a hard one that he wasn't sure he could've done.

"I owe you far more than just an apology," Brant admitted. "But that's all I've got to offer tonight."

Kamren nodded.

"Wasn't there, but seeing Riley's wounds, the depth and severity..." Brant's jaw twitched. Emotion clotted his voice. "You made the right call. The injury is severe, permanent loss of mobility in her hand assuming she can keep it, but anything less and..."

Rachelle could've killed Riley.

RILEY LOOKED SO pale and fragile within the bed. Thick gauze coiled around her throat like an unwanted rattler. Tubes and needles protruded from her. Monitors beeped and flashed on both sides of the bed. A nurse flitted in and out, carrying bedding for the large sleeper-style chair they'd rolled in when Dallas and his brothers informed them their mother would be staying with Riley overnight.

The nurses had frowned but had wisely remained silent and

moved into action. They must have sensed the intensity within the Mason men, or their reputation was known even in Nomad. Either way, Momma Mason was set for the night, though Kamren suspected she wouldn't be the only one remaining at the hospital.

Riley's eyes opened, eyes so blue like Dallas's that Kamren nearly collapsed beside the bed. She'd almost died tonight. Tears streamed down Kamren's face unchecked. She'd tried hard to keep a firm grip on her emotions, but seeing the damage...it was too much. Dallas stood at her back, gripping her shoulders as she sat in the chair beside the bed.

"Thank you," the woman mouthed.

Kamren nodded. "I'm sorry."

"Not your fault. We all failed her." Riley squeezed her hand. "Gonna need you translating for a while."

Kamren chuckled. "I'm thinking your brothers are gonna have a bit of fun with that."

"Probably," Dallas admitted. "Ma's set to spend the night. Nolan and Cord are staying, too. Marshall's on his way back."

"I'm fine." Riley's gaze shifted to Kamren. "Thanks to you. Besides, I have street cred now, right?"

"What'd she say?" Dallas asked.

"She asked if she has street cred now."

"No, but you just earned yourself a few more self-defense classes with me and Jud. Advanced takedown techniques. I've treated you with kid gloves, hadn't taken the threat potential seriously because Jud is your partner. We all see the error of that decision now, sis."

"I'll be ready." Her eyes drifted shut.

"She needs to rest," the nurse chided.

Kamren rose, looked at Dallas's sister one more time, then followed her man out of the room.

"Come on, let's get you home."

Kamren exited the hospital room but halted in the middle of the hallway when her gaze landed on Cliff. His eyes were bloodshot, his face was red. Hair wild and clothes wrinkled and dirty, he looked at her with the same lost, desperate expression from the night their dad had killed their mom.

She hadn't seen life in his eyes since that night and would gladly rewind time to erase what all had happened to never see that much pain in his expression again. She closed the distance and wrapped her arms around her brother, who remained tense within the embrace. "I didn't have a choice. She was going to kill Riley."

"This is all my fault. I should've handled her a long time ago. I didn't want to hear what you were saying, sis, didn't want to admit we'd failed her. Didn't want to see she'd gotten more of Mom's crazy than I wanted to admit. She was my little sister. I was supposed to keep her safe."

"She's alive, Cliff. She's gonna get the help she needs." Kamren desperately needed to believe the words she offered her brother. "The best thing we can do for her is to move forward, find our new normal and live. We aren't abandoning her. She's family."

"The shit she did out at the farm? She killed Wayne." Cliff's ravaged voice trembled. "She's not ever getting better, Kam. Not ever."

Kamren's heart ached as she silently accepted the truth within her brother's words. In many ways she wasn't ready to accept what a part of her had known all along. "We can't help someone who isn't ready to accept it."

"I didn't want to believe you," Cliff said. Gaze averted, he sighed heavily and ran a hand across his face. "I didn't want to accept that Dad was murdered because a part of me always suspected she was somehow responsible. Looking back, I remember the way she was after, when you weren't around. Happy, downright gleeful. He was a son of a bitch, but he tried to keep us safe."

"We couldn't have known it was her," Kamren whispered. She hugged her brother again. "We've gotta move past this, Cliff. You and me, we've gotta move past this."

"Not sure I've got it in me," he admitted. "I think I'm gonna head out for a few days, think some things through. I fucked up big time, sis. I've wasted my life away a long time, let you carry the load while I numbed myself with too much smoking and drinking. Seeing the way your new man and his brothers had your back, the way all of them at The Arsenal were there for you when I was too fucking lazy to even worry about it..."

"Cliff..."

"No. You don't get to excuse what I didn't do. I wasn't there when you needed me, sis. I was never there. All those times Mom dragged you to the barn, even when it wasn't your fault. All those times Dad made you go hungry to teach you a lesson you didn't ever need to learn. I didn't do shit."

"Cliff, they're gone. We've moved on."

"Yeah, you did. Somehow you dragged yourself from that hellhole and then turned around and went right back in for me and Rache," Cliff whispered. "I should've been there for you."

She couldn't deny his statement because he was right. In so many ways, he was absolutely right. He'd ignored so much and chosen to live in his pretend world where there weren't any problems or stresses. There weren't bills and dramas unfolding, or a sister spiraling to a new level of troubled. "It's over. Rachelle's gonna get the help she needs; Dad can rest in peace—even if he doesn't deserve it. We can move on from Mom and Dad and just be Kamren and Cliff. Don't waste another day wallowing in self-pity and blame. It won't do you a damn bit of good. You're right. You fucked up, Cliff. Big time. Accept the blame, learn from your mistakes, and move on. Grow the fuck up and make something of yourself. Prove Mom and Dad wrong. They never thought we were gonna be worth a damn, but I know better. We are worth a damn, way more than that."

"You are," Cliff said.

"So are you." She patted his cheek and smiled. "If you need to step back from Marville, then go up north. Tanner and his crew could always use some help."

"Thinking I'm not good enough to fill your shoes up there," he admitted.

"Then don't try. Be yourself. No one's expecting you to be the same as Dad, or me, or anybody. Stop avoiding life just because you don't want to live it the way you think you should. Just live."

Cliff nodded, motioning behind Kamren. She half turned and smiled at Dallas, who remained close, but far enough to offer a bit of privacy. "He's a good man, sis. They all are."

"Yeah."

"Proud of you," Cliff whispered against her forehead as he kissed her there. "I'm sorry I wasn't the brother I should've been. I swear I'm gonna get there, though. One day I'll make you proud."

"You already have just by being here," she whispered. "Go. Live. Stay in touch, or we'll hunt you down."

Cliff laughed and nodded, then turned and left. She expended a weary and pained breath as the last of her kin left the area. Everyone she had clung to for so long was gone. Strong, warm arms wrapped around her as Dallas settled at her back.

"Let's go home, sweetheart."

Home.

She had a new family. While she wouldn't ever abandon her blood, it was time she focused on the man she loved and the life she wanted to live. "Take me home, Dallas."

26

Kamren smiled as she leaned against the doorway and listened to Dallas reading TJ and DJ a story. The boys had woken when they'd arrived at the house. Although both boys had been drowsy, they'd been alert to the fact that something had happened. To calm them down, Dallas had crawled into bed with them and read them a story.

Dallas flashed her a grin as he looked down at DJ, who was sacked out on his left. TJ, drowsy but ever the alert protector, blinked up at him. The boy reached up. "Can we call you Dad?"

Wow. Kamren swallowed the lump of emotion in her throat as Dallas smiled. Eyes watery, he leaned down and kissed TJ's forehead. "I'd love that, son."

"Gramma says you'll make an honest woman outta Kam soon, then she'll be Mom."

Oh wow.

"That so?" Dallas chuckled and mussed TJ's hair. "Your grandma's got a way of accelerating timelines."

"'No sense wasting time or drawing out the obvious.' That's what she said when Uncle Nolan said that."

"That so?" Dallas chuckled again. "I suppose she's right. You good?"

"Someone hurt Aunt Riles."

Kamren wasn't sure when all the aunt and uncle business had started, but its weight filled the room. The boys were settled deep into the Mason family, entrenched in a way no one would ever dig them out. No way someone could. Protectiveness rushed through her. She'd do anything for the man she loved. His kids. His family.

"Yeah, but she'll be home soon. She's gonna be okay."

"'Cause Kam and you made it so. Uncle Jesse. Uncle Nol. Everybody made it okay."

"Yeah, we did."

"I miss Lilly," DJ whispered.

Kamren's heart clenched at the admission. The woman had refused their offers of help. Whoever she was, whatever she was into, she didn't want to have any help resolving whatever had gotten her captured and shoved into a hole in the middle of a forest.

At least she'd agreed to remain at one of Tanner's remote cabins for a while, long enough for the man to agree to an Arsenal team going up and assisting with upgrading their security and training a few of his men on hand-to-hand and defensive techniques.

Lilly would be safe because, even if she didn't want help, she was getting it from a distance. Mary, Vi, and Zoey were all digging. The three determined women wouldn't stop until they had answers. Who was Lilly, and why had she been in that nightmare?

Dallas extricated himself from the bed and tucked both boys in tight as TJ shifted closer to his little brother. "Know it's tough, little man, but I need you to stop listening when grown folks talk. No one's gonna hurt you or your little brother. Things around here get real intense sometimes. Your uncles and I have gotta do a better job separating that from the house and you two, but I need you to be less 'little man' and more 'little kid'."

The boy looked up, seriousness etched on his face. "You need me to stay tapped out."

"Yeah, so you can go to school, meet kids your own age, get friends. Play."

"Jacob says he can teach us how to make whirlies. Said it was real simple."

Given Jacob was nineteen and was a stone's throw from finishing his graduate degree at MIT, Kamren suspected everything was simple to the young man. But he and his dad had entered the fray in a big way when they'd returned to the compound. She hadn't spent much time with Danny yet, but if he was anything like his son, he was an amazing man.

One who'd undergone his own personal hells and come out a victor in a way that left every operative at The Arsenal respecting the hell out of him, according to what Dallas had shared earlier when they'd met. It'd take her months to learn everyone's names, but she would, because they were extended family. Not by blood. But by choice.

Team.

Cliff had left the compound and gone back to the farmhouse. He'd head up north in a couple days. For now, the troubles Kamren had invested herself in were handled, which left her open to explore a future with Dallas.

Marriage.

The possibility ignited anticipation as his intense gaze strolled over her, a long, slow glide filled with enough inherent promise to pool arousal between her legs and harden her nipples. The man was lethal in many ways, but they were a long way away from her becoming Mrs. Dallas Mason. Not that the name meant a damn thing. She was his and he was hers in all ways that mattered.

"You two can do anything you want. You're both so smart and strong," Dallas said. "But you aren't ever alone. There's nothing we can't talk about. Whatever it is, you can come to me. Kamren. Your uncles. Anyone on this compound. Anytime. With anything. Okay?"

TJ nodded. "I'll make sure DJ knows. He's had loads of questions."

DJ had lots of questions and scares and frights, per TJ—aka the mouthpiece for the boys. From what Doctor Sinclair had shared with everyone, TJ was transferring his own scares and emotions onto his younger brother to continue coming across as strong. It was one of many things she was working on with them both.

"We'll go out tomorrow and see if we can get some of those questions answered."

"Can we get Bubba's again?" TJ asked. "DJ really liked it."

"Yeah, though we need him to start talking more," Dallas said. "That's part of the tapping out. It's time to let him be a little man, too."

"That's what Doc said."

"We'll talk more about it tomorrow." Dallas grinned. "At Bubba's."

Such a pushover.

Kamren smirked as he flicked off the lights, got the nightlight situated, and extricated himself from the room. She meandered toward the bedroom they'd been sharing in the Mason house. Tomorrow they'd move into the cottage so Riley could take her room back. She grinned at her man as she walked backward.

God, he was so sexy. He walked with such a lethal grace it was a prowl. Quiet. Confident. Her womb contracted. Having his kid? Yeah, she wanted lots and lots of little Dallas'es. She hadn't known his father well, but if he'd been half as sexy and wonderful as Dallas, she now understood why Dallas's mom had seven kids. The woman had enormous restraint in Kamren's opinion.

"What's that look?"

"You're such a pushover," she said. "You can't give them everything they demand."

"No, but Bubba's isn't a demand. It's a necessity." He snagged her by the waist and tossed her on the bed.

Her laughter echoed within the room as he covered her, then proceeded to kiss the breath from her. He pulled up, settled above her, then looked down. Happiness danced within his gaze. "I love you, Kamren Garrett."

"I love you, Dallas Mason. Now shut up and make love to me."

And he did. Again and again until she knew without a doubt her life had begun again. This time she wasn't alone, nor was she having to be the strong one. Together, she and Dallas could do anything, including raise two boys. And a whole bunch more. She curled her toes. One step at a time. But one day, one day she'd take her vows, stand before God and all his family and their friends and reaffirm what she'd already declared.

Dallas Mason was hers in a way no one could ever deny.

27

Two weeks later...

Dallas looked over at the woman beside him. She'd been quiet, tense as a mouse in a cathouse the entire way to Huntsville. To say Daniella DeMarco was not a fan of him, Nolan, or anyone else with the last name Mason was an understatement. She'd crawled into the back seat of the large truck, donned a pair of earbuds and shrunk against the window.

He glanced over at his big brother, who'd taken the woman's obvious hatred of them hard, mainly because no one knew why—not even Kamren. Sooner or later, they'd unearth the truth. Until then, she was within their protection because she was extended family via her friendship with Kam.

The buzzer sounded as a guard opened the door to the private room they'd secured. Dom shuffled in, pausing at the entry as his restraints were removed. Tears shimmered within Dani's gaze as it remained locked on her big brother.

Her entire body shook with the emotional tsunami striking her. Dallas set a hand on her back and glanced at Dom, whose entire demeanor of murdering badass died with one glance at his sister.

"Go." Dallas shoved Dani enough to motor her forward in a rush of limbs. She slammed into her brother, the impact enough to emit a groan from the man, who pulled her into a hug so hard it lifted her from her feet.

Dallas leaned against the back wall beside Nolan, as far away as they could get from the brother and sister as they reunited for the first time since he'd gone down for murder.

Nolan held out the folder they'd brought.

"You sure this is the best play?"

"Yeah, Jud's down for continuing the Marville cleanup. This is part of it."

With Rachelle secure in a facility and Henry Mills locked away for kidnapping and under investigation by the FBI, there were still a few loose ends to tie before The Arsenal could consider the Marville matter fully handled. Jesse and Marshall were in San Antonio speaking with the Texas Rangers and handing over all the evidence they had—which was mostly pictures and data HERA had pulled because of Kamren's investigations.

Sheriff Haskell's operation in Marville was about to crumble, which would likely unearth other assholes who needed to be taken down. Dallas would help Jud consult with the Texas Rangers until everyone was brought to justice. But he'd also help Riley investigate a mystery that'd gone unsolved too long.

"Riles needs something solid to focus on that's not us or what went down with her best friend. She's got a good head on her shoulders, a natural talent for ferreting out truths. She'll figure out what went down that night."

"You need help, let me know," Nolan said. "At least the Marville Dogs aren't a problem any longer."

"No, and Haskell won't be much longer." Life was shifting into cruise control, and Dallas couldn't be happier. At Kamren's suggestion, they'd asked Ellie to help TJ and DJ catch up on their studies via private home study.

Ellie had recently joined their team and had taken on the perilous position of Office Manager, but she'd been an elementary school teacher in Marville until recently. Dallas didn't know why she'd shifted careers, but she was great with his sons. That's all that mattered.

While socialization was vital, the doctors didn't want them rushed. Slow acclimation. Bubba brought Sam and Shane over frequently. A passel of other children had made their way out to The Arsenal, typically on Saturday afternoons when the compound turned into more of a large family commune than a paramilitary organization. If they weren't wheels up, everyone gathered around grills or in the mess hall and enjoyed life.

"D." Dom's voice dragged him back to the present. Dani was wiping at her face as Dom prowled toward Dallas. Hand out, the man's expression turned soft, the way it'd always been back in the day —when Dallas had been considered a second brother. "Got no words to show my appreciation. Seeing Dani..."

The man's speech halted as he dragged Dallas into a hug.

"Whatever you need," Dom said.

Dallas passed the folder off to Dom. "Here's the rest. Pains me to pass this on, knowing there're more questions than answers because of what's inside, but we're working it. We'll get answers. Jud, Riley, and I are on point. Everyone else will pitch in as needed. Whatever went down that night you supposedly killed someone, we'll figure it out."

"Your sis, she good?"

"She'll get there. She's strong. Stubborn."

"Anything you need." The man opened the folder and tightened as he scanned the contents. He glanced over at Dani, who smiled at him as she sat at the table. "You show her this shit?"

"Fuck no," Nolan responded. "She won't ever see that shit."

The man grunted. "I'll make some calls, tighten the security around her."

"Leave that to us," Dallas advised. "You did right by her in disbanding the Marville Dogs. Let her breathe free."

"And Ricardo?" The man thumbed through the contents. "What about him?"

"We'll find him," Dallas promised.

THREE DAYS LATER...

Early morning had barely dawned when Kamren snuck out of bed to help Momma Mason undertake the last portion of her preparations. Leaving Dallas sleeping in bed had been tough, but she couldn't help but take a certain measure of pride that his mom had trusted her with final preparations. She peered out into the large field on one of the back portions of the Mason property.

Folding chairs covered in slate gray and blue so dark it shimmered deep purple filled the area as far as the eye could see. A large tent was a distance away, along with a makeshift stage and dance floor. Brant's brothers were in the process of laying flooring down between the seats to intersect with a long, wide path to what Kamren assumed was the reception area.

Today was Mary's and Vi's wedding day and neither they, nor their grooms, had any idea. More than half of Resino was already there helping to set up and get the elaborately large seating area arranged. Roses in the same beautiful colors were interspersed with white as far as she could see.

"This is beautiful." She breathed the words on a sigh as her heart thundered wildly. Perfection.

She'd gotten to know the two women very well the past couple weeks. They deserved a happily ever after as big, beautiful, and brilliant as they were. Momma Mason had pulled out all the stops to make sure they got it. Jud's mom and dad flitted around a large tree near where the altar had been set up. She watched as they argued about which direction to wind the decorations around the thick base. Momma Mason clucked her tongue and settled a hand on Kamren's arm. "Those two remind me of me and Monty."

"He must've been a hell of a man to land you and have so many wonderful children. You and he did good raising them," Kamren said.

"I like to think so. In all honesty, I'm thinking a lot of it was sheer luck." She smiled. "Monty's grandpa proposed to his girl right there under that tree. He always said any marriage that starts under its branches will last for an eternity."

Kamren's eyes watered as her heart swelled. An eternity with Dallas would be awesome. She already missed him, even though they'd only been separated a short while. "Are you sure this is a good idea? Shouldn't Mary and Vi be getting ready? Like, hair appointments and makeup and stuff?"

"Those two are beautiful just as they are, inside and out. A couple of the women from Resino Hair and Nails are coming by in a bit. Once they're here, we'll wander over and let the brides and their men know they've got plans today. Until then, we'll leave them be. No sense in getting those two women worked up, and their men are gonna have hemorrhages about security."

Kamren looked around, a bit worried about security herself. "Did you happen to mention all this happening today to Marshall? Or Nolan? Maybe Jesse?"

Dallas didn't know. Either that or he hadn't told her.

"Those boys have bigger things on their minds. Zoey's running interference with the drones so the others don't see anything they shouldn't. Gage is handling the gate, along with Fallon and that wonderful new man, Marcus. The Burtons were kind enough to take down the fence where our two properties meet so folks can sneak in the back when they're ready to come on over."

"Great." Just what Dallas and his brothers would love to hear.

"And Bree and Rhea have drones up."

Oh, thank goodness. If the two scientists were running drones, then maybe this wouldn't be so bad. She tried to imagine Vi's and Mary's surprise when they woke up to find out today was the day.

"Now come on, time's wasting. Brian Burton's daughter has a bad stomach bug today, so he wasn't able to get out here and finish welding the arc at the entrance to the reception area. We haven't even started decorating it yet." Momma Mason's voice lowered. "Bree mentioned you could weld and said you'd shown her a few things. I hate to impose, dear, but..."

"Lead the way," Kamren said quickly. She was glad to have a

purpose, a way to help get the festivities underway, but she needed to give Dallas a head's up this was going down today.

Though she doubted Momma Mason and her well-meaning partners in crime (and there were a lot of them) had flown under the radar. Dallas and his brothers, not to mention all the other operatives at The Arsenal, were pretty observant. Nearly a hundred women, most old enough to be their moms or grandmas, would definitely not go unnoticed.

Kamren hoped.

She followed the woman to the back of the large tent, where a pile of supplies sat beside a welding machine and all the necessary supplies. Gage crossed his arms and glared from his sentry position beside said equipment. Unsure whether the glower was for her or Dallas's mom, she kept quiet. When the woman beside her shuffled over to Gage, smiled, then pinched his cheeks, Kamren rolled her lips into her mouth and fought the laughter tumbling from her.

"Such a nice boy. When this is all done, you and me are gonna sit down and you're gonna tell me why you're giving that nice woman Zoey such fits." She shook her finger at him. "I know you were raised better than that, Gage Sanderson. Why, I was just on the phone with your sister the other day."

The man shifted, his eyebrows up near his hairline. "You were on the phone with my sister? When did you two get tight?"

"Oh, she called one day a while back, when you all were looking for DJ. She was having some man troubles, and I happened to be there." Momma Mason looked up at Gage, seemingly unfazed by the look on his face. "See, dear, that's what I'm talking about. You're just like my boys. Protective to the core. Don't give that girl such a hard time. Take my word for it, she's a keeper."

Kamren bit her tongue to not laugh.

"Well, I'll leave you to it, dear. Thanks again. You let me know if you need anything at all."

"Thanks, I'll be fine," Kamren assured her. She waited until the woman was headed toward whatever the next crisis was before she laughed long, hard, and belly deep.

Gage joined in as he pinched the bridge of his nose. "Jesus, I've never even spoken to her, and she's already meddling."

"Just go with it. It's way easier," Kamren advised. "So...Zoey?"

"Don't," the man warned. "I'll go ten rounds with Dallas if needed, but I'm not taking your shit, too."

With that, Kamren laughed her ass off and got to work.

"WHAT DO you mean you can't tell me?" Dallas leaned in, letting the full brunt of his rage loose so the woman peering up at him could experience it fully. He'd never had much reason to have a one-on-one conversation with Zoey, but if she didn't tell him what he needed to know, they'd be having more than a conversation.

They'd be having a war.

"It's a secret." Zoey peered up at him. "How did you get in here? The door was locked."

"You forget what my last name was?"

"Hardly possible," she muttered.

"No door's locked with my last name, especially around here. Where. Is. Kamren?"

"Yeesh, you're worse than Gage. Listen." She stood and stretched to her full height by raising on her toes. She barely reached his shoulders. Her eyes widened when he shifted his stance and crossed his arms. "Right. I'll break this down real slow, Dallas. Kamren is helping with something and cannot be disturbed, most especially by a Mason. So be a good son and go tend to *your* sons. They just woke."

Shit.

Dallas glared at the woman and headed back to the main house in a jog. That's when her last statement struck. Be a good *son*.

Son of a bitch.

His gaze swept the area. His mom had been AWOL since he'd woken a few minutes ago. Come to think of it, where the fuck was everyone? No operatives or Warrior's Path participants were milling about. Dread uncurled in his gut.

He entered the family farmhouse and grinned. DJ and TJ had Jesse on the floor. The three were in the midst of a tickle war. All the dread he'd chewed on disappeared beneath the grins of the three people on the ground.

Family.

His family.

Love and happiness filled him as he joined in. By the time he and Jesse had mock surrendered to the two young boys' tickling prowess, a good twenty minutes had passed.

"You wanna tell me why you looked like you were about to declare war on someone when you walked in here?" Jesse asked.

"Kamren's AWOL, Zoey's acting shady, and it's all somehow tied to Ma."

Jesse grunted. "You mean the Ma that snuck out of here at three in the morning and tripped the silent alarm I'd added to the house?"

"You added a secondary alarm system to this house? One not tied to HERA?"

Jesse shrugged as he rose, taking TJ with him. The boy curled around him and grinned.

"It's the big day," DJ said as Dallas stood.

"What's the big day?" Dallas asked.

"Dunno. That's what Gramma was singing when she left."

"You aren't supposed to say anything," TJ chastised his younger brother. "Remember? She said they'd all worry and ruin the day if they knew too soon. That's what she told Gage outside."

Dallas debated whether to get onto his eldest for listening in on conversations. It was an ongoing battle, one he couldn't set aside simply because the boy had information he wanted. Fortunately, Jesse handled it for him.

"Appreciate the info, but we shouldn't listen in on conversations. If people want us to know something, they'll come and share."

"I know," TJ said. "She was just so happy it made me happy and I wanted to know what to do to make her like that again if she got sad."

Dallas's heart clenched. Ma had been beside herself with worry over Riley's injuries. Little sis was recovering well, though. He glanced up at the upstairs area. If anyone knew what Ma was up to, it'd be her. "I'll be right back."

It didn't surprise him when Riley opened the door the moment he took the last step. He, Jesse and the kids been louder than a thundering herd of buffalo downstairs, which didn't exactly translate to the ideal environment for sleep. He smiled as she closed the distance and wrapped him in a hug.

"Hearing your laughter. Jesse's. Your sons making that laughter happen." She looked up, her blue eyes shimmering with unshed tears. Her voice was soft, hesitant from nonuse. "Best damn medicine in the world. And I get my second dose later today."

Dallas tensed as he glanced down at little sis. The pieces clicked together. A chuckle escaped him as he realized what the big day meant. "Shit. Has she even told them?"

"Nope."

Dallas wasn't sure whether to laugh or curse, so he opted for amusement. Only Ma would think it was okay to not tell two couples they were sleeping through their wedding day. "I don't know much about wedding days, but I'm thinking Mary and Vi would like to know so they can get ready. What time?"

Fuck. Security.

"And this is why she didn't tell any of you." Riley swatted Dallas's arm. "It's covered. I helped with the details and insisted she call in some of the team leads to help security. Bree, Rhea, and Zoey are helping by manning HERA. The geeks have enough drones flitting about to take on a second-world country. The only thing happening today is a wedding. Or, well, two weddings."

Son of a bitch.

It was the day.

And he wasn't ready. "Gotta go, sis. Can you help wrangle the boys? I'll be back in a bit."

"What are you up to? Don't you dare go out and spoil the surprise."

He didn't pretend to not know where the big event was being held. He and his brothers had figured that out a few days ago when the Burtons pulled them aside to give them the heads up that the back pasture fence between their properties was going down. Security overrode surprises, even for the townsfolk. They understood and respected the need for security.

But he should have known when they'd broached them meant the big day was coming fast. Son of a bitch. His chest tightened and his stomach did awkward somersaults as he sprinted toward the small cottage beside the one he and Kamren were now in with his sons. He banged on the door and waited. Banged again.

Then again.

He had his fist raised to give it a fourth go when the door opened. Dylan glared as he drew the drawstring in his pants. "There a reason you're knocking my door down?"

"It's time."

"Time?" Dylan swiped his hand across his face.

"Making an honest woman of my nephew's mom today." Dallas grinned. "I'm taking my life into my hands by giving you a heads up. Ma's flying under the radar thanks to our team leads."

Dylan froze. Eyes wide, body tight. "For real?"

"Not gonna lie about something like that." Dallas grinned and drew his big brother into a hug.

Dylan tightened the hold. "You ready?"

"Fuck no." Dallas grinned, pulling back. "You?"

"Fuck yes."

Dallas gave himself the moment to laugh his ass off. Dylan was marrying one of the best women in the world today. So was Jud. And Dallas was proposing to *the* best woman in the world at the reception. He'd had the plan in place for a week, but he hadn't expected the wedding to happen so quickly.

Then again, Mary was pregnant. Her round belly was so cute. "Gotta go get some stuff together for tonight," Dallas said with a grin.

"I'll give the heads up to Jud. We'll keep it quiet for now. I'm sure Ma's got a plan for the women."

Knowing Ma, she likely had more than a few plans underway.

Dallas grinned. Hopefully she'd be willing to do it all over again on a much smaller scale for him and Kamren soon.

"Hey." The woman in question startled him when she stopped a couple feet away.

"Jesus, I was so in my head I didn't even hear you." His gaze swept across her coveralls. They were baggy and faded with holes all along the legs and torso, evidence they weren't for show. His woman worked her ass off. Dirt was on her face.

He smiled and swiped her cheek with his thumb. She leaned into the contact, closed her eyes, and sighed. "That's what I needed."

"You okay?"

"Not really." She rocked back on her heels and dragged her bottom lip into her mouth. "I kind of got dragged into a secret I don't think I should keep."

"Riley just told me." He motioned to the house he'd just left. "Dylan knows, he's giving Jud the heads up. We'll keep it from Vi and Mary for now."

"Good." She sighed and smiled. "What your mom's doing is sweet, but I'm not good with surprises. I'd want to know. And holy wow, there are gonna be too many people here."

She squeezed him tight as she settled her head against his chest. He inhaled her scent and smiled. God, he loved this woman.

"They're starting a new chapter of their lives today and have no idea," she whispered. "That's so sweet, but so sad. They should know."

"They will, sweetheart."

"I'll bring the boys back here after the wedding. They'll get nervous with all those people there. She's planning for the whole tri-county to be there. I don't even know where she got all those chairs from. She's got the full Burton Construction crew laying down flooring in a field, Dallas."

"Jesus." He muttered as the laughter tumbled from him. "Why?"

"Danny's wheelchair and likely others with mobility issues." She leaned back and whispered up to him. "You gotta warn them about that, too."

"About what?"

"Danny. Your mom asked him to give the two women away."

"Fuck." They definitely needed a heads up about that. He didn't think either Mary or Vi would want the entire tri-country witnessing their emotional reaction to that decision.

Which was brilliant.

The two women had rescued the man from hell. Not once, but twice.

Dallas pulled out his cell and texted Dylan and Jud. Once it was done, he returned the phone and claimed Kamren's mouth. Her anxiety was palpable, and a dose of reality that choked out the elaborate plans he'd concocted in his head.

A proposal of that magnitude, him standing before everyone in the tri-county and asking for her hand was sweet. A fairytale ending.

But it wasn't him.

And it sure as fuck wasn't her.

He severed the kiss, letting their breathing return to normal a moment. "Marry me, Kamren."

"What?" She leaned against him.

"I was going to do this in front of everyone at the reception, but I can't wait. Marry me."

"Yes!" She cheered. Tears ran down her cheeks. "I love you, Dallas Mason."

"I love you, Kamren Mason."

"You can't call me that yet, not until the wedding."

"A piece of paper doesn't make that decision, sweetheart. We do. You were a Mason the day you exploded a truck outside this compound. You became *my* Mason when you found my sons. Actually, you were mine the day I walked into the Sip and Spin, turned that stool around, and looked into your eyes." He cupped her face. "I knew you were about to rock my world right then."

She took his hand. "That, Mr. Mason, has just earned you a special preview of our wedding night."

Dallas chuckled as he lifted her up and jogged to their home. Her laughter rolled through the area, dissolving any residual fallout from what all they'd gone through the past few months. Today, four of the best people he knew were taking vows. One day soon, he would, too.

But the only vows that mattered had been decided the moment he met Kamren Garrett.

~THE END~

ABOUT THE AUTHOR

Born in small-town Texas, Cara Carnes was a princess, a pirate, fashion model, actress, rock star and Jon Bon Jovi's wife all before the age of 13.

In reality, her fascination for enthralling worlds took seed somewhere amidst a somewhat dull day job and a wonderful life filled with family and friends. When she's not cemented to her chair, Cara loves travelling, photography and reading.

Newsletter|Facebook|Twitter|Website

THE ARSENAL SERIES
Jagged Edge
Sight Lines
Blood Vows
Zero Trace – Coming November 2018
Battle Scar – February 2019

Want more of The Arsenal Series? Subscribe to my newsletter or join my Facebook group for the first peek at exclusive bonus content. Links to free short stories in the series can be found on my website at www.caracarnes.com